JOHN SANDFORD
STORM FRONT

London · New York · Sydney · Toronto · New Delhi

A CBS COMPANY

First published in the US by G. P. Putnam's Sons, 2013
A division of the Penguin Group (USA) Inc.
First published in Great Britain by Simon & Schuster UK Ltd, 2013
A CBS COMPANY

This paperback edition first published, 2014

1 3 5 7 9 10 8 6 4 2

Simon & Schuster UK Ltd
1st Floor
222 Gray's Inn Road
London WC1X 8HB

www.simonandschuster.co.uk

Simon & Schuster Australia, Sydney
Simon & Schuster India, New Delhi

A CIP catalogue record for this book
is available from the British Library

A format ISBN: 978-1-47113-217-9
B format ISBN: 978-1-47113-216-2
Ebook ISBN: 978-1-47113-218-6

This book is a work of fiction. Names, characters,
places and incidents are either a product of the
author's imagination or are used fictitiously.

Book design by Nicole LaRoche

Printed and bound by CPI Group (UK) Ltd, Croydon, CR0 4YY

1

His bags were packed and sitting by the door. Nobody thought that was strange, because four diggers were jammed into each small living suite. With two eight-by-ten bedrooms feeding into a tiny sitting and kitchen area, and an even tinier bathroom, there was hardly anyplace to keep clothing, so they kept it in their bags.

Elijah shared a room with a middle-aged volunteer from Alabama named Steve Phelps. When Elijah's cell phone vibrated at two o'clock, his first move was to roll up on one shoulder, turn it off, and listen to Phelps breathe.

Phelps was a sound sleeper, and he was sound asleep now. Elijah often got up to pee at night, and hadn't awakened anyone doing that for two weeks—the days in the sun were exhausting, and once his roommates were familiar with his night moves, they never twitched.

When he was sure of Phelps, Elijah rolled out of bed, moving as quietly as he could. He'd loaded all of his personal items—wallet, passport, small cash—into his pants the night before, so all he had to do now was get into them. His socks were already rolled into his shoes, which he would put on outside.

When he was dressed, he listened again to Phelps, then eased through the door into the sitting area. Here was the tricky part. Another of the diggers, who slept in the adjoining room, had keys to one of the dig cars—and the keys were sitting on a radiator in his room.

Elijah stepped to the door of the other bedroom, and again, listened for a moment. Both of the men snored, which was why they'd been put together. When he was sure that he could distinguish the separate snoring, he eased open the door (he'd put a dab of Crisco on the hinges the night before, when the others were out) and stepped silently into the room.

The men continued to snore, which helped cover his movement as he stepped barefooted across the room and picked up the car keys. Two seconds later, he was out of the room; a minute after that, he was outside with his bags, in the cool of the Israeli night, sitting on the steps, tying his shoes, and again, listening and watching.

It had been an exciting day—maybe somebody else had been restless?

But nothing moved anywhere on the kibbutz as far as he could tell. He'd been through one tricky part, and now here was the second one. When his shoes were tied, he walked down to the first floor with his bags—a nylon backpack and a leather satchel—and around behind the dormitory to a low wooden building used to sort and classify pottery and other finds at the dig.

There were no lights inside the building. He reached into his bag, took out a large screwdriver, and pried open the door. Inside, navigating without lights, he went to a row of metal lockers, felt for the fifth handle down, and with the same screwdriver, pried open the locker door.

A stone sat on the locker shelf. He couldn't see it, much, but he could feel it, and it was heavy. He put it in his leather satchel, closed the locker door and the outer door.

A HALF HOUR LATER, Elijah the Mankato-ite sped west in a stolen car past Jezreel, where, roughly 2,850 years earlier, Jezebel the queen had been thrown out a window. Her body had been eaten by dogs—all except for the palms of her hands and the soles of her feet—just as predicted by the other Elijah, the prophet guy.

As they didn't say at the time, *Bummer.*

The latter-day Elijah paid no attention to Jezreel, as the former royal city was now just another stony field. Ten minutes later, he rocketed past Armageddon—Megiddo to the locals—where there was no battle going on, penultimate or otherwise. At Megiddo, he turned northwest toward Mount Carmel and the Mediterranean coast at Haifa.

Elijah was in a hurry: he had to be gone before the diggers got up, and some of them got up very early, at four o'clock. He kept his foot on the floor, and the much-abused Avis rent-a-car groaned with pain. Out the passenger-side window, as he went past Megiddo, he could see the lights of Nazareth twinkling across the farm fields of the Jezreel Valley.

It was pretty, all right, but he'd been to Israel too often to be impressed. He remembered that first naive astonishment, forty-five years earlier, when he found that the Mount of Olives was full of fake religious sites, that the Sea of Galilee was full of Diet Coke bottles, and that Jesus' hometown was an Arab city where a good Christian could get his ass kicked if he wasn't careful.

Not that he didn't love the place, because he did. He loved all of it, from the green and blue mountains in the north to the sere desert in the south, and especially the *shephelah*, and above all, Jerusalem. But he loved it more like an Israeli than an American; that is, despite its faults.

THE FLANKS OF CARMEL were still dark when he drove into town. He'd leave the Avis car outside the dealership, he'd decided, where they'd find it when they opened at eight o'clock. He had a legitimate set of keys for the car, but it had been rented on a credit card provided by a credulous American graduate student from Penn State. The student would be mightily pissed if Elijah lost the car. In fact, he'd be mightily pissed if Elijah left the car outside the Avis agency, but Elijah had more important things to worry about than the feelings of grad students.

Luckily, the Avis agency wasn't far off Route 75, and not far from the harbor, either. He found it easily enough, dumped the car, left a message on the dashboard, and called a cab.

As he waited, he fumbled a couple of pills from a bottle that he kept in the backpack, swallowed them without water.

THE CABDRIVER didn't speak much English, but Elijah had excellent Hebrew, so they got along. The cabdriver asked, "Only that luggage?"

Elijah had the nylon backpack and the leather duffel with brass buckles. "That's all," he said. "It's only a day trip."

"I don't go on the water," the cabdriver said over his shoulder. "If the water grows too deep in my shower, I get seasick."

"Never been a problem for me, though I live as far as you can get from an ocean," Elijah said.

"This is in the States?"

"Yes, Minnesota," Elijah said.

The driver noticed that his fare was sweating, even in the cool of the early morning. He also had the expensive leather bag clenched in his lap, as though it might contain an atomic bomb. The driver didn't ask.

Strange things happened in Israel every day of the week, and asking could be dangerous. Though in this case, the driver thought, danger was unlikely: the man wore a black snap-brimmed hat, a white clerical collar under his black polyester suit, and he had an olive-wood cross hanging from a silver chain around his neck.

He was a type. He would have been a type anywhere, but in Israel, he was *really* a type. Give a guy a black suit, a clerical collar, a wooden cross, and a sick, screaming baby, and he could walk through any checkpoint in Israel with his socks full of cocaine or C-4. Because he was an annoying, proselytizing, American Christian *type*—the kind who usually came with slightly noxious religious and political opinions, and who was almost always chintzy with the tips.

Though not in this case. The driver dropped Elijah at the Fisherman's Anchorage at HaKishon, the mouth of the Kishon River, and Elijah gave him a hundred-shekel note, which was way too much. He didn't ask for change, simply hustled away, the pack on his back and the leather bag clutched in his arms, like a sick baby.

ELIJAH HAD BEEN to the port four days earlier, where he'd found the people he'd been looking for: a German couple, drifting around the Med on an ancient fiberglass sailboat with an engine that worked some of the time. He'd offered them five hundred dollars to transport him, without questions, across the water to the Old Port at Limassol on the Greek half of Cyprus.

The Germans had been reduced to eating pilchards fished from the dirty port waters and cooked over an alcohol stove, so a little human smuggling wasn't really a central ethical problem for them. The woman, a lanky blonde named Gerta, told him that she could provide carnal entertainment during the trip for an extra two hundred, but Elijah declined, citing conservative religious values.

When Elijah arrived on the dock, the Germans were awake and waiting, perhaps nervous that their five hundred dollars had gone somewhere else.

Gerta's partner, also lanky and blond, but improbably called Ricardo, pushed them off the dock within thirty seconds of his arrival. He fired up the engine, which coughed loudly before resuming its silence. Ricardo whacked it a couple of times, and got it running well enough to get them out into open water, where the Germans launched the sails.

Ricardo said, "Such a nice day for sailing. Should I put your bags below?"

"No, no, they make a place to sit," Elijah said, in German. His German, like his Hebrew, was excellent, and their English was no better than the cabdriver's, so it was what they had. He sat on his pack and clutched the leather bag in his lap.

"So you are carrying your valuables there," Ricardo said, as Haifa slowly lowered itself on the horizon. He was eyeing Elijah's bag as a great white shark might examine a dog-paddling fat lady.

"Yes, but I'm afraid some of them will have to go over the side before we get to the Old Port," Elijah said.

"Over the side?" Ricardo was puzzled.

"Yes, over the side," Elijah said. He pulled an older-looking Beretta 92F from the bag, a gun that may have migrated from Iraq to Israel, looking for work. It fit well in Elijah's rugged hand, a hand that might have seen an early life throwing bales of hay onto a horse-drawn wagon. "It's a shame, because it is a fine piece of weaponry. Fast, powerful, and accurate."

The muzzle was not pointed at Ricardo, but neither was it pointed far away. Ricardo, who'd been sitting unnecessarily close to the reverend—for Elijah was indeed an ordained minister in the Lutheran Church in America—eased away. "Perhaps not over the side," Ricardo said. "When we get to the port, I could find a place to put it."

Such a fine piece of weaponry would sell for a couple of thousand dollars on the right stretch of the Med, Elijah thought, and come to no good end.

"Perhaps," Elijah said.

AND PERHAPS NOT.

The trip took all that day, the next night, and most of the following day. The winds were perfect: strong enough to give them a good run, but not so overwhelming that the seas got trashy. Elijah spent the time on deck, reading books on an iPad, wrapped in a nylon rain suit during the cool of the night. He'd come prepared.

When Cyprus hove in sight, and when Ricardo was preoccupied with getting the engine started again, Elijah dropped the pistol over the side. As they came into the marina area, Ricardo, who'd properly understood the display of the pistol as a counter to any possible ambitions concerning the reverend's valuables, asked about the gun.

"Fell over the side," Elijah said. And, "I think the man on the dock is trying to get your attention."

Dockside, they told their story: Elijah Jones was an American who'd joined his German friends for a sail in the Med, but who'd unexpectedly begun urinating blood and was in great pain. Elijah explained that he was dying of colon cancer, and was making a last trip around the eastern Mediterranean to say good-bye to friends in Greece, Egypt, and Israel. Now he just wanted to get home to Mankato, Minnesota, so he could die in peace.

He would need to stop at the local hospital, he said, and then go on his way. As proof of his condition, he showed the customs man his bag of medications and a treatment letter from his physician at the Mayo Clinic.

He was also sweating and stifling groans, and as the customs officials conferred over his documents, he asked to be excused to the dockside, where he promptly peed blood into the Mediterranean Sea. The chief customs agent stamped his passport and expressed the wish that God would bless him.

TWENTY MINUTES after they reached the port, Elijah was on his way to Larnaca International; six hours later, on his way to Charles de Gaulle in Paris, and six hours after landing there, on his way to Minneapolis.

At Minneapolis, two uniformed paramedics, one male and one female, were waiting in the customs area. Elijah, sweating like a boxcar loader, was pushed into the baggage area in a wheelchair. The customs guys asked him if he had anything to declare, he groaned, "No." A drug dog gave him a perfunctory sniff, and they waved him through to the EMS techs and the waiting ambulance.

The male paramedic carried his bags, and joked, "What you got in here, a rock?"

Ninety minutes after that, Elijah checked into the Mayo Clinic in Rochester, and told the techs to put his duffel bag on the floor by the bed.

Three days later, when his condition had again been stabilized, and he was no longer peeing blood, he checked himself out.

But he didn't tell anybody. He just walked.

With the heavy leather bag.

2

I t was one of the great Minnesota summers of all time—or maybe it just felt that way, after one of the most miserable springs in history. On April 22, in a nasty little snowstorm, he'd skidded off a highway in Apple Valley, and had had to call for a tow to get his four-wheel-drive truck out of the ditch.

On May 1, he'd gone north to a friend's cabin near Hayward, Wisconsin, to do some early-season fly-fishing for bluegills, and it had snowed the whole day, and the day after that, totaling sixteen inches of the stuff, and then it had spent two days raining old women and sticks, as the Welsh would say, although they'd actually say something more like *mae hi'n bwrw hen wragedd a ffyn.*

But the summer . . . ah, the summer, which was now coming to its peak, the summer was a joy to behold, even from the inside of a diner.

VIRGIL FLOWERS was sitting sideways in a booth in a Perkins restaurant on Highway 169 in Mankato, Minnesota, his cowboy boots hanging off the end of the seat. He was talking to Florence

"Ma" Nobles about her involvement in a counterfeit lumber ring, of which she denied any knowledge. He'd been investigating her for a while, and had even met three of her five intra-ethnic fatherless boys—Mateo, Tall Bear, and Moses.

Virgil picked up a french fry and jabbed it at her: "Dave Moss said you sold the same barn fifteen times, Ma. He says your boy Rolf has another two thousand board-feet of lumber down at the bottom of the Minnesota River, getting old. Dave says you'll be peddling that all over New England next year."

Ma made a rude noise with her lips, and Virgil said, "C'mon, Ma, that's not necessary."

Ma said, "That goddamn Moss can kiss my ass—though, to be honest, he already did that and seemed to like it all right. This is more a domestic dispute than anything else, Virgie. I broke it off with him, and he's just getting back at me."

Virgil said, "I'm not sure I can believe that, Ma. There's a fellow named Barry Spurgeon who spent forty-four thousand dollars buying lumber from your boy, so he can build some sort of a barn-mansion in Greenwich, Connecticut. He got suspicious and did a tree-ring test and that tree was cut down last year. *Last year*, for Christ's sakes, Ma. You didn't even let it go *five* years. Spurgeon wants that money back because he paid for real old-timey barn lumber."

His phone rang and he picked it up and looked at it: Lucas Davenport.

"I gotta take this," he said. He pushed the "answer" tab on the phone and said, "Hang on a minute, Lucas," and to Ma, "You sit right here. Do not run away."

"Instead of talking about barn lumber we oughta talk about how to scratch my itch," Ma said, pushing out her lower lip. "Here it is July and I ain't been laid since March the eighteenth. You're just the boy to get 'er done, Virgie."

VIRGIL SLID out of the booth and walked back toward the men's room, where nobody was sitting. "What's up?" he asked Davenport.

"Got an assignment for you . . . easy duty," Davenport said.

"Aw, man. I left my shotgun at home."

"No, no, nothing like that," Davenport said, though he'd been known to lie about such things. "There's an Israeli investigator who needs to talk to a professor at Gustavus Adolphus, though the professor actually lives there in Mankato. Probably on your block. He's a minister named, uh, let me look . . . Elijah Jones. A Lutheran minister, like your old man."

"An Israeli? What's that about?"

Virgil was keeping an eye on Ma as he spoke to Davenport, and it wasn't particularly hard to do. She was undeniably a criminal redneck, but she was also a pretty blonde, only thirty-four, though she had five children, including a nineteen-year-old. She had a long, thick pigtail down her back, and a short, slender body. If, purely hypothetically, she were lying on a California king with that hair spread out over her . . .

". . . some kind of precious artifact—"

"What? Say that over again," Virgil said. "I'm sorry, I'm trying to keep an eye on a local criminal here . . . that barn-lumber scam I've been working."

"I said, the Israeli's coming into MSP and it'd be nice if you'd pick her up," Davenport said. "This Jones guy supposedly stole some kind of precious artifact from an archaeological dig and smuggled it back to the States. He apparently left Israel illegally—the Israeli cops tracked him to a port and he caught a boat to Cyprus and then flew home from there."

"What kind of artifact?" Virgil asked, now semi-interested. "Does it have mystical powers?"

"I don't know about mystical powers, but supposedly it's a piece of a stele—a steelee? I don't know how you pronounce it—that's got some ancient writing on it. The whole thing has apparently got the state of Israel in an uproar," Davenport said. "Anyway, the Israelis want it back and the State Department says if Jones stole it and brought it into the country, he broke about nine laws. I'll send you a sheet on it."

"That sounds like a federal case," Virgil said. "Why don't the Israelis talk to the FBI?"

"Well, it *is* a federal case. The feds have issued a hold on Jones, based on information from the Israelis, and also because he said he had nothing to declare when he came through customs, which was a lie. The feds asked us in because of local knowledge—that'd be you—and because we owe them one this month, and the boss okayed it," Davenport said.

"I bet the stone does have mystical powers," Virgil said. "Maybe the Israelis can use it to blast Iran, or something. Or maybe it curses the person who has it—your balls rot off, or your seed only falls upon barren ground, so to speak."

"My seed's already got me in enough trouble, so I don't care anymore," Davenport said. "Just bust the fuckin' minister, get the fuckin' stone, and get the fuckin' Israelis out of here. Okay?"

Ma caught Virgil looking at her, and her tongue came out and stroked her upper lip. Just in case Virgil might have missed it, she did it again. Davenport said something else, but Virgil missed *that*, and he said, "Goddamnit, I'm up to my ass on this lumber thing. What time is she coming in?"

After a moment of silence, Davenport said, "I just told you that: I don't know. Today, tomorrow, the next day. She'll either call ahead or send you an e-mail when she knows for sure."

"Sorry, I'm really . . . I'm afraid this guy's gonna run. What's her name? The Israeli?"

"Yael Aronov," Davenport said. He pronounced it "Yale."

"Is that Y-a-e-l?"

"Yeah."

"That's pronounced Ya-el," Virgil said. "In the Book of Judges, Yael meets this enemy commander named Sisera, and gets him in her tent, where, and I quote, 'Yael, Heber's wife, took a nail of the tent, and took a hammer into her hand, and went softly unto him, and smote the nail into his temples, and fastened it into the ground: for he was fast asleep and weary. So he died.' End quote."

"See, you're the perfect guy for this," Davenport said. "You not only know the Bible, but your third wife was just like this Yale chick."

"Ya-el," Virgil said. "And when you're right, you're right."

THE LUMBER SCAM did not get resolved. As they walked out to the parking lot, Virgil told Ma that she'd have to find another person to scratch her itch. "Not," he said, "that you don't have a pretty attractive itch."

"I appreciate your sayin' that, but sayin' it don't solve the problem," Ma said.

"You better get it scratched right quick, because if you keep selling that lumber, I am gonna put your ass in jail," Virgil said.

"You're one mean cowboy," Ma said. She left in a new red Ford F-150, which seemed to Virgil to be some sort of a taunt, since she'd been poor-mouthing about the depressed state of the architectural salvage business.

VIRGIL DIDN'T HEAR from the Israeli woman that afternoon, and he didn't have much on his investigative plate, so he made a quick run over to the Mississippi River, where he hooked up with his old friend Johnson Johnson to do some evening walleye fishing. He wound up spending the night at Johnson's cabin, where Johnson and his current girlfriend, Shirley, made a nice dinner out of baked walleye and fresh handpicked watercress. Virgil and Johnson did a little northern fishing in the early morning, and then Virgil headed back home.

At Rochester, he stopped at a McDonald's, got a Quarter Pounder with Cheese, declining the offer of a Double Quarter Pounder, checked his e-mail on his iPad, and found a message from the Israeli: she'd be arriving at Minneapolis–St. Paul at one o'clock. Virgil checked his watch and figured he'd have enough time to cut cross-country to the Cabela's outdoor superstore at Owatonna on his way north.

VIRGIL FLOWERS was a tall, thin man, two inches over six feet unless he was wearing cowboy boots, which he usually was, and then he was three and a half inches over six feet. He wore his blond hair long, curled over his ears and the back of his neck; in general, he looked like a decent third-baseman, which he'd been in high school and for a while in college, until he found out he couldn't reliably hit a college-level fastball.

After college, he did time in the army, expecting an assignment in the infantry or intelligence. The army made him a cop, which, to his surprise, he liked. He was a captain when he got out, landed a job with the St. Paul cops, and a few years later, moved to the Minnesota Bureau of Criminal Apprehension. Now he was the only resident agent in the southern end of the state. He would work six or eight murders in the course of an average year, and spend the rest of his time chasing down people whose criminal activities required more range than an individual sheriff's office could normally cover. Ma Nobles, for example, lived in one county, her son in another, a suspected accomplice in a third, and the lumber might well be hidden underwater, precisely on a county line.

In addition to his cop duties, Virgil was an outdoor writer, though he'd recently branched out and had stories printed in both the *New York Times* magazine and *Vanity Fair*. Despite a mild disregard for money, between the state job and the writing, he found himself edging toward affluence.

So that's what he did. Meth labs had been his special curse for quite a while, generating a number of the killings he'd worked, but now they were beginning to fade away.

Tough, on-the-ball law enforcement, Virgil was proud to say, had forced Minnesota criminals to go back to stealing.

VIRGIL GOT OUT of Cabela's for two hundred dollars, not a bad price, considering the possibilities, and made it into the airport's short-term parking a half hour before Yael Aronov's plane was scheduled to land. He bought a fishing magazine at a newsstand and a croissant at Starbucks, and settled in to wait.

He was deep into a pro-and-con article on the use of bucktails when his phone rang, a call from an unknown number.

"Yes?"

"Is this Agent Flowers?"

"Yes, it is."

"The plane has landed. Your supervisor gave me this number and said you would meet me. Are you here?"

"Yes. In baggage claim. You're at carousel nine. I'm a tall, thin man with cowboy boots and a straw hat, sitting in the chairs facing the carousel."

"Very good. I will be there as soon as I can."

————

SHE WAS another twenty minutes. Virgil finished the bucktails story and was reading about Bulldawg technique when people began gathering around the carousel. He put the magazine away, and two minutes later, a woman walked up and said, "You're the only cowboy. You must be Virgil?"

"Yes, I am," Virgil said, unfolding from the chair.

They shook hands and she said, "Yael Aronov," and, "I have two large bags."

"That's fine," Virgil said. "Where are you staying?"

"At the Mankato Downtown Inn? Is that correct?"

"That's correct," Virgil said.

Yael was a tall woman in her late twenties or early thirties, athletic, with dark hair cut short, regular features, an olive complexion, and quick, dark eyes. She was pretty, but if Virgil had been asked what she looked like, he would have said, "Tough."

"I'm tired. It was straight through—Tel Aviv to Newark, and then a long layover in Newark and then to here," she said. "I need to sleep."

"I was never told who you work for, exactly," Virgil said. "I understand you're looking for an artifact of some kind."

"I work for the Israel Antiquities Authority, the IAA. I'm an investigator—really, the only investigator," she said. "We're looking for part of a stele"—she pronounced it *stella*—"that was stolen by this Reverend Jones."

"I don't know exactly what a stele is."

"Okay, I will tell you," she said. "In the ancient Middle East,

the various kings, Persian, Egyptian, Assyrian, when they con-
quered a place, would sometimes put up a stone pillar boast-
ing about their conquest. They often inscribed the pillar with
more than one language, usually their own and the local language. Then, after they died, another conqueror would come
along, and the old pillars would get thrown down and broken
up, and maybe new pillars set up. What Reverend Jones found was
a piece of one of these pillars, a piece of a stele. Unfortunately, he
stole it, and carried it out of the country."

"You're sure?"

"One hundred percent," she said.

Jones, she said, had been working on Israeli digs since the late
sixties, most recently at an excavation on the Jordan River east
of the town of Beth Shean. He was one of the most trusted
diggers—a man with long experience, decent Hebrew, and good
friends all over Israel.

Then, a little more than a week earlier, there'd been a stunning
find: a fragment of a black limestone stele, a little more than a
foot long and about ten inches thick at the thickest part.

SHE BROKE OFF TO SAY, "Here are my bags."

They were, in fact, two of the largest suitcases Virgil had ever
seen come off an airplane. But when he pulled them off the carousel, they were light, as though they were almost empty.

"They weigh—"

"Nothing," she said. "But believe me, they will weigh much
more when I go home. I will put refrigerators in them, if I can."

"Why is that?"

"Israeli taxes," she said. "Israel would tax words, if that were possible. Would tax air. This way . . . no taxes."

"All right."

THEY TOWED the two bags out to Virgil's truck and threw them in the back. Out of the airport, he said, "So, keep talking. The stele was a foot long and ten inches thick . . ."

"Yes. Everybody was jubilant, excited," she said. "The director of the dig, Rafi Frankel, this is the greatest find of his career. It came out late in the morning—they stop digging at noon because of the heat. Reverend Jones was actually the one who found it. We have photos from the earliest moments, when all you could see was one dressed edge of the stone coming up through the dirt."

More photos were taken as the stone was dug out of the ground, she said, and as it was removed from the dig pit and carefully wiped. When it was out of the ground, it was driven back to a dig house, put on a table, where more photos were taken.

"Frankel is a professor at the Hebrew University of Jerusalem, in the Institute of Archaeology," Yael said. "He called friends there and told them of the find, and of course, the word spread instantly. He said he would transport it the next day to Jerusalem. Some of the people from the dig stayed up late, until ten o'clock, examining the stone. Then it was secured in a locker, and the room was locked, and everybody went to bed. When they got up at four-thirty, the stone was gone. So was a car, and Reverend Jones."

Frankel immediately called the Israeli cops, who eventually traced the Avis rent-a-car to the city of Haifa. There, they lost the trail for a couple of days, fooled by a false scent: the report of a tall man in a dark hat and dark suit walking near the Avis dealership with a couple of big bags. They tracked the man down, but he turned out to be an Orthodox Jew who lived in the neighborhood, and had nothing to do either with the dig or with Jones.

Backtracking, they eventually found a cabdriver who had taken Jones to the port. A yachtsman there told investigators about two Germans who had vanished with their boat that same morning that Jones disappeared. The Germans were identified by customs, and four days later, they were found in the Old Port of Cyprus.

The Germans said they'd taken the American for a sail, but he'd become seriously ill, had begun vomiting and urinating blood. They'd dropped him at the Old Port, they said, as the fastest place they could get to, and had last seen Jones getting into a taxicab.

"We didn't believe all of that, of course. We think they were paid to take him out of the country. But, mmm, it was a hard story to break because a Cyprus customs official actually witnessed Reverend Jones urinating blood," Yael said. "When we continued to trace his travels, we found that he came here, and was taken to the Mayo Clinic. He has terminal cancer. After three days, he left the clinic, without permission, and his whereabouts are now unknown."

"And you have reason to believe that he had the stone with him," Virgil said.

"Oh, yes. He was carrying a large leather bag, which he would allow nobody to touch. The cabdriver said he carried it like a baby."

"What could he do with it?" Virgil asked. "If you have all those photos, he couldn't sell it."

"Ah. But he could," she said. "For a lot of money, if he made just the right connection. Perhaps he saw it and went a little crazy. He's dying . . . maybe he thought this would be a big thing, if he could publish it himself."

"You know what's on the stone? What it says?"

"No, no, that will take some study," Yael said. "One side is in Egyptian hieroglyphics and the other, perhaps some primitive form of Hebrew. Nobody really knows for sure," she said. She yawned, and then said, "Maybe I sleep for a few minutes. This day catches up to me."

"There's a pillow right behind your seat," Virgil said.

"Thank you. This is excellent," she said, as she fished the pillow out of the back and then snuggled against the passenger-side window. "I sleep now."

And she did, as Virgil drove along, thinking about the story she'd told. The story interested him for two reasons: he'd grown up as a minister's son, and Bible tales had been a big part of his youth. The other thing was, she'd told the truth right up to the end, and then she'd begun lying. She was good at it, but Virgil had been listening to liars for years, and he could hear the lies in her voice.

There was something about the stele that she didn't want him to know—or that she didn't want to talk about.

He wondered why. Mystical powers? Hmm.

He drove on.

3

Virgil dropped Yael at her hotel. She was still dazed from the jet lag, she said, so he led her inside, got her checked in, agreed to pick her up for breakfast the next morning, and sent her up to her room.

He lived a mile away, and decided he might as well get going on the Jones case: with any luck, he could have it settled by the time he picked Yael up in the morning. There wasn't much of the working day left, but Gustavus Adolphus College was only fifteen minutes away, and Jones lived even closer.

At home, he cut up an apple and moved to his den, where he got online with the college. Jones was listed as a professor emeritus in the Department of Sociology and Anthropology. His online vita said that he'd graduated from a seminary in St. Paul and had been ordained there, and later graduated from the University of Iowa with a Ph.D. in early and primitive religions.

When he'd been working full-time, he'd taught Archaeology of the Holy Land, the History of Religion and the Hebrew Bible.

He'd worked on archaeological digs in Israel, Jordan, Syria, Egypt, Turkey, Cyprus, and Greece during the late sixties and the seventies, and after becoming a tenured professor at Gustavus, had led annual student treks to Israeli archaeological digs.

Attached to the site was a note that he was leading a dig that summer, with the dig scheduled to start on Sunday, June 23, and continue for six weeks.

Judging from the dates of graduation listed in his vita, Jones must have been in his late sixties. His departmental photo showed a thick—but not obese—bearded man dressed in a short-sleeved blue shirt and long khaki pants and boots, standing with a group of smiling students both male and female, on the edge of a dig, with odd-looking black tents in the background. On closer examination, the tents appeared to be swaths of some kind of fabric held up with PVC drainage pipes.

As with Yael, if asked to describe Jones, Virgil would have included the word "smart." Jones looked like a smart, tough prairie preacher, Virgil thought, and he'd met a number of those.

With Jones's background in mind, Virgil went online with the Department of Motor Vehicles and took a look at his driver's license. While the online photo at the college had shown a man with jet-black hair and a thick black beard, the license photo showed a thinner man with graying hair and beard, though both were more black than white; but it was the same guy, and he lived only eight blocks from Virgil.

Virgil thought, *Pick him up tonight, wring him out, get the rock back, give it to Yael in the morning, and send her on her way. Warn Jones about not running, and let justice take its course. Whatever that might be.* With any luck, he could be back investigating Ma Nobles by noon the next day.

Ma, he thought, was a much more interesting case. With that thought, he shut down the computer, put the remains of the apple in the garbage disposal, washed it away, and headed over to Jones's house.

JONES LIVED in a plain-vanilla clapboard house that had a porch with a wooden swing and a picture window that looked out over the porch steps to his small front lawn. A flower box hung under the window, but had no flowers in it; a big but barren flowerpot sat on the porch at the top of the steps.

The front door had a wide, short window that was covered with two curtains, with a crack between them; he peered through the crack and simultaneously rang the doorbell. Nothing moved. He rang again, and there was none of the vibration you got from an occupied house.

After a third ring, and another minute on the porch, he walked over to the detached garage and looked in the window: there was an SUV inside, but it appeared to be covered with a thin layer of dust, as though it hadn't been moved for a few weeks. Had Jones been home at all? He'd certainly had the time.

After looking in the garage window, he wandered into the backyard and looked in a window in the back door, but couldn't see anything but the inside of a mudroom, with a bunch of coats hanging on pegs.

He'd climbed down off the stoop when a woman shouted,

"Hello?" He looked around and saw her next door, standing on her own back stoop, an old lady with a cane and Coke-bottle glasses, looking at him with suspicion.

He called back, "I'm a police officer. I'm with the state Bureau of Criminal Apprehension."

"Elijah isn't home. He's in Israel," she called.

Virgil walked over, took his ID out of his pocket, and showed it to her. "He's actually back in the country—he's been here for a while, over at the Mayo," Virgil said.

"Hasn't been here," she said. "He always stops here first thing—he leaves a set of keys with me."

"His biography at the college said he's married," Virgil said. "Is his wife around? Or did she go with him?"

"That's Magda, poor thing. She has Alzheimer's," the old lady said. "She's in a home now. He couldn't take care of her anymore. No, he lives here by himself. His children are gone. One lives up in the Cities, one is out on the West Coast, San Diego, I think. I haven't seen either of them, either."

"How old are they?"

"Oh, the oldest one, Dan, he must be . . . forty-one or forty-two? Ellen must be in her late thirties. I think she's three years younger than Danny."

"Would you have their addresses or phone numbers?"

"Well, no, no, I don't. Ellen works for the state, her last name is Case. You could probably find her that way. Did something bad happen?"

"There's some kind of an argument going on with this dig that Reverend Jones was on," Virgil said, evading the question. "Listen, I'm going to leave a note on his front door. If you should see him, tell him to call me, right away. The moment he gets in."

WHEN VIRGIL left Jones's house, he checked his watch. If Gustavus Adolphus operated like most colleges, he might be too late to talk to anyone, but he wasn't doing anything else anyway, so he decided to take fifteen minutes to run up to the town of St. Peter, where the college was.

Gustavus was a mixture of old and new buildings set on a rolling campus; in the late nineties, it had been hit by a huge F3 tornado that tore the campus apart, but luckily during spring break, and none of the students were killed.

Virgil had to poke around for a few minutes before he found the administration offices, and from there was sent to Jones's department, where he found a woman pecking at a computer keyboard in a small book-stuffed office. Her name was Maicy, she said, an assistant professor. She'd been working every day, she said, because she couldn't afford to go anywhere that summer, and had not seen or heard from Jones.

"We've had a lot of calls, though," she said. "We just haven't been able to help. We can't even believe what they're telling us— that Elijah stole this stele? I mean, if so many people weren't telling us the same story, I would have said it was nonsense. I don't think Elijah ever stole a single thing in his entire life. To steal a stele? It's hardly credible."

She was insistent, and said that if Virgil tracked down other department members, he'd get the same thing from them: until

they saw the proof, they would not believe that Jones was in any
way involved in any theft.

Virgil thanked her and left.

He'd run out of time. The college offices were closing, and
there wouldn't be much more that night. He stopped by Jones's
house again, found his note still on the door, leaned on the bell,
got nothing.

It occurred to him that Jones might be inside, dead. If another
day passed with no sight of the man, he'd go talk to a judge about
that idea—or call the daughter, when he found her.

Virgil went home, ate, and resumed work on a magazine story
about fly-fishing for carp, the part about stalking tailing carp in
shallow water.

YAEL WAS bright and cheerful and drinking coffee when Virgil
arrived at the hotel's restaurant at eight o'clock the next morning.
He slid into the booth across from her, and she said, "I am completely screwed. I slept well until one o'clock this morning and
then I woke up. I haven't been back to sleep since. About four
o'clock this afternoon, I am going to die."

Virgil said, "Maybe we'll be done by four. I couldn't find him
last night, I looked, but he only lives about a half-mile from here.
We'll check his house again, and if we don't find him, we'll
check with his daughter and see if she knows where he is. If she
does, we'll pick him up, get the stele, and send you off to Macy's."

"Macy's and then this Best Buy. Everybody says I should go to
Best Buy for good prices."

"Well, there are lots of them around," Virgil admitted.

"But first, the stele," she said.

"First, I need some pancakes," Virgil said.

During the pancakes, he quizzed her on the investigation of Jones, trying to figure out what she'd been lying about the day before: "I don't want to hassle the wrong guy."

"He's not the wrong man," she said. She detailed the investigation into Jones, including his positive identification by several unconnected individuals in two countries, as well as some exit photos at the airport in Cyprus, and entry checks at Minneapolis.

"It was him, all right," she concluded.

Virgil said, "You know, just off the top of my head, I would have thought that if you were going to steal an Israeli stele, you might try to sneak it out of the country. I mean this place he stole it from—is it in a town, or out in the countryside, or what?"

"Out in the countryside, east of the city of Beth Shean, very close to the Jordan River."

"Okay. Now, Jones has a Ph.D. from an actual legitimate university, so he's probably not stupid. If he'd stolen the stele and then reburied it, say, a few hundred yards away, who would have known? He could have pretended to be as mystified as everyone else. When it was time for him to leave, he could dig up the stone, pack it in his luggage, get a boat out of town. Who's to know?"

"But he didn't do that," she said. "I told you what he did."

"That doesn't make any sense," Virgil said. "I mean, look at it. He finds the stone, digs it up, steals it, steals a car, drives it to the car agency, where it can be traced instantly—he could have left it in a parking lot somewhere, and you might still be looking for it.

Then, dressed as an American Christian minister in a big black
suit with a white collar, who speaks good Hebrew, he calls a taxi
and overtips the driver. Then he gets a ride out of the country with these Germans, who everybody in the marina knows. He
then pees blood into the harbor in Cyprus, so that everybody will
be sure to remember him there, and flies home, where he's met
by an ambulance crew. He couldn't have left a clearer, faster trail
to follow if he'd been dropping ten-dollar bills at each step."

"We considered that," Yael said. "It does seem a little curious—but."

"But?"

"But he stole the stele," she said. "That's very clear. I don't care
if he snuck out of the country by getting Tinker Bell to sprinkle
fairy dust on his ass. I just want the stele."

"Your English is very good," Virgil observed.

"Thank you."

"And you know about Tinker Bell?"

"Of course. My parents have had a condo on South Beach, in
Miami Beach, for forty years," she said. "I was born there. I've
been to Disney World eight or nine times."

"Ah. So you're actually an American?" Virgil asked.

"No. I could have been, but I chose Israel," she said.

ON THE WAY OVER to Jones's house, Virgil went back to Jones's
departure from Israel. "Are you telling me that he stole the car,
drove to this city on the coast . . ."

"Haifa."

"Yeah, Haifa. Then he drops the car at the Avis agency, which he just happens to know where it is, catches a cab before dawn, gets a ride to a specific marina, where he finds two Germans willing to smuggle him out of Israel, no questions asked . . . and he didn't prearrange it? And, of course, he couldn't prearrange it, because he didn't know the stele would be found."

"The diggers left the *tel* at noon and locked the stele up at midnight. He could have easily taken a *sherut* to Haifa, and back, in that time."

"A *sherut*?"

"Like a minibus," she said. "Or he could have taken a taxi."

"So Haifa's not far?"

"Maybe an hour and a half," Yael said.

"You checked to see that he was gone for at least, say, five hours in that period? Time enough to catch a bus, get there, make arrangements, and get back?"

"There seems to be some controversy about that, but I don't care," she said.

"And you don't care, because he stole the stele, and that's what you care about."

"Correct," she said.

At Jones's house, Virgil's note was gone from the door. He rang the doorbell again, and a second time, then reached out to the doorknob . . . and it turned in his hand. Hell, this was Minnesota. He pushed the door open and called, "Hello? Anybody home?"

He heard the creak of a floorboard from the back of the house. "Hello? This is the police. Anybody there?"

He heard two quick steps and then the back door banged open and Virgil was running through the house. It occurred to him, as he cleared a china cabinet full of blue-and-white Spode dishes and cups, that usually, in this situation, the cop had a gun. His was in the truck, and not for the first time, he thought, *Jeez*.

He went through the kitchen and took a wrong turn, into a dead end that led to a stairs down into a basement. He reversed field, and through a back window saw a tall, dark-complected young man with long hair, in a T-shirt and jeans, hop a back fence and dash between the two houses that backed up to Jones's house.

Virgil ran back through the kitchen and through the mud-room, out the back door and across the backyard. There was a four-foot fence separating Jones's yard from the house it backed up to. He clambered over the fence and ran to the front of the house; but none of that was as fast as the runner had done it, because Virgil was wearing cowboy boots and the runner was wearing running shoes.

He was in time to see a champagne-colored Camry pull away from the curb a hundred yards farther on, and accelerate down the block and then around the corner. The car was too far away to get the tag, but it was from Minnesota, and he noted a basketball-sized dent in the left rear bumper.

"Shoot." He felt for his phone, and remembered it was on the charger in the car.

He jogged back around the block, got the cell phone, and

called 911 and identified himself and asked the Mankato dispatcher to have her patrolmen take the tag numbers on any champagne-colored Camrys they saw in the area. "The driver is tall, with long dark hair. He looked sort of like an Apache. Or, because of what I'm doing, he could have been Middle Eastern."

The dispatcher said she would do that, but, "There are probably two hundred champagne-colored Camrys in town. That's probably the most common car in the world."

"Yeah, but . . . do it anyway," Virgil said. "The car had a dent in the left rear bumper. And you might send a car around to a probable burglary."

HE'D BEEN TALKING to the 911 operator from Jones's front lawn. When he got off the phone, he went back inside the house, where he found Yael innocently standing in Jones's living room, examining a wall of photographs.

"Did you look around?" he asked.

"Of course not," she said. "That would be illegal. I don't have a search warrant."

"Good. If I were to get a search warrant and look around, do you think I'd find a body? Or a stele?"

"No, I don't think you would," she said.

"Then there's no reason to hurry," Virgil said.

"Well, when I came to look at these photos, I noticed a smear of some kind on the floor in the hallway, there." She pointed at a hallway that probably went back to a bathroom and some bedrooms. "Perhaps you should check it."

Virgil went that way. The smear was three feet from the point where the hallway entered the front room and was about the size of Virgil's index finger.

"Looks like dried blood," Virgil said.

"I couldn't really tell from this far away," Yael said.

"Right," Virgil said.

"The police are here," she said.

Virgil walked back through the living room and saw two city cops coming up the walk. He stepped out on the porch and said, "Hey, Jimmy. Paula."

"Hey, Virg," Jimmy said. "You got a burglary?"

"Well, I got a runner, anyway," Virgil said.

He told them about chasing the Camry man out of the house, and introduced Yael, and she told them about the search for Elijah Jones. Neither of the cops knew Jones, and Virgil said, "I'm going to walk around for a while, see what the neighbors say."

"We'll take a look around," said Jimmy. "Paula, get the basement."

Yael said, "I should stay here with Paula and Jimmy. I would recognize the stele."

Virgil went first to the house on the right, but nobody was home. Then he went back to the old lady's house. She answered the door and said, "I think he was back last night. He didn't come over, but I saw lights in the house, late."

"You didn't see him this morning?"

"No, and I get up early. I went and knocked on his door, but nobody answered, and your note was gone."

"But you're not sure it was Jones himself."

"No, I guess not. Could have been Ellen, I suppose."

VIRGIL THANKED HER, and walked back to his truck and called Davenport. "This may be a little more complicated than you thought," he said.

After a moment of silence, Davenport asked, "Why can't anything you do be simple? Get the steelee and send Yale home."

"Well, I went over to talk to Jones this morning, but he wasn't there, but a burglar was, and I think there's blood on the floor."

"Ahhhh . . . shit."

"Yeah. But it might not be from violence. He's got cancer, and he's apparently been leaking a lot of blood." Virgil told him about the runner, and about the smear, and about how Yael was lying about something, and then he asked, "Do you have any hint what this stele might involve? I mean, it looks like Yael's not the only one who wants it. And wants it bad enough to break into a house."

"No idea," Davenport said. "But if there's blood, and a burglary, then put the screws to this chick. We need to know."

"I don't think she'll tell me," Virgil said.

"How about the other people on this dig? They must know something. Couldn't you call one of them?"

"I was just about to do that," Virgil lied. "I'm tracking down some names now. But I wanted to update you on the blood thing."

"Okay. Don't bother to call me unless you've got something

serious. If this is gonna be another fuckin' Flowers circus, I don't want the details."

DAVENPORT occasionally had some good ideas, Virgil thought, as he rang off. Like calling people from the dig. It should be late afternoon in Israel, so if he could call soon . . .

He dug his iPad out of the pocket of the passenger-side seat-back. He signed on, went to the Gustavus Adolphus website, got the names of the other faculty in Jones's department, and the main number for the school. After hassling a bit with a function-ary in the school's office, he got home phone numbers for four other faculty members. He struck out on the first one—no answer—but the second one, Patricia Carlson, picked up on the first ring. Virgil identified himself, and asked her what she knew about the dig, or anyone else on it.

"Hang on a minute," she said. "I need to go online here."

A minute later, she said, "There are seven Gustavus students at the dig, and one parent. I have the emergency cell phone number for the parent, in Israel. Her name is Annabelle Johnson."

The miracles of modern communication, Virgil thought. He'd gone online from a computer in his truck, which coughed up phone numbers for a college faculty in a different town, and from there, had gotten a phone number for a woman half a world away.

Earlier that year, he'd been fishing at a fly-in camp in north-west Ontario, fifty miles from the nearest road, and another guy, whose wife was pregnant, and whose father was seriously ill, had a sat phone, and had daily conversations with them both, routed through his personal satellite link.

ANNABELLE JOHNSON was in a dormitory at an Israeli kibbutz. She'd been taking her afternoon nap when Virgil called. He explained the problem, and she said, in a hushed voice, "We're not supposed to talk about it. We're shocked, here. Shocked when Elijah ran away."

"I'm working with an investigator from Israel," Virgil said. "I'm not sure she's being entirely up front with me. I could really use some help."

He told Johnson about the encounter at Jones's house and about the smear on the floor. "I can't find Reverend Jones, and that worries me—especially if that smear turns out to be blood. Can you tell me if Jones was behaving differently on this trip? I know he's sick . . ."

"He's dying," Johnson said.

"That's what I've been told," Virgil said. "Even given that, how was he behaving? Was there anything unusual about him, in the days before he found the stele?"

"Listen, this dig is really rough work. It's like excavating a basement using nothing but trowels, in a hundred-and-four-degree heat. People feel bad all the time. There's always somebody who's dehydrated, who can't make it out in the morning. So it's hard to tell when something unusual is going on," Johnson said. "Elijah was sick, and sometimes he didn't make it out. But he tried, every day. I was so happy when the stele came up—I was right in the next square, and when he found that first edge, it was like, 'Okay, this could be amazing.' But we'll find something that could be amazing several times every dig, and they usually turn out to be disappointments. But this—this was even more amazing than anything we'd ever expected."

"Why would he run away with it?" Virgil asked. "He'd have to know that everybody would be on his trail. What could he accomplish?"

Johnson said, "I think he saw what was on the stele and he freaked out. Something just broke. All the stress from the dig, from the heat, from the cancer, from worrying about his wife . . . and then this. I think he snapped."

Virgil: "The Israeli investigator here said it'd be quite a while before they knew *what* was on the stele. You mean . . . he already knew?"

"Oh, God," Johnson said. "We're *really* not supposed to talk about that. Too many people already know. There are all kinds of photographs. Even some of the kids have photographs, although they're supposed to have turned them over to the Israelis. It's bound to get out."

"What is it?" Virgil said. "Is it really a big deal?"

"Oh, yeah. About as big as it could get," Johnson said.

"What is it?"

Johnson told him about it.

4

When Yael walked out of the house, Virgil was in his truck, talking to Davenport.

". . . up my ass," he said. "This thing is gonna turn into a screaming nightmare."

"I didn't know. Nobody knew," Davenport said.

"I'll tell you what, Lucas. We gotta find Jones in the next ten minutes, get that stone back, and get Yael out of here," Virgil said. "If that's blood in there . . . And with that runner this morning, there's gotta be somebody else involved. Yael says she has no idea who it might be."

"I'm hearing you. When will we know if it's blood?"

"Pretty quick. The Mankato crime-scene guy will be over in a few minutes. I mean, I could probably get a paper towel and put a little spit on it . . ."

"Maybe you ought to wait for the crime-scene guy," Davenport said.

"Yeah, yeah. Ah, poop. Here she comes. I'm gonna jump down her throat."

"Go ahead. Do it in a nice way. Remember, they're our allies."

HE HUNG UP THE PHONE as Yael popped the passenger-side door and asked, "Am I invited in?"

Virgil said, "Yeah, climb in."

"I was talking to the police officers," she said, as she got into the passenger seat and closed the door. "They think it's blood. They're almost sure it is." Virgil eyed her for a moment, and she finally asked, "What is it?"

"Yael, you've been lying like a mm . . ." He suppressed the "motherfucker." "You've been lying, and you forgot that everybody has cell phones. I talked to some people at the dig, and they all know what the stele said. I can guarantee it'll be in the *New York Times* in the next few days."

"That'd be terrible."

"Whatever. Now, what I think is, you're going to tell me everything you know or I'm gonna kick your ass out of the truck and you can do your investigation from a taxicab," Virgil said.

"That's not fair."

"Not fair? Gimme a break," Virgil said. "You think it's fair that I should go looking for somebody and not know who else is around, when there's blood on the floor? Am I gonna get shot investigating this thing? Is somebody else going to get shot? Has somebody already been shot? Is this thing worth killing for?"

She didn't answer.

He said, "Answer! Is it worth killing for?"

She mumbled, "Who knows? Maybe. To some crazies."

"Israeli crazies? American crazies?"

She shrugged. "Palestinian crazies, Syrian crazies, Egyptian crazies, maybe a couple of Israeli crazies. Turks. Some Americans, too, I suppose. Maybe the Pope."

"The Pope?"

"Okay, maybe not the Pope." She hesitated, and said, "Then again . . . maybe."

"Maybe? Why didn't you tell me that last night, or this morning?" Virgil asked. "You walked me right into a place where there was probably a crime under way, and you gave me no warning."

"All right, all right." She waved a hand at him, as if to dismiss unwarranted whining. "I'll tell you. There may be some propaganda value in this stele, if it's real. That's a big *if*. I didn't know anybody else would be here, or I would have warned you. Now that I do, it's obvious what happened."

"Oh, really? It's not obvious to me," Virgil said.

"Okay, so let me tell you. Jones is trying to sell it. Being in Israel as much as he is, he knows about the antiquities market, and he knows who the big buyers are. He also knows what this thing is worth . . . if it's real."

"Well, is it real?"

She seemed to be thinking for a moment, then sighed and said, "It's got a very good provenance. It was uncovered at a major dig site, by people of the highest reputation and the greatest experience, with thirty witnesses. They actually photographed it coming out of the ground. Highly detailed photographs taken with a Nikon D800. I don't know if you're familiar with this camera . . ."

"I own one. Keep talking."

"So, I looked at the photos and the earth around the stone did not appear to be disturbed at all . . . and usually you can tell. Or, at least, the diggers can. Old compacted dirt is different than new compacted dirt. So it appears to be very real."

"The people I talked to at the dig . . . What's a *tel*? She said she was at a *tel*."

"It's a hill, a mound, that covers the site of an ancient city."

"Okay. The people working on this *tel* said that there are several people there who can read Egyptian hieroglyphics, and they had a hieroglyphics dictionary, too, and that they're pretty sure it's about some guy called Semen and about Solomon—"

"It's not semen. Semen is—"

"I know what semen is. Just tell me."

So, SHE TOLD HIM.

"There was a pharaoh named Siamun. Not semen. He became pharaoh around 986 BCE, which was about the middle of the reign of King David," Yael said. "That's according to the traditional dates. He overlapped with King Solomon, who was David's sole surviving heir . . . after he finished killing off David's other sons, anyway. If you believe the Bible."

"Do you believe in it? The Bible?"

She shrugged. "Some parts of the histories, yes. Most of it is foundation myths, tall tales, and literature. Do you believe in Moby Dick?"

"*Moby Dick* is a novel, not a history," Virgil said.

"Do you believe in the details about whaling ships and whaling boats and all that? All the detail in the novel?"

"Some of it, I guess. Yeah, most of it."

"That's the Bible," Yael said. "I believe some of it."

"So . . . what does the stele have to do with this?" Virgil asked.

"It's a triumphal stele, that may have been in secondary use—"

"What does that mean?"

"It means that it might have been brought from somewhere else, thousands of years ago. It was originally a pillar, then got thrown down and broken up, and finally might have been used as a foundation stone or a cutting block or something, by people who didn't know what it was," she said. "This *tel* is only about five klicks east of Beth Shean, which was an Egyptian administrative city, off and on, over the centuries. Anyway, there is an inscription on it. . . ."

The inscription, Yael said, was in two languages: an extremely primitive form of Hebrew, and in hieroglyphics.

"The problem is, mmm, Hebrew is a more or less phonetic language, but in the very earliest versions, there are some unfamiliar letters that are not yet fully evolved, and perhaps the phonics, the *sounds* made by the individual letters, had not yet completely solidified."

"Okay . . ."

"Okay . . . so the stele seems to describe a routine victory by

Siamun, over a not-very-big city. We don't know which one. That part of the stone is missing."

"So what?"

"So . . . the Hebrew version, on the other side of the stele, seems to describe exactly the same victory, in very much the same words, but this time, the victory is ascribed to Solomon."

Virgil thought about that for a moment, then said, "I don't know what that means, either."

"Well, there are a lot of odd things about Solomon," Yael said. Then: "That police officer wants you."

Virgil looked up at Jones's house, where one of the cops beckoned to him. He leaned past Yael and called, "Give me two minutes."

The cop waved and went back inside.

VIRGIL SAID to Yael, "Keep going."

"If you read the Bible closely, and if the Bible is correct, you realize that David was not a rich and powerful king. He ran a small kingdom—in the beginning, you could walk from one end of it to the other in a single day, and it was mostly rural and poor. It got much larger during his reign, but never particularly rich. It was almost like David was the leader of a motorcycle gang, instead of a real king."

Virgil nodded: "I remember that much, from Bible class. But Solomon . . ."

"Solomon suddenly has enormous riches, and a huge treasury, and seven hundred wives and three hundred concubines, and the

Queen of Sheba comes all the way from Sheba, which is way at the far end of the Arabian Peninsula, in Yemen, to sleep with him," Yael said. "That doesn't make a huge amount of sense for a ruler of an insignificant kingdom that had always been under the thumb of the Egyptians."

"I still don't know what it means," Virgil said.

She slapped him sharply on the thigh with an open hand: "Think, idiot. If this stele is real, it suggests that Siamun might have been the model for Solomon. Might have been the *real* Solomon. That there *was no* Jewish Solomon—that David's kingdom was taken over by an Egyptian pharaoh named Siamun, who became the Jewish Solomon in the early tales, probably through transcription errors and changes in early Hebrew phonetics. The Bible wasn't put together until three or four hundred years after Solomon, or Siamun, died, so the Bible writers were relying on oral histories and maybe a few inscriptions. Things get *warped*."

"So, uh, the biggest king of the Jews . . ."

"Yes. Was an Egyptian. If the stele is real. In Israel, that's a development we'd call 'unfortunate.' David's important both to Christians and Muslims, too—in fact, the Messiah is supposed to be descended from David. Well, Solomon killed all of David's surviving sons, according to the Bible. He was the last one left. So if you trace the lineage back . . . Jesus is descended not from the Jewish David, but the Egyptian pharaoh Siamun."

"That's not something you hear every day," Virgil admitted.

"No kidding. The crazies all over the Middle East already deny that Israel is a legitimate Jewish homeland. If it turns out that

Solomon was an Egyptian, well, it's another stick on the fire. A pretty big stick, too."

"And if you had some kind of proof of that, like a stele, you could probably sell it for the big bucks."

"That's what we think."

"Ah, boy," Virgil said. "Yesterday, I was investigating a redneck woman who was selling fake antique barn lumber. Today, I'm up to my crotch in Solomon."

"Who'd want *real* antique barn lumber?" Yael asked.

"Rich people," Virgil said. "Mostly on the East Coast."

"Ah," she said, as though she understood completely.

A city van pulled up, and a man hopped out. "That's the crime-scene guy," Virgil said. "Let's go see if it's blood."

She opened the truck door but before she got out, Virgil said, "One more question."

"Yeah?"

"Does this stele have any special powers?" Virgil asked.

"What?"

"I mean, if you mess with it, could you be struck by lightning or be carried up in a whirlwind, or something?"

"Maybe you could be struck by lightning, if you carried it out on a golf course during a thunderstorm," she said. "Or, you could drop it on your foot. It's heavier than a concrete block, because it's not hollow. It's got a really sharp edge. That would hurt a lot."

"Still, that'd be better than taking a hundred million volts in the back of the neck because you pissed off Yahweh," Virgil said.

"Virgil . . ."

"Just pulling your weenie," he said. "Let's go see what the cops want."

INSIDE, THE CRIME-SCENE GUY, whose name was Simon Hamm, and who was often called Simple, even to his face, was kneeling in the hallway with his eye about a quarter inch above the smear on the floor.

Virgil said, "Hey, Simon. Is it blood?"

Hamm looked up and said, "Hand me one of those paper towels from the kitchen."

Virgil walked across the living room to the kitchen, got a paper towel, and brought it back. Hamm said, "We got the main smear, but we've also got a couple little drops that are otherwise useless." He spit on the paper towel and scrubbed one of the spots, then looked at the towel.

"Yep, it's blood," he said. He held up the towel so Virgil could see the crimson smear.

"That makes my day," Virgil said. "Though it's not much blood."

"Not much, but it's more than you'd get from nicking your finger with a bread knife," Hamm said. "The other thing is, it's all in one spot. It's not like he was dripping a little blood—it's like he was bleeding and not moving."

"This doesn't seem good," Yael said.

"See, recognizing that—that's why you're a highly paid investigator," Virgil said.

"So what do we do next?"

Virgil looked at his watch. "First, we'll go through the house,
in detail, to see if he hid the stone here. Then, we'll run up to the
Twin Cities and see if we can surprise his daughter. Maybe Jones
is hiding out with her."

HAMM ESCORTED THEM through the house. He didn't want them
in it at all, because of the possibility that a violent crime had been
committed, but Virgil insisted on looking for places that the stele
might be hidden.

"The problem with that is, the guy who was here when you
came in—he might have left prints, but we don't know where,"
Hamm said. "If you go digging around, you'll ruin them."

"So *you* open the doors," Virgil said. "We'll just look."

And that's what they did. They went through two bedrooms, a
third bedroom that had been converted to a study, two bath-
rooms, a small home office niche, the living room, and the basement, and then out to the garage. They found no sign of a stele,
no body, and no further evidence of violence. The Nissan Xterra
was still in the garage, still covered with garage dust. Although
Jones had apparently been home, he hadn't moved the truck. Virgil looked inside, to see if he might have stashed the stone there,
but the truck was empty.

In the house, one living room wall was devoted to photo-

graphs, mostly small, and mostly taken at a variety of digs in Israel, featuring Jones and a cheerful, slightly overweight woman
Virgil thought was probably Jones's wife. Yael pointed out various
well-known Israelis, posing with Jones. "This is Jones with Yigael
Yadin, probably the most famous archaeologist in Israel, after the
War of Independence," Yael said. "They look very friendly together. I confess, I am impressed."

"This can't be right," Vigil said of another. "He's playing golf
by the Pyramids."

"I don't know, I've never been to Egypt," Yael said. "But I tell
you, in my job, I travel to sites all over Israel, and there are sites
here that I haven't seen. I believe this one is Samaria, on the West
Bank, it must have been years ago. He was digging near Jericho . . .
here." She tapped a photo. "Not the best place for a Jew."

"Maybe not so bad for a Lutheran," Virgil said. "Especially one
with a bushy black beard."

"Perhaps," she said.

There were three or four photos, wide-angle shots, taken in
Minnesota at what looked like ministerial conferences. Virgil examined them closely, then said to Yael, pointing at a sandy-haired
man at the edge of one of the shots, "This is my father. Must've
been twenty years ago. He would have been maybe ten years
older than I am now."

She nodded. "I see the resemblance. Was he disappointed that
you didn't follow in his footsteps?"

"No, he knew I'd never had a call to the ministry. He was just
hoping I wouldn't become a moonshiner or a stock-car driver.

Being a cop was just fine with him: he imagines that I'm on the side of the angels."

"You're not?"

Virgil shook his head: "There're not many angels around any-more. Not in my work."

HAMM THREW THEM OUT when they didn't find the stone, or anything that might have the stone in it, and told them not to come back too soon. "This will take a while. What do I do if Jones shows up?"

"Bust him," Virgil said. "We have a warrant for him and an Is-raeli extradition request."

"I haven't arrested anyone in fifteen years," Hamm said.

"So, get one of the other guys to do it. Or, you know, just say, 'You're under arrest,' and make him sit on the couch until some-body else gets here."

"So that's how it's done now," Hamm said, scratching his neck. "I don't remember it being that easy."

Two minutes later, Virgil and Yael were on their way to the Twin Cities. Virgil had gotten Jones's daughter's name from the old woman next door, and had found her phone number on a list tacked inside a kitchen cabinet, next to a telephone.

He called Davenport with that information, and asked for a callback, detailing where Ellen Case worked. Davenport said he would give it to his researcher, Sandy, and Sandy called back ten minutes later with a home address and the information that Case was a highway engineer with the state Department of Transportation.

"Call her and tell her to stay where she's at, so we don't have to chase all over town," Virgil told her. "We'll be there in an hour and a half, or so."

"I'll call her," Sandy said.

When he was off the phone, Yael said, "If she's involved in this plan, she may warn her father."

Virgil nodded. "Maybe."

"That doesn't bother you?"

"No, because I plan to scare the shit out of her," Virgil said. "I'll draw her a picture of how her career ends in disgrace, how she might spend fifteen years in an Israeli prison. Or maybe a Minnesota prison. I'll tell her about the blood on the floor, and that if she lies to us, she may be involved in a murder conspiracy, which is thirty years' hard time in Minnesota. She's a bureaucrat: she'll know all about cutting her losses."

Sandy called back a few minutes later and said, "She's not working. She's on vacation. A guy at her office said she's getting over a divorce, and decided to take a long wandering trip to Alaska. By car."

"Well . . . that's a poke in the eye," Virgil said.

"That's what I thought," Sandy said.

Virgil got off the phone, told Yael, who said, "I suspect this is a ploy. It's too convenient that she is on a vacation so far away, while her father dies."

"You really do speak good English," Virgil said. He pulled onto the shoulder of the highway and waited for a line of traffic to pass so he could make a U-turn. "I've never heard anybody use the word 'ploy.'"

"Perhaps because you live in a rural state?"

"What?"

HE MADE THE U-TURN and they headed back south, and had gone about three hundred yards when he took another call, this one from a Mankato cop named Georgina. She said that Mankato had collected tag numbers on forty-two Toyota Camrys that might have been considered champagne, depending on who was considering it.

"I would say it would probably run from gold to silver," she said. "Anyway, you said something about this guy might be a Middle Easterner, so when I ran the numbers, I was looking for something that might be relevant. The good news is, an Arab-sounding guy popped up, a student here at the U, so I thought I'd give you a ring. His name is Faraj Awad. You want the address now?"

"I do," Virgil said. He wrote it on a notepad. "Thank you. Now, what's the bad news?"

"My husband gets back tonight, unless he gets stuck in Chicago," she said. "I probably won't make it down to the Coop."

"Aw, man—Wendy's playing."

"You know I'd give anything to be there," she said. "But Ralph's gonna want his pound of flesh."

"Well, shoot—make it if you can. Don't bring Ralph."

"He wouldn't be caught dead doing a two-step," Georgina said.

"THIS COULD BE INTERESTING," Yael said, when Virgil told her about Awad. "If we can get passport details, maybe I can talk to somebody in Israel and get more information."

Virgil called and told Davenport about the change of circumstance. Davenport put him on hold, and came back in one minute: "He's got a Minnesota driver's license. Been here for at least two years."

ON THE WAY BACK TO MANKATO, Virgil and Yael spent most of the drive time talking about the Solomon stone, archaeology, and about the differences between Minnesota and Israel. There were many; in fact, there were almost no similarities, geographically, climatically, ethnically, or culturally. Minnesota was about nine times larger than Israel in land area, but Israel had about two million more people.

"Everything here is so green. In Israel, we have more tan," she said. She examined a farm they were passing, and sniffed at the distinctive aroma: "And you have far more pigs."

She also tried to nap, but without success: "I hate jet lag," she groaned, after ten minutes with her eyes closed. She sat up and smacked her lips. "My mouth tastes like a hoopoe has been roosting in it."

"A what?"

"A hoopoe. It's our national bird."

"Ah," Virgil said. "Minnesota's state bird is the rotisserie chicken."

"A chicken?"

"It's because we're a rural state," Virgil said. "You know, the politicians have to please the farmers."

"I'll have to look them up, these chickens," Yael said. "If you see one, point it out."

"I will do that," Virgil said.

5

araj Awad, according to his driver's license, lived at North Star Village, an apartment complex for students not far from the university. Virgil had driven past it, but had never stopped.

As he turned into the parking lot, he judged it as an okay place, but not great: the four rectangular, yellow-painted concrete-block buildings in the complex were neatly kept, but offered neither individual garages nor an underground parking garage. Given Mankato's winter weather, a garage was a serious consideration.

But not today.

Temperatures would be reaching well into the eighties, and could touch ninety. They cruised through the lot, and found Awad's car—the exact shade that Virgil remembered, with a basketball-sized dent in the left rear bumper—in the second row.

"There we go," Virgil said, pleased with himself for making the call on the Camry.

When they got out of the car, Yael said, "This is another difference, from Israel to here. I am drowning in the humidity. The air feels thick."

"It gets worse," Virgil said. "On the other hand, this is the most beautiful place in the world, in August. If you like water and natural color. And rural states."

He opened the truck's back door, used a key to unlock the gun safe hidden under the backseat, took out his pistol, already in a soft waistband holster, checked it, and tucked it behind his belt at the small of his back. Then he took a sport coat that had been folded in a plastic bag out of the back and pulled it on.

"You prefer the Glock?" Yael asked with a frown.

"It's preferred by my agency," Virgil said. "You're familiar with them?"

"Yes. I'm much happier with a Sig 229 in .40 Smith & Wesson," she said. "Though I would also take a Beretta, if it was well turned."

"I don't know much about pistols and I'm not that good a shot," Virgil said. "When there's a problem, I prefer an M16 or a good solid pump shotgun."

Yael said, "Hmm. Have you ever had to shoot at a human being?"

Virgil said, "Yes, unfortunately," and headed for Building B. She hurried to catch up, and Virgil half-turned to ask, "You're a good pistol shot?"

"Very good," she said. "But as an IAA investigator, I mostly arrest people for digging holes in *tels*. Or illegally selling antiquities to tourists, on those rare occasions when the antiquities are real. I've never had a chance to test myself in combat."

"It's not all that it's cracked up to be," Virgil said.

"You will have to tell me," she said. "Such experience is rare."

"Have to get me drunk first," Virgil said.

THE APARTMENT BUILDINGS each had an interior porch, with unlocked doors to the outside, but a second set of locked doors
going in. Awad was in Building B, "The Sunflower." Virgil leaned
on the buzzer for the manager's office, but no one answered.

They'd waited three or four minutes when a young woman
popped out of an elevator inside and walked out through the interior doors. Virgil caught it when it opened, and held it for her,
but she stopped and said, uncertainly, "You're not supposed to
do that—go in."

Virgil fished his ID out of his pocket and said, "I'm with the
state Bureau of Criminal Apprehension. We've been buzzing the
manager, but nobody answers."

"That's no big surprise," the woman said. "She considers all
calls to be a pain in the butt, so she mostly doesn't answer anything."

"I'll talk to her about that," Virgil said. He ushered Yael inside,
and the woman went on her way.

Just inside the door were a series of mailboxes, and 220 said:
"Awad."

"We should talk to the manager?" Yael asked.

"Why? She doesn't want to talk to *us*," Virgil said. "Let's go
upstairs and knock on his door."

THE INTERIOR of the apartment building resembled a lower-end
travel motel, with a central atrium going up three floors to a sky-

light, and two sets of red-carpeted stairs winding up on either side of the atrium's core. There were also elevators, but Virgil took the stairs, with Yael at his elbow.

There appeared to be about a hundred doorways down the corridors stretching north and south from the central atrium, the doors painted in varying shades of red, blue, and yellow in a failed effort to make them look stylish. Awad's was blue-green. Virgil knocked on the door, and a second later, heard a thump from inside.

"Somebody's home," he said. He stepped a bit sideways from the door, gestured to Yael to get behind him, knocked again, and put a hand on his pistol. A moment later, the door opened two inches, and a man peered out through the crack behind a chain: Virgil could see a single dark brown eye. "What?"

Virgil held up his ID. "We need to chat with you, about Reverend Jones."

The man's eye narrowed, and Virgil thought he'd slam the door, but then he said, "Ahhhh . . . I will take the chain."

The door closed an inch, and the chain rattled and the man said, "Come in," to Virgil, and then, "Why are you bringing an Israeli?"

Virgil was inside, with Yael a step behind him. "How'd you know she was an Israeli?"

The man shrugged: "She looks like one."

Virgil: "You're Faraj Awad?"

"Yes, but everybody calls me Raj," the man said. "And you're . . . Virgil?"

"Virgil Flowers. Yes."

Virgil looked around. Awad's apartment was small, with a

kitchenette, a fourteen-by-twelve living room, and a tiny balcony overlooking the parking lot. A bedroom was off to the right, and through an open door Virgil could see that it was barely big enough to contain a queen-sized bed. The bathroom was apparently out of sight off the bedroom.

The living room was furnished with a couch, two chairs, a coffee table, and a worktable with a laptop and a printer in the middle, and a small flat-panel TV sitting on one end of it, facing the couch. A soccer ball was half hidden under the coffee table, along with stacks of books, American magazines and newspapers, and two twenty-five-pound dumbbells.

Awad was an inch or two shorter than Virgil, slender and square-jawed, with a short, carefully cut beard, longish black hair, and large dark eyes. He had a gold earring in one ear. He would, Virgil thought, do well with the Mankato State coeds, if he was inclined to. He said, "Come in and sit down. Even the Israeli, as long as she builds no settlements behind my couch."

Virgil asked, "Why'd you break into Jones's house this morning?"

Awad dropped on the couch and shook his head, not bothering to deny that he'd been there. "I didn't. I was invited to come over to look at a stone. I was on time, I knocked, but nobody answered. I knew he was sick, so I went inside—the door was not locked—and called to him. Nobody answered. I was writing a note to him when you came in . . . I suppose it was you."

"It was," Virgil said. "Why did you run?"

"I thought you might be the Turk," Awad said.

"The Turk," Yael repeated.

"Yes. You definitely do not want to mess with the Turk. He cut your good parts off. Well, maybe not you, but"—he pointed at Virgil—"you."

Virgil thought, *First things first*, and asked, "Where's this note you were writing to Jones?"

"Should still be there, in the kitchen."

Virgil said to Yael, "Don't let him run—I'm going to make a phone call."

"Yeah, I'll stop him," she said. "I'll hit him with my purse."

Awad said to her, "Your personality alone would be enough. You are one very attractive Jewess."

"Keep talking," she said.

"Ah, Jesus," Virgil said.

VIRGIL CHOSE to step into the hall, leaving the door mostly open, in case one of them tried to strangle the other. He called Mankato PD to get the cell number of the crime-scene guy, and when he had it, called and asked about the note.

"It was on the floor by the kitchen counter. All it says is, 'Dear Mr. Minister Jones . . .' That's it."

"Thanks," Virgil said, and rang off. He had no case on Awad, even if he wanted one. Not unless Awad's fingerprints were found on the patch of blood.

Back inside, Awad was saying to Yael, "Think about it. I am a young single Lebanese Arab man who is attending a flight school. You think I want to get caught by the American police for breaking and entering? I'm surprised Virgil didn't bring Homeland Security with him, to kick down the door. Not even my large and succulent personality could help me then."

Virgil came in, sat on the couch, winced, took the gun out of the small of his back and put it in his jacket pocket. "So," he said, "who's the Turk?"

"One minute," Awad said. He went to the worktable, picked up the laptop, came back to the couch, touched some icons, and a note page popped up: "He is a man named Timur Kaya," he said, looking at the laptop page. Virgil moved closer, looked over his shoulder, took a notepad out of his jacket pocket, and copied the spelling.

Awad continued: "He represents another man named Burak Sahin." He tapped the laptop screen, and Virgil noted that name, too.

"According to my uncle, Kaya spent his earlier days in Turkish Army intelligence, cutting the testicles off Kurds, when they would not tell him where the other Kurds were hiding," Awad said. "My uncle told me to be careful with my testicles." He looked at Yael. "I am very fond of them."

"I'm sure they are quite valuable," she said.

"This is correct," Awad said. "Mmm. So: he is employed by Sahin, who is a big collector of important artifacts from former Turkish lands. Like Israel. The rumor is that he will pay five million for this stone the minister has."

"Five million?" Virgil was incredulous. He knew a guy who'd killed a friend's wife for ten thousand dollars and the papers to a three-year-old Buick. He looked at Yael. "It's worth five million? You didn't tell me that."

"We weren't concerned with how much it would sell for—we're only concerned that it's stolen property," she said. "We're not going to pay to get it back."

"Then I think," Awad said, performing a full-dress Middle Eastern shrug, which involved the entire body, "that you will not see it again."

ACCORDING TO AWAD, his uncle had called him from Beirut and said that a man he knew was interested in buying the stone, and would pay a large amount of money for it. Awad was not being asked to make the payment himself, but to simply verify Jones's possession of the stone. If he did that, then Awad would arrange for the buyer to meet Jones for the exchange.

"Who is this that your uncle knows?" Virgil asked.

"I do not know the answer to that question," Awad said. "I asked, and my uncle said it was best that I did not ask."

"The Party of God," Yael said.

"This is possible, but I would not venture, under any conditions, to say so myself," Awad said.

"The Party of God—is that bad?" Virgil asked.

"You may know them as the terrorist group Hezbollah," Yael said.

"Okay, that's not desirable," Virgil said.

"So, with three killers seeking this stone already, I think it's time for Raj Awad to preserve his testicles and take a vacation,"

Awad said. "Perhaps to New England. New England is supposed to be nice in the summer."

Virgil: "Three killers? This Kaya guy, the Hezbollah buyer—who's the other one?"

Awad looked at Virgil, as if not believing his ears, then at Yael. When Virgil still didn't catch on, he poked a finger at her.

"She's with the Israel Antiquities Authority," Virgil said. "She does antiques."

Awad snorted. "They sent an antique dealer to compete with the Turk and the Hezbollah? I tell you, Virgil, I use an American idiom here. Your head is placed where the sun don't shine."

Virgil looked at Yael, who said nothing, then back to Awad: "The sun don't shine?"

"She is Mossad, Virgil. Or Shabak. She cut your throat like a young goat." Awad drew his index finger across his throat.

"A young goat?" Virgil looked at Yael.

Yael said, "He's been on the *kief*. I'm with the IAA."

Awad snorted again, and Virgil said to Yael, "You were talking about favorite pistols? You prefer a Sig or even a well-turned Beretta? And you're an antiquities expert?"

"Israel is different," Yael said, looking away.

"This is true," Awad said. To Yael: "I am told that young, attractive Mossad women are sometimes used to seduce their Arab targets."

"I wouldn't know," Yael said. "But I wouldn't get your hopes up."

"I would gladly volunteer for this interrogation," Awad said.

"Ah, Jesus," Virgil said, and he went back to the hall.

HE CALLED DAVENPORT. "I haven't found the stone yet, but I'm making some progress. I wanted to update you in case I'm found dead."

"Virgil . . ."

"Lucas, I found the guy who was in the house. He's acting as a kind of representative for Hezbollah, the terrorist group, in Lebanon. He says there's another character in the hunt, a former Turkish Army intelligence officer, known for cutting the testicles off Kurds. He also tells me that Yael is not from the Israel Antiquities Authority, but from the Mossad. Or . . . uh . . . I think he said Shabak, which is apparently some other Israeli intelligence agency that kills people. She denies it, but she's lying."

Davenport was silent for a moment, typing on a keyboard, then said, "Shabak . . . I'm looking at Google. It's Israeli internal security. I guess here in the States we call it the Shin Bet. They do seem to kill some people. Interesting."

"Interesting? I'm dealing with a Turk who cuts your balls off, a Middle Eastern terrorist group, and an Israeli gun moll, and you say it's *interesting*?"

"It *is* interesting. You need some help?"

"Yes. The first thing is, I want you to get onto whoever it is you get onto, your fed friend in Washington, that Mallard guy. Find out if they have anything on a Turk named Timur Kaya." Virgil spelled it.

"I'll get on that," Davenport said. "And I could spring Jenkins and Shrake if you need more manpower."

"Not yet, but I might. I'm going to poke this beehive a couple more times, but you tell those guys to get ready, in case I call."

VIRGIL HAD just stepped back through the door when Awad took a phone call. He listened for a moment, and said, "I will call you back. I cannot talk at this moment."

He hung up and said to Virgil, "Football friend." He tapped the soccer ball with a toe.

Virgil said, "Raj, I swear to God, if you run, I'll have you arrested and shipped to Israel. Not Lebanon, but Israel, for complicity in this theft. You know what they do to Hezbollah agents in Israel? They string them up by their testicles."

"Do not," Yael said.

"So I'm going to give you my phone number, and you'll give me yours," Virgil continued. "If I call, you drop everything and come running. You understand?"

"Of course, but I did nothing," Awad said. "I am not Hezbollah—I'm a Lebanese from birth, not a Palestinian."

"Okay, I'll accept that, at least at this point," Virgil said. "Did you know that we found blood on the floor of Jones's house?"

Awad's eyebrows went up, and he said, "No," and then, "The Turk," and then, "Much blood?"

"Not much, but it wasn't done shaving."

Awad shook his head. "This is not good."

———

VIRGIL AND YAEL LEFT, after one more warning to Awad. Back in the truck, Virgil muttered, "Mossad."

Yael said, "You cannot believe this Arab."

"Shut up."

He pulled out of the parking lot, drove onto a neighboring street, then around the block, and then around another block, and finally parked on a hillside two blocks from Awad's apartment parking lot, with a view of Awad's car.

Yael said, "We do this because he lied about the football call?"

Virgil said, "Yes." He unsnapped his safety belt, got out, popped the back door on the truck, got a pair of image-stabilized Canon binoculars out of his equipment box, got back in the truck, and handed the glasses to Yael. "You watch. I'm going to close my eyes and think about this."

He thought for thirty seconds, then sat up and called Davenport again. "I've got a cell phone number. I need to know where the calls are going, and where they're coming from."

"We can do that," Lucas said. "Hope it's a smartphone."

"It's an iPhone," Virgil said. He gave Davenport Awad's cell phone number.

"Piece of cake."

VIRGIL CLOSED HIS EYES AGAIN, then asked, "Will you guys have a file on this Turk?"

"Somebody might," she said.

"Get it."

"I will ask," Yael said.

No mention of the handicap of working for the antiquities authority, Virgil noted.

A minute later, Yael said, "Here he is."

Virgil sat up: "That didn't take long."

"Just long enough to call back to his football friend," Yael said.

AWAD WAS NOT ELUSIVE. He drove a half-mile into the downtown area, with Virgil a few cars back all the way. Once downtown, Awad dumped the car in a parking space, got out, looked at his watch, and hurried down the street. Virgil pulled into a space at a fire hydrant, and they watched as Awad crossed the next street, looked at his watch again, and disappeared into the Pigwhistle bar and grill.

Virgil drove a half-block down the street, found a parking space, and put the truck in it. "C'mon," he said to Yael.

"Surveillance?" she asked, as they got out of the truck.

"If the guy he's meeting came out of the bar first, would we know which one he was?"

"Maybe," she said, "if it's another Palestinian."

"And maybe not," Virgil said. "You want to do surveillance, do it on your own."

"What are you going to do?"

"I'm gonna go see if it's the Turk in there," Virgil said.

"How?"

"I'm gonna ask him."

"This is a most unusual technique," Yael said. "I shall enjoy watching it, but I have little hope for its success."

6

The Pigwhistle bar and grill had a painting of a woodchuck—a groundhog—in the front window under a flickering neon Blatz Beer sign, because that's what a pigwhistle is.

In this case, the pigwhistle had been painted by a refugee from the Mankato State fine arts program, and looked, at first glance, like a dachshund, and was the reason that people familiar with the Pigwhistle called it "the Dog," as in, "Meet you at the Dog." You had to live in Mankato, and be of a certain *boulevardier* class, to know that. Virgil qualified.

He stepped inside, with Yael just behind him, and waited a few seconds for their eyes to adjust. In addition to a wide range of exotic beer, and excellent pizza, the Pigwhistle had an extreme degree of bar darkness, along with high-backed booths, the better to attract adulterers. When he could see, Virgil walked down the line of booths, checking each one, until, at the back, by the bowling machine, he found Awad.

And Derrick Crawford, the local private detective.

Virgil looked down at Crawford and his battered pinch-front fedora, and asked, "Whazzup, Derrick?"

Awad looked up, startled, and asked, "You followed me?"

Virgil said, "Of course. What, you thought we were here by accident?" To Crawford, he said, "Move over, Derrick."

Crawford said, "Jesus Christ on a crutch," and slid over, taking a half-glass of beer with him, and Virgil sat down. Yael sat across from him, next to Awad. She said to Awad, "You want to move your leg, please?"

Awad moved a quarter inch, which seemed to satisfy her, and she said to Virgil, "Proceed with the interrogation."

Virgil nodded and said to Crawford, "Tell me everything you know about this whole thing with the stone." He pointed to Awad. "And about this Awad guy."

Crawford pushed back his hat—he wore a fedora because he thought he looked a little like Harrison Ford in *Indiana Jones*, and, in fact, he did, except that he was several inches shorter and perhaps fifty pounds heavier, and, when his hat was off, bald—and asked, "Right from the beginning?"

"That's probably the best place," Virgil said.

"Well, this guy"—he pointed at Awad—"called me up and said that he wanted some surveillance done on this Reverend Elijah Jones, to see who he was talking to. We met up, I told him two hundred bucks a day and expenses, and he gave me a grand, in cash. Said there was more where that came from."

"Your uncle?" Virgil asked Awad.

Awad nodded.

Crawford took a sip of beer—he was one of the few people

Virgil knew who could drink beer while keeping a wooden kitchen match firmly in the corner of his mouth—and said, "I asked around and found out that Jones was at the Mayo, so I went over there and talked to him about this stone. He denied knowing anything about it, and that was that. Then, he checked himself out of the place, and a nurse I know called me up and told me, so I put a watch on his house."

"How did you do that?" Yael asked.

"Parked down the block," Crawford said.

"He showed up?" Virgil asked.

"Yup. Last night, after midnight. Driving a rental car, which I thought was a little odd, because his own car is in the garage."

"Why do you tell him all of this?" Awad asked. "This was secret communication, like with a lawyer."

Virgil looked at him and said, "Quiet." And to Crawford: "Go ahead, Derrick."

"So anyway, when he got to the house, I called up Raj, here, and he said thanks, he'd give Jones a ring. He told me to stay on the job until he called and let me go," Crawford said. "So fifteen minutes after that, another car pulled up. A rental. I checked on the tag, ran it through a couple of databases, and it turns out it was rented to a guy named Timur Kaya, who's traveling on a Turkish passport. I happen to know he's staying at the downtown Holiday Inn."

"How do you know this?" Yael asked.

"I followed him there," Crawford said.

"Good work," Yael said. "Which room?"

"One-twenty."

"When the Turk left, he didn't leave with a body-sized bag, did he?" Virgil asked.

"He didn't leave with any bag," Crawford said. "Not even a stone-sized bag."

Virgil: "So you followed the Turk to the Holiday Inn? Then what? You talk to him?"

"Hell, no. Raj told me about the Turk and this thing with testicles, and I said to myself, *That's not necessarily a guy I want to know.* So I went back to Jones's house, drinking lots of coffee, making two hundred bucks an hour. I'm standing behind a tree, taking a leak, when another car pulls up."

"It was like a traffic jam," Virgil said.

"Yeah," Crawford said. "I oughta mention, it's two o'clock in the morning by now, and the light's still on at Jones's house. It's like he was expecting these people. Anyway, a guy gets out of the car and goes up to the house, and I see Jones let him in. I check the tag on the car, it's a Cadillac SUV. I find out it's private, owned by a guy named John Rogers Sewickey from Austin, Texas."

"How do you spell that?" Virgil asked. He was taking notes. Crawford took his own notebook out and spelled the name.

"Never heard of him," Awad said. "Who is he?"

"He's a professor who specializes in Ancient Mysteries," Crawford said, orally capitalizing Ancient Mysteries. "I was about to tell you that when Virgil arrived. He teaches the Ancient Mysteries core course at the Center for Transubstantial Studies at University of Texas."

"Hook 'em, Horns," Virgil said.

"Exactly. He's written a lot of books and papers and so on. I looked at his bank account, don't ask me how, and he has four-teen thousand dollars in checking and in an investment account. He appears to be writing two alimony checks a month."

"Then he's not here for the stone," Yael said. "He couldn't afford it."

"The Turks are agents for somebody else, so maybe he's an agent for, like, the Iraqis," Crawford said. "I know he's been there—he led the search for the Garden of Eden. I guess he found it, at the junction of these two big rivers, the Euphrates and the Ganges."

"I believe the Ganges is in India," Virgil said.

"Okay, then it was something else," Crawford said.

"Where's he staying?" Virgil asked.

"Well, conveniently at the downtown Holiday Inn, in room two-seventy," Crawford said.

"Then what?" Yael asked.

"After I watched him check in, I went back to Jones's house, and the lights were out and the rental car was gone."

"Ah, crap, you missed him," Virgil said.

"Yeah, I did."

"Did you try going in the house?" Virgil asked.

"No, no, I didn't. . . . You know why."

"Okay. Do you know anything else? Anything at all? Or have any guesses?"

"Well, before you got here, Raj told me that you'd found blood on the floor?"

"Just a smear."

"Then I suspect the Turk probably created that," Crawford

said. "When Jones came to the door, to meet Sewickey, he looked like he was blowing his nose in a hankie. Now, if there was blood on the floor, I think he might've been trying to stop a nosebleed. I mean, how many people would meet somebody at the door while blowing their nose? And keep blowing it?"

"That's a legitimate question," Virgil said.

"Thank you," Crawford said. "Also, when Raj first called me, and before I found out that Jones was at the Mayo, I walked across the street to the courthouse to look up his tax records, to see where he lived. Turns out he has two places—the one here in town, and he's got what looks like an old family farm off Highway 68 West. I haven't gone out there yet, just looked at the tax file."

"Where is it? Exactly?" Virgil asked.

Crawford looked at his notebook again, and gave Virgil the location, which Virgil noted in his own notebook. Crawford spread his hands. "And *that* is all I've got. Well, except for one thing. It was the Euphrates and the Tigris."

Virgil said, "Ah. Good catch."

Virgil turned to Awad. "Why didn't you go over to Jones's house last night, after Derrick called you?"

"Because he told me to come this morning. So I did."

"Exactly how close are you to the Hezbollah?" Virgil asked. "Don't lie to me."

"I am not close, I promise you," Awad said, holding up his right hand, as though swearing an oath. "I am now calling my uncle and telling him what has transpired here, and telling him I want nothing more to do with it."

"Probably a little late for that," Yael said. "Especially if you plan to go back to Lebanon. The Hezbollah do not like people who say 'no' to them. They'd cut off more than your testicles, though they might start there."

"See, I don't want to hear this," Awad said. "I am an innocent pilot-in-training. I don't need 'Hezbollah agent' on my résumé."

BOTH VIRGIL AND YAEL asked a few more questions, but got nothing more of substance. Crawford swore he'd told Virgil everything he knew, and Virgil said, "If you find out anything else, call me up."

"I think I'm done with this case," Crawford said. "Hezbollah, the Turk, Mossad. And you *know* if a guy's from Texas, and he's driving a Caddy, he's gonna be carrying a gun."

"Yeah, probably," Virgil said. "Staying clear might be a good idea."

Crawford switched the kitchen match from one side of his mouth to the other, and back. "I understand you're chasing after Ma Nobles."

"You got something on that?" Virgil asked.

"Nope. Not other than the observation that Ma has some excellent headlights. I personally wouldn't mind examining her high beams."

"Thanks for that," Virgil said. "I'll put it in my report."

"What is this?" Yael asked.

"Car talk. American men love cars," Virgil said.

"There were ambiguous undertones," she said.

"You really do speak great English," Virgil said.

WHEN THEY WERE back out on the street, in the dazzling sunshine, Yael said to Virgil, "I will confess, this was an amazing interrogation. He tells you everything, because you ask."

"He's our only private eye," Virgil said, as they walked back to his truck. "There's not a lot of private detective business around here, so he makes ends meet by selling marijuana to the college students. He's probably got a hundred pounds of it down in his basement, which is why he's careful about committing any other crime—like going into Jones's house. If we find a reason to search Crawford's place, he'd be in trouble."

"You're saying that he's a drug dealer, and yet you don't arrest him."

"Well, he sells only California-grown pot, and none of the heavier stuff like cocaine or heroin," Virgil said. "That mostly keeps the Mexican dope out of here. I mean, we can bust as many people as we want, but somebody will still be selling weed. Better to have it somebody we know, who buys only California, instead of letting the cartel in."

"Also, it gives you an excellent lever when you need one."

"That's the other reason," Virgil said.

"Interesting," she said.

"Pretty sophisticated for a rural state, huh?"

"Yes. So, what is next?"

"Next we check out Jones's farm."

"Perhaps we should go to the Holiday Inn, instead?"

Virgil said, "Here's what I'm thinking: if we get hold of Jones, we could probably get the stone. Once we get the stone, everything stops, and right quick. We no longer have to worry about the Turk or the Texas guy, or Hezbollah, because we've got the stone. But another possibility would be for me to drop you at the Holiday Inn, you could check in there, too, and keep an eye on the place, while I go out to the farm."

Yael mulled that over for a moment, then shook her head. "I think I ride with you. You're a lucky guy. One of my advisers tells me, 'Good intelligence is important. Good luck is critical.'"

"That would be one of your advisers at the antiquities bureau?"

"Of course," she said.

THEY'D JUST CLEARED TOWN running northwest, when Virgil saw a red Ford coming up in the rearview mirror, and it gave off a certain vibration. He said, "Shoot," and looked around the interior of the truck for a baseball cap—anything but the straw hat he'd been wearing—saw nothing handy, but then spotted a farm driveway coming up. He stood on the brake and swerved down the drive, and pulled up toward the house.

"This is it?" Yael asked, frowning. Instead of an old farmhouse, they were looking at a newer ranch-style house with an aboveground swimming pool and a children's play set in the side yard.

"No. I'm just . . ." Virgil was watching the mirror, and fifteen seconds later, Ma Nobles went by in her pickup. As far as Virgil could tell, she never looked down the drive. He put the truck in reverse, backed down the drive, and edged out to the highway. "The woman in the truck ahead of us . . . I'm interested in where she's going."

"This is not about Jones?"

"No, it's a different case. Be patient, this won't take long."

THE HIGHWAY RAN PARALLEL to the Minnesota River, where Ma and her son had allegedly stashed the fake barn lumber. Virgil stayed well back and they drove along four miles, then five, and finally Ma turned north on a gravel road toward the river. Virgil pulled to the shoulder of the road, hooked his iPad out of the pocket on the back of the passenger seat, and called up a satellite view of the area.

"No bridge down there," he said. "The road does go along the river for a while."

"She made a lot of dust on that road. If you go down there, she could see it."

They never had a chance. Ma's truck reappeared at the corner, and she turned toward them. As she went by, she smiled, twiddled her fingers at Virgil, and continued back toward town.

"She saw us," Yael said.

"I was almost sure she didn't," Virgil said. "She never looked at us when she turned off."

"Then . . . she has an outlook. They saw us coming behind, they saw us go to the shoulder, they telephoned her."

"Lookout, not outlook," Virgil said. "Yeah, that's what I'm

thinking. Which means the real turnoff is somewhere between here and the driveway we turned down. That's helpful."

"She won't be going there now."

"No. And Jones's place ought to be about a half-mile up the road."

JONES'S PLACE WAS just what Virgil had expected from Crawford's tax-roll information. The house was old, and in poor shape: an early twentieth-century frame farmhouse in need of new paint, new roof, new windows.

New everything.

A garage at the end of the driveway had a hayloft and was in the same shape; a machine shed farther down the drive was falling apart, and a head-high stone foundation was all that remained of what had once been a barn. All of it stood on what looked like ten acres, most of it covered with lumpy fescue and knee-high weeds. A cluster of old, arthritic apple trees stood to one side of the house, while overgrown bridal wreath and lilac bushes lined the driveway. A "For Sale" sign, with a "Reduced" card fixed to the top, faced the highway, and looked as though it had been there for a while.

A black ragtop Jeep sat in the driveway.

"Here we go," Virgil said. He pulled in behind the Jeep, to within inches of its back bumpers, pinning it between two lilacs. If anyone managed to get to it, to flee, they'd have to go forward and then across the front yard to get out. Virgil popped the door, got his pistol out of the back, and stuck it in his belt at the small of his back.

Yael was pointing at the front door like a Weimaraner. Virgil said, "There'll be a side door. That's where you go in."

She said, "Yes?"

She and Virgil walked down the driveway and as they did, a slender dark-haired woman with green eyes walked out of the side door and asked, "Can I help you?"

Virgil took her in. She was pretty in a reserved way, and when their eyes met, they went "clank," like eyes sometimes do. She would not be a candidate for marriage. "We're looking for Elijah Jones."

"Dad's not here," she said. "He lives in town."

"We've been there," Virgil said. "I'm an agent with the Bureau of Criminal Apprehension. We have a warrant for Reverend Jones's arrest."

"His arrest?" Her hand went to her throat. "What for?"

"On a hold request, for theft, from the nation of Israel, and for failure to declare the importation of an artwork or artifact of value more than eight hundred dollars, which is a federal offense," Virgil said.

"My God, what'd he do?" she asked. But Virgil saw the flicker in her eyes, and Yael glanced at Virgil to see if he'd picked it up. He nodded his head a quarter of an inch. Not only was the woman not telling the truth, but that kind of pickup put Yael distinctly with the Mossad.

"You're his daughter who works with the DOT?" Virgil asked. He dug around in his memory and came up with, "Ellen?"

"Yes, how did you know?"

"We tried to get in touch with you, but were told you were on your way to Alaska," Virgil said.

"That was a joke about getting away from my ex," she said. "But about Dad . . . You can't find him? I'm sure he never smuggled anything, or stole anything, that's crazy talk. He's very ill. We tried to talk him out of going to Israel this summer. We were supposed to meet out here this morning, to see if there's anything anybody might want in the house before they burn it down—"

"You're going to burn it?"

Ellen looked back at the place and nodded. "I'm afraid so. It was my great-grandparents' place, but I can hardly ever remember even coming here. My grandfather was a preacher, and then Dad. The land was all sold off, the house can't be fixed . . . the land's more valuable with the house gone. We'll burn it, then clear it with a bulldozer, fill in the basement, and then maybe Chuck Miller will add it to his farm."

Virgil said, "Nice to have apple trees . . . and asparagus." He could see the feathery bush-tops of asparagus growing down the far fence line.

"The apple trees are pretty much shot. Mostly good for firewood, now."

Virgil came back to the case: "We went to your father's house this morning. He wasn't there, but he was last night. We haven't been able to locate him, but we did find a spot of blood on the floor."

"I just can't help you," she said. "I've tried calling his cell, but it goes right over to the answering service, so it's probably turned off."

Virgil said, "He's not in the house. This house."

"No, of course not. You think I'm lying?"

Virgil said, "No, I just have to ask—because if I ask, and if it turns out that you *are* lying, then you've committed a crime, and I can come back to you on that. I mean, you can refuse to talk to me, but you can't lie to me to cover up a crime or hide a criminal."

She put her fists on her hips: "That's a mean thing to say."

"I try not to be mean," Virgil said. "But this is a serious matter, Ellen, and you should not be fooling around with it, thinking otherwise. Your involvement in this, if you're involved, could jeopardize your whole career."

Yael chipped in: "He is trying to sell this artifact he stole. The people he is trying to sell it to are extremely dangerous. People who might kill him, if they need to, to get the stone."

Virgil added, "Hezbollah, among others."

Yael added, "And Texans."

Ellen nodded. "I will keep trying to get in touch. I'll go into town and look for him. I'll leave messages. I'll do everything I can."

"Don't get too close," Virgil said. "Like Yael said, these people could be dangerous. There's a lot of money involved."

"I promise: I'll tell you the minute I find him."

They exchanged cell phone numbers, and Virgil got her father's phone number, and then, like an afterthought, she asked, "Before you go, do you want to look inside? To see that I'm telling the truth?"

Yael said quickly, "I would."

Virgil said, "Go ahead. But old houses can be dangerous— Ellen should go with you. I'll take a look at the machine shed and garage."

THE TWO WOMEN WENT INSIDE, and Virgil headed toward the garage. He stepped inside, saw nothing, then checked to make sure the two women were out of sight in the house. They were; he hurried back to the truck, got inside, and dug into Yael's handbag.

She carried a small clutch purse inside, with a snap, which he unsnapped. In one of the credit card slots he found two key cards for the Downtown Inn. Like most seasoned travelers, she'd gotten two, so she wouldn't lock herself out on a quick trip to the Coke machine. He took one of them, and put the purse back in the bag.

He got out of the truck, eased the door shut, walked quickly behind the row of lilacs, to the end of the driveway, into the machine shed. Nothing there, either, except one piece of an old hay rake, a rusting fifty-five-gallon drum full of ashes, with two ancient yellow Pennzoil cans sitting on top. They were empty as they always are, with two triangular punch-holes in each of them.

He looked at the weathered boards, then stepped outside, looked in his directory, and called Ma Nobles.

She answered by saying, "Were you following me, Virgie?"

"No, I wasn't," Virgil said. "I was actually on my way out to an abandoned farm owned by a guy I'm investigating, which is about a mile on down the highway from where you saw me. On the south side. Got an Edina Realty sign on it. They're about to burn it down. I was looking at it, and realized the whole thing is made out of the kind of lumber you're selling."

"In good shape?"

"Authentic antique shape, but a lot of the boards look solid, like they could be cut and reused. Anyway, I could talk to the owner about giving it to you, free, or almost free, if you'd tell me where I might find a bunch of lumber at the bottom of the river . . . and how to get it out of there."

After a long silence, Ma said, "Free, huh?"

"They don't want to burn it," Virgil said.

"I'll take a look at it, and call you," Ma said.

"I'll tell you, Ma," Virgil said. "We got a couple people looking at you real hard. This would be a good way to keep your ass out of jail. And your boy's, too."

"I'll take a look," she said again, and hung up.

VIRGIL WAS WALKING back up the driveway when the two women came out of the house. Yael shook her head: nothing inside. Virgil told Ellen about Ma Nobles.

"Well, sure, she can have it if she wants it," Ellen said. "Maybe . . . for a few dollars."

"You'd have to work that out with her," Virgil said, looking up at the house. "But you know, it's just sort of old and neat. I'd hate to see it go up in flames."

Virgil gave her Ma Nobles's phone number, and he and Yael got in his truck. As they backed toward the highway, Yael said, "She knows where her father is."

"Yeah, I know. The blood."

Yael nodded: "You told her there was blood on the floor of the house, and she never asked about it. She knows he's not injured badly, and that he was bleeding in his house. And she did not ask about the artifact."

"Mmm. I'd hate to put her in jail, though," Virgil said. "Probably doesn't want to betray her father, which I can understand."

"It seems to me, after some discussion and observation, that you do not wish to put anyone in jail."

"Not true," Virgil said. "I know about nine people right now that I'd like to put in jail, and who deserve it. Just not anyone you've met."

She asked, "Now what?"

7

The Reverend Elijah Jones, sweating like a pig in Miami, walked down the hillside through the trees toward the picnic tables, carrying the bowling bag in his left hand, his right hand in his pants pocket, pressed against the right side of his groin.

He was not hurting, but only because he'd taken so much oxycodone that he wouldn't have felt anything less than an amputation. Yet something down there, in his groin, something vital felt like it was coming loose. Without the pills, he thought, he'd have felt like he'd just dropped his balls into a bear trap.

Walking two hundred yards down the hill hadn't helped. He didn't have much time left, he thought, before he'd be so clouded that he'd be incapable of pulling off any kind of deal, much less one with a Hezbollah agent, two Turks, or a famous TV star.

He got to the bottom of the hill, walked across a patch of scrubby grass to the concrete table, had to lift the bowling bag to its surface, groaned as he did it.

Not a groan of pain, but of incipient death. How much longer,

Oh Lord? Two weeks? The docs had told him that the cancer in his brain would kill his ability to breathe, before it got to his reasoning faculties. He'd get to enjoy every minute of his own death.

A hundred yards away, two men, remarkably out of place in the bucolic park, were watching him carefully. He'd told them to wait there, when they arrived, so he could be sure that they were alone, that there wasn't a troop of Turkish cavalry over the hill. Now they were looking at him, a black-bearded man in a black suit and ministerial collar, and he lifted a hand and waved them over.

They walked up, peering around as they came. The park had two softball diamonds down at the far end, where fifty kids and forty parents and coaches were either playing or watching two separate games. Closer to the picnic area, a half-dozen teenagers were kicking a soccer ball around, and at the other end of the picnic area, three stoners, two male and one female, were playing Hacky Sack. Poorly, and passing a joint.

The stoners glanced at the Turks as they came up, then turned away. The two gave off a specific vibe: they didn't want to be looked at, so you'd best not do it. They were both broad men in silvery suits, with wide pale shimmery neckties, like the sides of king salmon. The broader of the two had a gray Stalin mustache. The other one was wearing round sunglasses as black as welding goggles, which made him look like a malevolent Mr. Mole. He was carrying a briefcase, and Jones felt a quick spark of hope: maybe it would happen.

The broader man led, came up, stopped ten feet away, and asked, "Reverend Jones. Good to see you again. You seem better."

"The bleeding stopped," Jones said. "That's always good. You have the money?"

"Do you have the stone?"

"I do."

"May we see it?"

"You may," Jones said. He fumbled with the zipper on the bowling bag, got it open, reached inside with both hands, and with some effort, pulled out the rock and placed it in the center of the table, where it seemed to soak up most available sunlight; the atmosphere around it literally seemed to grow dimmer, and the two Turks looked around uneasily. Jones looked into the sky and saw that a bass-boat-sized cloud had momentarily covered the sun.

The sun came back and the bigger Turk stepped forward and seemed about to reach toward the stone, when Jones put his arm around it and pulled it toward himself. "Uh-uh," he said. "Not until I see the money."

The Turk straightened. "We don't have the money, here, exactly, because we thought it unwise to walk about with five million dollars in a briefcase."

"Then where is it?" Jones asked. The spark of hope was dying.

"At our hotel."

"You left five million dollars in cash in your hotel room, where fifty minimum-wage workers have keys to your room? You can't possibly be that dumb, so I can't possibly believe you." Jones pulled the stone closer, and again fumbled with the bowling bag, to put it away.

"Don't do that," the big Turk said. "We will take it with us."

"I don't think so," Jones said. He lifted a hand overhead. He said, "I have a friend in the woods with a deer rifle. If you try to take the stone, he will shoot you dead. All I have to do is drop my hand."

The big Turk said, "This is, mmm . . ." He turned to his smaller partner. "The American idiom. The one we spoke of."

The smaller man—who was not small—said, "Shit from the cow."

The big man shook his head and said, "No, no, no, this is one word, this . . . cowshit. No, bullshit."

"Same thing," said the smaller man.

"But this is not how you say it," the big man said. He turned back to Jones. "This gunman, this is bullshit. Drop your hand, tell him to shoot me."

"Ah, you're right," Jones said, and dropped his hand.

"The stone, please," the Turk said.

"Nope."

The Turk slipped his left hand into his jacket pocket and took out a switchblade. He squeezed once, and the blade flicked out. He kept it against his leg, so the stoners couldn't see it, smiled to show his thick white teeth, and said, "We insist."

Jones smiled back, showing slightly bucked but yellower teeth, and said, "There is another American idiom that you should know: 'Don't bring a knife to a gunfight.'"

With the right hand, he pulled back the right side of his jacket, to display the stock of a handgun tucked under his belt buckle.

The Turk considered it for a moment, and then said, "I have some experience with the knife. Do you think you can withdraw the gun before I can reach you with the knife?"

Jones said, "You're fifteen feet away. You'd have to jump over the picnic table to get to me. I don't have to jump over the picnic table to get to you."

The bigger man said, "We will take the stone."

"No."

The smaller man said to his companion, "Be very careful. I think he is tense."

The bigger Turk said, with a quick backward glance, "He is a man of religion. He will not shoot us. We will take the stone."

He took a step forward and Jones pulled the gun, a large frame revolver. One of the stoners said, "Holy shit," and Jones sensed all three of them running away.

The Turk said, calmly, "You will not shoot."

Jones said, "Well," and looked down at the pistol, and then up at the Turk, and the Turk lifted a hand as if to say, "Wait," but Jones shot him in the middle of the chest and he went down.

And he didn't stop. The other Turk half-turned and Jones shot him in the neck, the gunshots echoing like thunderclaps off the amphitheater-type hills to the side of the park. The bigger Turk rolled and climbed back to his feet to run, and Jones shot him in the back, then turned to the other and fired two shots at him, into the back and the back of his head, then fired another shot into the big Turk's back.

They were both half-running, half-stumbling away, and Jones lifted the stele and put it back in the bag. The stoners were half-way across the park, the two men far in the lead, the woman running frantically after them; and at the far end, parents were screaming for kids, and both parents and kids were running out of the park toward cars—balls, bats, and gloves forgotten.

Jones felt a moment of pride. He'd given thousands of sermons in his life, and had never before gotten a response so universal and enthusiastic. *Everyone* was running.

He had time for only that spark of pride. Then he took the bag and shambled back into the trees, and up the hill. He'd just gotten to his car when he heard the sirens, some way off, yet.

By the time they arrived, he'd gone around three corners and was accelerating away.

WHEN VIRGIL AND YAEL got to the park, eight patrolmen and four detectives were walking the area, with two crime-scene people crawling around the picnic table, and three highway patrolmen parked on the street watching. Part of the turnout was the result of children being nearby, and the school-shooting scares. The other part was sheer excitement: this just didn't happen much in Mankato.

The cops were basically looking for anything they could find, and had rounded up two stoners, a boy and a girl, and said that a third one had been with them, but he'd kept running and hadn't yet been located.

"I called you because of that Reverend Jones thing," said the lead detective on the scene, whose name was Don Scott. "We think this was Jones. Big guy, black beard, wearing a black suit with a ministerial collar."

"Yeah, that's him," Virgil said. "You find anything that would point to him?"

"Well, we're doing the crime-scene things, because he apparently wounded the two guys he was talking to. We haven't found them yet, but we will—the witnesses said they were shot bad. Head, stomach, back wounds. One guy, who seemed like he knew what he was talking about, said they drove off in a Mercedes-Benz SUV. We got all the hospitals looking out for them, and we're looking for the car. We found a switchblade where the two unknowns were, so Jones may have been threatened. We'll get at least one good print off the knife, because I could see it, just looking at it. And we're doing the usual—footprints and so on, got some blood from the ones that got shot."

Virgil filled him in on what he'd found, and Scott said, "Well, if he's dying, then he doesn't have much to lose."

Yael said, "We have considered that, and you are correct. I think his behavior, from the time he stole the stele, is influenced by his illness. This is not an excuse for him, but a motive."

Virgil asked, "You mind if we talk to the kids?"

"Go ahead. I think we wrung them out, though, and they don't have much."

"Just want to hear it, myself." Virgil ambled over to the two stoners, who were perched on a picnic table, introduced himself and Yael, and said, "Tell me what you saw."

They told the tale of the two men walking up to the reverend, about the stone coming out of the bowling bag, about some kind of dispute—they hadn't been close enough to hear the words, but they could hear the tone of it. The discussion hadn't turned into a screaming argument, but had been tense.

"I'll tell you what," the boy said, "that sucker opened up with that pistol, the first thing I thought was, he was gonna hit some of those kids for sure. They were lucky he didn't, too. They were right in the line of fire."

"That wasn't the first thing you thought," the girl said. She was way past a simple pout. "The first thing you thought, *asshole*, was, *Run*. You completely left me behind, you, you, *stupid*."

"What was I gonna do, carry you?" the boy whined.

Virgil broke in: "Did this minister look sick? Or hurt?"

The girl shrugged. "We were playing Hacky Sack and didn't pay too much attention until they started talking louder . . . but he seemed okay to me. After he started shooting, I didn't see him. I just ran."

"The two men who were shot—they didn't get the black stone?"

"No. They just started running like everybody else," the girl said.

Virgil got descriptions of the men who were shot, and looked at Yael, who said, "Turks. Two of them."

"I think so. Let's get some cops and go down to the Holiday." He thanked the two kids and walked back to Scott and said, "If you could give us a couple of cops, we have an idea where the two wounded guys might be . . . if they haven't checked into the hospital."

"Here in town?"

"Holiday Inn downtown," Virgil said.

"Well, hell, let's go," Scott said.

THE HOLIDAY INN was an older building downtown, left over from the sixties or seventies, slowly failing in place, with most potential patrons going to the Downtown Inn, where Yael was, or the City Center Hotel, or a newer Holiday Inn Express out on the edge of town.

On the way down, Yael said, "I don't understand how they could flee . . . if they were shot so badly. Why didn't they stay? Why aren't they in a hospital?"

"Good question. Ellen Case said he'd never hurt anyone."

"He's gone crazy from the illness, or the pain, or the drugs."

"Maybe," Virgil said.

AT THE HOLIDAY INN, they all unloaded, Virgil, Yael, Scott, the other plainclothesman, and three patrolmen. One of the patrolmen said, "You see the ass end of that green SUV down there?" He pointed to the far end of the hotel parking lot. "That's a Benz."

Scott positioned the patrolmen around the parking lot and exits from the hotel, and he and the other detective, along with Virgil and Yael, walked down to the Mercedes and looked in the windows. Both the front seats were stained with what looked like blood, and Yael said so.

"Doesn't *look* like blood, it *is* blood," Scott said.

Scott told the other detective to sit on the car, but the cop said, "Bullshit, I'm coming with you," so they got a patrolman to watch it, and the four of them walked down to the hotel office and explained the problem to the manager, who then summarized what they'd said: "They're bleeding to death in my room?"

"That's why we need the key," Scott said.

They got the key and walked down to the Turks' rooms—they had two rooms, as it happened, with a connecting door. Virgil listened at the first one, and heard two men talking. He listened at the second and heard nothing. So he pointed at the first one, and Scott knocked.

"Who knocks?"

"Mankato police. Open the door, sir," Scott said, and he and the other detective pulled their pistols. Yael looked at Virgil, who said, "Back in the car," and she rolled her eyes.

Scott pounded on the door again. "Mankato police. Open up."

A chain rattled on the door, and a man looked out. He was bare-chested, had a bloody bandage on his ear and neck, and was holding a pair of tweezers.

Scott said, "Step back, please."

The man stepped back. Inside, a larger man sat on a chair, also shirtless, with a bloody patch on his furry chest.

"We are . . . cleaning up," he said.

Scott turned to the other detective and said, "Get a goddamned ambulance over here."

"We are not hurt so bad," the bigger man protested.

"You've been shot."

"But only with these baby bullets." He looked at a room service menu by his elbow, whose black plastic cover was dotted with tiny lead shot.

"Snake shot," Virgil said.

Scott said, "You're going to the hospital anyway. You can't just sit here and pick shot out of your skin. You could get infected. And we need to talk to you about the Reverend Jones."

"We have no time for hospitals," the big Turk said.

"You're gonna take time," Scott said.

"You did not get the stele?" Yael asked.

The Turk looked at Scott: "Why is there an Israeli here?"

Scott: "How'd you know she is an Israeli?"

"She looks like one," the Turk said. "Why is she here?"

"We are trying to recover property that belongs to the state of Israel," Yael said.

The big Turk said to the smaller Turk, "Mossad."

"It's so," the smaller Turk said.

Yael, impatient, asked, "You did not take the stone?"

"What stone?" the big Turk asked. To Virgil: "Why am I in the USA, and yet I am interrogated by the Mossad?"

"Beats me," Virgil said.

THE TURKS did not want to talk: about Jones, about the stone, about what they were doing in Mankato. Six minutes after the cops went into the room, the other plainclothesman said, "The ambulance is here."

"I can't understand why you won't help us," Scott said to the big Turk. "Jones shot you guys."

The big Turk shrugged: "It's only business."

YAEL ASKED, "Now what?"

"Stop asking that," Virgil said. He scratched his chin, then said, "We could go back to the farmhouse—he might've run there. He's gotta be staying somewhere. Or we could see if the guy from Texas is upstairs."

She thought for a moment and then said, "We can always find the man from Texas—besides, I looked, and there is no Cadillac in the parking lot. If we hurry to the farmhouse, perhaps we will catch Jones."

But they didn't.

They did find Ellen Case talking to Ma Nobles. Ma walked over to them as Virgil and Yael got out of the truck. It was a warm day, and Ma had a fine mist of sweat on her face, and hadn't bothered to encumber herself with a brassiere. She said, "Hey, Virgie. Want to thank you for this. We got a deal. I'll get Rolf and Tall Bear over here to pull it down and load it up."

"So you gonna tell us where that fake lumber is?"

She ignored him, and instead took a long look at Yael. "Who's this?"

"An investigator from Israel."

"Ah, looking for Ellen's old man. She was telling me about that, about this stone," Ma said. She looked back at Yael. "So, you're a Jew?"

Yael said, "Yes. You have trouble with this?"

"No, no. Moses is a Jew, I guess. At least half."

Yael: "Moses?"

"My third boy. His daddy was one good-lookin' Hebrew, if I do say so myself. Line-dance instructor, met him down at the Coop. Used to wear these silver and turquoise bracelets around his wrist, and custom cowboy boots. That sonofabitch could talk. Talked me right out of my undies. Next thing I know, I looked like I swallowed a watermelon, and he was run off to Mexico."

Yael said, "Watermelon?"

Ellen walked up. Green eyes, cool, even in the heat. She asked, "Did you find Dad?"

"He just shot two Turks, down in Mankato," Virgil said.

This time she showed the shock. "Shot them? That's impossible. There's no—"

"Didn't kill them," Virgil said. "He used snake shot. But they identified him—and he had the stone."

"That snake shot, that had to sting," Ma said.

"And would have put out their eyes, if he'd shot them in the face," Virgil said.

"Is that why you're back here?" Ellen asked Virgil.

"Yeah. He's gotta be hiding out somewhere, and after the shooting, he must have been in a hurry to get out of sight."

"Well, he's not here," Ellen said. "Ask Ma. Or look around."

Virgil said, "Ahhh . . ."

Yael said quickly, "I'll look. We're here, I'll look. Can I borrow your Glock?"

"No."

Yael muttered something in a foreign tongue and stalked off to the truck, got her purse, and headed for the house.

Ma looked after her and said, "Hope she doesn't want to use the bathroom. I can tell you, Virgie, there's no old man in there, but there is a whole bunch of yellow jackets in the upstairs bathroom."

"Why would you think she's headed for the can?" Virgil asked.

Ma caught the speculative tone in his voice, and asked, "Why else would she take her purse?"

"Okay." To Ellen: "Your father is now being hunted by everyone, for aggravated assault. If you know anything about what he's doing, or where he is, I can talk him down. If you don't tell me, or if you really don't know, and he runs into a nervous cop, there's a good chance he'll be shot to death."

"He never even called me when he got back in the U.S.," she said. "He didn't even call me from the Mayo. He did call me when he left there, and told me not to look for him, told me he was in a lot of trouble, but he didn't tell me what it was. He said he thought he'd be dead in two or three weeks, and that was almost a week ago." Her lower lip trembled. "But he would never shoot anyone. Never."

Virgil said, "Well, he did. You have to understand, he doesn't seem to be acting like himself. Could be drugs, maybe the disease is affecting his brain, who knows?" He took out his notebook and asked, "Who are his friends? Who might be inclined to hide him? Who'd keep hiding him after the evening news? Because he's going to be on the evening news, big-time."

She gave him a half-dozen names, but said that she doubted

that any of them would hide him after word got out of the shooting. "They're all very respectable. They would tell him to give
himself up, and they would give him up themselves, if he didn't."

"So where do you think he is?"

She had to think about it for a moment, and then said, "From
what you tell me . . . I suspect he went back home to get his hiking gear, and he's probably camping out somewhere. He hunts
and fishes, knows all of southeast Minnesota like his own backyard, every nook and cranny. When he was healthy, he probably
spent thirty or forty nights a year in his sleeping bag."

"Where'd he keep his hiking gear?"

"A big gear closet in his garage. If his gear is gone, then . . ."
She shrugged. "He's in the woods."

"Does he have any special outdoorsy friends?"

"Yes, on the list I gave you? Sugarman," she said. And, "Virgil,
don't hurt my dad."

YAEL CAME BACK, unstung by yellow jackets. "Now what?"

Virgil said, "I'll tell you what." He stepped past her, as though
on his way down the driveway toward the machine shed, and as
he passed her, he yanked the purse off her shoulder. She tried to
grab it as it came free, but he twisted it away.

"What are you, what are you . . ." She danced around him trying to get it back, but he dug inside and pulled out a pistol—a full-
sized 9mm Beretta.

Yael shouted at him: "You can't do that."

"It's against the law to carry a concealed weapon in Minnesota without a permit. Since it takes a while to get one, you don't have one, because you just got here," Virgil said. He said to Ma, "This is another reason why women take their purses with them: they're packing heat."

"Got me there," Ma said.

Virgil said, "Yael works for the Mossad. Or Shabak. She's like an Israeli killer."

8

The conversation languished on the way back to Mankato. Virgil had put the Beretta into his backseat gun safe, and after a couple of protests, Yael crossed her arms and went into a sulk, refusing to speak to him, even to answer questions.

Finally, Virgil said, "All right, don't talk. I'm going to see the Texan. You can come if you want, or walk back to your hotel. It's only a couple of blocks."

Not a word.

"I'm not giving you the gun back. I'll send it up to BCA headquarters in St. Paul. If you can get it back from them, or your embassy can get it back, then so be it."

Not a word.

Not a word until they'd parked at the Holiday Inn, where she got out of the truck and said, "You're hunting a man who shot two Turks. You don't carry a gun yourself. You say that when you do, you can't shoot it. You're risking both our lives."

"Jones wasn't trying to kill anyone," Virgil said. "In my estimation, you're more likely to get killed when you carry a gun than when you don't. Besides, if we run into Jones, I have a feeling that you'd kill him. I don't think that's necessary. Not for some rock."

She stepped back and crossed her arms again, and Virgil sighed and led the way up to Sewickey's room. When they got to the right door, Virgil lifted a hand to knock, but Yael's grabbed his wrist before he could, and pulled him back.

"What?"

"Listen."

She was standing with her ear next to the room's window, and gestured to it. Virgil put his ear to the glass, and after a second or two, separated out the background noise. What was left was the sounds of vigorous sexual activity, and a woman having a screaming orgasm. And she didn't stop. And she still didn't stop.

After a minute of the woman not stopping, Virgil said, "Ah, he's watching porn."

"I hope, or this woman is going to explode."

Yael put her ear back to the glass as Virgil knocked on the door, and three seconds later, she said, "The orgasms have stopped. At least on the TV."

"That's because the TV has been turned off," Virgil said.

"But is Sewickey?" she asked.

VIRGIL KNOCKED AGAIN, and they felt the footfalls of somebody moving inside, then the door opened and a short, thin, black-eyed man, with thinning black hair, peered out over the door chain.

"What?"

Virgil held up his ID. "I'm with the Minnesota Bureau of Criminal Apprehension. We're investigating the theft of a stele from the state of Israel, and a shooting earlier today at a park here in Mankato. We think you can help with that. Could you open the door, please?"

He didn't open the door. Instead, he asked, "Who got shot?"

"We want to talk about that," Virgil said. "Could you open the door?"

"This room is my temporary domicile, and as such, you're not permitted entry unless I give you permission, which I'm not," Sewickey said.

"Mr. Sewickey, I don't want to get all lawyerly here, but I have no intention of searching your room, unless I see something illegal the moment I step inside," Virgil said. "Several crimes have been committed, you were seen speaking to the man who committed them. If you don't let us in, I will arrest you as a material witness, and have you sent to St. Paul for questioning. That will take several days, to effect the transfer and so on. If you want to spend the next several days in jail, that's fine. If you don't, you need to speak to me now."

"I'm going to call my attorney," Sewickey said.

"Fine. We will wait out here for ten minutes," Virgil said. "If it's any longer than that, I'll arrest you."

"I don't think that's a reasonable amount of time."

"I don't care what you think," Virgil said. "I don't have to give you even one minute—I can arrest you now. I don't want to have to do all that paperwork. We can still avoid that, but you do need to answer some questions."

Sewickey held Virgil's eyes for a second, then looked past him at Yael. "Who's the Jew? Or perhaps, in the circumstances, I should ask, who's the Egyptian?"

Yael snorted, and Virgil said, "She represents the state of Israel in an effort to recover stolen property."

"That property belongs to all of mankind," Sewickey said.

"Yeah, but somebody in mankind has to hold on to it, and in this case, it's the Israelis," Virgil said. "Now, time's a-wastin'. Call your lawyer or not, but I'm putting you on the clock."

"I'll be back," Sewickey said. He closed the door.

Yael said, "I hope there is no other exit."

SEWICKEY WAS BACK in eight minutes. The chain rattled, and he opened the door and said, "I reserve the right not to answer questions that may be incriminating."

"You have that right," Virgil said. Sewickey backed up and Virgil and Yael pushed into the room, which smelled a little funny. Virgil said, "Why don't you sit on the bed, and Yael and I will take the chairs."

Sewickey had the tense look of a man who lived with excessive stress. He was perhaps five-eight or -nine, tightly muscled, with gnarled hands and a nose that seemed to be carved from cheese: soft, but with sharp edges. His fingernails, Virgil noticed, were bitten down to the quick, and he seemed constantly to be on the verge of trembling. He was wearing black jeans, a turquoise shirt with a string tie, and pointy black cowboy boots, in crocodile hide.

He sat down and said, "I will tell you that I did speak to the Reverend Jones, and he allowed me to look at the stele."

"When was this?" Virgil asked.

"Late last night. Very late. I drove here from Austin—how much do you know about me?"

"We read your entry in the wiki," Virgil said.

"All right. That's not particularly accurate, but neither is it particularly inaccurate," Sewickey said. "My age is incorrect. I'm forty-one, not forty-three."

"Fine," Virgil said. "I'll make a note. What did Jones tell you?"

"He told me that he'd found the stele on an archaeological dig, and he fled the country with it because he realized its importance, and because the Israelis were already taking steps to hush up the discovery."

"This is untrue," Yael said.

"Whatever," Sewickey said. "In any case, he said he is dying of metastasized colon cancer, and expects to be dead within the month. I believe he is trying to sell the stele, but I told him I was interested more in documenting its religious and mystical significance, than in actually purchasing it. As long as I know the stone is legitimate, and if I have photos to work from, I will be satisfied."

"So you're not a buyer?" Yael asked.

"No, I'm not. I don't purchase what might be considered by the narrow-minded to be stolen goods," Sewickey said. "In any case, Reverend Jones allowed me to make a number of photographs of the inscriptions on the stele. He is exceedingly anxious to make sure that the Israelis can't cover up this momentous discovery."

"I think he is exceedingly anxious to advertise this object for sale," Yael said.

Virgil: "Have you made arrangements to meet again?"

"I will have to refuse to answer that on grounds that it might possibly incriminate me," he said. He frowned. "By the way, who did he shoot?"

"Couple of Turks from downstairs," Virgil said. "They weren't hurt too bad—he was shooting snake shot."

"Perfectly appropriate, if it's the two Turks I'm thinking of," Sewickey said. And then, "Have you heard anything about Hezbollah becoming involved in this question?"

"Why would you ask?" Virgil asked.

"So you have," Sewickey said. He rubbed his chin. "This matter is becoming complicated. We can't allow either the Turks or the Hezbollah to gain control of this artifact. This thing has tremendous power. This might be the most powerful artifact since the discovery of the True Cross, which discovery I recount in my book, *Cross of Christ, Blood of Hope*."

"I hadn't actually heard that the True Cross had been discovered," Virgil said.

"Oh, yes, yes, it has," Sewickey said. "It's currently being hidden by the Vatican. I had found it sealed in a lead capsule, probably by Constantine's wife, Saint Helen, thirty feet underwater in the Golden Horn, and had taken it ashore. I was preparing to move it to a safe location when we were hit by a Jesuit commando team, who . . . Well, it's all told in my book, which is available on Amazon. Suffice to say, I was lucky to escape with my life."

"I've found that usually does suffice," Virgil said. "I will tell you, the Jesuits might have let you off easy, but if I find out that you're hooking up with Jones, I will put your Texan butt in a Minnesota jail. If you see him, hear from him, find out somehow where he's at—I want to know about it. I'm deathly afraid that somebody's going to get killed in the hassle over this thing."

"Somebody probably will," Sewickey said, his voice gone somber. "The Solomon stone—many people would think its power worth killing for. Beside this rock, an atomic bomb is nothing."

"Nothing?"

"Nothing."

They talked awhile longer, speculating about Jones's location and motive; Sewickey's anxiety increased as they talked, and he looked at his watch several times. Then there was a knock on the door and he got to his feet, stepped to the motel hanger bar, took down a suit coat, and slipped it on.

"I'm afraid I'm going to have to call an end to the interview," he said. "I've told you everything I know."

"That wouldn't be Jones knocking on the door, would it?" Virgil asked.

There was another knock, and Sewickey called, "One second, please." And to Virgil, "No it wouldn't."

"I told you, you should be carrying your gun, or let me have mine," Yael said.

"Hmm," Virgil said. He pulled the door open.

And found a man in jeans and a T-shirt, with a large video

camera, and a chunky man in a suit with a hairdo that was, compared to most other men's hairdos, as the Matterhorn is to Bun-
ker Hill; with pink cheeks. He said, "Virgil. Hey man, what're you
doing here?"

"Ah, boy," Virgil said. To Yael: "It's Channel Three."

YAEL WANTED to watch the interview but Virgil didn't. He took
her down the motel hallway until they were out of earshot of the
TV crew, and said, "I'm going to get something to eat. Can you
walk back to your hotel?"

"Yes. We are done for the day?"

"I have nothing more to do—I might try to find some of
Jones's hunting and fishing friends, and ask where he likes to camp
out. If I find out anything that seems promising, I'll call you."

She nodded and turned back to Sewickey's room, where Sewickey was talking to the TV crew about the best place to set up
the interview.

VIRGIL CALLED the duty officer at the BCA and told him he
needed an address for a David Sugarman somewhere in the
Mankato area, stopped at the Howlie Inn for a chicken sandwich,
got a call back and was told that Sugarman lived across the river in
North Mankato. He was, the duty officer said, a mailman.

Virgil crossed the river, found Sugarman's address, and Sugarman riding a lawn mower in diminishing squares on his half-acre
lawn. Virgil flagged him down.

Sugarman was a balding, sweating man in a Hawkeye T-shirt, with a short blond mustache, who could have played a half-dozen different roles in Hollywood movies, just by changing clothes: outlaw biker, truck driver, friendly neighborhood bartender, fat guy on the other side of the fence, the Number Three movie cop who has one line and uses it to crack wise, probably about somebody's bowel movement or manhood. This version said he hadn't heard from Jones. "You know he's dying?" he asked, as he wiped his face on his shirtsleeve.

"I've heard that," Virgil said. "He just shot a couple of guys over in Mankato—didn't hurt them too bad, but we need to find him. The whole cancer thing, the drugs and pain pills and all, may have pushed him over the edge. We think he could be camping out somewhere."

Sugarman suggested one riverside camping spot, plus a lakeside hunting cabin in a chunk of woods east of town. "I'd check the cabin first," he said. "It's pretty comfortable, there's nobody around, and it's out of sight. You can drive right up to it."

Virgil got directions, and pulled up a satellite view on his iPad, and spotted the cabin exactly. Sugarman said, "You know, to be honest, I wouldn't help find him, even for a cop, but if he's shooting people, that's not the Elijah Jones I know. He's a good guy, or used to be. Give you the shirt off his back. Take it easy on him."

VIRGIL THANKED HIM, got back in his truck, turned around in the street and was headed out when he took a call from an unknown number.

"Is this Agent Flowers?" a woman asked in a husky, strongly accented voice.

"Yes?"

"This is Yael Aronov. I'm in Chicago, and was told I should call you. My plane will arrive in this Minneapolis airport at seven o'clock. I was told to tell you this, that you could find me there and help me to this Mankato."

Virgil thought about that for a second, rubbed his forehead. "You know, you speak really good English."

"Thank you," she said. "I was actually born in Miami Beach, where my parents have a condo."

9

Davenport was not amused.

"So you've got two Israelis claiming to be Yael Aronov, and the one you have now . . ."

"I'm calling her Yael-1," Virgil said.

". . . was carrying an illegal gun and you suspect that she knows how to use it and think she may be *willing* to use it."

"Eager, almost. She said she hadn't had, and I quote, a chance to test herself in combat, unquote. If she's the real Yael, most of the people who've looked at her think she's with the Mossad. Or this Shabak. Apparently something about her . . . Everybody who's looked at her also thinks she's an Israeli, so she probably is."

"Sounds like you've got a conundrum," Davenport said.

"Really? I thought it was a clusterfuck," Virgil said. "So, two requests: I need somebody with some clout to get on to the Israelis, the antiquities authority or whatever, and get me a picture of the real Yael Aronov. Without, you know, getting anybody too excited."

"I'll have Sandy call, and if that doesn't work, maybe Rose Marie would wade into it, speaking for the governor," Davenport said. Rose Marie Roux was the state commissioner of public safety. "What's the other thing?"

"We got that bunch of magnetic GPS trackers in the other day. We had a class. I'd like to borrow four of them, along with a tracking tablet."

"I'll check," Davenport said. "When do you need them?"

"I'm going up to the airport to get Yael-2. I've got a little time, I thought I'd stop in St. Paul on the way. I think Jones is talking to at least the Texas guy and the Turks and maybe his daughter, and maybe even Yael-1, or she might find out where he is: so I want to cover all of them."

"I'll call you back," Davenport said. "I'll e-mail you the photo of the real Aronov, when we get one."

"Quick as you can. I'll try to get a shot of Yael-1. Maybe the feds could identify her. They've gotta have a file on Mossad agents. If not, they might want to start one."

VIRGIL WENT back to the Holiday Inn. The Channel Three truck was gone, so he called a Mankato cop named Georgina, the same one with whom he went dancing, when her husband wasn't in town, and asked her for a favor. He described the favor, and she asked, "This won't get me in trouble, will it?"

"Don't see how," Virgil said. "Just read the script and hang up."

"All right. But if I get in trouble, I'll blame you."

"That'd be a change," Virgil said.

———

VIRGIL DROVE two blocks to the Downtown Inn, where Yael-1 was staying, and parked fifty yards away. He got out of the truck, dug a Nikon D800 out of his equipment box, mounted a huge Nikon 400mm f2.8 lens with a fast-release plate, attached a monopod, sat in the cargo space, and ran the rear window halfway down.

Five minutes later, a cab pulled up out front of the motel, and Virgil focused on it. One minute later, Yael walked out, and he fired off nine automatically bracketed shots, in three sequences of three. The cab pulled away, headed for the Coop, a bar that backed up to the Minnesota River, where the Reverend Jones would not be, unless by a terrific coincidence. Which should, he thought, teach Yael-1 a lesson: just because a woman calls you and says she's Reverend Jones's daughter, you shouldn't necessarily believe her. Would a member of the Mossad make that mistake?

When the cab was out of sight, Virgil plugged the Compact Flash card into a reader, plugged the reader into his Mac laptop, imported the photos into Lightroom, and cleaned them up. Two of them were okay; one was really good. He turned on the Verizon Jetpack, switched the laptop to the Verizon WiFi, and exported the three best photos to Davenport as hi-res JPEGs.

Davenport called a minute later and said, "I got the pictures. I don't have the GPS units yet, but I'll get them before I leave, and I don't have a picture of the real Yael Aronov, but Rose Marie is talking to somebody at the American embassy in Tel Aviv. We ought to know something soon."

Virgil: "Okay. I'll see you in a couple of hours. If you're gone, leave the units on Shirley's desk."

"I'll do that. If more Yales show up, I'll be in a meeting."

"Ya-els," Virgil said, but Davenport was gone.

SOMETHING ELSE was about to happen, Virgil thought, but he didn't plan to call Davenport about it. He sat in the truck for a couple of minutes, in case the taxi came back, and while he waited, changed the lens on the Nikon to a 60mm macro. When that was done, he watched another fifteen seconds, then got out, walked down the block, into the Downtown Inn, and up a flight of stairs to Yael-1's room. He took out the stolen room key as he walked, and at the room, knocked a couple of times to see if he'd get an answer—there was still an open question of an accomplice or associate who'd supplied Yael with the pistol—and then used the key and stepped inside.

The lights were on. One of the huge suitcases was open, showing a mesh bag full of clothes. He picked up the bag, squeezed it, and put it back. He picked up the other suitcase, but it was so light it was obviously empty. A laptop sat on a side table, but was turned off. He felt that he dare not turn it on, because it was too likely that it would be alarmed, and she would know that somebody had opened it.

He spent five minutes searching quickly through the room, found nothing of interest except another mesh bag, the size of an envelope, with a few papers inside. He checked them out, and found a passport and some letters in Hebrew, one with an En-

glish translation on the letterhead that said: "Israel Antiquities
Authority."

The passport was in both Hebrew and English. Her picture
was current, and her name was given as Aronov, Yael; the birth
date looked more or less right.

He flipped through the back of it and found a few entry stamps
for European countries, and one for Jordan. Virgil didn't know that
Israelis could go to Jordan, but he wasn't sure they couldn't, either.

He was leaving, giving the room one last look-around, when
he hesitated, then went back to the empty suitcase and thought,
The old empty-suitcase trick. He unzipped it, and found it empty.

Of course it would be empty. He pushed his fingers against
the interior fabric, and dragged them down the length of the
suitcase . . . and found a thin lump where there shouldn't have
been one.

It took him a minute to figure out how to get to the lump:
it was easy enough, a professionally neat slit in the fabric, right
where the seam was, closed with Velcro. He pulled the seam
apart, and found another passport.

A diplomatic passport for a Tal Zahavi, with a current photo
of Yael-1. The same birth date as in the other passport. The interior must have had fifty entry stamps for European and South
American countries, plus the U.S., Japan, and South Korea. The
woman traveled a lot.

Virgil put the passport on the worktable, flattened it along
the edge with a magazine, and took a photo, checked to make
sure the photo was good, and took a backup just in case.

When he was done, he returned the passport to the suitcase,

zipped it back up, put it back where it had been, and took another look around, and left. One minute later, he was in his truck.

Tal Zahavi.

With a diplomatic passport . . .

DAVENPORT CALLED again when Virgil was halfway to St. Paul. "The incoming Yael is the real one, unless there are three of them. I sent you a picture of her, you'll have it in your e-mail. Anyway, Yael-1 doesn't look anything like the photo we got from the embassy."

"I wonder who the hell she is?"

"Maybe Yael-2 will know," Davenport said.

"She's gotta be working with somebody," Virgil said. "Listen, the gun's gonna have her prints on it, and I've got it locked up in my truck. I'll drop it off with the guys upstairs and see if they can pull anything off it."

"I'll make sure somebody waits for you. I'm going home," Davenport said.

Virgil rang off. It would be convenient if the feds were able to identify Tal Zahavi by name. If they could, there'd never be awkward questions about how Virgil had identified her, if it became necessary for him to reveal her identity.

WHEN VIRGIL got to the BCA building on St. Paul's north side, he found a latent print specialist waiting; she was reading a *Kick-Ass* comic, which she set aside as he brought in the gun.

"It has your prints all over it, of course," she said.

"Mostly on the slide. I didn't touch the stock, but I'd think the magazine would be the best possibility," Virgil said.

"Give me a half hour and I'll tell you if there's anything there," she said.

"Call me," Virgil said. "I'm on my way to the airport."

He stopped at Davenport's office, where he found a single GPS and a tracker tablet, along with a note from Davenport. "Apparently, right after the class, everybody wanted one of these things, so there was only one left in the house. I could get a couple more tomorrow or the next day if you still need them. Let me know."

Probably guys tracking their girlfriends, Virgil thought. He went back to his truck and headed to the airport.

He got a call from the latent prints tech as he was walking through the skyway into the main terminal: "We've got prints. Partials on the brass, a couple of good ones, thumb and forefinger on the magazine. I'll get them off to the feds."

"She's a foreigner, so there might not be anything," Virgil said.

But: if she were really with the Israeli government, a Mossad agent, would she have left fingerprints on the magazine?

Virgil had taken his laptop and the phone/WiFi link with him. At baggage claim, he found a seat, turned all the electronics on, and first checked his e-mail, where he found the photos of Yael-2. Then he went to the Israel Antiquities Authority website at www .antiquities.org.il, clicked on "About Us," and then on the "Organizational Structure" and "Curriculum Vitae" tabs, and harvested as many names, with positions, as he could find. He transferred the data to a Microsoft Word document.

He was still doing that when Yael-2 called from the plane, which had just touched down.

YAEL-2 WAS a middle-sized dishwater blonde, who looked more German than Virgil's idea of an Israeli—pretty and a little plump, and exactly like the photos Davenport had forwarded to him. She had a more pronounced accent than Yael-1. She shook hands as she introduced herself, apologized for arriving later than expected. "I went through Amsterdam, there was some stupid problem with my passport. I had to stay there two extra days before they would allow me on the plane."

"You were arrested?" Virgil asked.

"No, no, they even arranged for a hotel, though I had to pay for it. Then it turned out, there was no problem, and they arranged for me to get on the same flight I would have been on two days before. Annoying. I thought the computer systems were better than that. And sometimes, when things like this happen, I think, the Europeans don't like Israelis so much."

"Annoying." And delaying, Virgil thought. *Mossad.*

"At least I'm not so jet-lagged as if I came straight through. Going west is easier than going east." She looked past him to the luggage carousel. "My suitcase is going around."

Virgil retrieved the bag, which was extremely light. "You travel light—doesn't feel like there's much in here."

"Not yet," she said. "Do you know this place . . . Sam's Club?"

———————

YAEL-2 HAD a room reservation at the Holiday Inn Express in Mankato, which was out of the town center, and not the same one housing either the Turks or the Texan. On the way down to Mankato, Yael-2 told Virgil almost exactly the same story that Yael-1 had, of the theft, the flight, and the importance of the stone.

She did not try to hide the fact that the stone had been translated, and gave Virgil about the same information that he'd eventually squeezed from Yael-1.

Yael-1, he thought, had been very well briefed.

At Mankato, he told Yael-2, "We have to stop at my house for a moment. We need a private conversation, which I will explain when we get there. I need to look at my laptop while we're doing it."

She was mystified. "Have I done something?"

"Probably not, but somebody else has," Virgil said.

Virgil parked in his driveway, took Yael-2 in through the kitchen, paused to water his cactus, which appeared to be dying of thirst, and then asked her if she'd like anything to eat. She inquired about the possibility of fruit. Virgil opened the refrigerator, looked inside, and said, "Apples, oranges, green grapes, a few bing cherries, and an unopened tub of cantaloupe slices."

She took some grapes and cherries, and they moved to the living room. Virgil opened his computer, apologized insincerely about the test, and asked her to identify the people whose names he'd taken from the IAA website. He ran through twenty names, and she nailed them all.

He shut the computer and said, "All right. I believe you. I believed you before, but better safe than sorry. The reason I had to ask is that two nights ago, a woman arrived here in Minnesota and identified herself as Yael Aronov from the Israel Antiquities Authority. She's been working with me for two days, trying to find the stone. There's some reason to think that she might be Mossad."

"Why would you think that?"

"Because everybody who has seen her said so—Turks, Arabs, Texans."

"Texans?"

"One, anyway," Virgil said.

Yael-2 sat for a moment, looking down at her hands, but her eyes flicked back and forth as though she were working down a pathway, and then she said, "This fucking Mossad. This is why I had trouble in Amsterdam. Not because the Dutch hate Israelis."

"But why would they do it?" Virgil asked.

"Because only three things can happen with this stone," Yael said. "One, we prove it is authentic, which it appears to be, and we rewrite the history of Israel. Or, anyway, we rewrite the Bible. Two, we prove it is a fake, but many people don't believe us, especially not the Arabs. Then we engage in another propaganda war about whether Jews have land rights in Israel, and the French again call us a shitty little country. Three, we drop it in the sea and the issue does not come up. *They think.* This would be very tempting for the large brains at the Mossad—to simply destroy the issue."

"And your organization would not approve?"

"Of course not," Yael-2 said. "Throwing it in the sea? This

would be a sin. And since there are already photographs, it would not kill the legend of the stone anyway. It might even make things worse—if the Mossad is found to have thrown the stone in the sea, then our enemies would say we did it to cover up."

"Which you would have."

"Yes, and maybe unnecessarily," she said. "It still could prove to be a fake."

"Nobody seems to think that," Virgil said. "Except, maybe, me."

"You think it's a fake?"

"I can't make any sense out of Jones's run out of Israel. It all seemed like a con job."

"I don't understand this phrase," she said.

"It seemed too . . . contrived to me," Virgil said. "Like he knew the stone was going to appear, and he was prepared for it."

"I see. Interesting. This has been mooted at my agency," Yael-2 said.

"In any case, we need to find the stone."

"Yes. Now, more than ever."

"So let me tell you about our other competitors here," Virgil said.

HE TOLD HER about the Turks, the Hezbollah, and the Texan, and about Jones shooting the Turks, and about Jones's daughter. "He'll be dead soon. So why is he trying to auction the stone? He can't use the money—and it's a lot of money."

"For his children?" Yael-2 suggested.

"Maybe, but I'm not sure they really need it," Virgil said. "I've

warned his daughter to stay away, but I can't think of anything
else that Jones could do with the money. He's asking for it in cash,
and he'll have to pass it to somebody."

"So you track her," Yael-2 said.

"I'm going to do that. And I'm thinking maybe I should
call a conference with all the competitors and explain to them
that they'll all be going to a pretty nasty prison if they don't co-
operate."

"I know the boss of the Turks," Yael-2 said. "He lives in Istanbul, and does not leave very often. His collection from the
Ottoman lands is huge—perhaps the biggest in existence. I don't
think you will convince his people to go away. The Hezbollah, if it
is like you say, would literally kill to get this stone. This man you
say that you like, this Raj Awad, he is playing a dangerous game.
And this Mossad agent . . . perhaps we can warn her away, if we
can find her."

"She's at the Downtown Inn," Virgil said.

Yael-2 shook her head. "Not anymore. If the Mossad stopped
me in Amsterdam, then they know that I am now here talking to
you. She will be gone."

"To where?"

Yael-2 shrugged. "Who knows? Maybe an Israeli sympathizer
here, or maybe another hotel under a different name. You say she
had a gun, there must be somebody. If they could get a gun, they
could get a car and a room."

"Well, poop," Virgil said. "But tell you what: let's go look.
Maybe you'll know her."

"Good," she said. She spit the last of the bing cherry pits into the bowl Virgil had given her, then said, "Let me tell you something."

"Yeah?"

"There is something going on here that we don't understand. Something fundamental."

Virgil thought about that on the way downtown, and finally concluded that Yael-2 was wrong. There wasn't *something* fundamental that they didn't understand: there were a whole *bunch* of things they didn't understand.

At the Downtown Inn, they pulled into the parking lot and almost the first thing Virgil saw was the Texan's Cadillac. He pointed it out to Yael-2 and said, "That's one thing we don't understand—why those two are talking to each other."

Up at Yael's room, Virgil knocked, but got no answer. He knocked louder. Nothing. He had the room key in his wallet, but wasn't willing to use it around witnesses, just in case this should ever move to a courtroom. They went down to the front desk and talked to an assistant manager, whose name tag said Vivek Bhola. Bhola checked his guest list and said, "She checked out two hours ago."

Yael-2 said, "Of course."

"You haven't cleaned the room?"

"Not until tomorrow morning," Bhola said.

"Get the key," Virgil said.

Bhola programmed a key and they went up. The room was empty, except for two huge suitcases, apparently abandoned. Virgil checked the one where he'd found the passport: the passport was gone.

"Now what?" Yael-2 asked.

"Do me a favor," Virgil said. "Don't ever ask, 'Now what?'"

What they did was check Sewickey's Cadillac, though not until Virgil had loaded the two giant suitcases into the back of his truck. "They are abandoned, and I may find a use for them," Yael-2 said.

"Take some refrigerators home?"

She eyed the suitcases for a moment, then said, "I don't think refrigerators."

When they checked the Cadillac, Virgil found the driver's side unlocked—and the keys sitting on the driver's seat.

Yael-2 said, "Well, I can't ask you . . . to rephrase it, what now?"

"Let's run down to the Holiday Inn," Virgil said. "Maybe Sewickey's there. This Caddy with the keys, that's very curious."

WHEN THEY got to Sewickey's room, Virgil knocked, and got no response . . . but did hear a distant *thump*. "Did you hear that?"

Yael-2 said, "Like something fell?"

"Yeah." He knocked again, and this time, there were four thumps. Like, *thump*, pause, *thump*, pause, *thump*, pause, *thump*.

"This doesn't sound good," Yael-2 ventured. "We should call the hotel manager, and enter this room also."

They did that, and the assistant manager, Arjun Sharma, programmed a key and took them up. They knocked again, heard more thumps, and Sharma unlocked the door and stepped back.

Virgil pushed the door open with his fingertips and flipped on the light. He didn't immediately see anyone, but then saw the cowboy boots sticking out past the end of the bed, toes down. The moment he saw them, the boots lifted off the floor and landed with the thump they'd heard from outside. Virgil walked around the bed and looked down at Sewickey, who was largely wrapped in duct tape, looking something like a joint in a Cheech & Chong movie.

He was lying on his stomach, his hands taped behind his back, with more loops around his arms, his knees, his ankles, and his mouth.

Virgil said, "We need a knife," but nobody had one, so he jogged down to his truck and got a knife and jogged back, flicked it open, and started by cutting the tape behind Sewickey's head, gently unwrapping his mouth, and then his hands and his body.

Sewickey, breathing hard, finally pushed himself up and fell on the bed and groaned, "Finally. I was afraid I'd vomit and choke to death."

"What happened?" Virgil asked.

YAEL-I HAD CALLED HIM, he said, and asked to meet—she thought they might be able to work out an alliance. When he opened the door, she stuck a gun in his face, taped him up, and then tore his room apart.

"She got all the photographs of the stone, my camera and

my cell phone—Jones has that number, it's the only way he can reach me."

"So you have nothing that would prove the existence of the stone?" Virgil asked.

He shook his head. "Nothing." He glanced at his watch and frowned.

"Then what?" Yael-2 asked. She glanced at Virgil and said, "Sorry."

"Then nothing," Sewickey said. "I just kept trying to breathe through my nose. I thought I might be lying there until the maid came in the morning. I was afraid that she might have put the Do Not Disturb card on the door."

They all looked at the door, but she hadn't done that. "Still a crime. Another one, a felony this time," Virgil said. "When I find her, I'm going to put her in jail, and let the Mossad get her out."

"I can tell you one thing," Sewickey said, pulling at the sticky tape residue in his hair. "She's working with somebody. She called him and told him that she'd drive my car down to her motel, and for him to meet her there."

"Sure it was a him?" Virgil asked.

"Well, no. But she was going to meet somebody." Sewickey got shakily to his feet, rubbed some sticky stuff off the side of his mouth, and asked, "It's almost ten o'clock?"

Virgil: "Yeah?"

"My interview. It'll be leading the news at ten."

Virgil said, "Ah, man, did you really have to do that?"

Sewickey said, "Hey. You think I'm here for my health?"

10

The interview actually led the news, and from the tenor of it—and from the lack of actual news later in the broadcast—Virgil realized that the trouble had only begun: the real storm would arrive the next day, when every reporter south of the Canadian line would be in town.

Because it was just too good. Even worse, it'd been a slow news day, and the stone was definitely something to talk about.

The report started with the portentous, hard-fat anchorman pivoting to face the TV audience in a raking light, and saying, in his best serious-news voice, "A famed archaeological explorer and specialist in ancient relics, often compared to a real-life Indiana Jones, has come to Minnesota in search of a stone that he says could quite literally rewrite the Bible and perhaps damage claims that the Jewish people have to the land of Israel. Reporter Jayden Noah Ethan has the story exclusively from Mankato."

The taped story featured the reporter, whose questions appeared to have been written by Sewickey, interviewing Sewickey as he stood in front of his Cadillac. Virgil noticed for the first time

that it had auxiliary lights and a winch on the front end, to em-
phasize the explorer motif.

Sewickey told the story of Jones's discovery and flight from Israel, about the stone, and about Siamun/Solomon. When the report was done, Virgil took his phone from his pocket and turned
it off: Davenport would be calling.

Sewickey said to an astonished Yael-2, "It's this kind of report-
ing that has made the American media what it is."

She nodded. "You are correct," she said.

VIRGIL DROPPED YAEL at the Holiday Inn Express with her own
suitcase and Yael-1's two enormous empty bags, told her that he'd
pick her up at seven o'clock the next morning, and that he had a
few more leads they could chase down.

Then he had to think about it. Ellen, he believed, was back in
the Cities. The Turks were available, and right there, but they'd
had a falling-out with Jones, and Jones might be done with them.
Eventually, he drove over to Awad's apartment, located his car,
unpacked the magnet-mounted GPS tracker, fixed it to the Toyota's frame, and made it doubly secure with a few turns of black
duct tape.

Then he went home.

Unable to help himself, he checked his phone, and found that
Davenport had called at 10:14, and had left a message. He turned
the phone back off. His best response to Davenport would be to
call him in the morning, at about seven o'clock. Davenport never
got up before nine, but Virgil did.

Virgil got in bed, and thought about the day: and thought, uneasily, that he should have checked out the campsites mentioned by Sugarman, the lawn-mowing guy. If he could only get hold of Jones and the stone, then everybody else, with all their motives, money, and impulses, became irrelevant. They'd go home, and leave him alone to investigate Ma.

He considered getting up and going out, but then he thought about driving down a dirt track at midnight, coming up on somebody about whom he knew only one thing for sure: he was willing to shoot people.

He thought, *Screw it*, and went to sleep.

VIRGIL WOKE the next morning at six-thirty, did his usual twenty-minute shave and cleanup, microwaved some instant coffee and poured it into one of several stolen paper cups from Starbucks, and called Yael-2. "I am awake," she announced.

"I'll be there in ten minutes. We'll find a place to get breakfast, and plan the day. I have a couple of places we need to check."

"I will wait," she said.

Virgil got his bag and carried it out to the truck and fired everything up. He sat in the driveway and checked the GPS tracker tablet, which showed Awad's car still at the apartment complex. Virgil backed out of his driveway and headed east toward the Holiday Inn Express, checked the time—6:59—and called Davenport.

Davenport answered on the fifth ring, groaning, "This better be important."

"Hey, you called me in the middle of the night," Virgil said, as brightly as he could manage. "I didn't get it, but I figured it must be critical."

"Fuck you," Davenport said, and hung up.

As Virgil had expected, Davenport had called to rag on him about the TV interview. The whole episode cheered him up, and he was whistling when he pulled in at the Holiday Inn Express.

Yael was ready to go. Virgil asked, "Are you carrying a gun?"

"Good God no," she said. "Why would I do that?"

"Atta girl," Virgil said. "Let's go get some bacon 'n' eggs."

"Maybe not," she said. "I prefer not to burn in Jewish hell. I would like a nice morning salad, with some olives."

"That'll be a Mankato first," Virgil said.

THEY HAD just ordered breakfast at a downtown café—Virgil told her about the GPS tacking unit on Awad's car, and about the two places that Jones could possibly be hiding—when Awad called. He said, "This is Raj. I need to speak with you on the telephone."

"Well, you are," Virgil said.

"Yes, good. I now drive to the airport," Awad said.

"You need some flying advice?"

A moment of silence. "No, no, I wish to speak to you confidentially."

"That's my middle name," Virgil said. "Confidential."

Another moment of silence, then Raj said, "I doubt this. For many people, this would be an unusual name. For you, it would be ridiculous."

"So what do you want to talk about?" Virgil asked.

"I have a big problem which I have considered all night, and I finally have decided to put my life into your hands."

"Hang on a second, my pancakes just got here," Virgil said. Raj hung on, and when the food was delivered, Virgil started soaking it in maple syrup with one hand, and went back to the phone with the other.

"What's up?" he asked. "You know where Jones is?"

"No. But I tell you this with great confidentiality, that an important figure in Hezbollah will arrive this afternoon in Minneapolis, and will take a car, and will come here to stay in my apartment, and then I am supposed to meet him with Jones. This frightens me, and I have decided that the only way I may survive this is to become an informant. So, this is what I do."

"Very, very smart," Virgil said. "What's this guy's name?" To Yael, "Pass me the pepper."

Awad said, "What? Pepper?"

"I was talking to somebody else," Virgil said.

"I don't know this name, but I am told he is important, and will call me," Awad said.

"All right, I will tell you what," Virgil said. "You're now my official informant, and I will do everything I can to protect you. If any of this ever comes to court and you are implicated somehow, I will protect you."

"This is good," Awad said. "How should we proceed?"

"Whenever you learn anything, call me on the telephone. I will listen for you all day and all night."

"I will do this," he said. "Do not shoot me."

"I won't," Virgil said.

"This other figure, you may shoot him."

"I'll try to avoid that, as well," Virgil said. "He will have to call you to make arrangements to meet. Call me as soon as you hear."

"I will. I thank you, and my father would thank you, if he was here to do that."

Virgil rang off, pleased with himself, and Yael asked, "What was that?"

"A man put his life in my hands," Virgil said. "That's always good."

THE BIGGER of the two Turks, the one with the knife, whose name was Timur Kaya, looked at the face of his cell phone, then pressed the "answer" bar and said, "Mr. Kennedy."

Kennedy, a rental car clerk, said, "I have a location for you."

"That is excellent. This comes through the hijack mechanism?"

"LoJack," Kennedy said. "He shouldn't be running from the cops in one of our cars, anyway."

"You are quite correct," said Kaya. He thought it was interesting how people who took bribes usually found a way to justify them as the right thing to do.

The location, which they got from Kennedy and spotted on their iPad, was at a nearby lake. By zooming in on Google Earth, they could see a cabin; by switching to the map view they could get an exact route to the place.

"This Google, I love this Google," said the smaller Turk.

"When we are in the car, I will tell you my famous Google story," the big Turk said.

They both had guns, and checked them before they went out to the Benz. "This time, this snake shot will not stop us," Kaya said.

"Americans have a lot of very interesting sporting equipment," the smaller Turk said. "Guns, everywhere."

ON THE WAY out to Jones's location, the smaller Turk said, "So tell me this famous Google story."

Kaya said, "In 2008, I was sent to Iraq in coordination with the American Air Force. To Balad Air Force Base to observe operations. While I am there, I find that some of the Americans call this air base 'Mortar-ita-ville,' because, you see, the resistance fighters hide in the farm fields around the base, with a mortar dug in the ground, and they drop in a shell and walk away. So, five, ten times a day, a mortar shell lands on the base. Since the Arabs don't shoot so well, nothing happens, except that the Americans make an announcement of the event on the loudspeaker. I don't know why, but this is what happens—a woman makes this announcement. The people on the air base call her 'the Big Voice.' While I am there, an American sergeant shows me his laptop, with his Google Earth. He calls up Balad. You can see everything—buildings, runways, even individual helicopters parked on the flight lines. He shows me that you can find an intersection outside the base—a canal crossing, a deviation in a road, a group of palm trees. Then,

using a Google measuring stick, on the Google Earth, you can get
the distance to your target in precise meters, and the precise direction. So this, with a mortar, should be like shooting a paper target.
But, the Arabs fail to do this. Why? I don't know."

"Lucky for you, they don't," the smaller Turk said.

"Yes. But I wonder. Does this Google work with the American
government, with the CIA, to change distances and directions? Is
this why the mortars never hit? Is something to think about."

"I don't have to think about it," the smaller man said. "Of
course they do. The CIA is everywhere."

THE RURAL LANDSCAPE in Turkey and the rural landscape in
Minnesota differed in one fundamental way: the roads in Turkey
followed the contours of the land and connected specific places to
each other. The Minnesota roads—the smaller roads, anyway—
were built on a grid, with little regard for the movement of the
land. The Turks found this disorienting. In Turkey, if you wanted
to go somewhere, a road usually led directly to it. In Minnesota,
you could often see your objective, but getting there was another
matter, and often meant a series of zigzag turns until you found
the road that went through that place.

In the case of Jones's cabin, they could see where they wanted
to go, but couldn't get there in the car, without giving themselves away. They wound up leaving the car in a roadside pull-off,
and after consulting with their iPad, walking through swampy
ground around the south end of the lake where Jones was hiding.
Their iPad didn't show the minor vagaries of the route: on the

way, they pushed through some stinging plants, which left little white dots on their hands and arms that itched like fire; and they stepped on patches of what looked like solid ground, only to find themselves up to their knees in muck. The smaller Turk momentarily lost an Italian loafer in the stuff, and when he managed to retrieve it, it smelled like rotten eggs.

And it was hot. Turkey could get hot, but this was hot and humid, and in crossing through the woods, sweating, they stirred up clouds of mosquitoes, which attacked like hawks. Pursued by mosquitoes, stung by nettles, ruining their shoes and slacks, they became annoyed, to the extent of about a nine on a one-to-ten scale, where eight was "murderous."

And they were not quiet.

They didn't know exactly where they were going, and they kept detouring around fallen timber, and crunching through some kind of heavy reed that grew in swampy areas. Then they were there.

They knew they were there because Jones shouted, "Who is that? Who's there?"

As luck would have it, Jones's car was parked thirty meters from the front of the small wooden cabin, and they'd emerged halfway between them. They could see Jones standing in the doorway, looking toward the area where they were standing. He had what looked like a pistol in his hand.

The smaller Turk said, "He has a gun."

Kaya said, "A warning shot." He lifted his pistol and fired a shot over the roof of the cabin.

Jones threw himself sideways, and Kaya was about to call to

him, when glass broke in a window left of the door, and Kaya saw what appeared to be the barrel of a gun, and BOOM, from the muzzle flash, the blast, and the sound of a falling tree limb, he knew he was no longer dealing with snake shot. He dropped and rolled into the roadside weeds, which he would later discover were called "poison ivy," and from there scrambled back into the trees.

"Go away," Jones shouted.

The smaller Turk fired two shots into the cabin, and Jones fired back, a shot right through the wall of the cabin, spraying wood splinters up the driveway, but missing the Turks by a good measure.

Kaya said, "I will move closer to talk to him. You cover—"

The smaller Turk fired two shots into the cabin roof, moved sideways, fired another one, moved again.

Kaya was getting closer, and did a peek from behind a tree, saw a fallen log that looked like a good place to negotiate from. He dropped to his knees and crawled toward it, shook a sapling as he passed. That was one sapling too many and Jones fired at it, low, and Kaya felt the stinging impact in his buttocks. He rolled and scrambled deeper in the woods, and reached back, to touch the wound. His hand came back bloody. He called to the smaller Turk, "This donkey's asshole has shot me."

The smaller Turk, well covered by a burr oak, emptied his pistol at the cabin and then ran through the deeper woods, in a semicircular path, until he came back to Kaya. He knelt next to the big man and asked, "How bad?"

"In the back. Can't see it . . ."

"Roll over."

The smaller Turk looked at the bigger Turk's butt and said, "Not bad, but it will hurt."

"Did it go through?"

"It didn't go in. It's a trough. A bad cut."

"Then a bandage will work. We should go."

"Yes."

"Before we do that . . ." The big Turk pushed himself up, braced against a tree, and emptied his pistol at the cabin. "Goddamn him," he said. He limped away, through the nettles and poison ivy, through the cattails and alders and prickly gooseberry bushes. They were coming up to the Mercedes, muddy nearly to their knees, the big Turk limping and cursing, bunching his trousers against the wound, staunching the blood, when the smaller Turk said, "Listen."

In the distance, they could hear a siren.

"Now we are in a hurry," the smaller Turk said.

VIRGIL WAS just finishing the pancakes and had asked the waitress for one last cup of coffee, when the phone rang again. Ellen—Jones's daughter. He said to Yael, "Jones's daughter. Could be something."

He said, "Hello?"

Ellen started screaming at him.

Virgil couldn't make out what she was screaming but pinned the phone to his shoulder with his ear and stood up and dug out a twenty and threw it at the table and headed for the door with Yael trotting behind, and on the sidewalk he started shouting, "Slow down, I can't understand you, slow down—"

"My father," she screamed. "Somebody's trying to shoot my father. I'm going there, I'm going there—"

"Where is he? Where is he?" Virgil piled into the 4Runner and fired it up, barely noticed Yael belting herself into the passenger seat.

"A cabin—he's in a cabin off County Road 18, West Elysian Lake Road, north of Janesville."

"Ah, Jesus," Virgil groaned. The cabin that Sugarman had told him about, that he'd spotted the night before. "I know exactly where it is," he shouted into the phone, as he swung through a U-turn. "I'm on my way. Where are you?"

"I'm still west of town, I'm coming, but I'm way behind you. My dad just called three minutes ago, said somebody was shooting at him, he's shooting back. He doesn't think he can hold out."

"I'm going," Virgil shouted, and clicked the phone off and hit the truck's sirens and flashers. When they'd made the big turn on Highway 14 and were rolling, he called 911 and told the dispatcher where they were and what was happening. "Are there any sheriff's cars in the area?"

"Let me check, Virgil," the dispatcher shouted at him. "Goldarnit, this is more exciting than string-cheese night at Lambeau Field."

"What?"

"We got Frank Martin is about, mmm, fifteen or twenty miles south of you, but he's not in his car, can't get there for a couple minutes. We got Fred Jackson. He's over to the west."

"Get them started and anybody else you can find."

"On the way."

VIRGIL HAD BEEN out to Elysian Lake a few times, caught a few bass and pike, and more carp than he'd admit to, so he knew the area: they were about twelve miles out. If Jones was being shot at, it had to be either the Turks or Yael, because he knew where Awad and Sewickey were.

He just finished thinking that when Yael said, "I find it very suspicious that this Arab called you just before the shooting started. He said he was driving to the airport and the GPS says his car is going to the airport . . . so he has this alibi that you provide."

Virgil thought about that for a second, and said, "I couldn't live with that kind of paranoia."

"This is because the Hezbollah is not trying to fly a missile into your window every minute."

"All right. I'll put Awad back on the suspect list," Virgil said.

"I think this is a good idea."

"But I think it's either Yael-1 or the Turks."

"Let us hope it's this *katsa*, and not the Turks. I don't think she would kill us. The Turks . . . I don't know."

"Katsa? That's her name? How—"

"Not her name. It's her type. Spy . . . or agent. I ask you this: Why do you use your bell? They will hear us."

"I hope so," Virgil said. "We're still eight or nine minutes away, that's forever in a gunfight. Most gunfights last a few seconds. If he's holed up inside this place, maybe it'll take longer, maybe whoever is shooting will hear the siren and run."

"Good analysis," she said. "We want the stone, not the shooters."

"I want the shooters, too," Virgil said. "But mostly, I want to keep anybody from being killed."

SEVEN OR EIGHT MINUTES after they left town, Virgil threw them off Highway 14 and onto 390th Street to West Elysian Lake Road, and then north, and then they were coming up on the side road that took them into the stand of timber that hid the cabin, and a couple of deer stands that overlooked a cornfield.

With the siren still wailing, Virgil took the truck to within a hundred yards of the trees, then stopped, killed the siren, jumped out of the truck, shouted at Yael to "stay there!", got his vest and his M16 out of the lockbox in the back, slapped a magazine into the gun and put another under his belt line, ran into the road-side ditch and then started running through the weeds toward the trees.

The ditch was wet, so he moved left, and ran along the slope of it. He heard no shooting, nothing but the siren still wailing behind him.

Fifty yards from the tree line, he slowed down, looking for any kind of movement; saw nothing. He dropped into a crouch and moved forward, stopping, listening, although his hearing hadn't yet recovered from the screaming siren.

Twenty-five yards out, he knelt and crawled for a way through the thick weeds, then sat and listened some more. Nothing but silence, and the high-pitched whine of mosquitoes.

He waited another half-minute, then started the slow approach. At the tree line, he crossed the fence he'd been crawling parallel to and stepped back into the woods. The aerial photos he'd looked at the night before had shown the cabin perhaps a hundred yards ahead, but he could see almost nothing in the tangle of trees and brush.

He waited, then moved, slowly, still hunting—avoided a nasty-looking patch of shiny green poison ivy—the muzzle of the M16 leading the way. Fifty yards into the trees, he'd seen or heard nothing at all.

Another ten yards and the road twisted to the left, and as he rounded the turn on the inside of the track, he saw the cabin; the visible windows were shattered.

He stopped, listened for another few seconds, then shouted, "Anybody there? Police. Anybody there?"

He heard, in reply, a weak, "Help . . ."

"Who is that?" he shouted.

He heard, "Me. Jones. They're gone. I heard them go."

All right. Virgil thought he understood that. Still, it could be a trap.

"Are you okay?" he shouted. He'd wait for backup, if he could.

"I've been shot."

"I'm coming," Virgil shouted back. "But I'm coming slow. I have a machine gun. If you or anybody else tries to shoot me, if I see a gun, I'll mow down the whole goddamn forest."

"I got an empty gun, but that's all," the man's voice said.

Virgil moved in, tree by tree, always looking for something from another direction, listening. When he got close to the cabin, he could see that the front door was closed but the windows were all shattered, and he could see what looked like fresh broken wood across the front wall of the place.

Bullet holes.

The cabin was surrounded by a small open space, half grass, half dirt. A Toyota Corolla sat at the far end of the opening. Virgil had to make a move sooner or later: he called, "My backup will be here in a minute. We're cutting off this whole field. You'll have to wait another couple of minutes."

"Don't make me wait too long or I'll be dead," the man said. "I'm bleeding pretty good."

Virgil made his move, bolting from the cover of the tree, across ten or twelve yards of the clearing, and up onto the porch.

The man inside laughed. "You were lying about waiting. You might as well come on in. Door's unlocked. I got nothing left."

Virgil risked a peek at the window to the left of the front door and saw the top two-thirds of Jones's body protruding from behind a heavy kitchen table, which had been overturned to provide some protection. Jones was lying on his side, more facedown than faceup. Virgil could see his hands, and his hands were empty.

"I'm pointing an M16 at you. If you show a gun, you're gonna find out what a real hosing is all about."

"Are you gonna come in here and help me, or are you going to stand there and bullshit?" Jones asked.

Virgil went inside. Jones showed a trail of blood on the floor behind him, and as Virgil stepped through the door, he pushed a revolver across the floorboards toward Virgil's feet. "Nothing left in it," he said, "So I hope you really are the police."

"I am," Virgil said. "Don't move."

He patted Jones down, picked up some blood off his pants, wiped it on the back of Jones's jacket. "Do you know where you're hit?"

"In the hip. On the side. The hip that's up in the air."

Virgil asked, "Do you have a knife?"

"There're a couple of kitchen knives on the counter."

Virgil got a paring knife, came back and cut away the pants where the blood was showing through. The wound was a bloody channel through skin and fat on the outside of Jones's hip. It was bleeding, but not pumping blood. "There's some blood," Virgil said. "We need to get an ambulance out here, but I don't think we have to do anything radical. I'll call for one. What about the shooters? How long have they been gone?"

"Five or six minutes. I heard them crashing off towards the lake. I suspect they parked on another track over on the other side. They'll be gone by now."

"You know who they were?"

"No. I was too busy looking for cover," Jones said. "They really shot the place up."

"Maybe because you shot them, in the park?"

"The Turks? I doubt it. How'd they find me?"

"Good question," Virgil said. "To which I don't have the answer."

"Ah, golly, that hurts," Jones said. "That really hurts. I mean, a lot."

VIRGIL STOOD, called 911, and got an ambulance started. The dispatcher told him a sheriff's car should arrive in the next minute or so, and when Virgil hung up, he could hear a distant siren.

He went back to Jones. "You didn't make any arrangements to meet somebody here?"

"No. Nobody knew I was here. I heard them coming. They were on foot, coming in from the back, then around to the side. They cut me off from my car. There was more than one—maybe two. I got my gun, and called out to them, and then they started shooting. Didn't even say how-do-you-do? Just opened up. Good gosh, it was like a war. I got between the table and the cookstove, and called Ellen and she said she'd call you."

"She's on the way," Virgil said. "Where's the stone?"

"What stone?"

"Reverend Jones, I'm about to arrest you for aggravated assault on a couple of Turks, so you won't be peddling any stones for a minimum of six to ten years," Virgil said. "You might as well tell us. It's an ethical responsibility, a moral responsibility, as much as anything else."

"I'm not about to do *anything* for six to ten years. I'm not going to do anything for more than two to three weeks, at the outside. And I don't need a cop to tell me where my moral and ethical responsibilities lie," Jones snapped, and then he groaned again and said, "Don't make me mad. It hurts when I shout."

Virgil said, "You're a friend of my old man, Lewis Flowers from Marshall. I went to church every Sunday and Wednesday for eighteen years, and got lectures on ethics and morality twice a week. You can't tell me that stealing a country's national heritage, and using a gun to assault a couple of people, put the fear of death in them, is all that moral or ethical."

Jones just said, "Really? You're Lewis's kid? I think I've read about you."

"That's really great," Virgil said. "About the stone?"

Jones groaned again and said, "Hey, Officer Flowers?"

"Yeah?"

"I want a lawyer."

VIRGIL LEFT HIM on the floor and walked out to the truck. Yael was waiting at the front bumper, and as he came up to her, a sheriff's patrol car turned off the road and onto the track and accelerated toward them.

Virgil said to Yael, "He's been shot, but he'll live. For the time being, anyway. He says he doesn't know anything about the stone. I'm gonna arrest him, and send him to the hospital, and then we'll see."

Virgil climbed in the truck and killed the siren.

In the deafening silence, Yael asked, "What happened with the assassins?"

"I don't know—they walked in, they probably had a car over on the other side of the woods, Jones said. They're gone. I'll get the sheriff's people to see if anybody saw them."

The sheriff's deputy came up, climbed out of the car, and called, "Do I need my shotgun?"

STORM FRONT   147

"Don't think so," Virgil said. "We got one down, got an ambulance on the way. C'mon, I'll show you the layout."

Yael and the deputy followed Virgil back down the track, and Virgil said, "We're gonna take the cabin and his car apart. I can't believe the stone is far away."

JONES'S CAR WAS a rental, he said, and he asked Virgil to ask Ellen to turn it in for him. "Costing me a hundred bucks a day," he said.

Virgil got the keys, and he and the deputy and Yael worked through it, and concluded that unless Jones had sewn the rock into one of the car seats, it wasn't in the car.

They were just finishing when the ambulance arrived, and two minutes later, Ellen Case. She got out and ran after the ambulance guys and their gurney, paused as she was passing Virgil, catching his arm: "Is he alive?"

"Yeah, but he's hurt," Virgil said.

She ran inside after the ambulance guys, and Yael, Virgil, and the deputy followed. Inside, a paramedic was wrapping a big white bandage across the wound, as Jones told them about his cancer, and he said, "You gotta pick me up really careful, 'cause I'm like a big sack of loose guts. It could all fall apart."

"Aw, Dad," Ellen cried, and patted his arm.

"Take it easy, kid," Jones said.

When the wound was wrapped, the paramedic and the ambulance driver talked about the best way to half-roll, half-lift him onto the gurney. They did that, with Jones gritting his teeth, and then Jones, his face covered with sweat, said to Virgil, "Hand me that red bag over there, Flowers. That's got my pills. Say hello to your dad for me."

Virgil got the bag and the paramedic put it on Jones's chest, and they carried him to the door, dropped the legs, and began rolling him down the track to the ambulance.

Virgil said to Ellen, "You better follow them in. When you've got the time, you can come back here with a friend and get the car. He wants you to turn it back in to the rental agency."

Virgil told the deputy to follow her out: that Jones was under arrest, and should be restrained after treatment. The deputy left behind Ellen.

Yael said, "Now . . ."

"Now we take the cabin apart," Virgil said. "See if that goddamned stone is here. We'll get a crime-scene crew out here later, to look at the place. If they can figure out where the gunfire was coming from, maybe they can locate some brass. If God is smiling on us, we could get a fingerprint."

"I'm not sure God would smile on anything to do with all this," Yael said.

"Unless it's all a joke to begin with," Virgil said. He opened the oven. "Okay. Not in the oven."

11

Virgil spent the rest of the morning and part of the afternoon cleaning up the aftermath of the shooting, including reports for two different law enforcement agencies; that part was never as swift as anybody would like it to be. He also spent an hour with Yael walking around in the woods behind the cabin, following game trails and peering into gullies, hoping to find a fresh patch of earth where the stone might be buried.

They found nothing.

He checked the GPS tracker tablet a couple of times during the day. Awad's car was at the airport for four hours, and then had been driven back to the campus. He had, he thought, put his one tracker on the wrong car.

When he'd finished all the reports, he drove to the hospital, asked where Jones was, and found him in a private room in the surgical area, with a drip of some kind plugged into his arm, another drip of a specific kind coming out from under the blanket and into a bag near the floor, and a massive bandage wrapped around one thigh and also anchored with a strip that went at an angle around his waist. There was a security cuff on one leg, which was attached to the bed frame with a steel chain.

Ellen was sitting in a visitor's chair, reading a newspaper, and when Virgil came in, she said, "Oh my God, I'm so grateful that you got there in time."

"Has he told you anything about the Solomon stone?"

Jones, who was awake, said, "Hey, I'm right here. I've got a lawyer. You're not allowed to question me."

"I'm not questioning you, I'm questioning her," Virgil said, pointing at Ellen. "She's a witness. Before you toddle off to the Great Hereafter, you might like to know that if she lies to me, I'll put her in the women's prison at Mankato, as a result of your moral and ethical failings."

"You're a vicious little rat," Jones snarled.

"No, *you're* the rat. I'm trying to keep people from being killed," Virgil snarled back. "You're trying to *get* them killed. If your daughter here ends up one of them, which seems possible since these people are willing, I hope you live long enough to see it. I'd want that blood on your head and I'd want you to know it."

"Virgil!" Ellen said. "What a horrible thing to say."

"Yeah, well, fuck him. He's about to die, so he's taking no risks messing around with these crazies. He's all about the money, that's all he is. But you're not—you've still got a whole life to get cut short," Virgil said. "I'm really tired of him."

"Virgil—"

"Do you know where the stone is?"

She looked straight at him: "No. I don't."

He looked over at Jones, then thought, *Screw it*, and walked out. Jones called, "Hey! Hey!" but Virgil kept walking. As he headed down the hall, it occurred to him that Jones was on the edge of death, and so *somebody* else had to know where the stone was . . . or how to find it. Jones could no longer rely on his own ability to recover the thing.

He believed Ellen when she said she didn't know—he didn't think she could lie without flinching. He wondered about the son in San Diego. Was it possible that he was out there somewhere? He suspected, though, that the answer was closer by: that Jones hadn't told Ellen where the stone was, but he *would*. She didn't know now, but she *would*. When he got to the truck, he checked the tracker tablet and found that Awad's car was in the apartment parking lot, five minutes away. He drove over, pried the unit free, drove it back to the hospital, and attached the tracker to Ellen's car. He felt a little bad doing it, because she seemed like a nice woman, but, in the end, he didn't feel all that bad.

HE WAS THINKING about going home when he got a call from the woman who ran the BCA crime-scene team. "We found a clue," she said.

"No shit," Virgil said. "That's gotta be a first."

"Hey."

"Just kiddin', Bea. What is it?"

"It's a note. Written with a ballpoint pen. What happened was, Jones was shot and thought he was dying, so he started writing a note to his daughter. You probably ought to come take a look at it."

"Can't you just read it?"

"Yeah, but you oughta see it," she said.

"All right. Give me twenty minutes."

When Virgil got back to the hunting shack, the place had been lit up with work lights run off a gas-powered generator. The generator was also driving a Dell computer with a couple Logitech speakers, currently playing the Bangles' "Walk Like an Egyptian," which Virgil recalled from his childhood; a song about right for Bea Sawyer's teenybopper days, and, when he thought about it, appropriate for the current investigation.

Sawyer was crumpling up a pair of disposable Tyvek pants in which she'd been crawling around the cabin. When she saw Virgil, she said, "The note," and pointed to the table where the computer sat.

The note was in a transparent plastic evidence bag. Virgil sat down and peered at it, and Sawyer said, "You can see it better with a flashlight," and passed him an LED flashlight.

The note was on a piece of paper torn from a notebook, and was heavily creased. "It was a paper wad when I found it," Sawyer said. "When you showed up and saved his ass, he wadded it up and threw it in the corner, hoping we wouldn't find it."

"Wonder why he didn't eat it?" Virgil asked, peering at the note. The handwriting was cramped, and nearly illegible.

"Probably no spit," Sawyer said.

"What?"

"When you get shot at, your mouth tends to go dry. Can't eat paper with a dry mouth."

"Huh," Virgil said. Sounded like bullshit. He flattened the note out and struggled through it. He got this:

> Ellen: I'm not going to make it this time. So far there are three bidders for the stone. You have to recover it; the buyers will come to you, but it might take them a while. Be careful. I put it where the sun comes through. You know I've always loved you and Danny, and the greatest pain is knowing I won't see your faces anymore. I always hoped . . .

The note ended and Virgil said, "The sun comes through?"

"Comes through what?" Sawyer asked.

"I don't know. The drapes, the attic window, the branches on the old oak tree or down the well . . ."

"The well?"

"Probably not the well," Virgil conceded. "How in the hell would I know? It's some kind of reference that his daughter would understand."

"You gonna brace her?"

"I need to think about it for a while."

Sawyer snorted. "Good luck with that."

IN BED THAT NIGHT, reanalyzing his moves, Virgil decided that he had to confront Ellen about the note. If he could just get his hands on the goddamned stone, all the maneuverings would collapse.

He spent some time wondering about the "three bidders." The Israelis supposedly weren't bidders, Sewickey said he didn't have any money, and Jones knew that. So the bidders were the Turks, if they were still involved—after the park shooting, they might be less interested—and the Hezbollah agent. Who was the third bidder?

He had no answer to that.

Then he thought about God for a while, and wondered why He would allow one of His preachers to drift so far from the paths of righteousness, especially on his, Virgil's, time. The only answer, he decided, had to lie within Jones's personal psychology. Some twist, some juke, some repository of wrong chemicals. You saw it often enough in preachers who taught hate, bigotry, intolerance, or who preyed on their own flocks.

Which led him to another thought. Did the Jesuits really have commando teams? The concept was oddly attractive.

And he thought for a few moments about Ellen. When he met attractive single women, he tended to assess their potential personal compatibility; he didn't think he was unique in this—in fact, he thought everybody did it, automatically. There was never any mystery when somebody found somebody else attractive, or unattractive; the mystery came when somebody was obviously attractive, obviously right down the centerline of his taste in females . . . and there wasn't even a flicker of response in his own self. Ellen was like that: she was very good-looking, had eyes like emeralds, was most of what he looked at in women. And yet he felt almost nothing. It was almost like a sisterly response. He could like her very much, but there'd never be a sexual urge involved. He sensed that she reacted to him in the same way. Strange.

Then he went to sleep . . . for a short time.

MA NOBLES had eavesdropped on the conversation between Ellen Case and Virgil Flowers, and had been deeply impressed by two things: first, the money they were talking about, which apparently could involve millions of dollars; and second, that they were talking about Case's father, the Reverend Elijah Jones.

When she mentioned to Virgil that she'd known Jones, she'd choked back an impulse to be effusive about it, and had let it go with the comment that she'd known him long ago, when she was a child.

That wasn't the whole story; that wasn't even much of it.

JONES HAD long ago been called to preach at a dying Lutheran church out in the countryside. He'd agreed to do it out of charity—he was already a full professor at Gustavus Adolphus, and didn't need the small amount that he'd be paid at the Good Shepherd Lutheran Church of Bizby, Minnesota, pop. 321.

In fact, his church salary barely covered gas and an afternoon cheeseburger at Carl's Diner & Fuel, Bizby's only business. Jones had done it not because he'd been called by the Good Shepherd Church, but because he'd been called by God.

In any case, it was at Bizby where he'd encountered Florence McClane before she became Ma Nobles. She'd been nine years old at the time, the youngest of three children of Helen McClane, part-time and later no-time wife of Hank McClane, who left for anywhere else when Florence was seven.

After Sunday services, Jones had a children's class, and had noticed that Florence and her brothers never brought lunch. They were supposed to tell Jones that they always ate lunch at the table with their mom, but Florence confided to him privately that, on most days, there was no lunch—perhaps an early sign of her ability to manipulate the world around her.

So Jones, true minister that he was, went back to a youth group at Gustavus and got them to pledge a hundred dollars a week to help out the McClane family until Helen McClane could find something permanent. The hundred dollars a week got the family through the bitterest summer of the young girl's life. She would never again eat lemon Jell-O with little marshmallows and sliced onions. . . .

In the fall, Jones found Helen McClane a meat-cutting job at the Hormel plant in Austin, Minnesota, and the family said goodbye to the trailer in Bizby.

Life in Austin hadn't exactly been a bowl of cherries, with a single mother on the night shift, and three growing children, but it was approximately fourteen thousand light-years better than Bizby. Austin had libraries and movies and local TV stations, and kids her own age. Right up to the time when Florence got knocked up in ninth grade, she'd been a happy girl; even after that first kid arrived, things had been okay. She'd managed to graduate from high school, and get a couple years in at the community college, before she got knocked up again and had to get a job.

She got a spot in the same plant where her mother worked. When her mother began suffering from carpal tunnel syndrome— meat-cutting did that to you—Florence, who was already called "Ma" by her friends, decided to take the latest offer of marriage, to a man called Rick Nobles. She knew going in that the marriage wouldn't last, but it would carry her through to another job.

Nobles had his own towing company, which actually picked up with Ma doing the books and calling around for business, but he couldn't keep his hands off the customers. When he got one of them pregnant, three months before Ma would produce yet an- other son, she called it off.

Nobles was decent about it, and Ma got out with a three-year- old Ford F-150 and fifteen thousand in cash. From there, it was a series of office jobs, and a second marriage to a man who had a small farm, a part-time salvage business, and a big hunger for Wendy's Baconators. One Baconator too many, a failed Heimlich maneuver, and Ma was on her own again.

She'd felt bad when he died—cried off and on for a month— but then had gotten on with it.

WHEN MA realized the minister that Case and Flowers were talking about was her very own Reverend Jones of the big beard, big teeth, and wide red suspenders, she nearly spoke up in praise of the man. But some instinct made her keep her mouth shut— possibly because of the money they were also talking about.

She couldn't help wondering if Jones might need . . . an assistant?

There was no way she could contact him to ask that question, until she heard about the shoot-out at the hunting camp—and that Jones was on the surgical floor at the hospital in Mankato.

She was familiar with the surgical floor.

Two of her sons had been there: Mateo, after jumping out of a hayloft with a bedsheet for a parachute, which had resulted in two badly broken legs; and young Sam, who'd gotten pissed off when Ma handed him a spading fork and told him to get busy in the garden, digging potatoes, and he'd hurled the fork down in disgust. Unfortunately for Sam, before the fork got to the ground, two tines had gone through the tops of his Nikes, through his feet, and most of the way through the soles of his shoes. He'd been standing outside the chicken house when he did it, and some chicken shit had penetrated the wound. They had taken him to the hospital for the necessary repairs, which had been complicated.

Jones's arrest had been all over the news, along with the fact that he was listed in good condition. Ma figured that she at least owed him a visit.

When her boys had been hurt, she hadn't had a lot of money— she still didn't, though things had gotten considerably better since the family got back in the salvage business. Anyway, when the boys had gotten hurt, a woman from the cashier's office had pursued her through the halls of the hospital like a hound from hell. Ma had eventually worked out a way she could visit them without bothering with the front entrance.

Her latest trip to the hospital began with a phone call:

"This is Mable Diarylide with the Bureau of Criminal Apprehension. I am calling for Agent Flowers. We have a crime-scene crew that needs to speak with Reverend Elijah Jones. We need the room number."

That got her the room number.

WHEN HER KIDS had been hospitalized, the visiting hours had gone until 8:30 p.m. She'd usually gone in late, to avoid the harridan from the cashier's office, and because the kids had been young, she had been allowed to stay later than was normally permitted.

Good training.

She went in that night through the emergency room, her hair covered with a babushka. She took a circuitous route to a back stairway and went up one flight. The nursing station was down to her right, so she could push the door open just a crack and see if anyone was there. For the first few minutes, there was. The last time, she pushed open the door just in time to see the nurse pick up a clipboard and exit, stage right.

Ma was across the hall in five seconds, and into Jones's room. Jones was asleep, but not very.

She touched his arm, and he opened his eyes: "What?"

"Do you remember me?" she whispered. "I'm Florence McClane."

He looked at her for a long time, in the dim light, and then shook his head. "No."

She told him about being a little girl in Bizby, and even then, he wasn't sure: "I remember Bizby. . . . I do remember *something*

about your family. Didn't your father get hurt in an industrial accident, or something?"

"Not unless he cut himself on a pull-tab," she said. Ma was
disappointed. He was a major character in her life, and she apparently wasn't even a minor one in his. Oh, well.

"I feel like I owe you," she said. "I feel like I've always owed
you. Now you seem like you need some help."

"What? You came up here to bust me out?" He tried to
laugh, and wound up coughing. "You think you can take the
bed with you?"

He rattled his good leg, which was chained to the bed at the
ankle.

Ma said, "I brought a bolt cutter, just in case," and pulled it out
of her bag to show him.

She'd caught his interest. "Maybe you do owe me," he said.
"But even if I could walk, I wouldn't get far."

"If you could get down one flight of stairs, I could pick you up
in my truck," she said.

"I could do that," he said, pushing himself up. "I couldn't run,
but I could hobble that far. I think."

"I can't take you home. That state cop, Virgil Flowers, is all
over me. On another matter, not about you, but he's how I found
out where you were. Do you have a place where you could go?"

"Yes. If you can get me there."

They heard the nurse coming down the hall, and Jones pointed
across the room and whispered, "That door—it goes into the
bathroom."

She slipped inside just in time. And then thought, getting

caught in the bathroom wouldn't be good. The bathroom was shared: she tried the door on the other side, and it was unlocked. On the other side, she found a sleeping man. A pair of crutches leaned against one corner.

LATER, WHEN SHE cut Jones free from the bed, he said, "I'm not sure how I feel about stealing a man's crutches."

"They're hospital crutches," she said. "They'll give him new ones—and you can always send them back when you're done with them."

"My clothes are in the locker." He pushed himself up, and groaned. "I'm so damaged. . . . Young lady, you are definitely a godsend, but I tell you, I am a very damaged old man."

"I'm sorry, sir," she said. She got him his clothes, and looked at her watch. "They'll be checking you in six or seven minutes, and then not for another half hour. Put your clothes under your pillow, and put them on before you come down. I'm going now. You have to fake being asleep when they check you, but then, as soon as they leave, come down. The door is down to your right, and across the hall."

"God bless you," he said.

SOMEWHAT TO MA'S SURPRISE, it worked out. The reverend, flailing with the crutches, appeared outside the stairway door, and looked both ways. She flashed her lights at him, and he turned toward her as she pulled through the parking lot, bumped over the curb onto the grass, and rolled up to the side of the building. She jumped out, ran around the truck cab, and helped boost him into the passenger seat.

"I don't mean to be a complainer," he said, as she got back behind the wheel. "But I hurt, and I'm going to have to take a pill. They make me a little woozy. I understand what's going on, but my reactions aren't so good. Before I do that, I need to tell you where we're going."

So he told her, and as they pulled away into the night, she asked, "Will this involve a burglary?"

"No, no, I have a key."

"Are you bleeding?"

"I don't know. I wasn't hurt that bad, I guess," he said, rubbing his forearm, where he'd pulled out a catheter. "They weren't really giving me any treatment in the hospital—after they patched me up, it was just pain medication and observation. But you will have to help me into the house."

"I can do that," Ma said. She watched as he gobbled down a couple of pills, and then asked, "How long before they take effect?"

"It's pretty quick," he said. "Now. Tell me your story. When the pills kick in, I may look a little sleepy, but I do understand what people are saying."

"What do you want to hear?" she asked.

"Your story—the whole story, from the time your mom got the job at Hormel, right up until now."

So Ma told the story: and when she thought about it later,

it was a pretty good story, with some nice high points, and the usual lows for a single mother with five fatherless boys.

"We were in trouble," she said. "The people in Bizby were okay, but nobody around there had any money, except some of the farmers who lived out of town. We were on welfare, but we didn't have any clothes. . . ."

By the time they got to Jones's hideout—actually, a pleasant middle-class home—he looked like he was out of it. But when she parked, and walked around to help him out of the car, he looked up at her from the passenger seat and said, "That was one of the best stories I have ever heard, in my entire life, and I was there at the beginning. It's one of the things that made my life worthwhile, and I'm grateful to you for telling it to me. I will think about it every day until I die, and rejoice a little."

Later, driving away, she thought about his sincerity in saying that, and it made her cry.

12

Virgil's phone rang at 3:37. He knew that because his clock was the first thing he looked at when the phone began ringing; 3:37 phone calls were not usually lawn-furniture sales, and more often than not, left him fumbling for his pants in the dark.

He took his cell phone off his nightstand, looked at the caller ID and saw "Unknown," which usually meant a cop. He answered: "Virgil Flowers."

"Virgil, this is Shane Cobley over at Mankato. We just got a call from the hospital, and they said your guy Jones has taken a hike."

"What?"

"They said—"

"I heard that. He was chained to the bed."

"They say he cut the chain off. That's about all I know. I called Don Scott, and he said he'd go over there, and he told me to call you."

"I'm going," Virgil said.

But he would not, he thought, fumble into his pants in the

dark. He turned the lights on before he fumbled into his pants, and a clean T-shirt, and yesterday's socks. He was out the door in five minutes, at the Mayo in ten.

Scott was standing in the hallway talking to two nurses, one each male and female, and a young man in a white jacket, when Virgil arrived. The nurses' names were Max and Jane, and the resident's name was Mark.

"Don't know what happened," Jane said. "I checked on him every half hour, and at three o'clock he was sound asleep. At three-thirty, he was gone."

Mark, the resident, said, "I was asleep in the physicians' room, and Jane woke me up. We ran around looking, but there was no sign of him. His clothes are gone, so he's probably outside somewhere."

"Can he walk?" Virgil asked.

"He's hurt, but he's pretty bound up in bandages. We would have had him on his feet in the morning."

"We got three patrol cars covering the area," Scott said.

"What about the cuff on his leg?" Virgil asked.

"Take a look," Scott said.

They went into Jones's room. One of the two cuff bracelets was still attached to the bed, with a short length of chain hanging from it. Virgil squatted to look at it. "Bright metal. Cut with a real bolt cutter—this was no side-cutter. Snipped right through it."

"There was nobody up here that I saw," Jane said, and she then glanced sideways at the male nurse, Max.

Max said, "I just got out of an elevator and I saw a woman walk down the hall toward me, and then she went down the stairwell. I didn't see where she was coming from, but she shouldn't have been here. I thought maybe she was a nurse I didn't know, but she was dressed in civilian clothes."

"A dirndl," Jane said.

Virgil: "She was wearing a dirndl?"

Max said, "That's what Jane says it was. You know, a low-cut dress, cut square across the top. She went through the stairway door, and I thought it was odd, something odd about her, so I pushed open the door and looked down after her, but she was already going outside at the bottom."

"Did you mention it to anyone?" Virgil asked.

"Yeah. Jane. She's the charge nurse tonight," Max said. "That's how I found out about the dirndl."

"She was never around the station, I never saw her," Jane said. "The thing is, the stairway door is only two rooms down from Reverend Jones's. So . . . I wouldn't have seen her, if she was just quick in-and-out."

"What time was this?" Virgil asked.

"A few minutes before three, I guess," Jane said. "Because a little while after I talked to Max, about this woman, I went and did my room checks, at three. Reverend Jones was asleep. Then . . . well, you know. I did the three-thirty check, and no Jones."

"What did this woman look like?" Virgil asked Max.

"I wasn't that close to her . . . blond, maybe, very fair-skinned. I didn't see her hair. She was short, she had . . . uh . . . ." He'd unconsciously cupped his hands, then glanced at Jane, who crossed her arms, and he uncupped his hands and finished, "A pretty good figure."

"Couldn't see her hair?"

"No, she was wearing like a handkerchief over her hair."

EXAM TIME.

Virgil asked himself, who did he know who was short, blond, would cause a witness to cup his hands, and who very likely would have instant access to a bolt cutter, and who knew about the stone and the search for it, and the money involved?

He said aloud, "Goddamnit, Ma."

Scott: "Who?"

"Ah, that goddamned Ma Nobles. You know her?"

"Yeah. What's she got to do with this?"

Virgil explained how she'd been around the edges of it. "She has a nose for money, and she probably gives every one of her kids a bolt cutter when they graduate from elementary school."

"She lives out in the country, right?"

"Yeah. I'll go on over there," Virgil said. "But by this time, she's ditched him someplace. Unless his daughter picked him up."

He explained that, then excused himself, went down to his truck, pulled out the tracking tablet, and found that he'd lost Ellen—according to the map, she'd driven off the north edge of the tracking radius at nine o'clock, apparently heading back toward the Twin Cities. Possibly, he thought, because she was creating an alibi.

————

VIRGIL PICKED UP his cell phone and peered at it, reluctant to make the call, but he really had no choice.

Davenport said, "Goddamnit, Virgil."

"Listen, one phone call, and you can go back to sleep. I need Jenkins and Shrake. Like now."

Davenport wanted to know what had happened, and why Virgil was up at four o'clock in the morning.

"Jones took a walk," Virgil explained. He finished with, " . . . so I need somebody to keep an eye on her. Shrake has that pickup, that'd be good, but Jenkins sure as shit can't come down in the Crown Vic. He oughta get a company car, I guess. The more dusty and beat-up, the better."

Davenport said that he'd get them started. "What're you going to do?"

"I'm going to find a place where I can watch Ma's driveway, see if anybody's coming or going," Virgil said. "Tell those guys to call me as soon as they get close. If Ma sees me, she'll know I know."

VIRGIL STOPPED back at his house, got an olive drab REI bivy bag, a couple of pillows, and two Dos Equis, threw them in the truck, and drove north out of Mankato. On the way out, Jenkins called, and Virgil had him pull up a map on his iPad, and spotted Ma's house for him. Jenkins said they'd be there sooner or later, depending on traffic.

MA LIVED on what had been a run-down farm. She'd been re-building it since her second husband died in the epicurean tragedy at Wendy's, and it had come a long way back—too small to be really successful as a farm, but with some of the better land leased out, and extensive subsistence gardens, some chickens and an annual calf, they did okay. Virgil looked at a satellite view before he went out: the place appeared to cover a half section, a near-perfect rectangle a mile long and a half-mile deep.

Two of the back forty-acre chunks were wooded, with the beginning of Ayer's Creek running through them. Five of the remaining forties were covered with corn and soybeans, and the last forty included space for the house, barn, garage, machine sheds, a chicken house and pen, maybe ten acres of pasture. The satellite shot showed what appeared to be a corral with a trodden dirt circle inside, as though Ma might be training horses.

Virgil could see almost none of that on the ground, as he arrived in the faint predawn light. He checked the mailbox, and in his headlights saw "Nobles" painted on the side of it. A single mercury-vapor yard light hung from a pole at the end of the drive, and he could see the red pickup parked under the light. He went on by, to the first turnaround, then back past the house. He could see no lights, other than the yard light.

He continued up the road for a half-mile, to the remnants of a woodlot, turned in, found a spot where the local children probably came to screw, and parked. He walked back out to the road and then a half-mile down it, crossed the ditch into a soybean field, spread out the bivy bag, zipped himself inside, propped his head on the pillows, cracked one of the Dos Equis, and began the surveillance.

Nothing happened, and eventually, as the sun came up, he dozed.

A couple of trucks went by between six and seven, and then Jenkins called: "Where you at?"

"I'm laying in a bean field. Excuse me. I meant, I'm lying in a bean field."

"We're on the job. We've got her pickup and her plates and her picture, so we're good."

"She'll be looking for you."

"Like I said—we're good. You can go on home."

"Call me if she moves," Virgil said. He gathered up his gear, put the empty beer bottles in his pockets, went home and went back to sleep. When his phone went off, he jerked awake and looked at the clock: it was after ten, and he picked up the phone.

Yael-2: "What are we doing today?"

"There's been a problem," Virgil said.

He explained the problem to her, and she said, "To use your American idiom, our grave is in the water."

He had to think about that for a minute, came up with "dead in the water," and said, "Yeah, pretty much. Have you made any inquiries about our Mossad agent?"

"Yes, I called my embassy and they told me that they know nothing. This is not true."

"Is there anyone there who I can call?" Virgil asked.

"Mmm, I think this would cause trouble," Yael said.

"Probably, but so what?"

"Mmm. If you wish to explore this direction, I think you should make the exploration yourself. To determine who to call."

"I can do that," Virgil said. "If you want to go off to the Sam's Club, now would be a good time to do it. Just not much happening."

"Okay. But be cautious in your phone call," she said.

"What could they do to me?"

"To be honest, I worry not so much about you," she said, and hung up.

So VIRGIL looked up the embassy on the Internet, found that it had a "police and security" division, called it, identified himself, and wound up talking to a colonel, an "aluf mishne," who was described by an underling as second in command.

"Good enough," Virgil told the underling.

A moment later, a man said, "This is Colonel Ohad Shachar speaking. And who are you again?"

"I'm Virgil Flowers, I'm an agent with the Minnesota Bureau of Criminal Apprehension. I've been assigned to help an Israeli investigator from your antiquities authority recover an artifact stolen from a dig there a couple of weeks ago."

"I have heard of this," Shachar said.

"Yes. Well, the problem is, while the real investigator was delayed by Dutch police in Amsterdam by what now seems to be a phony or spurious charge against her, another woman, who several people have suggested to me is a member of the Mossad, impersonated her in an effort to recover the stone."

"This sounds very unlikely and unreasonable," Shachar said.

"I think so, too. Now, the problem is, this person apparently tried to assassinate the holder of the stone, to recover it—this happened yesterday."

"This sounds increasingly unlikely. The state of Israel does not conduct any such operations in the United States—"

"I'm sure you don't, so you probably can't help me much. But I thought I would call, and you could perhaps talk to your Mossad contact in the embassy. If there's any small sliver of a possibility that the Mossad knows who this woman really is, and if they can reach her, they should tell her to surrender herself to law enforcement authorities. They should warn her that she is being sought for attempted murder, attempted robbery, aggravated assault, conspiracy to receive stolen goods, illegal entry into the United States, and reckless discharge of a firearm, as well as other state and federal felonies carrying a minimum prison sentence of one hundred and sixty-five years. Also, because of the assassination attempt yesterday, all police officials have been warned to treat her as armed and exceptionally dangerous. If I see her, I will deal with her with an M16."

"This sounds very . . . bleak," Shachar said.

"An excellent choice of words, Colonel."

After some more back-and-forth bullshit, in which the colonel assured Virgil that no Israeli government employee would ever knowingly violate American laws and friendship, and Virgil assured him that he believed that, Virgil rang off and went to make breakfast.

SHRAKE CALLED while he was eating: Ma was in her pickup, driving toward town. Ten minutes later, Jenkins reported that she was at a Hardware Hank. Virgil took more calls as Ma headed west, and wound up at what Virgil recognized as Jones's country place, where she met two young men. They walked around looking at the buildings, prying random boards off and examining them. Then Ellen showed up, and when Virgil checked, he found her back on his tracker tablet.

"That's probably a couple of Ma's kids," Virgil told Jenkins. "They're gonna tear those places down for the lumber."

He told them to keep watching, and Jenkins said they'd have to keep the watch very loose, because there was no place to hide.

"I have full confidence in your professionalism," Virgil said. He went to get cleaned up.

SOMEWHERE, HE THOUGHT as he smoothed the shaving cream on, Jones was hiding out. He had help, from someone. From Ma? From Ellen? He probably couldn't walk very far. Was it possible that somebody had checked him into a motel?

This was the worst kind of police work, aimlessly looking for somebody who didn't want to be found. Virgil had once spent two weeks looking for a hillbilly that everyone said was so insular, so repressed, that he was probably hiding in a culvert under a road. He was picked up six months later by Los Angeles cops, who busted him for trying to shoplift Maui Jim sunglasses from a Rodeo Drive accessories store.

His telephone went off. He picked it up and looked at the screen: Awad. He put him on the speaker. "Yo. How they hangin', big guy?"

"The Hezbollah gentleman is here—he arrived unexpectedly an hour ago. He has one suitcase, and it is not so good. It is this ultra-suede. I think he has no money."

"Is he staying with you? Or in a motel?"

"With me, unfortunately. I sleep on the couch. He is locked in the bathroom even now, in the shower."

"It's very important for everybody's future to tell me if he has an appointment," Virgil said. "You understand?"

"Clearly," Awad said. "Would you like his car and license plate number?"

"That would be nice," Virgil said. "You're an excellent spy."

A BREAK? MAYBE.

The Turks had met Jones, had seen the stone, but hadn't coughed up any cash. Maybe they didn't have any. Maybe this guy wouldn't have any, either, and the whole scam would fall apart.

He continued shaving, and a moment later the phone rang again. It was Scott, the Mankato investigator who'd been at the park and at the hospital. Virgil put him on the speakerphone. "Yeah? You get him back?"

"No, but you know those Turks?"

"Yeah. How they doing?"

"I imagine they still hurt a little—some of that shot got in pretty deep, and had to be dug out. Anyway, they called me and said they wanted to talk to you, since you're the state big shot."

"Don't be bitter," Virgil said. "You know what they want?"

"No, but they're waiting at the motel. I said you'd rush right over."

"Well, you're right. I will."

Virgil finished shaving, picked out a fine old Wilco shirt, pulled it on, with his jeans, boots, and tan linen sport coat, and headed out the door. Hot. Sun. Went back inside for the straw cowboy hat, got in the truck, put on his aviators, and felt complete. On the way downtown, he stopped at Jones's house, used his key to open it, took a fast lap around the place, found it empty, checked the garage to make sure the Xterra was still there—it was—and continued on his way to the Holiday Inn.

WHAT THE TURKS had to say was interesting, in its own, non-problem-solving way. Virgil knocked on the motel room door, and the small Turk answered, looked back into the room and said, "Here is the Virgil."

"Send him in."

Virgil stepped in, and found the big Turk buttoning his shirt. Their suitcases sat on the two beds. They were open, but fully packed. "You are this fucking Flowers," he said. "We hear this from Officer Scott. But this is a friendly saying, correct?"

"I hope so," Virgil said. "You asked to see me?"

"This is also correct," the big Turk said. "We are announcing that we going home. To Istanbul. We do not buy the stone, we do not talk to Jones. Our plane is at four o'clock, so we must hurry."

"I think this is a wise decision, although I'm not one hundred percent sure that I believe you," Virgil said. "Speaking only in a friendly way."

"I shall announce to you why we are going," the big Turk said.

"I'm listening," Virgil said.

"We are going . . . because my . . . mmm . . . principal . . . also has dealing in Israel and other places where the Israelis have some authority, and he has received a telephone call from the Mossad asking him to withdraw. He is pleased to do this."

"Really? You mean, because if he doesn't, the Mossad will kill him?"

The small Turk wagged a finger at him: "People in the U.S.A. speak too much of killing. This is not true in our country."

The big Turk, the one who supposedly cut the testicles off recalcitrant Kurds, said, "Of course, the Mossad doesn't say this. And they don't do this, anyway. Well, maybe they do it, but not to Turks. But, for a man who does business in Israel, business could become difficult. So, he telephones us, and tells us, we are done. So we go."

Virgil: "The arrival of the Hezbollah has nothing to do with it?"

"Mmm. We did not know that the Hezbollah has arrived. This information would also be of interest to our . . . mmm . . .

principal. Perhaps he can make friendly with the Mossad, telling them this."

"All right. That's good," Virgil said. "Is it okay if we keep you under surveillance until you go through airport security?"

"Of course," the big Turk said. "It will be an honor."

"Try to stay away from those Kurds, too. You know, when you get back," Virgil said.

OUTSIDE, VIRGIL CALLED the Mankato chief and asked if he could shake a patrol car loose for the afternoon. "Maybe. What do you need?"

"You know those Turks that got shot?"

"Yeah. Everybody knows, Virgil," the chief said. "Everybody in the state. Everybody in Iowa, too. Everybody—"

"Okay, okay. The Turks are supposedly leaving for the airport up in Minneapolis. I'd like one of your patrol cars to follow them. Not subtly."

"A little encouragement . . . I think we can do that. We always welcome foreign investors, of course, but perhaps these gentlemen should be on their way."

"Have to be quick," Virgil said. "They're already packed up."

"We'll have somebody there in two minutes."

VIRGIL WALKED across the street for a piece of breakfast pie and a Coke, sat in the window and watched the Turks pack the Mercedes. The patrol car pulled into the parking lot, and the cop on the passenger side got out and said something to the Turks. The big man said something back, and flashed a smile. A moment later, the Turks pulled out, with the cop car fifteen feet behind.

When they were gone, Virgil called the Homeland Security chief at the airport, told him about the situation, and asked that the Turks' bag be checked carefully, and that somebody watch them get on the airplane.

That would be done.

Virgil was happy to see them go; and the fact was, from their attitude after the shooting, he suspected that he might like Turks in general, if not these Turks specifically.

But then, he liked most people.

13

Three bidders, Jones's note had said. Hezbollah, the Turks . . .

Maybe Sewickey would know, Virgil thought. Might as well check in, anyway, since he was right there. He walked back across the street to the Holiday, up the stairs to Sewickey's room, and found a note on the door: "TV Personnel: We have gone to Custard's Last Stand."

Custard's was a diner and party room, six blocks away.

When Virgil arrived at the diner, he almost kept going: three white TV vans were parked outside. Sewickey, he thought, was having another press conference. He thought that for almost four seconds, at which point Sewickey exploded through the front door, one hand wrapped in the jungle shirt of a man who was punching him in the head.

A half-dozen reporters followed them out, plus two cameramen, rolling. Virgil said to the truck, "Ah, Christ Almighty, now what?"

He stuck the truck into a fire hydrant space, threw it into park, pulled the keys, and jumped out. The cameramen were following the fight, which now had gone to the pavement. Virgil broke through the screen of cameramen, grabbed Sewickey, who was on top, by the shirt, and threw him across the sidewalk. The man who'd been beneath him said, "Thanks," and dragged the back of his hand across his mouth, smearing some blood across his attractively dimpled chin.

Sewickey, showing a trickle of blood from one nostril, was rolling to his feet and Virgil said, "Do not start again, or I'll kick your ass and then I'll arrest you."

One of the reporters shouted, "Who are you?" and another one answered, "Virgil Flowers, he's with the BCA."

Virgil looked at the fighters, then the reporters and cameramen, and said to Sewickey and the other man, "You two, get in the truck." He pointed at the man with the bloody lip and said, "Passenger seat," and to Sewickey, "Backseat. Now!"

The man with the bloody lip grinned at the reporters and said, "I guess we'll talk later." He picked out a female reporter, wiggled his eyebrows at her, and said, "Sheila."

He was, Virgil realized, disturbingly good-looking, with curly dark hair, somewhat oversized brown eyes, square shoulders, and a three-day beard. He was wearing an olive drab jungle shirt with pockets on the sleeves. The sleeves were rolled up over the elbow, with a buttoned flap holding the rolls up high, showing just a hint of muscle. A loop of Tibetan beads, turquoise alternating with lapis lazuli, decorated one wrist, but in a purely masculine way. The shirt was tucked into khaki cargo shorts, over waffle stomper boots with the socks rolled down.

He was maybe thirty, Virgil thought.

He was going to say something more to Sheila, the reporter,

until Virgil repeated, "Now!" Sewickey headed toward the truck, and the good-looking guy nodded apologetically toward Sheila and went to the truck.

IN THE TRUCK, Virgil turned in the driver's seat and said, "All right, what was that about?"

Sewickey said, "This cocksucker—"

"Whoa! Shut up," Virgil said. To the other man: "Who are you?"

"He's a charlatan," Sewickey said.

"SHUT UP!"

Sewickey shut up and the other man dug a business card out of one of his shirtsleeve pockets and said, "I'm Tag Bauer. You may have heard of me."

Virgil looked at the card, but only one faint bell rang. "You mean . . . like the watch?"

In the backseat, Sewickey laughed. "Yeah, like the watch. Another useless fashion statement."

"SHUT UP!"

"That's Tag Heuer," Bauer said. "My last name is Bauer."

The card said, "Field Archaeologist—Host of *The Bauer Crusade* on PBS."

"You've got a TV show?" Virgil asked.

"That's why he's wearing makeup," Sewickey said. "Unless he's gone transvestite on us."

Virgil: "If you don't shut up, I'll cuff you to the truck bumper. I'm serious, man. Shut the fuck up."

Sewickey shrugged and looked out the window at the TV corps. Bauer said, "You may have seen my name in the *New York Times*, and just not remembered. I'm the person who found the Siddhartha's begging bowl in an obscure Tibetan monastery, smuggled it past the Chinese guards and across the Himalaya, and returned it to the Dalai Lama in Dharamsala."

"I may have seen a book," Virgil said, tentatively. He hadn't, but there was bound to be one.

"Yes, *Bowl of Clay, Ark of the World*," Bauer said.

"Available on Amazon?"

"Yes, both in paper and in Kindle form. Also, through Barnes and Noble, for the Nook."

"This Sidhay dude . . ."

"Siddhartha," Bauer said. "The Buddha."

Virgil's eyebrows went up. "Like, the *Buddha* buddha?"

"That's right. . . . Look, maybe I should explain."

"Uh-oh," Sewickey said from the backseat. "Watch his lips. If they move . . ."

Virgil looked at him, and Sewickey held up his hands and nodded again. To Bauer, Virgil said, "Yes. Explain."

"I roam the world in search of ancient mysteries and artifacts of power," Bauer said. Sewickey made a farting noise in the backseat, but Bauer continued. "Through my work, my writing, and my connection with PBS—"

"And your inheritance from Daddy," Sewickey interjected.

". . . I am fortunate enough to be able to rescue various artifacts that have been lost or hidden, and return them to their rightful and historic owners."

"When you say, 'fortunate enough,' you mean . . . buy them?" Virgil asked.

"Sometimes these artifacts have been in the hands of the 'new owners,' if I may call them that, for centuries," Bauer said. He moved his hands as he spoke, in the practiced arcs of the TV presenter. "They naturally feel they have a proprietary interest in them, and if they are valuable, want recompense for their delivery. For example, when I located the gopher wood planks from Noah's Ark, in Tsaghkaber, Armenia, I was required to make funding available to the current Armenian owners so that the planks might be brought to the United States."

"Gopher wood," Sewickey said, laughing again. "They really saw you coming that time." To Virgil, he said, "You know where he took delivery of the gopher wood? At a gas station in Glendale, California. I'm surprised he didn't wind up as an extra on *Keeping Up with the Kardashians*."

For the first time, Bauer seemed disturbed. "Where did you hear that? I did not. That's a slander, and believe me, I have the legal means . . . I took delivery of them on the shores of the Black Sea, and brought them to America on, first, a lugger out of Vakfikebir, and then on my own boat, *The Drifter*, out of 'Stanbul."

Virgil asked Bauer, "Have you made a bid on the Solomon stone?"

Bauer said, "Maybe."

"Don't lie," Virgil said.

"Well . . . yes. I spoke to Reverend Jones three days ago, and rushed here, on my private plane, *The Wanderer*."

"Out of Hoboken," Sewickey said. "Just like I came here in my Cadillac, *The Holstein*, out of Austin."

"I keep *The Wanderer* at Kennedy International," Bauer said. "I may have to be somewhere at a minute's notice."

Virgil thought, *Okay. The third bidder.* He said, "Listen, you guys. That stone is stolen property. Three people have been shot over it so far, and it's only been by a ridiculous streak of good luck that we've avoided any deaths. Now. If you go after the stone, and get it, I will arrest you for receiving stolen property. If anyone is killed in the pursuit of it, and if you are one of the pursuers, I will see you charged with felony murder—that's a death in the course of a commission of a crime. You do not have to pull the trigger. All you have to do is commit a felony that's relevant to the death. That's thirty years without parole, in Minnesota. I also want you to know that the Mossad is after it, and their agent here has bragged to me about how good a shot she is."

"The Mossad," Bauer said. His eyes flicked back to Sewickey. "I first encountered them in Aswan."

Sewickey said, "A rough bunch. They've already attacked me here—I might be dead if it weren't for Virgil and some Zen-based self-disciplinary techniques, to keep from choking to death. Reminded me of the time I ran headfirst into Yaniv 'Che' Offer in Jaguaruno, Brazil, in my *Search for Hitler's Heart*."

"I refueled *The Drifter* there, two years ago," Bauer replied. "I didn't know you were familiar with the place. Or that Che was hanging out there."

"Hey, hey. Listen, guys, let's try to focus," Virgil said. "Yaniv 'Che' Offer is gonna look good to you if you keep fuckin' around, chasing this stone. I keep telling people this, but they don't seem to believe me. I will put your ass in prison. Understand? *Prison.* Look up 'Stillwater' in the dictionary, and you'll find a picture of your ass."

"I got that," Bauer said.

Sewickey nodded, looked out the window. "You'll have to excuse us, Virgil. The reporters weren't finished yet."

"No more fighting," Virgil said. "I'll—"

"We know," Bauer said. "You'll put our asses in prison."

"That's right," Virgil said.

ONE O'CLOCK, and Jenkins called. "Ma's gone back home."

"Goddamnit, I'm going over there," Virgil said. "But I've got somebody else for you to watch. Gotta be careful. This guy is a terrorist, or something. Hezbollah. He's driving around in a red Kia rental car." He gave Jenkins the tag number, and told him where they could pick him up at Awad's apartment. "Watch for a meeting with Jones. I don't care much about this Hezbollah guy, I just want Jones. And the stone."

"How much money are we talking?"

"Maybe a couple million. Maybe five."

"I could use some of that," Jenkins said. "I could put in a new kitchen."

ON THE WAY over to Ma Nobles's, Davenport called. "I saw you on TV one minute ago. A brawl outside some diner."

"Yeah, it's a couple of these stone hunters. They were fighting each other, I was breaking it up. You got a problem with that?"

"Hell no, I was happy to see that you were actually working, and weren't towing your boat," Davenport said. "Keep it up. And keep in touch."

"I will."

"You're not hurt?"

"I'm good."

AT MA NOBLES'S PLACE, Virgil turned in the drive and nearly ran over a towheaded kid, maybe eight, dressed in a Cub Scout shirt and neckerchief, headed out on his rattletrap bicycle. He stopped, rolled down the car window, and said, "Sorry."

"Scared me," the kid said.

"Are you Sam?"

"Who's askin'?"

"I'm a cop, I need to talk to your mom."

"Sam I am," Sam said. "Ma walked down to the crick for a swim. There's a path out past the barn."

"You going to a den meeting?"

"Yup. Up to the Wilsons'."

"Take care," Virgil said.

The kid nodded and took off. Virgil drove down the drive, parked, then walked back out to the end of it, peeked around the edge of the cornfield that came almost to the driveway, and saw the kid pedaling away.

Virgil walked back to the house, pounded on the door, got no response. Thought about going in for a quick look around, decided it was too risky. He walked out to the barn, and past it—a red chicken was pecking gravel around the barn door, and stopped to look at him cockeyed—and saw the trail headed off toward the hill behind the house. What the hell.

The walk took ten minutes, past a sweet corn patch, already showing a little browning silk, and through a pasture dotted with dried cow pies, back to a line of cottonwoods that marked the path of the creek across Ma's property. He followed the path to the edge of the water, which was not more than ten feet wide, and probably not more than knee-deep at the deepest point. Not a promising swimming spot. The path went north, toward the hill, and two minutes later, he found an old, partly broken-down dam, and Ma splashing around in a pretty little swimming hole behind it.

Her back was toward him, the water up to her neck, when he came up and called, "How you doing, Ma?"

She whirled in the water, saw him, and said, "Well, goddamnit, Virgil, why didn't you call me and tell me you were coming out? You scared the heck out of me."

"Excuse me. I just needed to talk to you about where you stashed old Jones."

"I'm sure I don't know what you're talking about," she said.

"Of course you do. Last night you went up to the hospital, dressed in a dirndl, with your hair up, and gave him some bolt cutters," Virgil said. "We got a witness. Probably picked him up after he cut himself loose . . . but that's water under the bridge. What I need to know is, where did you stash him?"

"I did not do any of that," Ma said. "I promise you. Cross my heart." She paddled a few feet closer, into shallower water, then stood up and said, "I cross my heart," again, and made the cross. Virgil tried not to goggle, because he was a trained professional. She said, "Why don't you come in here, and we can talk? It's too damn hot to be sitting up on some creek bank in the sun."

"I'm in the shade."

"Oh, so what?"

Virgil thought about it for a second, then said, "The last time I went skinny-dipping with a woman, somebody tried to shoot me."

"Virgil . . ."

"That water's probably so polluted with fertilizer and other crap that you'll grow another breast . . . not that you need one."

"That's pure water that you could drink," she said. "It comes out of a spring at the bottom of that hill, and there's not a drop of fertilizer that goes into it before it gets here. And—it's really cool. It's perfect."

She dropped onto her back and did a scissors kick into deeper water.

"Oh, all right," he said, taking off his hat.

So Virgil jumped in the water, which must have been thirty degrees cooler than the air temperature. The change nearly stopped his heart, and caused his testicles to retract up as far as his liver, but after a couple of minutes, felt delicious.

"I don't know why you think I'm a criminal," Ma said, as she floated around the pool on her back, doing a little finger paddle to keep herself moving. The water glistened on her breasts and belly, and it was better, Virgil thought, than seeing a fifty-seven-inch musky in the water. Or, at least, really, really close to that.

"I'll tell you, Ma, I don't see you so much as a criminal, as a woman trying to make her way in the world, without as many tools as other women might have."

"I've got a couple tools," she said. "I studied agronomy at South Central."

"Really? I didn't know that. I studied ecological science at the U up in St. Paul."

"Really."

So they floated around and talked about life, about the summer and the heat, and about the possibility that lumber was aging at the bottom of the Minnesota River, and about the likely location of Jones and the stele. Virgil told her about the fight at Custard's.

"Tag Bauer? Really? I mean, you know him now?"

"Well, I talked to him," Virgil said. "You know who he is?"

"Sure, he has a show on Channel Two. *The Bauer Crusade*. He's always looking for artifacts. He sails someplace on his yacht, *The Drifter*, or he flies someplace in the airplane . . ."

"*The Wanderer . . .*"

"Yeah. And he goes on expeditions in Jeeps, and he takes his shirt off when he swims these rivers, or when he's sailing."

Virgil could see that in his mind's eye. "Not when he's flying?"

"Not so much when he's flying," Ma said. "He's got this spider tattoo on his shoulder blade, given to him by a tribe in New

Guinea, and now he's a member of the tribe and is pledged to fight with them. Anyway, I'd like to meet him, you know . . ."

"Because of your interest in archaeology?"

Ma floated up to Virgil and wrapped both her legs around one of his and said, "C'mon, Virgie, I need this something fierce."

Virgil said, "Ma, if a guy takes it out and waves it at you, you get pregnant. I don't need any redneck kids running around my house, and even if I was inclined to scratch your itch, which is, I confess, not an entirely unattractive proposition—"

"I can tell," she murmured. "Judging from the evidence at hand."

". . . I don't happen to have any protection with me, and I'm not going to take the chance that you're on the pill—"

"They're not good for you, the pills," she said. "They cause hormonal imbalances."

". . . so, I'm going to have to pass. And, by the way, I suspect you already have hormonal imbalances."

"Well then, the heck with you," she said, letting go of the evidence. "Maybe I'll introduce myself to Tag."

"Why? Because you know where the stone is?"

"Of course not."

So, THEY GOT DRESSED and walked back to the farm, companionably enough, getting there just as Sam arrived back on his bike. He eyed them for a moment, both of them with wet hair, then said to Virgil, "I guess you found her."

Virgil said, "Yup. How was the den meeting?"

"Same old shit," Sam said. "You arrest her?"

"Not yet," Virgil said. "But you should talk to her, and tell her to stop messing with the law. And you shouldn't say 'shit.'"

"Okay," the kid said.

"That's really not fair," Ma said. "Bringing in the children."

"Ma, what the hell do you think is going to happen to the kids if you wind up in the joint for eight to ten?" Virgil asked. "You think that's going to be good for them? Sam'll be in college before you get out."

For the first time she looked a little shaken. "I gotta think," she said. She took her son's hand. "Come on, Sam. We gotta go think."

BEFORE VIRGIL LEFT MA'S, he checked the tracking tablet. Ellen was still showing at the farm, and he wondered if that might be where the sun came through. He turned that way.

As he drove, he called Shrake, who was watching the Hezbollah guy. "Nothing happening. They went out to a McDonald's, and then back to the Awad guy's apartment. I'm watching the back and both cars, and Jenkins is out front. It's really, really boring."

At Jones's old farm, Ellen's Jeep was parked halfway up the drive. Virgil pulled in, found the house and sheds unoccupied; one exterior wall of the house had had several boards removed. He walked past the last shed and saw Ellen on her hands and knees at the back fence line. He walked that way; she saw him coming and stood and waved. When he came up she asked, "Want some rhubarb?"

"Jeez, I wouldn't know what to do with it," he said. She had a pasta pot, which she'd half-filled with cut rhubarb stalks. "I don't cook much."

"If I'm down in the next couple of days, I'll bring you a pie," she said.

"I do eat rhubarb pie," Virgil said. "You're just getting a last harvest?"

"I'm thinking about trying to move the whole bed, and some of the asparagus," she said. "I'm going to have to talk to somebody about the best way to do it. And there're some old yellow farm iris I'd like to move. There're some roses and lilacs I'm afraid will have to stay. They're just gonna get plowed under, but they're so senile that they're not worth moving. Ma says she'll take down the apple trees—people like the wood to burn in their fireplaces."

"Sad," Virgil said. "It's happened all over, though, old farms going under."

She wiped a sleeve across her forehead and asked, "How come you look so cool?"

"I haven't been cutting rhubarb in the sunshine," he said. "Listen, I need to talk to you. Seriously. Let's find some shade."

"I know about Dad, but I don't know where he is," she said. "I couldn't believe it when the Mankato police called me."

They wound up sitting on the porch steps. Several planks had been removed from the porch floor, and Virgil said, "I hope you're getting some money from Ma."

"We will get some," she said. "I checked on the Internet, and we're getting an okay price from her. Better than burning it, any-way. I like her. She's an interesting woman."

Virgil said, "Whatever. The crime-scene crew went over the cabin where your father was shot. When the shooting was still going on, but apparently after he was shot, he began writing a note. When we got there, and he realized he wasn't going to die, he wadded it all up and threw it in a corner, behind some fire-wood, and hoped we wouldn't find it. The note was to you."

"To me? What did it say?"

"I'll tell you in a minute. First, I'd like to ask you to stop all of this. You *can* stop it. I think he calls you, I think you talk to him, I think you know what's going on here," Virgil said. "I need to know that. What in the heck is he doing? He's a lifelong minister, never broke a law in his life, and now people may die because of what he's doing? Ellen: tell me."

She turned away from him, staring off across the summer fields. Then, "I don't know the details. I had no idea about this stone. But it has to do with Mom. I think he's trying to get enough money together to make sure she'll have a place in an extended care facility, when he's gone. She's sixty-five. She has early-onset Alzheimer's, but other than that, she's healthy enough. She could live for years yet."

The extended care facility, she said, cost seven thousand dollars a month. She couldn't afford that, nor could her brother, even if they pooled their resources. "Dad tried keeping her at home, with a babysitter, but she needed professional watching. The thing is, she's healthy, and strong, but something happens, and she panics and tries to fight her way out of the house, or she sneaks out, and then . . . she's lost. When Dad got sick and had to go to the hospital, I tried to keep her at my place. It was impossible. I would have needed professional nurses sixteen hours a day, and there was just no way to pay for that. I couldn't stay home myself—somebody had to work."

"I'm sorry," Virgil said, and meant it.

"Dad's frantic about it. He knows he's going to die. There'll be some Social Security survivor's benefits for Mom, and we'll sell his house and put that in a fund, but it's not nearly enough. She'll wind up in a warehouse, minimal care, minimal conditions, unless we can come up with a solution. That's what this auction is—a solution. I don't know how he can set up the payments, but he's a smart man, and apparently thought of something."

"But . . ." Virgil took off his hat and smoothed his hair back. "But it came down to finding this stone? That's the solution? That's less likely than winning the lottery."

"I don't think he *had* a solution," she said. "He went to Israel to say good-bye to friends. He just saw his chance and took it."

"A miserable situation," Virgil said. He made a sneaky mental note to check on Jones's wife's location. Jones was probably looking in on her, he thought; but he couldn't ask Ellen where her mother was, because she might warn Jones away.

"Anyway," she said after a moment, "what did Dad put in that note?"

"He said he loved you kids, and the worst pain was thinking that he wouldn't see you again. He said he'd hidden the stone. Obviously, he hid it where you could find it. He was depending on you to sell it, apparently."

"Where did he put it?" she asked.

"You'll know where it is, and you have to tell me," Virgil said. "Ellen—three people have been shot. It's not reasonable to let people die, to make things better for a woman who won't even know that they're better."

She thought about that and said, "If I know where it is, I'll tell you."

Virgil took the chance. "He said it's where the sun comes through."

"Yeah." She stood up and dusted off the seat of her shorts, and said, "It's at the house. His house."

"We've looked through there pretty thoroughly," Virgil said. "I was there today, looking around."

"It's not inside, it's outside," she said. "The house next door to his has a big tree in the backyard, next to the garage. On exactly the day of the summer solstice, and only on that day, you can see the sun come up in the crack of space between the tree and the garage. He used to say it was like one of those ancient observatories. It'd put this shaft of light across our yard, and it'd hit this clump of hollyhocks on the fence on the west side of the yard. He'd get up at dawn on the first day of summer just to see it, and he'd make Mom and me and Danny get up, too."

"All right," Virgil said. "Let's go look."

"Might not be there," she said. "He might've figured you'd find that note, and that's why he ran away last night. He might've gone over to get it."

"Let's look anyway," Virgil said. "Then we'll know."

14

Virgil followed Ellen back into town, the sun sinking in his rearview mirror as they headed southeast through the bugs along the river, and the late-day heat waves coming off the tarmac. The evening would be spectacular, he thought, the air soft and cooling after the hot day, the moon coming up big and yellow; a good night for sitting on the back patio of a bar, talking with friends, the jukebox playing low, Guy Clark's "Rita Ballou," two-stepping with Georgina . . . or Ma.

The sun was down by the time they got to Jones's house. Virgil got a flashlight and Ellen led the way into the backyard, and pointed at the tree and the edge of the neighbor's garage, and by stepping back and forth and cocking their heads, they figured out where the shaft of sunlight would fall along the west fence.

The search took a few minutes: Jones had scraped fallen leaves and grass back over the hole he'd dug, and it was hard to see in the heavy shadows cast by the flashlight. Virgil eventually encountered a spot with an unnatural texture, and pushed into the earth

with an index finger. After a half-inch of soft, loose soil, his finger
hit stone.

He was shoulder to shoulder with Ellen—she smelled of
woman work-sweat with a touch of something, maybe Obses-
sion—both of them on their knees, and he said, "Here's something."

He scraped the dirt away, then more dirt, found the stone
was dark, at least, in the light of the flash, and heavy. They both
worked at it, clawing up the soil. Three or four minutes after
Virgil located it, the stone came loose, and he lifted it out onto
the lawn.

"Oh my God," Ellen said. "It really is . . ."

"That's it," Virgil said, shining the flash on the side of it. He
could feel the carvings, but not see them through the dirt.

"What should we do with it?"

"Take it back to my place, where we've got some good light,"
Virgil suggested.

VIRGIL CALLED SHRAKE and told him to get Jenkins and go home.
"I've got the stone. I don't care what the Hezbollah guy does."

"Good. I've been here so long I've been thinking about starting
a family," Shrake said.

Virgil called Yael. "Did you go shopping?"

"For a short time only, to survey the possibilities," she said.
"Has there been any progress in finding Jones?"

"No, but I've got the stone," Virgil said.

"You have the stone? This is wonderful. May I see it?" she asked.

"Sure. I'll come by and get you."

Ellen said she wanted to take a shower, and so she'd wait at her father's house until Virgil got back from picking up Yael. "But I'd like to be there when you guys look at it."

"Fifteen minutes," Virgil said.

YAEL WAS WAITING on the curb outside the motel. Virgil popped the passenger-side door for her, said, "Don't step on the stone," which he'd placed on the floor. Yael climbed in, then bent and lifted the stone into her lap. "Wonderful," she said. "I will ask my department to issue you a commendation."

"All part of the job," Virgil said.

They went past Jones's house again, waited a couple of minutes for Ellen to finish dressing, and then did a caravan over to Virgil's house. Virgil lugged the stone inside and said, "If it stayed buried for three thousand years, and is still okay, I don't think rinsing it off would hurt."

"That would be fine," Yael said.

They put it in the kitchen sink and sprayed it with warm water, until the dirt was gone and the water came clean. Virgil dried it with a dish towel, carried it into his study, put it on the desk, and pulled a reading light over.

The Solomon stone was pretty much as advertised—not quite a cube, a little longer than it was thick. The top was broken off nearly square, but the bottom had a fist-sized hole in it, as if there'd been some kind of inclusion there that had remained with the stone that this chunk had been broken from.

Under the raking light, they could clearly see the hieroglyphs, a lighter gray on a dark gray, densely covering two sides of the four-sided stele. The glyphs were small, about the height of a dime. The other two sides were covered with alphabetic forms. "Some of these could almost be modern—but some of them I don't even know," Yael said. "It's Hebrew, though, and very, very old."

She gently touched the Hebrew lettering, as if for good luck, or as a prayer.

"Can you read any of it?" Ellen asked.

"No, not really. I can read some of the letters . . . but the words elude me. This will take a lot of study. I think this"—she touched a group of letters—"could be the name of Solomon."

"Pretty cool," Virgil said.

"More cool than you know," Yael said. "Solomon, in the legend, was the last great king of the United Israel and Judah. Despite that, there is no contemporary mention of him. We have never found a stele, a coin, an inscription, anything, by anyone who lived around his time, who mentions him. Until now. This is the only thing, sitting here in Mankato, in the state of Minnesota."

"Amazing," Virgil said. "I'll tell you what: I'll keep it here overnight, then move it up to St. Paul tomorrow. We'll let the big shots turn it over to you, all official and so on."

"This would be very fine," Yael said.

"I wonder where the first Yael is?" Ellen asked.

"This I am not curious about," Yael said. "I hope she stays where she is, not in my sight."

"I'd like to know," Virgil said. "Maybe she went home, like the Turks."

"If my father calls me again, I'm going to tell him that you've got the stone," Ellen said. "Once everybody knows where the stone is, and that nobody's going to make a profit from it, maybe they'll all go home. And Dad can go back to the Mayo."

Virgil said, "He's got a legal problem."

She nodded. "Of course. But his time is very short. We've been told that when the final decline sets in, he will progress from a lucid state to death in a matter of a few days. He's already begun to lose bladder and bowel control, and that's the end."

"Then maybe he should just stay out," Virgil said. "If everybody agrees that this is the stone, it's not a decoy or something . . . I won't look for him at your house. Or at the Mayo, for that matter."

"Thank you," she said. "My brother is coming next week, or sooner, if Dad goes. So . . . I appreciate that."

"I am very sorry for your family," Yael said. "It comes to everybody, but is nevertheless a sad thing."

THEY TALKED for another five minutes, about the stone, and about where Jones might be, and then Ellen left, to go back to the Twin Cities and home. Virgil put the stone in the dishwasher, hidden behind a couple of plates, locked all the doors, then took Yael back to the Holiday Inn.

"I'll come for you at eight o'clock," he told her.

"I will stand here," she said, pointing down at the curb.

Back home, Virgil took the stone out of the dishwasher, made several high-res photos with his Nikon, and e-mailed a couple to his father, with a brief explanation. Then called Davenport.

Davenport picked up and asked, "You got Jones?"

"No, but I've got the stone."

"Good. If you've got the stone, you don't need Jones," Davenport said. "If everybody's reading this right, he'll be dead in a few days, and I suspect he'll turn up then. What're you doing with the stone?"

"I thought I'd bring it up there tomorrow morning, stick it in an evidence locker, and then let you guys talk to the embassy and authorize its return. Probably with the second Yael. Anyway, that's all diplomatic, it's not for a humble flatfoot like myself."

"That sounds about right," Davenport said. "Good job, Virgil. I've been watching all that bullshit on TV, and it was giving me an ice-cream headache. See you tomorrow."

Virgil was in the process of rereading all the George Mac-Donald Fraser "Flashman" novels, and the spy novels of Alan Furst. He was halfway through Furst's *Red Gold*, and picked up the book from the living room couch and carried it back to the bedroom.

Long day. Fistfights, a naked woman, an ancient relic . . . a relic that could reshape the way people thought about a couple of world religions.

He read Furst for a couple hours, realized he wouldn't be able to finish it, and reluctantly put it aside. He spent a short time thinking about God and one of His creations, Ma Nobles. He was beginning to see her as a bit more than a redneck woman, although she played that role.

And maybe even was one. She certainly wasn't uninteresting, though he recognized that he certainly wasn't exactly a disinterested observer in making that judgment . . . given the evidence at hand that day.

Virgil had been married and divorced three times, and wasn't eager to get back on the marriage market. But what he'd told Ma that day, about having a redneck kid running around the house, wasn't exactly true. He'd like to have kids. Maybe one of each. And if he was going to do that, he had to get busy. Ma might be a little much, but . . .

Jesus, what are you thinking? he asked himself. *Get a goddamn dog.*

Then he went to sleep. But not for long.

THE BIG PROBLEM with Bart Kohl, in Tal Zahavi's estimation, wasn't that he was a coward, it was that he was a whiner. She could handle the cowardice with blackmail; but the guy was a nudnik, pestering her with complaints and warnings, visualizing disaster at every turn, and worse, with all his visions of tragedy, his voice was like a band saw, high-pitched and nasal. Even worse than all of that . . . he was boring.

Like when Tal had called him and asked him to provide her with a pistol. "A *pistol*? Where am I supposed to get a *pistol*? I don't even know how to *do* that. When people asked me to help out, they said they'd just want me to *drive people around*. They never said anything about weapons. I'm against weapons. I signed the anti-handgun pledge."

So Tal, operating from Tel Aviv, had had to go online and find a gun show where he could buy a firearm. Even after he had the pistol, he bitched about having to drive it across state lines. "Now I'm committing a *federal* crime, delivering it across state lines without a permit."

Blahblahblah . . .

When she told him that they were going to grab Ellen Case, and use her to extort the stone out of her father, he'd nearly laid an egg.

"Kidnapping? Are you kidding me? No way. I'm out of this."

She had to remind him that he'd already committed a number of crimes, both state and federal, to get him to go along. "It's this way, Bart. Your name could be called to the police, and then what would you do? I will be back in Tel Aviv, but you will still be in Des Moines."

She'd had to plan the whole thing by herself, spotting and tagging Case, while Kohl sat next to her in the passenger seat of his van, twisting his hands and drilling into her head like a wood-pecker.

ZAHAVI HAD CASE'S ADDRESS, which turned out to be a small house on the south side of Minneapolis, near a creek or small river. When they spotted it, the house was dark. Zahavi told Kohl to pull into the driveway, and she walked up to the front door and knocked . . . and saw the lights of a security system.

Not too large a problem, she thought—especially if Case never got to it.

"Now, we have to be very careful," she told Kohl. "There may be cameras, there may be security patrols. We must keep moving."

Kohl said, "This is the end. The end of everything I've worked for. The end of all my dreams. My father said, 'You're an American, you're not an Israeli. Stop pretending.' Did I listen to him? Oh, no. I had to go to Israel. I had to sign up with the Interest Group. Interest Group? I thought I'd be giving lectures in Omaha, on Masada and Yad Vashem. Maybe I'd meet some nice young girls with small noses and low morals. But no—I have to go around and buy *guns*."

"Shut up, shut up, shut up . . ."

"And no, it's not just an Interest Group, it's a *Mossad* Interest Group. No young girls with small noses for you, Bart Kohl. No, it's some *meshugenah* bitch with a nine-millimeter."

Enough to drive her out of her goddamn mind, and she considered the possibility of standing him on the shoulder of a highway and unloading that 9mm into him.

Not really. She needed him.

They watched the house for six hours, almost until midnight. Zahavi was thinking of calling it off—the neighborhood was very quiet, but they'd seen a couple of police patrol cars, moving slowly, looking for trouble.

Then Case showed up; and they were right behind her.

"Pull over," Zahavi said. She got a gunnysack out of the back, purchased that afternoon at a Home Depot.

"Oh, Jesus," Kohl said, "I can't believe I'm doing this."

"And give me the tape."

"Please God, help me." But he handed her the role of duct tape, with the end pulled free and folded back on itself, to make a handy tab.

Case pulled up to the garage door, which was automatic. A light came on inside, and the door began to go up. Kohl pulled to the side of the road, at the front of the house, as they'd planned, and Zahavi got out in the dark, with the bag. Case pulled into the garage. Zahavi took another look around, and moved.

Case parked, and the garage door started down. Zahavi slipped into the garage with the bag, heard Case get out of the car, humming a little tune. Zahavi was at the Jeep's fender when Case, still humming, thumbed through her keys for the door—

Zahavi stepped up behind her and threw the bag over her head and dragged her to the floor, straddled her. Case was trying to scream, but instead made choking sounds, just as Zahavi had seen in a training film, and before she could actually scream, Zahavi hit her twice, in the head, with an open palm, stunning blows, and then Zahavi pulled the tape loose and began looping it around Case's head. Case began to fight, but it was too late, and too confusing, with the tape going on. Zahavi taped her up like a slow calf at the local rodeo, all the way down to her ankles.

The overhead light went out, and she started, listening, but couldn't hear anything but the muffled groans from Case.

She checked the tape, as best she could in the dark, then opened the garage's access door and waved Kohl into the driveway. He pulled in, and together they wrestled the struggling woman into the back of their van. She looked, Kohl thought, like a giant joint in a stoner film.

"You didn't have to hurt her?" Kohl asked, a pleading note in his voice.

"I might have had to slap her a couple of times," Zahavi said, with evident satisfaction.

"Another felony," Kohl said. He began to weep. "Oh, Jesus . . ."

"Pick another God," Zahavi said. "And slow down. Slow down. We do not hurry."

Case struggled and cried and begged, and was echoed by Kohl, but they made it out of town and south on I-35. They'd rented a hotel room, but it was two hours away, and they needed to drive circumspectly. A police stop would *really* have been the end. An hour south, they got off the interstate and turned east, cruising comfortably across the countryside in the dark. Case had gone quiet.

They arrived at the hotel, on the outskirts of the City of Rochester, after two o'clock. They had the two end units, and smuggled Case into the room at the far end.

"I'm going home," Kohl announced.

"Oh, no. No, no, no, no . . ."

"Please don't hurt me," Case begged, from inside the bag.

"No going home now," Zahavi said to Kohl. "Too late for that."

She sounded pleased with herself.

————

VIRGIL WAS ASLEEP before midnight. With the unconscious sleep-time clock that ran in the back of his head, he knew he'd been down for quite a while when he started dreaming that he was feeding automobile scrap into a hammer mill, and that garbage cans were falling down a stairway, that a Caribbean steel drum band was playing in his backyard. . . .

Then his eyes cracked open and he heard all of that, plus somebody screaming, "Virgil! Virgil! Get up, Virgil."

Virgil rolled out of bed, grabbed his jeans, started pulling them on as he stumbled to the front door. Somebody was pounding on the aluminum screen door, and they were panic-stricken. He got to the door, flicked on the porch light, and saw the bald head of his across-the-street neighbor, Robbie. He pulled his jeans up the last two inches and popped the door.

Robbie shouted at him, "Your garage is on fire."

"What?" He didn't comprehend that for a split second, and Robbie screamed again and pointed to his left, and Virgil saw the flickering light in the side yard.

He thought, *The boat!*

Virgil turned and bolted back through the house, into the kitchen, yanked open the cabinet under the kitchen sink, pulled out his fire extinguisher, ran through the mudroom, out the back door—barefoot—and around to the side of the garage.

An oval of flame was licking up the clapboard siding, and Robbie came running around from the front and shouted, "I called the fire department, they're coming. Where's your hose?"

Virgil shouted back, "On the other side of the back steps, it's already connected," and Robbie ran toward the steps. Virgil pulled the pin on the fire extinguisher and squeezed the handle, and foam began blowing out into the flames.

He could knock down the flames for a few seconds, but when he moved on to another section, the fire returned to the first, but he continued hosing it down, making some progress, and kept thinking about the boat: the boat was inside, his pride and joy, a like-new Ranger Angler, with a couple of years yet to go on the financing.

Robbie came running back, and Virgil realized the other man was still in his pajamas, and he was dragging the hose and turned the nozzle and fired it into the flames. The fire extinguisher ran out of foam and Virgil grabbed the hose and moved in close and Robbie shouted, "Watch your feet," and, "Here's the fire department."

The firemen came at a run, pulling hose, and hammered the fire with a flood of foam that the fire couldn't compete with: in less than a minute, it was gone, but Virgil shouted, "We gotta look inside."

He got the garage door up, but there was no fire inside. He started to step inside and a fireman caught his arm, held him back. "Don't do that, there might have been some structural weakening."

Virgil walked back out, calmer now, and asked, "What the hell happened?"

"Did you have gasoline out here or something? I can smell gas," a fireman said.

"There was no gas out here," Virgil said. "There's a can in the garage . . . still there, right by the lawn mower."

"Hate to say it," said another fireman. "It looks like a Molotov cocktail. Like somebody threw one at the side of the garage." He pointed to the top of the oval. "It broke there. Splattered, ran down the wall."

"He's a cop," Robbie said.

The second fireman said, "That could explain—"

Virgil said, "Yeah but . . ." And the thought struck him. "Ah, shit," he said, and he turned and ran back into the house, to the study.

The stone was gone.

Virgil felt like screaming, but he didn't. The first thing he did was look around, to make sure he hadn't simply moved it, and had forgotten about it, but he hadn't, and he knew that when he looked. Then he went to the tracker pad: no sign of Ellen's car.

But it *had* to be Ellen, one way or the other. Nobody else, other than Davenport and Yael, knew that the stone was in his house. He tried to call her, but after five rings, her phone sent him to the answering service. He left a simple message: "Call me when you get this, and I may not go for a warrant for your arrest on charges of arson, burglary, grand theft, and aggravated assault."

He took no satisfaction from the message: he'd warned everyone, several times, that they were playing with fire, and virtually every one of them had ignored him.

BACK OUTSIDE, the firemen were cleaning up, and the man in charge told him that the damage had been minimal, and confined to the garage siding. There were no structural problems, and the boat was untouched. "Not to say that it wasn't serious. If your neighbor hadn't seen it go up, and you guys hadn't gotten out there, the roof would have caught and then it'd have been Katie-bar-the-door."

When the firemen and the rubbernecking neighbors had drifted away, and Virgil had thanked and re-thanked Robbie, the guy who'd seen the fire, called 911, and come to help—he'd send him a couple cases of Leinie's Summer Shandy at the first chance—he went back inside the house and kicked an unfortunate wastebasket. He was a knot of frustration, four o'clock in the morning and nobody he could really call, or anything he could effectively do.

But sleep was impossible. Eventually, figuring that if he was up, everybody else should be, too, he cleaned up, and at four-thirty in the morning, drove to the Holiday Inn and woke up Sewickey. Sewickey came to the door looking stunned, and Virgil sensed that it wasn't an act. "We're having a meeting at eight o'clock in in the back room at Custard's. Be there."

Sewickey, confused, looked around at the parking lot, and then up in the sky, and finally asked, "What the heck time is it?"

He got a similar reaction from Bauer, who was at the Downtown Inn. Yael, however, was awake and staring at the television, still jet-lagged.

"The stone is gone?"

"Meeting at eight o'clock," he said.

"But why would I take the stone? I *had* the stone."

"Eight o'clock," Virgil said.

The Turks were gone, but he drove to Awad's apartment and pounded on the door until Awad opened it. He was wearing what appeared to be black velvet pajamas and yet another stunned expression.

Virgil said, "Invite me in?"

Awad looked over his shoulder and said, in a loud voice, "Of course, you are the police."

Virgil stepped inside, and saw a sheet and blanket crumpled on the floor next to the couch. He nodded at the bedroom door and raised an eyebrow, and Awad nodded.

Virgil stepped over to the bedroom door and knocked: "This is the state police. Please come out. Now."

A voice from inside: "Why?"

"We're having a conversation about the Solomon stone, and you need to be in it."

The door opened and an elderly gray-bearded man edged out. He was wearing Jockey briefs that were way too long in the crotch, and a white V-necked T-shirt. "What have I done?"

"I don't know," Virgil said. "Now: the two of you. You've been under surveillance. I know you're trying to buy the stone. You should know that I had the stone until earlier this evening, when my garage was firebombed and the stone was stolen while I was fighting the fire. So. We are having a meeting at eight o'clock at Custard's Last Stand."

And so on.

With some sense of righteous revenge—everybody was now awake and either frightened or worried—he headed back toward his house, but then thought, *Ma*.

Ellen and Ma had some kind of friendly relationship. Was it possible that Ma had stolen the stone? He continued past his house and out into the countryside, to Ma's house, pulled into the driveway and pounded on the door until lights went on.

Ma came to the door, peeked past a curtain, then opened the door. She was holding a Remington autoloading shotgun. "Virgil?"

"At eight o'clock . . ."

BY THE TIME he'd finished the rounds, it was almost six. He called Ellen again, and again got switched to the answering service—but the phone was ringing a half-dozen times before he was switched, so it wasn't turned off. She was either not hearing the ring, or was ignoring it. He called her every half hour until he got to Custard's at five minutes after eight, and never got an answer. Was she on the run?

CUSTARD'S BACK ROOM was usually reserved for cardplayers, but they never started until ten, so it was clear at eight. The meeting got held up because Sewickey, who arrived early, had ordered pancakes and bacon, and then Awad showed up with his Hezbollah associate, whose name was Adabi al-Lubnani, who ordered pancakes but got French toast by mistake, but was impressed by the name, and so accepted it; and by the time Virgil got there, everybody was fussing over food, and who had the ketchup and was there more syrup, except Ma, who was hunched over Tag Bauer, big-eyed about his television show. And not only big-eyed, Virgil thought sourly, as he tracked Bauer's eyes down to her cleavage.

He called the meeting to order by rapping on a water glass, and said, "This is gonna be short. I know you all want this stone, but as I keep telling everybody, if you buy it, you'll be violating a large number of laws. Do all of you understand this? That you could go to prison? I'd like a show of hands by those who understand this."

They all raised their hands.

Virgil said, "Further. For those with the money—I'm looking at you, Bauer, and you, Mr. al-Lubnani—there are some extremely suspicious circumstances involving the discovery of the stone, and its removal from Israel. If you wanted to bet me, I'd take either side of a fifty-fifty bet that the stone is a fake. Do you really want to spend, what, hundreds of thousands or millions of dollars for something that turns out to be a fake? I don't think so."

They all nodded into their pancakes, and al-Lubnani muttered something to Awad, who also nodded.

Virgil said, "You all know now that somebody firebombed my garage last night and stole the stone. I am beyond being pissed off. So I'm telling you: this is now personal, and you do not want to get in the way. Go home. I'm telling you: Go home. Everybody who understands that, raise your hand."

They all raised their hands, and Sewickey yawned.

Virgil: "You're yawning, Sewickey. You think I'm joking?"

"No, I don't," Sewickey said. "I'll talk to you about it in private. About the yawn."

Virgil looked at him for a moment, then said, "Right." And to everybody else, "Go home. All of you. Go home."

Then he turned and headed for the door, tipping his head, and said, "Sewickey."

SEWICKEY FOLLOWED HIM OUT into the main dining room and Virgil said, "The yawn?"

Sewickey pointed at an empty booth, and they sat facing each other, and Sewickey interlaced his fingers on the tabletop and said, "Virgil, you're a likable guy, and I don't want to see you or anybody else get hurt, but you don't understand what's going on here."

"What don't I understand? There's this precious artifact—"

"You don't understand that the stone isn't especially important. It's the *idea* of the stone, and what everybody can squeeze out of it. Blood, already," Sewickey said. "But the authenticity, the preciousness, the power? Nobody here really cares about that. Well, maybe this Israel archaeologist does, but the rest of us don't."

"I've read these, uh, books about the power these kinds of things can accumulate," Virgil ventured.

"Virgil, Virgil. It's all crap. It's a fuckin' rock. Some lunatic killer three thousand years ago wrote a note on it, and then he died and nobody gave a shit what he said. The stone was probably part of a fence or a foundation or something. Maybe a chopping block, and used when they cut the heads off pigeons."

"Then, what—"

"It's all about *us*. About me and Bauer and the Hezbollah and the Israelis. We aren't going home. We can't. We need this thing."

"So you don't even care about—"

"Virgil, listen. It's all crazier than a bucket of drunk rattle-snakes, but we've all got our needs and they need to be tended to," Sewickey said. "Bauer calls himself an investigative archaeol-ogist, but you know what he majored in, in college?"

Virgil thought for a few seconds, then guessed, "Television?"

"Drama. He wants to be a movie star. But he *needs* this stone. All that bullshit about the planks from Noah's Ark almost killed him off. *Nobody* believed him. That thing about getting the gopher wood at a Glendale gas station? That's the truth of the matter."

"The Hezbollah guy—"

"Al-Lubnani? You don't really want to go back to the Hezbollah leadership and say, 'Sorry, boys, that one kinda slipped off my plate,'" Sewickey said. "I mean, Virgil Flowers might put him in jail. The Hezbollah, on the other hand, will cut off his head with a chain saw. How hard will he think about that choice?"

Virgil regarded him for a moment, then said, "The Search for Hitler's Heart? The True Cross?"

Sewickey winced, then said, "Look. I've got a small depart-ment. It's me, an assistant professor, and two graduate students, funded by three rich oil and gas guys from Midland. You know what rich oil and gas guys want?"

"More oil and gas?"

"Well, yeah. But what they want from *me* is results. I pull down a hundred and fifty K from UT, get expense-paid trips to Istanbul and South America and Russia and a lot of other places, eat in some very good restaurants, get quoted on TV, especially in Midland, and occasionally get laid by undiscriminating museum ladies. If those rich guys go away, it's back to Mr. Sewickey's eighth-grade English in Bumfuck, Oklahoma. So: I won't risk my neck for the stone—you can send it into space, for all I care—but I *need* those photos I lost, because I *need* to be the American authority on the stone. If I could get those pictures back, I'd sit in the hotel looking at the porn channel and eating fried pork rinds and wait out the . . . the . . . climax of all this, and then go on TV at the end of it and become the *authority*. Make those guys in Midland *happy*."

"So . . ."

"So nobody's going home."

"That all sounds pretty cynical," Virgil observed.

"Virgil, have you even bothered to look at the economy? Another seven years and I'll have nailed down a substantial pension," Sewickey said. "If I'm kicked out of UT before then, it's thirty years of microwave dinners, thinning hair, and fattening waistline. I'll have spent fifteen years wearing a fuckin' string tie and these goddamned cowboy boots, for nothing."

Virgil thought about that, then said, "Tell you what. You hole up in your room. I took a bunch of high-res photos of the stone last night, and I'm a pretty goddamned good photographer. You hole up, stay out of this, and I'll get you a set."

Sewickey brightened: "Deal. You got yourself a deal, Virgil."

As he said that, Bauer emerged from the back room, trailed by Ma. Bauer asked, "What kind of a deal are we talking about?"

"Mr. Sewickey has agreed to withdraw from pursuit of the stone," Virgil said.

Bauer: "Really? Hard to believe. Once he gets his teeth into a project, he's a regular Chihuahua."

Sewickey half stood: "You want me to rattle a few of your fake pearly whites, wristwatch boy?"

Virgil: "Stop that."

They stopped it, and Ma said to Virgil, "You're getting pretty authoritarian, you know that?" and Virgil said, "Shut up, Ma," and she said, "Oh, no, I kinda like it. Gives me little shivers," and one way or another, thirty seconds later they all rolled together out the front door of the restaurant, and somebody yelled, "There they are!"

Somebody else screamed, "Virgil Flowers: Is it true somebody firebombed your house and stole the stone?"

Fifteen television people stampeded toward them, five of them with cameras on their shoulders.

Sewickey and Bauer surged past him, but the reporters ignored them and closed on Virgil. Virgil gave them one minute of non-committal answers, and then said, "That's all I got."

As he stepped back, the cameras still on him, his phone rang. He took it out of his pocket and looked at the screen.

Davenport.

Virgil said, "Ah, shit," and to the TV people, "You can quote me on that."

15

Davenport: "Why am I hearing about this on television? Somebody firebombed your house?"

Virgil was walking away down the street, leaving the TV crowd behind. "Ah, man, Lucas, I've been running around like a rat ever since it happened. I know who took the stone, or had to be involved."

He told Davenport how only three people knew that he had the stone, how Yael had no motive to steal it, so, "It had to be Ellen Case. She told her old man, and he firebombed me to get me out of the house. And it wasn't the house—it was my garage."

"Jesus, the garage? What happened to the boat?"

"The boat's fine. Not touched."

"That's a break. You got to give it to this preacher—he's got some balls."

"More like he's got nothing to lose," Virgil said.

They talked about the situation and finally Davenport said, "I'll send Jenkins and Shrake over to pick up Case. Show her that you're serious."

"I hate to, because she seems like a nice woman. I doubt she had anything to do with the fire."

"But she's involved, Virgil. There's nothing funny about a Molotov cocktail."

VIRGIL WALKED BACK to his truck and found Ma Nobles leaning against the front fender. "That Tag Bauer is a handsome young hunk. He has asked me out to dinner tonight, and I have accepted. However, my heart still belongs to you, if you act quickly," she said.

"What'd he do, tell you he's in love?"

"I figured that out for myself," Ma said. "Unfortunately, it's not with me. That boy's desperately in love with his own self, and it would take some serious spade work to break that down. But if you don't do something soon . . . I mean, I *got* a spade."

"You can tell by his hairline that he's gonna wind up bald," Virgil said. "He'll probably get one of those hair-replacement little sewing machine–looking things on his scalp." He sounded truculent in his own ears.

"I'm not talking about a long-term relationship," she said. "Anyway, you gotta admit, if him and me were to have a child, it'd be a good-looking one."

"Ma—"

"See ya," she said, and she pushed off the fender and walked on down the street, not looking back. Virgil watched her go, until she got in her truck, and then turned back the other way, where Bauer and Sewickey were doing an "old comrades" act for the TV cameras.

And he thought, *I hope Jenkins and Shrake aren't too rough with Ellen.*

VIRGIL WENT HOME and looked at his garage for a while, picking at the peeling paint. When he left the house that morning, he'd thought that the damage had been purely superficial—a matter of scraping off the burned paint and putting on a new coat. Now, he began to see that the damage was somewhat more substantial; nothing that threatened the building, but it needed new wood, a carpenter, and a painter.

He spent a few minutes talking to his insurance agent, who said that somebody would be around to take pictures and do an estimate on the damage. Virgil had worried that the policy wouldn't cover arson, but, as it turned out, it did, as long as he made an official report. He called the fire department to do it, and was told that he should also file with the cops. He did that by phone.

He was working on a computer report for Davenport when his phone rang. The screen said, "Unknown," and he clicked it and said, "Yes?"

"Virgil Flowers?" A man's voice, gruff. He'd heard it before.

"This is Flowers."

"This is Elijah Jones."

"Reverend Jones. I've been hoping you'd call, you miserable motherfucker."

"Well, I am, now . . . I need—"

"Wait a minute. Before we get to your needs . . . Did you take that stone from my house last night?"

"Yes. I also set your garage on fire. I hope the boat wasn't hurt."

"You're a goddamned sinner, you know that? You fire-bombed—"

"Shut up!" Jones shouted. "I got my back to the wall, Flowers. I've got the stone, but somebody's got Ellen."

"What?"

"She's been kidnapped. Whoever's got her, wants the stone. I never saw this, I never had any idea that anybody could go this low—"

"I told you, I told . . . Goddamnit, tell me what happened," Virgil said.

"I got a call, about forty minutes ago," Jones said. "A male voice, on the phone I've been using for the auction. They said they had Ellen, and would give her up, in return for the stone. They said they didn't want to hurt her, but they would if they had to. They said they'd start by cutting off her fingers and they'd leave them where I could find them, so I'd know that they were serious."

"Did you talk to Ellen?"

"Yes. They put her on the phone, but they wouldn't let her say much. She said she pulled into her garage, up in the Cities, and they were waiting for her, they threw a bag over her head and put her in a van and took her someplace, she doesn't know where."

"Did you drop off the stone yet?"

"Not yet. They said they'd hurt Ellen if I told anybody about this. They told me to start driving down Highway 83 south, and they'd call me and tell me when to turn and where to go, and if they saw anybody following me, they'd hurt her. I think it's the Turks, Virgil. Kaya likes knives, so I've been told. Anyway, I'm headed south now, back toward town. I don't know what you can do, but if I drop the stone, I'm afraid they won't want a witness. They won't have any reason to let Ellen go."

"The Turks went home," Virgil said. "At least, they got on an airplane to Chicago. Listen, did you get a phone number from the incoming phone?"

"No. It was blocked."

"Are you using the phone that Ellen calls you on?"

"Yes. They told me not to use the phone, but they only know about the auction phone, that's a different one."

"Give me the number—the number they called you on."

"Can you do something with that?"

"I don't know. I'm hoping the phone company can watch your phone, and if they call you on that again, see where the call is coming from. Or maybe tell where the first call came from."

Jones gave him the number. "Does the phone you're on now, does it have a speaker function?"

"Yes."

"So when you call me, put the phone in your lap and talk down into it. Don't put it to your ear, in case they're spotting you."

"Okay. Don't do anything that'll cause them to kill her."

"Just hold tight: I'll start bringing in help," Virgil said. "Are you in Mankato?"

"No, I'm coming down from the north."

"Don't drive too fast. Make me some time, before you get on 83."

"I'll try."

VIRGIL CALLED DAVENPORT: "Things got worse. . . ."

He recounted Jones's story, and Davenport said, "I got a call from Jenkins. He says Case is not at her house, but her car is in the garage. Her next-door neighbors didn't see her either last night or this morning. They're still checking the neighborhood."

"Okay. We need to alert the sheriff's departments south of Mankato, and any highway patrolmen down there. There's something a little odd about the call to Jones—if they took her last night, why did they wait until ten o'clock in the morning to call him? I can think of a couple of possibilities."

"Like?"

"Like they came from somewhere else, and have taken her somewhere else. Like if the Turks came back, but knew they couldn't be seen, so they hid out. Up there in the Cities, down in Albert Lea or over in Rochester. Maybe even down in Iowa, to get across a state line. They've got Jones driving south with the stone, so I suspect that they're not in the Cities."

"I'll check again on the Turks," Davenport said.

"Do that. There's also a possibility—maybe a better possibility than the Turks—that she was snatched by the first Yael. She disappeared so completely that I think she had to have help, and that help is likely male. The Mossad, if she's really Mossad, has done some of that kidnapping stuff."

"All right. What are you going to do?"

"Right now? I'm gonna talk to an Arab," Virgil said.

HE GOT on the line to Awad. "Where are you?"

"I am preparing for a training flight," Awad said.

"Good. I need an airplane ride. It's important. I'll pay. Can you do that?"

"I have no commercial license, but I accept pay, how do you say it, under the chair."

"Table," Virgil said. "Under the table. That's good enough. I need to go *now*."

"I will have the plane in two minutes. If you called me ten minutes from now, I would be in the air already," Awad said. "Is this a law enforcement matter?"

"Yes."

"Tell me in one seconds."

"A woman's been kidnapped."

"So I am helping to fight this crime?" Awad asked.

"I guess," Virgil said.

"This is A-1 quality," Awad said. And he did a perfect imitation of the *Cops* theme song, trilling, "Bad boys, bad boys . . ."

"Ten minutes," Virgil said. "If you have a pair of binoculars, that would be good."

JONES CALLED five minutes later, with Virgil halfway to the airport. "I'm coming into town, heading south. I'm driving a red Volvo station wagon. What should I do?"

"Call me when you get to the intersection of 22 and 83," Virgil said.

"Where will you be?" Jones asked.

"Close by—but out of sight," Virgil said. "You take care. You getting killed won't help Ellen one way or the other."

VIRGIL PARKED out front of the flight service, got his pistol, a cased M16, and a pair of image-stabilized Canon binoculars from the truck, walked into the flight service. The man behind the desk flinched when he saw Virgil coming, but Virgil had his ID ready and called, "Minnesota Bureau of Criminal Apprehension."

"What's going on? Is there trouble?"

"Where's Awad?"

"Raj? I always suspected—"

"I'm riding with him," Virgil said.

The man looked relieved for a half-second, then said, "In our plane? Wait a minute—"

"Don't have a minute," Virgil said. "We got a woman kidnapped."

"But—"

"And no time to argue about it. Where is he?"

He found Awad in the pilots' lounge with al-Lubnani. Al-Lubnani had a pair of binoculars around his neck. Virgil looked from al-Lubnani to Awad to al-Lubnani, and the old man shrugged and said, "Two binoculars are better than one."

"You're right," Virgil said. "Let's move."

Awad was dressed like a bush pilot, square-shouldered in a long-sleeved olive drab shirt with epaulets, jeans, and aviator sunglasses, like Virgil's. He was flying a Cessna 182, a four-seater. Virgil got in the front with Awad, who passed him a pair of headphones, and handed another pair to al-Lubnani in the back. Al-Lubnani sat behind Awad, so he and Virgil could look out opposite sides of the plane.

"Where do we go?" Awad asked.

Virgil said, "We need to survey the intersection of Highway 22 and 83. If you don't know it, I can point it out. We're looking for a red Volvo station wagon."

As they taxied out, Virgil saw the desk man standing with another man, and the desk man was pointing at the plane. If anything went wrong, Virgil thought, the governor was going to get a very large bill.

They were off the ground in ten minutes. The day was another hot one, with puffy gray-white clouds, and a haze that closed around them like a cotton-lined bowl. They climbed out and then Awad, showing an easy touch, banked left and headed due south. In one minute, looking down, Virgil said, "Okay, that's where 22 crosses 14—just follow 22 south."

Awad did, and in another minute, Virgil said, "That's 83 dead ahead."

The highway was a pale thread against the lush countryside. Virgil said, "We need to get as far away as we can and still see the intersection."

Awad said, "I shall find a convenient cloud."

Virgil's cell phone buzzed: Davenport. "You up in the air?"

"Yeah, we're waiting for Jones to call."

"I've got four patrolmen waiting down south of you, but they're pretty far out. They were running a big speed trap on I-35 over north of Albert Lea. We got some sheriffs' cars on the way, but I've told them to hold back unless you call. I got a dispatcher's number for you."

Virgil noted the number and Davenport said, "Tracking that incoming call is going to be a problem. We've got the phone companies working on it."

Virgil's phone beeped and he said, "I've got an unknown call coming in, it's probably Jones, gotta go, get me that phone if you can."

He switched over and Jones said, "I'm coming to the intersection."

Awad banked the plane and al-Lubnani said, "I see a red car."

Awad banked again, bringing the plane around, and Virgil put his binoculars on the intersection and saw the Volvo roll to a stop. "We got you," he told Jones. "As soon as they call, let me know."

Awad kept the plane in the hazy clouds, the Volvo barely visible, and at times, invisible, but since Jones was limited to following the highway, they couldn't lose him. They watched as the car crawled south a few miles, and then Jones called and said, "They just called me and said I'm supposed to go east on 30. They must be watching me somehow."

They watched as the car turned east, and Virgil told Awad and al-Lubnani, "If they're watching him, we might be able to spot their car."

They scanned the roadsides, but didn't see anything that seemed to be pacing Jones. After a while, Jones called again and said, "They say to go south on 13. They must be right on top of me. Do you see them? Where are you?"

"They are going to Albert Lea," Awad said to Virgil. "This is a training loop I fly."

"We're watching," Virgil told Jones. "Keep moving."

They followed Jones cross-country to Highway 13. The Volvo stopped at the intersection, then pulled onto the shoulder of the road.

"Watch him, watch him," Virgil said to al-Lubnani, who'd moved over so they were both looking out of the same side of the plane. "This might be the delivery point. See if he throws the stone out the window."

"We're too far away," al-Lubnani said.

Virgil said, "Raj, can you edge in a little closer?"

Awad tipped the plane toward the Volvo, and ten seconds later, the Volvo made a U-turn and started back the way it had come, accelerating, blowing past a car that it came up behind, and Awad said, "He is going a hundred and fifty kilometers an hour."

Virgil got on the phone, but Jones didn't answer. Virgil tried again, and a third time, and finally Jones came on and said, his voice curdled in anguish: "They saw you. They say you're tracking me in an airplane. They say they're going to cut a finger off and mail it to me."

"Why did you slow down there? Did you throw the stone out the window?"

"I'm going away. I'm not talking to you anymore."

And he hung up.

Virgil redialed, but Jones wouldn't answer. The Volvo continued speeding back west, and Virgil said, finally, "Raj, we've got to go back. I think he threw the stone out the window back at that intersection. We've got to go back and watch it until we can get a sheriff's car there."

"What about the red car?"

"We have to let it go. I'll get somebody else to run it down."

VIRGIL CALLED the dispatcher out of Mankato and had her vector a couple of city cars toward Jones, and to direct anyone available to the intersection. When they got back, Virgil said, "I hope we're not too late."

"I don't think so," said al-Lubnani. "We know they are watching us, but we cannot see them. So, they must be some time away. A minute or two. We have only been away for a minute or two."

"I hope," Virgil said. "Unless they were lying in that cornfield, there, and picked up the stone and walked back into it."

They circled the intersection for five minutes, watching the roads and looking for parked cars on the edge of the cornfield, seeing nothing, until finally a highway patrol car rolled up to the corner and stopped. Virgil got back to the dispatcher, who got a cell phone number, and Virgil called. The patrolman came on, and Virgil got him to walk the ditch.

"No stone here," the patrolman said. "They've cut this ditch, and there's no stone."

"So either they got it, or Jones never threw it in the ditch," Virgil said. To Awad, "We need to get back to Mankato. Fast."

He called the Mankato dispatcher again and was told that nobody had seen the Volvo. There was a net out around the city, but so far, no luck.

He tried Jones again, and this time, Jones answered.

"They're going to cut her finger off—"

"Did they tell you to do a U-turn and head back west?"

"Yes. . . . I don't know how they are tracking me."

"They're doing it with the phone. They know where you are. They will probably be coming for you. Where are you now?"

"I won't tell you that. Let them come. I just want Ellen back."

"Listen. If they call you again—and they will, if you keep moving, if only to tell you to slow down—if they call you, tell them that before they touch Ellen, to look at the television news tonight."

"What?"

"Tell them to watch the news," Virgil repeated.

"What are you going to do?"

"I'm going to send them a message."

Jones groaned then, and said, "I don't have any time. I don't have any more time." And rang off.

Virgil didn't bother to call again. Instead, he began calling television stations.

WHEN THEY LANDED, Virgil thanked Awad and al-Lubnani, jogged to his truck, locked up the guns, and raced through downtown Mankato, to his house. He printed a dozen photos of Tal Zahavi that he'd taken as she left the Downtown Inn for the last time. He paced impatiently as they chugged out of the printer, and when the last one popped out, he gathered them up and headed back downtown, to the Holiday Inn. When he saw the white vans, he said to himself, "Ah, boy." He'd gotten at least three responses.

The press conference was short, but hot; a sensation, in fact. There were four cameras and one radio reporter, and three newspaper reporters. Sewickey and Bauer were hovering in the background, attracted by the cameras.

Virgil announced that Jones had called him and told him that his daughter, Ellen Case, of Minneapolis, had been kidnapped and was being held, with the Solomon stone demanded in exchange. He passed around the photos of Zahavi and said, "We would very much like to speak to this woman, Tal Zahavi, who we believe is staying somewhere in southern Minnesota or northern Iowa. We believe that she is armed and dangerous. We are putting out an order that she is to be arrested on sight."

"Is she the kidnapper?" asked the Channel Three reporter.

"I don't know—but I would very much like to ask her that question," Virgil said. Everybody got the hint.

"Has the FBI been notified?"

"We don't know that the kidnappers have crossed state lines, but with Iowa so close by, it's possible. We will be talking to the FBI about the possibility."

As they closed the press conference, Sewickey stood up and called, "Could I have your attention? Virgil didn't say so, but this woman works with the Israeli Mossad. A few days ago, she robbed me in my hotel room, and bound me, and left me on the floor, where I'd still be if Virgil and a friend hadn't found me."

That resulted in another sensation, and another press conference, and another headache for Virgil; when it was over, he took Sewickey aside and asked, "Why?"

"Revenge," Sewickey said. "I want that bitch to be famous. I want to see you roll her ass right into whatever kind of hellhole you have for women in this state. If not that, I want to see her working in an Israeli dime store."

"Ladies' prison is not so much of a hellhole," Virgil said. "It's more like a dormitory."

"Send her down to Texas—we'll fix her clock," Sewickey said.

VIRGIL DROVE back to his house and called the Israeli embassy and asked to speak urgently to Colonel Ohad Shachar. When he came on the line, Virgil said, "I've put out an arrest order for Tal Zahavi, who I believe is a Mossad operator. I believe she has kidnapped a woman and taken her across a state line, which makes it a federal offense. You should be hearing from the FBI. In the meantime, I've sent very good photographs of her to every TV station in the area. I wanted you to know."

"You are misguided," Shachar said. "This woman has nothing to do with the Mossad—I doubt even that she is an Israeli. So, do what you must."

"I am telling you that I already have," Virgil said. "I'm not negotiating, I'm simply telling you. Let me give you a few of the television websites—you can watch the press conference yourself."

A while later, Davenport called: "Well, that's another weed in your cap. The legend of that fuckin' Flowers continues to spread, like Minnesota kudzu. At least you've got Jones and the stone."

"Not exactly," Virgil said.

Jones had vanished. He explained that to Davenport, who, after a silence, said, "I'm sure you'll find him right away. With the stone."

"Probably," Virgil said. "But I'm more worried about Ellen. Did you hear back about the Turks? Did they leave the country?"

"I haven't heard. We're still waiting."

"Not my day," Virgil said.

"Is there anything I can do?" Davenport asked.

"Yes. Get the DMV to do a computer run and figure out how many red Volvo station wagons there are in the state, and which ones are located around Mankato."

"I'll see what they can do," Davenport said.

"Goddamnit: I hope Zahavi gets the message," Virgil said. "If she gets the message, they'll let Ellen go. She had a couple of loose gears, but I don't think she'd hurt an innocent."

"You'd know better than me," Davenport said. "To tell you the truth, from this distance it looks like she's got more than a few loose gears. She looks like she's fuckin' nuts. For a stone? All of this for some old stone?"

To GET A DEGREE, Raj Awad was required to take general courses along with his pilot training, and so it was that after he returned from the airport adventure, he had to hurry off to "Introduction to Gender"—he'd been told that it was a good place to pick up chicks. He later decided that perhaps his American mentor had been pulling on his shirt, but by that time, it was too late, and he was in for the semester.

He was returning from the class when he found al-Lubnani standing in the kitchen holding a bottle of Stolichnaya.

Two concepts flashed through Awad's mind in a fraction of a second: (a) Hezbollah fanatic, (b) the Islamic ban on alcohol.

He stuttered, "Where did you find this? One of my silly friends—"

"Under the sink," al-Lubnani said. "I believe I saw a bottle of V8 in the refrigerator?"

A moment of realization. "And some celery," Awad said.

So that's the way it was. They mixed up a pitcher of Bloody Marys, got a couple of glasses, and sat on Awad's tiny balcony, in the heat, and made the best of it.

After a while, al-Lubnani observed, "I do not believe I see in you the best of the *mujahid*."

"I confess, this is true," Awad said. "I am a seeker of peace. I wish to be a pilot, and nothing more. The kind who lands his airplane at airports, and not in tall buildings."

"And I find a number of *Playboy* magazines under the bed," al-Lubnani said.

Awad sipped the Bloody Mary, said, "You know, this could use some pepper. I will get some." He stood up and said, "The *Playboy* magazines. I am all alone here."

"I understand this *Playboy*. I once bought them in Beirut, when

I was a younger man." Al-Lubnani frowned. "They're not so good anymore. They don't show so much, how do the Americans say it, this *qittah*."

"Pussy," Awad said. "That is not an exact translation."

"Not so clearly anymore, the photography," al-Lubnani said. "Back in the eighties, it was more clear."

Awad came back with the pepper, he sprinkled some on his drink and passed the shaker to al-Lubnani, who said, "I also sometimes become . . . weary of the conflict."

"Mmmm." Dangerous territory, but not uninteresting.

"Have you been to Paris?" al-Lubnani asked.

"Of course. I lived there for two years, when my parents sent me away from the fighting," Awad said. "I hope someday to fly for Air France."

"This is the most wonderful city, for me," al-Lubnani said. "The city of light. Strolling down the Champs-Élysées, or standing on the Pont Neuf, watching the boats, dinner on the Left Bank. I am an artist, you know, in watercolor. And I am half French. My mother was a Frenchwoman and I still have a French passport. My father was a diplomat, he is gone now."

"This is sad," Awad said. "About your father."

"Yes." Very long pause. "I have been thinking. I wish to be frank with you, and I sense that I may be."

"Mmmm."

Al-Lubnani laughed. "A careful noise, this mmmm."

"I am most interested in hearing you talk, but I am careful in such things."

Al-Lubnani, who was now lightly oiled, poured himself a third

Blood Mary. "You and I are much alike, despite our ages. We would like to live in peace. We are Lebanese, not Palestinian. We have grown up in one of the most sophisticated cities in the world, a place that was once the banker for the entire Mediterranean. I would have nothing to do with the Party, except, I was in the wrong place, and they asked me to speak for them, and I could not say 'no.'"

"Of course not," Awad said.

"So I spoke for them, and then . . . I was in the Party. I am Lebanese to my bones, I speak French and Arabic and English and a little Greek, and here I am, driving around with AK-47s in my car, bowing to illiterate gunmen and praying five times a day."

"I understand," Awad said.

Al-Lubnani sighed. "A man will come here and provide me with the funds to pay Jones for this stone, for this propaganda victory. This man, he is a killer—a real *mujahid*. The headquarters, they send me to make the transfer, because this man, this killer, he cannot risk exposure in the U.S. If the Americans find him here, they will put him in a box and never let him out."

"What is he doing here at all?" Awad asked.

"I don't know. You know, I am here unofficially, as a simple man from Lebanon, touring the country. I could not bring any money with me, because of American customs. This *mujahid*, his first mission was not here to deliver the money. He was here for something else, but the money comes to New York in the diplomatic pouch, is transferred to him, and he brings it here. I make the exchange, I take the stone to Lebanon, he goes back under the ground."

"Mmmm."

Al-Lubnani put his feet on the balcony railing. "But I ask myself, this only in theory: they wish to have this stone in Lebanon. I wish to live in peace in Paris, which is a very expensive city. This man, this killer, brings three million U.S. dollars in cash, in a satchel. For one million, plus my own funds, I could live, not brilliantly, but reasonably, in Paris."

"Mmmm."

"I ask myself, if Jones takes a bid of one and a half, who is to know that he has not taken all three?"

Awad said, "I ask myself, but only politely, why should I risk my life so that you could live in Paris in comfort?"

Al-Lubnani raised a finger: "You must do the mathematics. I believe Jones would take one and a half. I need one. That is two-point-five. For the additional five hundred thousand, one might buy a small airplane."

"I would like a small airplane," Awad admitted. "Although I would like to fly for an airline, becoming a bush pilot would also be acceptable."

"A bush pilot, here in the Minnesota?"

"Not in Minnesota. Too cold. I would be interested, perhaps, in some African bush. Or even Syrian bush. Well, any bush, as long as it is not shooting at me."

"Mmm. Syria. Syria might be difficult for the next thirty years," al-Lubnani said. "But Turkey, Turkey could have a place for you. Or Kurdistan."

"There is no Kurdistan," Awad said.

"There will be . . . and they might need bush pilots."

———

A MOMENT to sip the Bloody Marys. "This conversation is very interesting," Awad said.

"But it's all theory, of course," al-Lubnani said. "Nobody could be more loyal to the cause than Adabi al-Lubnani."

"I understand this," Awad said. "Tell me, do you know the name of this man who brings the money?"

"I do. Although, I hesitate even to utter it," al-Lubnani said. "One reason our conversation will come to nothing, is that this man might be sent to interrogate me, if they become uncertain of how the money was spent. Or if I do not instantly return to Lebanon."

"If you do decide to utter this name, I may have a way to work with it," Awad said. "As you know, I have an excellent contact with the American authorities."

"Interesting," al-Lubnani said. "This is Virgil?"

"Yes. I have been reading about him, on the Internet. He has contacts in the American government. If they would be interested in this *mujahid*."

"I tell you, very seriously, the world would be a better place without this man." Al-Lubnani took another sip. "Not that I am anything but a warrior against the face of these Israeli crusaders."

"Of course not," Awad said. "Still . . ."

"Another Bloody Mary?" al-Lubnani asked.

16

Virgil watched the evening news, and it was effective: Zahavi was now the most well-known young Israeli in America. Of course, if he was wrong about the kidnappers, she might wind up being the richest young Israeli in America, after the lawsuits.

He went to dinner at Applebee's, where he got a large slab of ribs, french fries, and coleslaw, and had managed to smear a substantial amount of deep orange barbeque sauce around his mouth when Ma walked in with Bauer.

They saw him instantly. Ma walked over and asked, "That sauce around your lips. You storin' that for later?"

Virgil wiped his face with a napkin and said to Bauer, "You asked her out, and took her to Applebee's? On a first date?"

Ma didn't let the man answer. Instead, she jumped in with a question. "Jones got away again?"

"Yeah. He's like a ghost."

"Well, something else for you to think about," Ma said. "Try not to burn your brain out. You need everything you got."

"Go eat your dinner," Virgil said. "Looking at you two, it annoys me."

VIRGIL THOUGHT about Ma's comment anyway, as he worked through the remaining ribs. So, he just thought about it all. About Jones, about his daughter, about Ma, about who was hiding Jones and where he might be hiding the rock . . . about who had Ellen, and whether Ellen and Jones could be faking the kidnapping to throw him off . . . and that was a disquieting idea.

Then he thought, why would any normal, sane person hide Jones, knowing that he or she would be complicit in several felonies, including aggravated assault and now kidnapping? And that while Jones would never pay, because he'd be dead soon, his little helper could go to prison for quite some time.

Virgil came to a conclusion: nobody would do that. Not if they were sane.

But somebody obviously was.

It took him a while, and a hot fudge sundae, eventually he got around to another thought: unless the person helping him didn't know he (or she) was actually doing that.

Hmm. He finished the ribs, then used all four of the chemical hand-cleaning cloths provided by Applebee's, took out his phone, went to a world time clock, and found out that it was 4:47 a.m. in Israel. Annabelle Johnson had said that they got on the bus every morning at five o'clock, to go out to the dig—so she'd be up. And if not, well, this was more important than sleep.

He found his previous call to her in the cell phone registry and punched it up again. After involving several ground stations and a couple of satellites, the call rang the phone in Johnson's backpack as she ate breakfast in a dormitory in northern Israel.

Johnson answered, sounding bright and cheerful. "Ken?"

"No, this is Virgil. Flowers. From the Minnesota Bureau of Criminal Apprehension."

"Officer Flowers. Have you found Elijah?"

"No, no. Could you tell me what kind of car you drive?"

"Why?"

"Just curious."

"Well, it's a Volvo," she said.

"Like a red Volvo station wagon?"

"Yes, exactly. Has something happened?"

They talked for another minute, and Johnson said that Elijah Jones certainly was not authorized to drive her car, or to sleep in her bed; but the keys to her car would have been easy to find, for anyone inside her house. They were in the top drawer of her bedroom dresser.

"Do you have your house key with you?" Virgil asked.

"Well, in my purse, somewhere."

"Could you check and see if it's still there?"

"Yes, of course." He heard her rummaging around, and a moment later, she was back on the phone. "It's not there. I can't believe this."

Virgil took down her address in the town of St. Peter, and she said that her next-door neighbors, the Jensens, had an emergency key to the house. Virgil gave her the phone number for the duty

officer at the BCA in St. Paul, asked her to call and have him record her saying that it was all right for Virgil Flowers to enter her
home. "Then have him call me and tell me he has it."

"Okay. Do you want me to call the Jensens and tell them to
give you the key?"

"Not right now," Virgil said. "I'll go there and call you from
there."

ON THE WAY out the door, he paused at Ma's table, where she and
Bauer were both eating shrimp platters, which Virgil had considered and rejected, feeling that Red Lobster would have given him
a better quality seafood entrée. Ma looked up as Virgil approached
and said, "What?" and Virgil bent over the booth and kissed her
on the forehead.

"Thank you," he said.

"For what?"

"I thought about it. Like you said."

JOHNSON LIVED in the northern part of St. Peter, on Inverness
Lane, a pleasant enough neighborhood probably three minutes
from where she worked at the college.

Virgil found the address and made a pass: no car was visible,
nor were there any lights on. He made another pass. Nothing. He
finally pulled into the driveway of Johnson's next-door neighbor,
where there were lights, and rang the doorbell.

A man came to the door, holding a magazine, looked out at Virgil, and opened the door. "Yes?"

Virgil identified himself. "Are you Mr. Jensen?"

"What'd I do?"

"You live next to Annabelle Johnson," Virgil said. He said he was interested in activity at Johnson's house; the coming and going of her car, the red Volvo station wagon.

Jensen's wife had come up behind him, to listen to the conversation, and she said, "I saw the car come and go a couple of times yesterday, but I assumed it was Roger."

"Roger?"

"Her son. He's supposed to be keeping an eye on the place while she's in Israel. He lives up in the Cities. Haven't actually seen him, though."

"She was on that dig with this Jones guy," the man said. "You think *he's* been using the car?"

Guy was no dummy, Virgil thought. He said, "We're just checking possibilities. Johnson said you have the emergency key to the house. I'd like to call her in Israel—she's waiting for me to call—so she can tell you to give it to me."

"Cool," said Jensen.

Virgil made the call, Johnson asked Jensen to give Virgil the key, and then Mrs. Jensen and Johnson talked for ten minutes on Virgil's dime, about what was happening in the neighborhood, whether Roger had been around, about a faculty dispute over an LGBT issue, and whether Johnson's lawn sprinklers had been on; and then Virgil got his phone back, and the key.

He told the Jensens to close the door and stay inside, at least for a few minutes.

HE MOVED his truck well down the block, got a flashlight and, as an afterthought, his gun, and walked back to the house. The house was single-storied, a ranch style, and he could see narrow basement windows set into the foundation. He went in through the back—the locks were single-keyed. Using the flashlight, he first cleared the top floor, and checked the garage, which was empty.

One-third of the basement held the mechanicals for the house, along with the laundry. The other two-thirds had been converted into an office, a small theater area with a large TV and a music system, with some exercise equipment in another corner. Two windows looked down into the office area, and both had been blocked with pillows—so Jones could hole up and watch TV, Virgil thought.

He looked at the couch facing the TV. A white garbage bag lay on the floor beside the couch, and showed what may have been a bloodstain. Jones, he thought, was trying not to bleed on his friend's couch.

Finished with the basement, he went back upstairs and looked at the rooms in detail. The bedcovers were badly rumpled, and when he pulled them back, he found two small patches of dried blood on the sheets below. He'd been careful in the basement, not so careful in the bedroom.

Nothing else. No stone, no clothes. The refrigerator was

stocked with beer and sandwich meat, and a loaf of bread sat on the kitchen counter. When Virgil squeezed it, it felt like it might be a couple of days old.

Would Jones be back?

No way to tell. But Virgil wasn't doing anything, anyway, and Johnson's house seemed like the best bet to find him. He called the BCA duty officer, got him to look up the phone number for the Jensens next door, and called them.

"I'm going to lie down on the couch here. I may be here overnight. Just carry on like you usually would," he said.

They said they would.

VIRGIL SAT in the living room for a while, realized that he wouldn't make it, sitting in the dark all night. He eventually went back to the basement, turned on a light long enough to browse Johnson's stock of movies, selected *Kick-Ass*, loaded it, turned the sound down as low as he could and still hear it, and turned off the lights.

He watched the movie, and nothing happened upstairs.

Then he watched two-thirds of *Watchmen*, and something happened. The phone rang, and when he answered it, Mrs. Jensen identified herself. "We worried about you sitting over there in the dark. I wondered, if I snuck over to the back door, would you like a slice of cherry pie?"

"Well, yeah. I would."

"Heated up?"

"Yes, ma'am."

"Ice cream?"

"That'd be great."

"I'll be over in five minutes. Back door."

Virgil really did like most people, because most people were pretty likable.

The pie was excellent. So was the movie, but he couldn't deal with a third one. At eleven o'clock, he raided the refrigerator for a beer, then curled up on the couch, placing his cell phone next to his ear.

He thought for a while about the whole ridiculous situation, and what he might do about it. Every cop in the south half of the state was looking for Ellen Case, but the only link to her was the phone in Elijah Jones's car.

Virgil often did his best thinking in a half-slumber. As he was about to go to sleep, he started thinking about the fact that Yael-1, or Tal or whatever her name was, had been able to track Jones's car, but they hadn't been able to spot the tracker from the air. Not only had Yael-1 been able to track it, but she'd been able to track it over several miles, and several turns . . . so had they placed a bug on the car? But how'd they known which car to bug?

"Huh." He woke up, picked up his cell phone, and called the duty officer again.

"When you lose your iPhone, can't you call up somebody and have them track it for you? Like, on a map?"

"I believe so," the duty officer said.

"This is what I need," Virgil said. "I need you to get in touch with Apple or whoever. They have this service where you can track your stolen iPhone on an iPad, I think, or maybe even another phone. Find out if somebody called them and asked them to track an iPhone through southern Minnesota today."

"I don't know exactly how I'd do that," the duty officer said.

"Well, figure it out. You're a smart guy. Look it up on the Net. When you do get hold of them, ask what number was calling, and ask where that phone is now located."

"I'll give it a shot."

"Don't call me back before seven in the morning," Virgil said. "I need the sleep."

WHEN THE PHONE rang at six o'clock, he groaned and rolled over. The couch hadn't been quite long enough, and he had a kink in the middle of his back, and his feet had gone to sleep, from being jammed between a seat pillow and the arm of the couch.

He picked up the phone and looked at the screen, which showed a 507 area code, an unfamiliar number, and "Rochester, MN."

"Hello?"

"Viiirrrrgilll . . ."

She was blubbering incoherently, but it was Ellen Case. "I'm walking down this road toward this gas station, I'm in the ditch."

Virgil sat up, his mind suddenly crystal clear: "Get to the gas station. Can you run? How far are you from the gas station? Is the station open?"

"The sign is on."

"What kind of sign?" Virgil asked.

"It's a Kwik Trip."

"How far away are you?"

"I don't know, not very far. I'm out in the country," she said.

"Could you run?"

"No, I'm all . . . I'm all . . . I'm so tired . . ."

"Just stay with me, stay on the phone," Virgil said. He was getting his boots on as he talked.

Virgil got her to the Kwik Trip, talked to the counterman, got the location, and then got the Rochester cops started.

When Ellen got back on the line, he said, "Just hang on, honey, every cop in the world is on the way."

Mankato, Minnesota, is about eighty-five miles from Rochester, and driving it takes no less than an hour and a half under normal conditions. Virgil made it in a bit less than an hour from the time he hit the street. On the way, he called the Rochester cops back and told them to press Ellen on exactly how and when she was dropped and anything she might be able to give them on where her kidnappers might be.

And he said he would be right there.

He'd just crossed I-35 south of Owatonna when it occurred to him that he should let Davenport know that Ellen had been found. Davenport was a bear if you woke him before eight o'clock in the morning, but he recovered.

So Virgil called and Davenport said, "You better not be in that fuckin' boat," and Virgil said, "No, no. I just got a call from Ellen Case. They cut her loose in Rochester."

"Aw, man. That's terrific. I was scared to death you'd stepped on your dick with that TV thing," Davenport said. "I was getting ready to tell people I didn't even know you. Where are you? You're going, of course."

"Yeah. The sonic boom that just woke up Owatonna was me going past. I've got the Rochester cops talking to Ellen, trying to see what she might give them on the kidnappers."

"You know what? I bet that Mossad chick is on her way to the East Coast, and I bet they've got a private plane to get them out of the country. They saw the TV show, freaked out, cut Case loose, and took off. You won't see her ass again, not this side of Jerusalem."

"You're probably right," Virgil said. "I hope I put a dent in her rep. Pisses me off."

"Call me again when you've talked to Case."

BY THE TIME Virgil got to Rochester, the cops had moved Ellen to the St. Mary's emergency room. A cluster of six uniforms and two detectives were loitering in the waiting area, when he hustled inside. One of the detectives recognized him, said, "Virgil," and Virgil said, "Donny," and "Where is she?"

"She's sitting on a bed. She says she's okay, and the doc says she's tired and probably could use a Xanax or something."

"I need to talk to her. Did she give you anything?"

"She's got no idea where she was," Donny Hall said. "They had her in a gunnysack from the time they grabbed her until the time they turned her loose. One man, one woman, they were in a motel somewhere. C'mon this way."

Ellen was lying on a hospital bed, her shoes off, but otherwise fully clothed. She opened her eyes when Virgil came in and sat up, tears leaking down her cheeks. "I just, I just . . ."

"Easy," Virgil said. "Can you talk to me? I don't want to upset you any more than you already are."

"I can talk, I'm not hurt. But I'm so *tired*. I thought they'd kill me. I'm never going to forgive Dad. This is so far over the top."

"Did you see the woman?"

"Only for a half-second, just from the side of my eye. They just, they just . . ."

She started to freak, and Virgil patted her leg. "Easy, easy."

"I was in my garage. I was wondering if I had anything good to eat in the refrigerator, and I never saw them coming. They threw this *bag* over me. It smelled like telephone poles smell. Then they threw me on the floor and the woman, I think this was the woman, she hit me, she slapped me, and I couldn't even scream. Then they started with the tape and then they threw me in the van, I'm sure it was a van. . . ."

The first ride in the van, the night of the kidnapping, had been a long one, but that morning, a short one. She'd never had any trouble breathing, because even though she couldn't see out of the sack, it was loosely woven. "Smelly, but I could breathe."

When she had to use the bathroom, the kidnappers pulled the tape off at the waist and led her to the toilet. The woman stayed with her in the bathroom. To give her food or water, they'd untape the sack again and pass the food or bottles of water under the edge. The sack never came off her head. The sack itself, she said, was back in the ditch by the Kwik Trip.

Virgil walked her through the whole story, and at the end, was ninety-nine percent certain that he'd made the right call on Zahavi.

When Virgil pressed her to identify the woman as Yael-1, or Tal, she couldn't—no names had ever been used—but she thought that yes, they may have been Israeli.

"Why?" Virgil asked.

"For breakfast . . . I had toast, cream cheese, and lots of vegetables and fruit. I went to Israel three times with Dad, and that's what Israelis mostly eat for breakfast."

There were a few details: a minivan, the first floor of a motel, but not a very good motel—the rooms had a stale odor about them, as if they permitted smoking, and were poorly cleaned. The rooms were not particularly soundproof, because she'd heard cars going by on gravel, and once, somebody calling to somebody else, but she hadn't heard anyone in an adjacent room.

In the morning, when she was released, she tried to keep track of where she was being taken, and thought she'd been driven only fifteen minutes or so—the motel was not far away.

"You think the motel parking lot was gravel, rather than paved?"

She thought for a moment, then nodded. "Yes. And when I think about it, I think we might have been in an end room."

Virgil continued pulling details out, and Donny, the detective, said, "I can think of two places she might have been. There might be more, but I'd bet it's one of those two."

"Can you send some guys around?"

"You bet."

He left, and Virgil patted Ellen on the leg and said, "I gotta ask you—can you talk to the media?"

"I . . . Do I have to?"

"We need to communicate with your father," Virgil said. "There's no better way. We've now had three people shot and a kidnapping. This is seriously ugly."

Virgil pushed her on the subject of who'd taken her father out of the hospital, and why. She was adamant: she had nothing to do with it, and didn't know who might have done it.

"I think, probably, it was Ma Nobles," Virgil said. "To tell you the truth, Ellen, I suspected that you probably briefed her on the whole thing."

"We did talk about the stone," Ellen admitted. "I might've . . . She seems . . ."

"What?"

"She seemed interested that the sale price on the stone might be, you know, a couple million dollars."

"So you talked about that?"

"Yes, we did."

"You knew that Ma had a little bit of a questionable history?"

Ellen said, "Well . . . she seemed nice enough. I mean, *you* introduced her to me."

Virgil winced: "I was trying to give her something legitimate to do."

"Well . . . that really didn't work out very well," Ellen said. "Do you think she'd know where Dad is?"

"I don't know. I don't know anything. Your old man is pretty good at hiding out, for a preacher."

ELLEN DIDN'T want to stay at the hospital. When the doctor
said she could go, Virgil drove her to the Rochester Law Enforcement Center to make a complete statement. While she was doing
that, he drove over to the Downtown Hilton, talked to the manager and reserved a space for the press conference, called Davenport and told him what he was going to do, and then began calling
TV stations.

He was at the Hilton when Hall, the detective, called and said
they'd found the motel. "It's a mom-'n'-pop called Foudray's out
where 54 crosses I-90. Jack Golden's out there."

"Are you done with Ellen?"

"Not quite. You need her?"

"Yeah, at the Hilton at eleven o'clock."

"We'll be done by then," Donny said. "I'll bring her over."

Virgil drove to the motel, a single-story building with a fifty-
yard strip of small rooms fronting on Highway 52. The parking lot was brown gravel, and Jack Golden was looking at the
end room, and talking to a shaky, unshaven old man who wore a
long-sleeved turquoise cowboy shirt and jeans. Golden and Virgil shook hands, and Golden introduced the old man as Bud
Anderson.

"Just saw one man, tall fellow, had a beard and long hair," Anderson said. "He looked kinda foreign, but he spoke English
pretty good. Didn't sound foreign."

"There was a woman with him?" Virgil asked.

"Yeah, I saw a woman getting out of that van, one time.

Skinny-looking. They had two rooms rented, the tall guy come in and asked for the two end rooms, because they needed some quiet, so, no skin off my butt. I put them down here."

Golden said, "The guy wrote down a tag number when he checked in. No such number. Signed in as Richard Johnson. Paid cash. Never used the room phone."

"They're long gone," Virgil said. "I don't even know if it's worth calling in the crime scene."

"Might find some fibers from that sack or something," Golden said. "But there's a bottle of 409 in the bathroom that doesn't belong to the motel. I suspect everything's been wiped."

"Of course it's wiped," Virgil said. "They're spies. Of course they wiped it."

Golden said, "Spies. I haven't actually dealt with spies before."

"They're all around us," Anderson said. "Spies." Then he looked up at the already hazy sky: "Gonna be another hot one," he said.

17

Virgil took a call from Hall, at the Law Enforcement Center: "We've got a small problem here. Case has decided to cancel your TV show."

"What?"

"She says she spent two days in a gunnysack, and she looks like it, and she's not going on TV looking like she does."

"I'll be there in five minutes," Virgil said.

THE FIVE MINUTES eventually cost him four hundred dollars at Macy's, but he did give her credit for haste: she had no purse, ID, or credit cards, and promised to pay him back. She settled for a couple of cosmetic products and a green summer dress, on sale, and a pair of low heels; and at the last minute went for some underwear, hair spray, and a comb.

On the way back to the Hilton, Virgil said, "Tell me what you *think* about the kidnappers. Was it the woman I introduced to you? Do you think they're still around? How organized were they?

What'd they talk about? Did they give you any idea of where they were from?"

She said that the female kidnapper was the one in charge. She was tough, and seemed organized, but a little overcooked. Ellen wasn't sure that it was Tal Zahavi, but thought it might be. "That same kind of executive attitude—if you won't do it, I will."

The man, on the other hand, lived in a state of panic: "He seemed more frightened than I was. Looking back, I don't think they ever planned to hurt me. The guy . . . he kept asking me if I had to go to the bathroom or needed a glass of water. He was an American, I think, but he used Yiddish slang a couple of times. I think he might have been an American Jew that they called on for help."

She had no idea of where either of them was from. Whenever the man began to ramble, the woman shut him up, and Ellen had the feeling that she was being pointed at—as in, "Shut up or she'll hear you."

The two kidnappers wound up watching a lot of TV, and the woman would go outside to make phone calls. At some point, they contacted her father, and then moved her back to the van and drove around for a while, apparently to exchange her for the stone, but the trade fell through when they saw an airplane tracking her father.

"That was me," Virgil said. "If I hadn't been up there, you might've gotten loose a day sooner."

"No way for you to know that," Ellen said, patting him on the shoulder. "I don't know how you would have seen them, either— they were hiding in cornfields when Dad went by. They were looking for cars or planes following him, and they saw the plane."

That evening, after the failure to make the trade, they'd seen Virgil on television, and they'd panicked.

"The woman was raving, she kept saying, 'What is this? What is this fool doing to me?' Then the man would say, 'Looks to me like he's fucking you, right there on TV.'"

"Then it must have been Tal Zahavi," Virgil said.

"Well . . . yeah, I guess it must have been."

They decided to release her near dawn, because the woman told the man that was when the fewest police officers would be around. When they'd kidnapped her, she'd been wearing a light gardening jacket, with her cell phone in her pocket. They took it away from her, but returned it when they left her in the ditch.

"That was nice," Virgil said.

"Not so much nice, as scared," Ellen said. "At that point, they didn't want anything to happen to me. They wanted me to call the police to come get me. The way they were talking, I'm pretty sure that they're not around anymore. The guy was saying he was going home, and the woman wasn't arguing with him. I don't know for sure if she took off, but I think he did."

AT THE HILTON, Virgil bullshitted the manager into giving them a free room for a couple hours, and left Ellen there to clean up.

When she emerged, fifteen minutes before the scheduled press conference, she smiled weakly and said, "At least I feel semi-human again."

"You look terrific," Virgil said. She did look okay, although behind the new clothes and makeup, her eyes looked haggard. If it had been Zahavi who'd done the kidnapping, and Virgil was virtually certain that it was, she owed Ellen something serious, because she'd taken away something serious: the sense that there's a safety and privacy in life, and that bad crazy things happen to other people.

He was inclined to give her a lecture about her father, and about any help she might be giving him, but after glancing at her, decided to let it go.

"You're going to get a lot of attention now," he said, as they started down in the elevator. "You will be doing everyone a great favor if you read your old man the riot act."

"I'm sure he's still focused on Mother," she said. "If he's still alive."

"That's a question we'll have to deal with—that I want to deal with in the press conference," Virgil said. "You have to make him call me. Or call you."

THE PRESS CONFERENCE was stacked with reporters. The kidnapping, and the stone, were the big story in the state, and for several states around, and it was beginning to get attention from the national cable channels like CNN and Fox. Both Sewickey and Bauer had been on early morning shows, Virgil had been told, and they had more on their schedule.

The press conference was being held in a meeting room, but they and a couple of Rochester detectives, including Hall, hid out in a conference room until it was time to go out. When it was time, the three cops led Ellen through the meeting room and around to the front, where a podium had been set up. Virgil counted seven cameras, and saw Ruffe Ignace, a *Star-Tribune* reporter, and sometime friend, taking up two chairs in the front row; not because he needed two chairs, but because he was a two-chair kind of guy, and he didn't like being touched, as he put it, by TV scum.

Virgil opened the press conference by saying that Ellen Case had been released early that morning, and that the kidnappers had fled, and were being sought by both local police and the FBI. He told them that the kidnappers had attempted to exchange Ellen for the Solomon stone.

He recounted her early-morning phone call, and his call to the Rochester police, and then turned the press conference over to Hall, who told about Rochester cops finding Ms. Case in the Kwik Trip store, about her trip to the hospital, her physical condition, and about the discovery of the motel where she'd been kept.

Hall introduced Ellen to the cameras, and she related how the kidnappers had taken her, how they'd kept her in the motel room, and then how they'd abandoned her on the side of the road.

"I think my father will either see this, or hear this, and Dad, I'm pleading with you, give it up. You're hurting people now. I can promise you, I'll never be the same. This whole thing is so crazy. Call Virgil, or call me—I still have my phone. Come in. Please, please, come in."

She began to tear up, to choke up, at the end of her statement. There were a lot of questions, which she answered, as best she could, and when the reporters began to repeat the questions, Virgil tried to end the conference.

Failed for a few minutes: a TV guy asked, "Is there any indication that this stone itself may be influencing the way Reverend Jones is thinking? Tag Bauer, the well-known archaeologist, says that these artifacts can be extremely psychically powerful and that Reverend Jones may no longer be in control of his own actions. That he may somehow be possessed by it."

Ignace slapped a hand to his forehead with an audible w*hap*.

Virgil said, "Ah . . . we think Reverend Jones is quite ill. We do think that he's in control, however."

Another reporter asked, "When you briefly had custody of the stone . . . did you notice any unusual effects from it? Did it glow, was it warmer than it should have been? Did the writing seem unusual in any way? Professor Sewickey said that with artifacts of great power, the writing sometimes changes."

Ignace turned in his seat and said, "It's a rock, you fuckin' moron," loud enough to be picked up by the microphones.

Virgil said, "No, I didn't notice anything like that. I've got to end this now, because we've got a lot of work to do. To reiterate, we need Reverend Jones to call us—either me, or his daughter."

He stepped back and one of the TV cameramen, a large man in a Sturgis T-shirt, said to Ignace, "You fuck up my tape one more time, and I'll pull your little fuckin' head off like a radish out of—"

He didn't get to finish it, because Ignace—not a tall man, but thick—dropped his notebook and went straight for his throat and the two of them tumbled through a rank of folding chairs amid screaming TV women and fast-moving cameramen still running their machines. The cameraman was on the bottom, and while he was much larger, Virgil saw Ignace land a really terrific right hand to the eye, and then another one, just before the Rochester cops got there and separated them.

Ignace, who as a child had fought in the 152-pound class in the Philadelphia Golden Gloves, gave Virgil a thumbs-up, and Virgil got Ellen and they went out the back door.

VIRGIL PLANNED to take Ellen to her home in the Cities, partly because it was the right thing to do, and partly because it would give him a lot of time to work on her head, on the chance that she'd tell him where her father was. They'd just started on the way when the day-watch duty officer called and said, "You wanted to know where that iPhone is?"

"Very much."

"It's at a McDonald's at the southeast corner of 14 and 169," he said. "We just got through the rigmarole with Apple, and we picked it up right away."

"On the way," Virgil said.

Ellen, who was sitting beside him, said, "I want to be there when you pick him up. He needs to go to the hospital now, and we need to get this stele out of our hair."

"Right," Virgil said. "And maybe he won't shoot me if you're there."

When they got to the McDonald's, there was no Jones to be found. The duty officer, however, said that he could see the phone location flashing on his computer screen. Virgil found the assistant manager, and asked him to dump the single external trash can. The assistant manager wasn't happy about it, but he did it, and after a couple of minutes of probing, Virgil came up with the phone.

"So he was here," he said to Ellen.

"He had a fondness for junk food, and after he got sick, he saw no reason not to eat it," she said.

"I have a friend who says he hopes that when he gets old, he contracts some painless but fatal disease, so he can get in a couple of years of smoking before he dies. He quit smoking for his health, but still wants them," Virgil said. "Makes sense to me."

THEY WERE halfway back to Ellen's place when Jones called, on Virgil's phone.

"I'd give up the stone in a minute in exchange for Ellen—but since I don't have to now, I won't," he said. "It'll all be over by to-morrow night, and I'll turn myself in."

"They're going to kill you," Virgil said, "unless you shoot first and kill somebody else. Is the stone worth killing somebody for? Or dying for?"

"Of course not—and that's not what's going to happen. This Tal woman . . . Did you figure out that it was her?"

"Yeah, we think so," Virgil said. "We think she might be look-ing for you."

"I think she might have been tracking me through that cell phone I had," Jones said. "I threw it in a trash can at a McDon-ald's. You don't have to bother looking for it."

"Are you at the hideout now?" Virgil asked.

"No, no, right now I'm out driving around, in case you can track this call. As soon as I'm done, I'll pop the battery out and go hide where you can't find me."

"Man, you gotta—"

"I don't gotta do anything, except die," Jones said. "Is Ellen still with you? Could I talk to her?"

"Hang on."

Virgil gave Ellen the phone, and Ellen shouted at him for a minute or so, and called him an asshole, and asked him where his principles were, and then told him she loved him and they hung up.

"I want you back in the Twin Cities, and I'm going to send somebody to your house to make sure you stay there, and that your old man isn't hiding out there. I want you somewhere safe."

"Don't hurt him," she said.

When they got to Ellen's house, Virgil pulled the tracker off her car. She was miffed: "You've been tracking me like some kind of criminal?"

"Ellen, you've *been* some kind of criminal. I've been overlooking that. Now, go inside, eat something healthy, get some sleep."

"Tell you what else," she said. "I've got my ex-husband's .22. I'm going to keep it right by my bed."

SINCE HE WAS in the Cities anyway, Virgil called Davenport: "Just wanted to see if you know anything I don't."

"All kinds of things, but one is relevant," Davenport said. "That is, I managed to pry loose another one of those trackers. You want it?"

"Yes."

"I gotta go out, but it'll be on my desk."

Virgil picked up the new GPS unit, bought some candy at the candy machine, talked to the fingerprint specialist about Zahavi's fingerprints from the gun—they'd gotten no return from anyone—and drove back to Mankato, to his house. He got a bowl of fruit and sprawled on his bed, the better to think about it, since that had worked so well the last time he'd tried it.

Three bidders: the Hezbollah, Tag Bauer, and the Turks. Plus three non-bidders, who were nevertheless pursuers: Tal Zahavi, Sewickey, and Yael Aronov. One outside interest, with unknown involvement: Ma Nobles, who Virgil thought had taken Jones out of the hospital.

The Turks were out of it, so if the deal was going down that night, it had to be with the Hezbollah, or with Bauer. Everybody else was probably out of it—or, at least, nobody else would be invited to attend.

Except, perhaps, Ma Nobles. Where was she in all of this?

Virgil thought about it for a moment, but didn't have anything to work with: she was an absolute wild card.

So: Bauer and the Hezbollah.

He picked up the phone and called Awad. "Can you talk?"

"I don't think I will be able to attend tonight—I have a sickness."

"He's listening to you?"

"Something I ate . . . Yes, it's a bad situation. I will try to do better."

"Can you sneak out and call me?"

"I think so. It's only a short-time problem. I will get better."

"Call as soon as you can," Virgil said.

VIRGIL GOT OFF the bed and headed downtown, to the Holiday Inn, and knocked on Sewickey's door. Sewickey didn't answer, which worried Virgil, given Sewickey's track record. He went down to the front desk, and the woman there said she'd seen Sewickey on foot, headed across the street toward the Duck Inn.

Virgil found Sewickey sitting on a bar stool, with a beer, talking with the bartender. Virgil got on the next stool down and ordered Heineken, since they didn't have Leinie's.

"You got any idea what kind of car Bauer is driving?" Virgil asked.

"Give you one guess," Sewickey said.

"Don't make me guess, just tell me," Virgil said.

"He's got *The Drifter* yacht, he's got *The Wanderer* airplane, so he's got to have a . . ."

The bartender, who'd been listening in, slid the Heineken down to Virgil and asked, "He's got a yacht, he's got a plane—can I play?"

"Go ahead," Sewickey said.

"Gotta be a Range Rover."

Sewickey pointed a finger at him and said, "Bingo."

Virgil said, "I was gonna say that."

"It's a white Range Rover, the new model, which, if I do say so myself, is still a pig," Sewickey said.

"Like you wouldn't want one," Virgil said.

"I really wouldn't," Sewickey said with a semblance of sincerity. "I'd take the Lexus GX if somebody offered me one, but the Caddy is fine. If I could find the right set, I'd like to weld a couple of nice longhorns to the hood, but that's about the only change I'd like."

"No itch for a horse trailer?"

"Horses don't like me," Sewickey said. "But that's okay, because I don't like them back. Though I did have a fairly good horseburger once, in Ljubljana."

"Fuckin' French," the bartender said.

"Ljubljana is in Slovenia," Sewickey said. "Had some really terrific horseradish mustard with it, too. It was one of those build-your-own horseburgers."

"Fuckin' Slovenians."

Virgil finished his beer and said, "I gotta run."

"I'll have another six or eight," Sewickey said, and the bartender said, "Attaboy." Sewickey asked, "Any idea of when we'll know about the stone?"

"Rumor is, the sale takes place tomorrow night, unless somebody is lying to me."

VIRGIL WENT back out into the heat, hitched up his pants, looked both ways, walked back to his truck, and drove to the Downtown

Inn, where he saw Bauer's Range Rover in the parking lot. Sticking the tracker to it was a matter of one minute, and then he was back in the truck.

Where was Awad?

Then Awad called and said, "I am going to the store to get potato chips. But: we must talk, face-to-face. I have found out something most important, for everybody."

"Tell me."

"Not on these phones. Who knows who listens?"

"Then let's meet. Now. I'm not doing anything."

"This afternoon, I fly. Let us meet at the airport, at four o'clock. You go there first, so if they follow me, they don't see you arrive. Now, I have to hurry back so I am not suspected. I tell them, ten minutes for these chips and soda water."

"Four o'clock," Virgil said. And after Awad was gone, thought, *Them?*

VIRGIL SAT in the truck for a couple of minutes—nothing to do, really—and thought about Ma. Since he *didn't* have anything better to do, and since Ma was the wild card, playing a game he didn't understand, maybe he could put some pressure on her.

He was about to head out to her farm, when he took a call from Yael Aronov: "I am at this Sam's Club. You should come here quickly."

"Jones is there?"

"No, not Jones. Is a woman I know from Israel. She is shopping. I do not know her, exactly, but I recognize her. She is the daughter of Moshe Gefen, who was the most famous paleographer in Israel. This cannot be a coincidence."

Virgil turned the truck around and headed for Sam's Club, while Yael explained that a paleographer studied ancient writing.

"So she would have an interest in the stone," Virgil said.

"Well—I don't know her, I have only seen her at picnics, but I believe she is involved in high tech. Computer programming. As far as I know, she has no interest in paleography herself."

"Maybe she's here for her father—but you said he *was* the most famous."

"He died six or seven months ago. Sometime like that. This was a big event in the archaeology circles. He was a winner of the Israel Prize, he was world famous in Jerusalem. But I tell you, if he were still alive, he would be the one chosen to lead the study of the stele."

"But if she's not a whatchamacallit, why is she here?" Virgil asked.

"Not for the shopping, I think," Yael said. "But the answer . . . we have to ask her."

Another bidder? Virgil wondered.

The woman's name was Yuli Gefen, and when Virgil got to Sam's Club, and managed to badge himself past the bulldog guard at the door, she was not to be found. In fact, he had to call Yael just to find *her* in the cavernous store.

"I'm sorry," she said, when they finally got together next to a pallet of generic toilet paper, "I didn't want her to see me, so I kept hiding, and then, once, I couldn't find her again."

"Maybe she saw you," Virgil said.

"This is possible," Yael said. She stopped to gaze, apparently awestruck, at the mountain of toilet tissue. Then: "But it's also possible that she is still here. We could look for a week."

"So let's look some more," Virgil said.

They did, but Gefen was apparently gone.

VIRGIL CALLED ELLEN CASE, who answered but said, "I'm not sure I'm talking to you."

"Things haven't changed—they're just as bad as they were," Virgil said. "I have a question for you. Have you heard the name Moshe Gefen?"

"Moshe? Sure—he's my father's oldest friend in Israel. Actually, oldest friend, period. His wife was my mother's best friend, period. They were. They're both dead now. They died early."

"How did they know each other? Your parents and the Gefens?"

"They knew each other forever," Ellen said. "Dad was in Israel at the time of the 1967 war, they were both students. Dad was studying Hebrew, and Moshe was studying German, which Dad spoke pretty well, so they were teaching each other. Dad had this old Ford that he'd fixed up, and they'd drive all over the country. When the mobilization started for the war, they were way up by Lebanon, and Moshe had to get to his unit, which was all the way down at the other end of the country, near Beersheba. Dad drove him down, but when they got there, his whole unit had already moved south, so Dad drove south toward the Egyptian border. . . . He had a whole car full of soldiers. Moshe got to his unit—he was wounded a couple of days later—and Dad wound up driving Israeli soldiers all over the place. It was chaos for a while, the way they told it. Then when Moshe got wounded, Dad picked him up at a field hospital and drove him back to Beersheba, to another hospital. They've been friends all their lives, Dad and Moshe, Mom and Hannah. Hannah died, let me see, four or five years ago, of a lung disease. Probably from going to too many digs, you know, they breathe in all that dust."

Virgil said, "Okay."

"Why?"

Virgil hesitated for a moment, then asked, "Do you know Gefen's daughter? Yuli?"

"Yuli? Of course. She's a good friend," Ellen said. "She dug with us a couple times, when we were there for the summer. How do you know about Yuli?"

"Because she was here this afternoon. Shopping at Sam's Club."

Long silence. Then, "Yuli? Really? She never told me."

"Why would she be here, Ellen?"

"Well . . ."

"Who was going to get the money from your dad, if he manages to collect it?"

"I don't know. I thought he'd probably arranged something."

"That's what I think," Virgil said. "I think he arranged it with this Yuli. If you see her, or talk to her, tell her that I'm looking for her. If she tries to leave the country with that money, she better be doing a backstroke across the Rio Grande, because she ain't getting it out legally. If I catch her—"

"I know, I know, you'll put her in jail," Ellen said. "You're sort of a broken record about that, Virgil. Let me ask this: Why don't you let it go? Let Dad sell the stone. You've got photographs, and you say they're really good—who cares who gets the stone? Are you going to kill somebody to get it?"

"No, but I'm going to get it," Virgil said. "I had it, and it was stolen from me by your old man, who damn near burned down my boat. I'm pissed. That stone ain't going nowhere but in my back pocket."

"Good-bye, Virgil," she said, and hung up.

"You HAVE solved the mystery?" Yael asked.

"Yes. Goddamnit, this whole thing is rolling downhill, now. Yuli Gefen is the bagwoman on the deal—Jones gets the money, she takes it out of the country, and Jones dies. Nice, neat, and tidy. And it's going to happen soon. Or as soon as Gefen gets out of Sam's Club."

"What about the stele?"

"Oh, you'll get the stele," Virgil said. "I promise you that."

18

Virgil took a taxi to the Mankato airport, just in case: everybody in the mix now had probably seen his truck, and if Awad was nervous, Virgil thought he ought to honor that. He did take his pistol, and when he walked into the pilots' lounge, he found the same man who'd been worried when Virgil had taken his guns on Awad's training flight.

"What the hell are you guys up to?" the man asked.

Virgil asked, "You read the papers?"

"I watch TV."

"You know about this minister, Elijah Jones, that everybody is chasing around?"

"I saw it on Channel Three. Tag Bauer's looking for him."

"Well, that's what it's about," Virgil said. "I would appreciate it if you'd keep this to yourself. When I say appreciate it, I mean I won't sic Homeland Security on you."

"Hey—I'm outa here," the guy said. "I really don't want to know."

"Just for future reference, Raj Awad has got some pretty high-up friends in Washington," Virgil said to his back.

"Got it." And the man was gone.

VIRGIL FOUND about four dozen various airplane magazines to read while he waited, but wasn't much interested in anything that didn't have either floats or skis. He did find an article about the rehabbing of Beavers and Otters, and that kept him occupied until Awad showed up.

Awad came in fast, hot, and stressed. "Virgil," he said. "I have news, but I do not know if it is good or bad. Or who it is good or bad for."

"Take it easy. Just lay it out," Virgil said.

"There is a man from Lebanon, but really, he is from Iran. Al-Lubnani tells me about him, because al-Lubnani is very, very worried. This man will deliver the money for the stone. The money comes through the Lebanese mission to the United Nations, sent here in the diplomatic bag. You understand this?"

"Sure. Nobody gets to look in the bag, except the mission staff. No customs, no nothing."

"This money is in hundred-dollar bills—three million dollars, which is Jones's asking price," Awad said. "But this is not important."

"It's not? Three million in cash isn't important?"

Awad wagged a finger at him. "Not important. What is important is the man who brings it. His real name is Soroush Kazemi.

He is an Iranian, but he pretends to be a Lebanese. He is known as
'the Hatchet' in this world."

"That's another bad sign," Virgil said.

"He came to my apartment to speak to al-Lubnani and myself. This is why I could not speak to you—the Hatchet was on
my couch." A wrinkle appeared in Awad's forehead. "He was not
exactly what I expected. He was very nervous. He sweated very
much."

"If he's from Iran, he's got reason to sweat," Virgil said.

"But here is the next important thing," Awad said. "Al-Lubnani,
who is very, very . . . very . . ."

"Worried."

"Yes. He says he does not know why Kazemi would come to
America. He must be here illegally, and he must be here to do no
good. The Hatchet only does no good. The Americans know all
about him, but they do not know he is here. If they find out he is
here, they will put one hundred agents on him, and carry him
down to the basement at the CIA, to where they keep the electri-
cal apparatus."

"We don't really do that," Virgil said.

Awad sighed and looked up at the ceiling, as if praying for pa-
tience. "Virgil, my friend, we will talk about this some other time.
But believe me, the American security agents would do anything
to get their hands on the Hatchet. The problem is, if he is taken
before he delivers the money, the controllers in Beirut will suspect
al-Lubnani or I. Even if they do not believe we betray him, they
will kill us, you know, just . . . mmmm."

"Just in case," Virgil said.

"Exactly. So we make a deal with you. We provide you details on where the Hatchet is, and you let the money through, and then follow him and arrest him far from here. We think he is coming from Washington, D.C., so maybe he has a ring there. This could be, very, very . . . very . . ."

"Important."

"Yes."

"Why are you telling me this?" Virgil asked. "You could have let this guy come and go."

Awad was shaking his head. "The big fear is, he will be caught, and he will be traced, every step of his time in the U.S. And then they trace him to an innocent Lebanese air pilot, who is taken down to the basement at the CIA—"

"Where they connect wires to your much valued testicles."

"That is the one problem. The two problem is, the Hatchet erases the pilot to eliminate any trace of his, the Hatchet's, arrival here."

Virgil stood up and put the Beaver/Otter magazine under his arm, intending to steal it. It was an old issue anyway. "You stay in close touch with me. As far as I know, this guy is the next Osama bin Laden—or he might be Father Christmas, and you're running some kind of hustle on me."

"I don't know this word, hustle," Awad said.

"You're trying to fool me," Virgil said.

"No, no, no, not ever," Awad said, making a wide-arm gesture like an umpire calling a runner safe at the plate. "I would never fool Virgil."

"Stay very, very much in touch, then," Virgil said. "Very. I will try to work something out. I'll call somebody, and see what they say."

He took a cab back to his truck, in town, called Davenport, who said, "'The Hatchet'? You gotta be shittin' me."

"Look, all I want to do is get to the bottom of Ma Nobles's lumber scheme," Virgil said. "I don't know about the Hatchet and I never did find out anything about the nut-cutting Turk. All I want is a phone number."

"I'll get back to you."

"Soon?"

"Five minutes," Davenport said.

More like fifteen minutes, but Davenport said, "I've got a number for you. This is going to sound weird, but the man on the other end will say, 'This is the colonel,' and that's all he'll say. You tell him about this Hatchet, and answer any questions he has, and then you eat the paper with the phone number on it, flush three times the next time you use the toilet, and then shoot yourself."

"Okay," Virgil said. "Who is this joker?"

"More asshole games from Washington," Davenport said. "You know how they are. Anyway, play along. We need the federal grants."

Virgil called the number, and a man picked up on the first ring and said, "This is the colonel."

Virgil said, "This is Virgil Flowers, I'm an agent with the Minnesota Bureau of Criminal Apprehension. A tall, good-looking blond guy, sort of a chick magnet, often compared to a younger Robert Redford. I was told to call you."

"You think you're auditioning for a comedy show?" the colonel asked.

"Maybe I got the wrong guy," Virgil said. "If you know the right guy, I need to talk to him about an Iranian citizen we've got coming in here. A Soroush Kazemi, aka the Hatchet, supposedly a big operator for the al-Quds Revolutionary Guard, now operating out of Beirut. He's got a bag with three million bucks in it, that came into the country in a diplomatic pouch through the Lebanese mission to the UN. He should be coming into Mankato, Minnesota, tonight. I've got contacts who'll give him up. If you're interested, or know somebody who is, give me a ring."

The silence was so long that Virgil thought that the colonel had either hung up or gone to sleep. "Colonel?"

"You were a major in the marines, served in Iraq."

"I was a captain in the army, and served in Bosnia."

"Somebody will call," the colonel said. "Sit right there in your 4Runner. Do not even walk across the street to the McDonald's. Sit right there."

Then he was gone, and Virgil looked uncomfortably across the street at the McDonald's and said, "Well, that was weird," and then, "They can't tell a man not to have a cheeseburger. Not in a free country."

So he went over to the McDonald's, got a Quarter Pounder

with Cheese, fries, and a strawberry shake, and carried them back to his truck. He'd finished the sandwich, the fries, and was sucking the last bit of the shake out of the bottom of the cup, when his phone rang.

"Flowers?" A different voice, with a Texas twang to it.

"Yes."

"Do you have a reliability score on your information?"

"Huh. I didn't really try to score it, but I'd say it's way better than fifty-fifty. My source has actually talked to the guy. I think the two guys who are getting the money are working some kind of hustle—probably planning to take off with it, and they don't want the Hatchet guy to come after them."

"Please don't use any specific names in this conversation. So you think it's better than fifty-fifty. I assume it has to do with this missing Solomon stone."

"Yes. The money is to buy the stone."

"And your contacts specifically identified the courier as the name you gave the colonel."

"Yes. And since one of my contacts is a member of a party of the highest kind—that's a hint—I think he knows what he's talking about."

"Hmm. All right, I understand that. The team leaders will see you in three hours at the Rochester airport. Be there."

Virgil said, "Before you go, give me a score on this incoming guy. You know, one to ten, ten being the highest."

"Eleven," the voice said. "Maybe thirteen. Three hours. Be there."

VIRGIL WENT HOME, cleaned up, put on a vintage burnt-orange Weezer T-shirt and a blue-black linen sport coat over his usual jeans and cowboy boots. With his straw hat and aviators, he thought, he should be able to hold his own with any stiff from D.C.

Before he left, he checked his tracker monitor to see where Tag Bauer was. The tracker put him either at the South Central College or the KEYC studio in North Mankato. Either was okay with Virgil.

Ma Nobles called as he was walking out to the truck: "Hot day," she said.

"Do you know where Jones is?"

"Why do you have to ruin a social call by asking something like that?" she asked.

"Because it's the only thing I can think about right now, no matter how hot it is," Virgil said.

"I just called to tell you I was heading out to the swimming hole, and thought you might like to come along."

Virgil said, "I can't. Believe it or not, some of us have to work."

"Working out my way?"

"No, I'm headed over to Rochester." Then he wanted to bite his tongue: no reason to tell her that she was free to run wild, with him out of the picture.

But she didn't seem to notice. "Be that way—but I'll be out there, in case you get a break from all that hard labor."

"Take a gun in case you run into any crazy rednecks out in the woods," Virgil said. "Oh wait—you *are* a crazy redneck."

"You are not advancing your cause, here, Virgil," she said. "I just may call Tag and see if he needs a swim."

"He can't go either. He's sitting in a TV studio and his makeup isn't waterproof," Virgil said. "But I'll be seeing more of you, real soon, Ma."

"I'll be holding my breath," she said, and hung up.

So much for intimidation.

Virgil had driven the highway to Rochester so many times that he tended to fall asleep at the wheel. On this day, though, he had too much to think about. Awad and al-Lubnani didn't have to know about the Washington team. If Awad and al-Lubnani were actually planning to rip off the Hezbollah's money, and he thought that likely, then he should be able to figure a way to blackmail them into telling him the exchange point, using the Hatchet as a sword hanging over their heads.

"I'll go on TV," he'd tell them, "and say you guys stole the money. Who's Hezbollah going to believe—the guys who disappeared with three million in cash, or a cop? But give me the stone, and I'll tell everybody that Jones got the money, and I'll tell Washington about the Hatchet, and no matter what happens then, he'll no longer be a factor."

Somewhere in that whole mix of threat and promise, he should be able to land the stele.

THE GULFSTREAM JET came into the fixed-based operator at Rochester, and after parking, dropped a ramp to the tarmac and a woman and two men got off. All three of them had tight skin of the kind you get by hanging around in deserts, all three of them appeared to be in their middle-to-late thirties, but generally looked like associate professors who happened to be in great physical condition. All three carried briefcases, and all three were packing guns, although they were discreetly out of sight beneath their jackets.

They spotted Virgil as the odd-man waiting, and the woman led the group over and asked, "Flowers?"

"Yes, ma'am."

She took in his T-shirt with neither a blink nor a question, offered her hand and introduced herself as Rose Lincoln. The two men were introduced as Tom Hartley and Wesley Moehl, and Virgil said, "My truck is out front."

"We should have two vehicles waiting for us," Lincoln said. "But we need to debrief you before we head over to Mankato. This FBO has a conference room."

"Let me get my briefcase," Virgil said, not wanting to be outgunned.

IN THE CONFERENCE ROOM, when Virgil arrived, the two men were sitting on one side of the table, and the woman on the other, all three with their chairs turned toward the head of the table and an empty chair. Virgil took it.

The woman had a thin stack of paper in front of her, and was flipping through it. When Virgil sat down, Lincoln said, "You're not exactly a virgin in this sort of stuff—you're the guy who shot up those Vietnamese agents a couple years ago."

"Yes, ma'am."

"And arrested a couple of high-level Homeland Security offi-cials for conspiracy to commit murder, which got your governor on every TV station in the country," said Hartley.

"Yes, sir, that's correct," Virgil said. "But the charges didn't stick. They were guilty, but the Department of Justice kicked it under the rug."

"I can tell you, for your own information, that those guys now have offices near the cafeteria at Homeland Security, where they spend their days making sure that nobody gets issued more waste-baskets than the regulations allow," Moehl said.

"I'm happy to hear that," Virgil said. "They weren't only dumb, they amplified their stupidity with their arrogance."

Lincoln said, "Hmm," and then, "The DEA likes you. They've talked about recruiting you for a fairly hot job."

"Yeah, I've chatted with a couple of their guys. The only prob-lem with their job is, I'd get killed."

"But you'd be paid well until then," Moehl said.

"True, but I've got a boat, and all the fishing and hunting equip-ment that I need. What would I use the rest of the money for?"

They all examined him for a moment, then Lincoln nodded and said, in a flat voice, "Tell us why we're here."

"Okay," Virgil said. "You have quite a bit of information about me in your computers, there, so you know I'm reasonably reli-able. Let me ask this: Are there more than three people assigned to this?"

Lincoln showed a tiny sliver of a smile. "You were in the army.

I'm the equivalent of a lieutenant colonel. I run the equivalent of a battalion. The battalion's being mobilized."

"You didn't say exactly who you're with," Virgil said.

"That's right," she said. "I didn't. Now: tell me what you've got."

So Virgil told the whole story, starting with the stone: about Jones, Zahavi, Aronov, the Turks, Sewickey, Tag Bauer, the Hezbollah contingent, and about Ma. All three of them took notes in the thickest laptops he'd ever seen, and every once in a while, made comments to each other that indicated that they were hooked into some kind of real-time research network.

When he told them about the Turks, and about the nut-cutter, Lincoln tapped a few keys and then said, "That could be true. The Partiya Karkerên Kurdistan seems to have a price on his head. They're offering a hundred thousand American dollars to anyone who brings it to them—the head. The rest of the body is not required."

"The party . . ." Virgil began.

"PKK—the Kurdistan Workers' Party," Lincoln said, without looking at her laptop screen. "But the Turks are gone, correct? We show them flying out of Kennedy International two days ago. Now, about this Ma Nobles. How does she fit in?"

"She sells this fake barn lumber," Virgil began, and by the time he was finished, he realized he sounded crazy. He said so. "But what can I tell you? I think she's got some kind of relationship with Jones."

"She's no dummy," Lincoln said. "According to her junior high records, she has a tested IQ of 151."

"Ma?" Virgil was dumbfounded.

"Uh-huh. So watch yourself. Now. Tell us more about al-Lubnani and Faraj Awad."

HE OUTLINED his relationship with the two men, and concluded by saying, "I think they've got an eye on all that money. Both of them seem to be pretty decent guys, other than that. Awad would just like to fly airplanes and get laid—he even made a weak pass at Zahavi, the Israeli agent. I don't think he plans to fly a plane into a building, or anything like that. He has a healthy fear of pain and death. He's afraid that you're going to take him down in the CIA basement and attach electric wires to his testicles."

Lincoln shook her head: "We'd never do that on-site."

Virgil suspected she was joking, but couldn't tell for sure.

He said, "So this is what *I* want. And with all due respect, you should listen to me, because, to tell the truth, the governor and I are asshole buddies, and if you don't want to get dragged kicking and screaming in front of the TV cameras by some large highway patrolmen . . ."

Lincoln shook her head. "Never happen. I'd never scream, no matter where I was being dragged."

And Moehl said, "We don't need threats. Just tell us what you want."

Virgil said, "You guys are a lot smarter than those Homeland Security people."

Hartley said, "We know. What do you want?"

Virgil laid it out: he needed to get the stele, so he could return it to Israel. He had no interest in arresting, or getting credit for the arrest of, the Hatchet. He wanted his relationship with Awad and al-Lubnani respected, although he understood that they'd have to be questioned by the feds—by *some* feds, anyway.

And he wanted the Hatchet taken down after the exchange for the stone, and at a long enough interval both in time and distance that Awad and al-Lubnani wouldn't be suspected of treachery.

Lincoln had been rolling a pen around in her fingers as Virgil spoke, and when he was done, she said, "What you've just outlined is what we've already decided to do, although we may put a wee bit more pressure on the Hezbollah guys than you're talking about. But, we're neither lawyers nor publicity seekers, and if they are what they say they are, we'll cut them loose without damage. If you can put us on Soroush Kazemi, we won't take him down until we've uncovered every single contact he has here in the States—could be weeks before we do that, unless he tries to run for it."

"Sounds good to me," Virgil said. "Oh, there is one thing more, since you guys have files on everybody. I'd like to see your file on Tag Bauer. I don't need anything top secret, I'd just like to see whatever you can give me."

Lincoln looked at him for a moment, then looked down at her computer, typed for a while, then said, "You've got it, check your e-mail. I stripped out the government sources for the information, but the information itself is good."

Virgil nodded. "Thanks."

Hartley said, "Now. To reiterate. You say that when you first heard about this stele . . ."

And Virgil had to tell the whole story all over again, with the three of them picking at the details. When they were done, Virgil asked, "What do you want me to do now?"

"Nothing," Lincoln said. "Keep looking for the stele, but don't do anything about Kazemi. His people will be talking to Awad and al-Lubnani, so he'll know all about you. If you act like you know he's out there, he'll figure it out. So: do nothing."

"All right, but if I bump into him . . ."

"Keep your powder dry," said Hartley. "He is a genuine, hard-core killer."

Lincoln stood up, dug in her briefcase, took out what looked like a very large, old-fashioned cell phone and a wall charger. "Turn it on, keep it with you, and keep it charged. It'll hold a charge for four days with normal use. It'll work anywhere. If you need us, push one. If we need you, it'll ring like a phone. Do not hesitate to call."

"I can do that," Virgil said, and they all started packing their briefcases.

"It's hot here," Moehl said conversationally, as they walked out of the FBO's building. "I didn't expect that."

"Gonna be a real scorcher tomorrow," Virgil said, looking up at the sky. "Ninety-five degrees, ninety percent humidity, fifty percent chance of thunderstorms in the afternoon. Could get a tornado."

Hartley asked, "You play the guitar?"

"Not so much," Virgil said. "Why?"

"'Cause Weezer was always, you know, so heavy into guitars. I thought maybe you were a picker."

"No, no, but I'm glad to know our spies are familiar with Weezer," Virgil said. "Makes you seem more human, and less reptile-like."

"Saw them a couple of times in L.A., back in the nineties, before I joined the Corps," Hartley said. He took out a pair of oversized Beverly Hills sunglasses as they walked out to the parking lot and put them on. "I liked them, okay, but they were always a little too . . . mainstream, I guess you'd say. Though I suppose if you're a cop, you'd wear a mainstream band T-shirt."

Virgil, though insulted to the core of his being, covered up and said, "I know what you're saying."

Lincoln asked, "So, you know Tag Bauer personally?"

19

Ma Nobles drove along the back road, not quite sure that she had it right, until she saw the "Sawyer Pottery" sign on the left side of the road, with a gravel driveway climbing up a low hill into an old, poorly maintained pine plantation.

At the top of the hill, she found a red-cedar-and-glass house, wrapped with a walkway at the second level. Visible out back were a gray wooden shed, built of boards that she could sell in thirty seconds, if she could get them to western Massachusetts; a garage; and farther away, a low, wide structure that looked a little like a yurt. She wouldn't have known what it was, except for a sign in a pathway that said, "To Wood Kiln."

She got out of the truck, and as she did, she heard a glass door sliding back, and then Jones came out on the balcony and said, "The door is open."

She went inside, and found Jones standing at the top of a short stairway. "Please come up," he said. "I'm too weak to go up and down too much."

"Nice place," Ma said, as she climbed the stairs and followed Jones to a sitting area. He dropped on a couch, and she took an easy chair.

"Yes. It's charming. Maybe a little too charming. But then, they're charming people," Jones said. "They would be somewhat unhappy if they knew I was here."

"Where are they?"

"England. Supposedly studying pottery," Jones said. "Maybe they are, and maybe they aren't, but I'll tell you what—they'll write it off."

"I brought the food," she said.

"Do you know where Flowers is?"

"He said he had to go to Rochester—I don't know what for."

"You believe him?"

"I asked him if he'd like to come over and go skinny-dipping, and he said he had to work. I know he likes to skinny-dip, so . . . I believe him. Hasn't called me today."

"Hmm. If I were younger, and not a minister, and not married, and not dying . . . anyway . . ."

"He would never find this place," Ma said. "I could hardly find it myself, and I knew where it was."

"I know that—that's not why I wondered," Jones said. "The thing is, Florence, I need another favor from you, and having Flowers on his way to Rochester is perfect."

"What do you need?"

"My wife is in a home in St. Peter. I need somebody to drive me up there."

Ma looked at him, then shook her head. "Sir, everybody in the state is looking for you, and your picture is everywhere."

"Yes, they know exactly what I look like. That's why I need another favor."

"Another one?"

"I need you to cut my hair. I can shave myself, but I can't cut the hair."

AFTER THE CONVERSATION with the spies, Virgil drove to the Rochester convention center, called Davenport on a hardwired phone, and filled him in. "I'm not sure I was supposed to tell you any of this, because I was sworn to absolute secrecy, but I want somebody at my back who knows what's going on."

"I got your back, but to tell you the truth, I'm confused as hell," Davenport said. "Assuming they take out this Hatchet guy, you've got the rest of it covered? The stele, the Israelis, the Hezbollah, this Bauer guy, and the Texan?"

"I'm not sure," Virgil said. "I'm trying to narrow things down—at this point, it seems to be coming down to the Hezbollah and Bauer. They seem to be the only ones with any money. If I get killed, pick up Ma Nobles and run her through the wringer. It's possible that she knows more than anybody about what's going on."

"You know I'd never second-guess you—"

"Yeah, right."

"But if it had been me," Davenport said, "I'd have sicced the

Iranian Hatchet man on the Turkish nut-cutter and called it a day."

VIRGIL HEADED HOME. When he was thirty miles out, he took a minute to check on Bauer's location: and his location was moving, out toward Ma's place. Nothing he could do about that—he was forty-five minutes away. Was it possible that Ma had Jones, and the exchange was about to happen?

He called Awad, who answered and said, "I can talk."

"What are the chances that an exchange could take place today, and that you're being cut out of the deal?"

"Do you know something?"

"I know nothing at all—that's my major problem," Virgil said.

"I don't think we're being cut out. Al-Lubnani talked to Jones— Jones called him—and al-Lubnani told him that the money was coming in cash, and Jones says, 'Good.'"

"All right. Stay in touch."

"What about that other thing we talked about?" Awad asked.

Meaning, the Hatchet.

"Don't even think about it," Virgil said. "This is no longer your responsibility. If you don't think about him, and al-Lubnani doesn't think about him, you'll be fine. If you think about him, this man will see it."

"I will not think, and will advise Mr. al-Lubnani to do the same."

"Is Mr. al-Lubnani there now?

"Yes."

"I need to talk with the two of you, together. It'll only take a minute," Virgil said.

"Come now. We will arrive at the laundry room on the first floor."

ON THE WAY INTO TOWN, Virgil had a stray thought: What if the stele was a bait, an artificial lure, so to speak, and Jones, who'd shown no reluctance to use a weapon, simply planned to hijack the money from both Bauer and al-Lubnani?

He'd keep the possibility in mind, but as he chewed on it, he decided that Jones probably was not doing that: in his own terms, it would seem unethical. The gunplay had all been in self-defense, which he would think of as ethically excusable.

But then, he *was* a thief, so his ethics, by definition, had to be somewhat flexible.

THE RIVERSIDE TRANSITIONAL CENTER looked like a small elementary school of yellow brick, with a flag circle out front, and two dozen cars in a narrow parking lot that was less than a third full.

Inside, the place was painted in colors meant to be cheery, and the bulletin boards were pinned with cartoons and felt animals and pictures of collies in pastures with fuzzy sheep.

"Place is like the waiting room for hell," Jones muttered as they went up the steps. He was using a cane he'd found in a closet at the pottery, and he needed it. It also worked as a disguise, because the athletic, bearded, long-haired Reverend Jones never used one.

Jones had always worn his hair preacher-long: not hippie long, but nothing like a military cut. Now you could see his pale scalp through Ma's buzz cut. And Jones had always worn a beard, and now Ma knew why. With the beard, he looked fierce, almost Old Testament warrior-like. Without it, he was a moonfaced man with a severely receding chin. The transformation was so complete that Ma could hardly keep from staring at him.

Inside, they went to a front desk, and Jones introduced himself as Clarence Haverford, Magda Jones's elder brother, "up from Iowa."

The cheerful woman led them into a locked dayroom, chatting cheerfully and filling them in on Magda. "She's very healthy, very cheerful, but she's not very aware of personalities or what's going on around her anymore. But always cheerful."

"She always was," Jones muttered. And then, "I bet you haven't seen that damn husband of hers around here. I've been reading about him."

"We don't talk about that. But I can tell you, we've got our eye out."

"Good," he said. "I'd like a few words with him myself. Or maybe not words. What I'd like to do is take this cane and shove it—"

"Clarence!" Ma said severely, as Jones turned toward her, and she thought she saw a twinkle in his eye. They were a good team.

————

THE DAYROOM was filled with people sitting in chairs, looking around, plus a couple of orderlies. That was it. People looking around, until an orderly walked up to a man and sniffed at him, and said, "Bob, we better go back to your room. You need to change."

"Change?"

Ma looked away.

Magda was sitting on a glider, gliding. She looked up and smiled when Jones and Ma walked up, and said, "Hi!" but there was no recognition in her eyes.

Jones got close and said, "Magda, how are you feeling?"

"I feel fine. Are you James?"

"I'm Elijah," Jones said.

"Where's Elijah?" Suddenly she looked frightened, and peered around the room, her smile disappearing. "Why don't they let me see him?"

Jones took her hand, and Ma suddenly realized she couldn't deal with it, and said, "I'll wait outside."

Jones looked at her, then nodded. "I'll only be a couple of minutes."

He was more like ten minutes, and Ma, looking through the glass plate in the locked dayroom door, saw him holding Magda's hand, talking gently with her, saw her shaking her head. But then the smile came back, and she began to talk. Jones listened to her for a minute or two, then said something to her, kissed her on the forehead, stood, kissed her again, and walked toward the door, looking reluctantly back. She was following him with her eyes, and he stopped and went back and kissed her on the lips, but she pulled away, as if shocked, and he kissed her on the forehead again, and then came through to the door.

Ma said, "I'm sorry."

"Yeah," Jones said, tears running down his moon face. "Tonight I'll pray to the Good Lord, and thank him for taking me with cancer."

Then Ma started to cry, and, leaning on each other, they went out the door.

VIRGIL MET al-Lubnani and Awad in the laundry room, and as Virgil had said, the conversation didn't take more than a couple of minutes. At the end of it, they all shook hands, and Virgil headed out to Ma's place, where his tracker said that Bauer's car was still parked. He was a few hundred yards out when a beat-up black Toyota pickup turned out of her driveway and headed toward him. As it passed, he recognized her oldest son, Rolf, at the wheel.

Virgil had been cooperating with the Blue Earth County sheriff's office on the lumber scam. He hadn't actually talked to Rolf, though he'd seen photos of him. On a hunch, he rolled past Ma's driveway—Bauer's Range Rover was parked in the side yard—and kept going until the black pickup was hidden in its own gravel dust. He made a quick three-point turn and went after it.

He was three hundred yards behind when the truck reached Highway 169, which paralleled the river as it turned north toward the Twin Cities. Virgil slowed as the pickup waited for a car to pass, hooked right onto the highway. Virgil drove to the intersection, thinking Rolf was probably going to Mankato—though he was taking a long way around—but then, a quarter mile down the highway, the pickup slowed, signaled a turn, and crossed over to a road on the other side, where it disappeared again.

Now Rolf was only a few hundred yards from the river. Virgil followed. The road down to the water dead-ended, but Rolf turned at the very end of it and disappeared again. An unmarked track? Virgil pulled to the side of the road, dug out his iPad, and looked at a satellite view of the area on Google Maps. As far as he could see, there was no track or other road extension. Rolf was right at the river.

Virgil drove on down, parked fifty yards out, got out, put his gun in the small of his back, and walked down to the end of the road.

The Toyota had been pulled off and parked in a notch in the riverside trees. Virgil found a path going back into the woods— more than a game trail, but less than a regular fisherman's access.

The problem was, the woods were so dense that if Ma's kid wanted to ambush him, he could. Virgil didn't think that was likely, because Ma's kids, those he'd met, seemed mellow enough. Still, he didn't know this one, and he really needed to see what was going on.

As he hesitated, the silence was broken by the sound of a gasoline engine, rough at first, then smoothing out, well down toward the river. Virgil plunged into the brush, moving quickly, but not trying to be especially quiet: he could still hear the engine, probably a gas generator, and nobody who was near it would hear

STORM FRONT   297

him coming. Two hundred yards in, he found that he was correct:
the kid had mounted an electric winch on a tree, and was using
the generator to run it. A steel cable ran down into the water,
where Rolf was standing, in hip boots. He was a muscular young
man, blond and round-faced like his mother, intent on the work.

As Virgil watched, a foot-thick stack of wire-bound boards sur-
faced, hooked up by the winch cable, and Rolf horsed them over
toward the shore. There, he threw the winch into neutral and
squatted to look at the boards. After he'd spent a couple of minutes scraping at them with a knife, he horsed them back out into
the river.

Not antique enough, Virgil thought. Not yet, anyway.

He thought about the possibilities, then eased back into the
trees. When he was a hundred yards back, he jogged the rest
of the way to his truck, turned it around, and headed back toward Ma's.

WHEN VIRGIL pulled into the yard, he got a quick flash of Ma's
face at a kitchen window, but she ducked away and Virgil thought,
Is Jones in there?

He walked up to the door and knocked once and then went
through and stood on the landing of the stairs that went down to
the basement and up to the kitchen, and called, "Anybody home?"

A moment later, Ma called, "Who's there?"

"Virgil. I thought we were going skinny-dipping."

Ma appeared at the top of the stairs, arms akimbo, and said,
"I'm entertaining."

"Well, hell, I'm happy to join in," Virgil said. "I'm a pretty good singer, actually."

Ma couldn't help herself, and smiled, and said, "I've got Tag Bauer on my couch."

"That's fine, Tag and I are old buddies," Virgil said, as he climbed the four steps up to her. She was wearing a cornflower blue linen blouse and white shorts, with flip-flops. "I was wondering, though, if you've got Elijah Jones under your bed?"

"I don't even know Reverend Jones—"

"C'mon, Ma, this is that fuckin' Flowers you're talking to." She backed into the kitchen, which smelled liked mashed potatoes and gravy, and maybe pie of some kind, and Vigil swerved around her and stuck his head into the kitchen and found Bauer sitting on the couch. His shoes, Virgil noted, were on and firmly tied, which meant that he hadn't gotten too comfortable. "How's it going, Tag?"

"Going fine," Bauer said, with a cheerful grin. "I'm thinking about leaving town, though."

"Not with the stele."

"I can't promise anything—I'd say that the recovery of the stone is something that we all are working toward."

Ma said, "Virgil—"

Virgil said, "Ma, Tag, let's sit down and have a little conference. I've been doing a lot of investigating and have things to report." He raised his voice and shouted, "And Reverend Jones, if you're up there, this is something you might want to hear, too."

There was no response, not even a squeaky board, and Ma said, "Virgil: he's not here."

"All right," Virgil said.

"So what'd you find out?" Bauer asked.

"I've been doing research, Tag, and I know a few things that I didn't know before," Virgil said. "You've got this urge to be a movie star, which is just fine with me and everybody else. And you've got some money—my best estimate is that when your father died, you probably inherited three or four million dollars. You spent a good piece of that on *The Wanderer* and *The Drifter* and so on. Then you've got that apartment out in the Hamptons, you pay on that time-share in Malibu, you rent a place in Paris."

"Cool," Ma said.

"You probably don't quite break even with your TV show, because they're so cheap about the travel money," Virgil said. "And there's a good chance that the show won't be renewed—there's been talk about *Bauer's Last Crusade* . . . and I figure you're probably down to your last million or so."

"They'll renew," Bauer said. "They know I could be on the History Channel in one second."

Ma: "If you're down to your last million . . . how're you gonna buy the stone?"

Virgil: "He can't."

"Well, poop," Ma said.

"This is all speculation," Bauer said. "I—"

Virgil cut him off. "Let me finish. The thing is, the information I've developed over the past day suggests that you've got no chance to win the auction, because you don't have enough ready money. Jones is dying, he's got no time to waste on promises, and Hezbollah is going to show up with three million dollars in hundred-dollar bills. He'll take it, if he has a chance. I've also found out exactly who we're dealing with. Now, you've got no chance to actually get the stone, but if you interfere with the deal, or if the Hezbollah guys think you're for real, they will kill you. And they won't be nice about it. They will cut your head off. I'm not exaggerating."

Ma and Bauer exchanged a quick glance, and Bauer said, "I'm sure there's a *little* exaggeration there—"

"No. There isn't. Ma knows me, and she knows I can be a pretty sincere guy. I'm telling you, they will kill you. They have a killer right here, on tap. I promise you, this is the truth."

Ma said to Bauer, "I think he's serious."

Virgil said to Ma, "And I've got some news for you, too. I know you're messing around with Jones. I haven't found out exactly why, yet. I know you're a little pinched for money, from time to time, but you've got that big red Ford, so you can't be too pinched. But Ma—I found out something in the last hour or so. I'm ready to let it go, but if you fuck with me on this Jones thing, your whole family is going to have a problem. I want you to know I'm serious about that, too. This is a threat, and I'll carry it out."

"What'd you find out?"

Virgil shook his head. "I won't tell you, but I give you my word: if you knew, and if you thought I'd act on it, you'd drop Jones like a hot potato."

"Something to do with Rolf?" Like she'd picked it right out of his brain.

"What do you think?"

So they all sat in a long quiet spot, and then Bauer said, "What should we do? Walk away? If we walk away, Jones will meet the Hezbollah someplace quiet, and you'll never see the money or Jones again."

"What I want is for you to go ahead with the auction, wherever you were planning to hold it. But I want you to tell me where it is—I'm going to bust it up. I want to grab the money, and Jones, and the stone, and the Hezbollah guys. If you go along with that, I'll tell the TV people that you, Tag, were instrumental in recovering the stone. I'll tell them that you were a hero. And Ma, I won't let you sell that fake lumber, I won't let you keep running that scam, but you go along with me, and I'll let bygones be bygones. You stop with this Jones bullshit, and I won't try to hang any old stuff on you or your kid."

They sat some more, then Bauer said, "I'll take your deal, but it really burns me up. Tell the TV people that I'm a hero? You know how long they'll remember that? About a nanosecond. But I don't see much choice. I don't want to get my head cut off."

"Where's the auction?" Virgil asked.

"I don't know yet. Jones said he'll call me tomorrow night at nine o'clock, and tell me where to meet him. He says it'll be a public place, and the other bidders will be there."

Ma said, "And I'll take the deal, though it's a bitter pill. I can't help you with Reverend Jones. I don't know where he is, but he wants me to back him up at the exchange. He's going to leave the stone for me, someplace, and call me at the last minute and tell me where. When he sees the money, I'm supposed to show up wherever it is, and flash the stone at them."

"That's . . . perfect," Virgil said. "You could drop the stone with me instead."

Ma shook her head. "Won't do it, Virgil. I won't leave the man hanging that way, with this killer. Now: I know he's going to do something tricky with the exchange, but he hasn't told me what it is. So what I will do is, I'll play my part. The money will be there, and I'll show up, with the stone, and if he's tricky enough, Reverend Jones will wind up with the money and you'll wind up with the Hezbollah and the stone. If he's not tricky enough to pull it off, then that's his problem, and you'll get all of it—Jones, the stone, and the money."

"You won't tell him that I'm going to bust it up?"

"No. I won't betray anybody," Ma said.

"Seems to me like you're betraying everybody," Bauer said.

She shook her head: "This is really starting to hurt me," she said.

Virgil sighed and said, "Ma, I really don't want to do that."

"Can't see how we can avoid it, now," she said. "We're all jammed up here."

"You really don't know where Jones is?"

"No," she lied, and steered Virgil in another direction. "I know where the red Volvo is, but I don't know where he is, or what he's driving now."

"Where's the Volvo?"

"Up in one of the Gustavus's parking lots."

"All right," Virgil said. "Now. Let's work through some details."

———

THEY WORKED through a plan for the next day. Bauer agreed that he would call Virgil with the exchange point as soon as he got it.

"You're not going to try to sneak up on me and take the stone away, when I get it, will you?" Ma asked.

"I'm not sure I could, out here in the countryside," Virgil said, but he didn't say yes or no.

"Think real hard about that, because I don't think you could, either. I'll make a whole bunch of stops, and if you jump me before I get the stone . . . I just won't show up at the auction, and the whole deal will fall through."

"I'll think hard about it," Virgil said.

When Virgil left, he looked back and saw a light go on, on the second floor. And he wondered, was Ma going up to the bedroom with Tag? Or was Jones up there, and now on his way down? Or what?

He watched for anyone looking out at him, then got in his truck, retrieved the extra GPS unit, stepped over to Ma's truck, and stuck it on the frame.

BACK AT THE HOUSE, Ma came down from the bathroom, paused on the landing to watch Virgil's taillights rolling out the driveway, then walked the rest of the way down and said to Bauer, "I don't know what to do. I'm stuck between two men."

"Take me," Bauer suggested.

"You're not in the running, sweetheart," Ma said. "I was talking about the Reverend Jones and Virgil."

"Flowers is pretty sweet on you," Bauer said. "That's obvious."

"I'm not sure of that, not at all," Ma said.

"Take my word for it: he is," Bauer said.

Ma sat on the arm of an easy chair. "So what do you think I should do?"

"Play it by ear. Get the stone from Jones, take it to the auction, like Virgil said. But meet me first. I've got a camera, we'll put it on a tripod. I want to handle the stone, show it off for the camera. That's all I need, and then I'll be happy."

"I guess I could do that," Ma said. "I don't see any harm in it."

20

Awad called: "Al-Lubnani just got a call from the Hatchet. He has just gone to a meeting now. He says he might be getting the money."

"Keep your head down," Virgil said. "This Hatchet sounds like a nutbag."

"I have thought to take myself out and get lost," Awad said.

"Do you have a favorite bar?"

"The Pigwhistle."

"Go there. Although, for a guy like you, it's a poor choice. No coeds at the Dog."

"As a man who knows these things, where should a man like myself go to meet women who will fornicate with me?"

"Ah, well, hmm, I'd try the Rooster Coop," Virgil said. "It's a cowboy bar. Don't tell them you're Lebanese—tell them you're part Apache. If a part-Apache can't get laid in the Rooster Coop, he can't get laid."

"I have cowboy boots," Awad offered.

"Then you're good," Virgil said. "But go to a drugstore first and pick up some protection. You don't want a bunch of little Apaches running around."

"I have many of those protections here in my apartment, which I buy, like you Americans say, just in case," Awad said. "I am going now."

Virgil got the double-secret phone from under the car seat, brushed some pizza crust crumbs off it, and pushed "1." Lincoln answered two seconds later: "Yes?"

"Al-Lubnani has gone to pick up the money from the Hatchet."

"We know. We're all over him. And Awad—we just heard you tell Awad to go to the Rooster Coop to get laid. That's fine. Now, you should just stay out of this."

"I'm starting to feel oppressed," Virgil said.

"That's your role in life," Lincoln said. "Go home." She hung up.

Is not, Virgil thought.

But he went home anyway, got online, read the news, thought about calling Ma, just for a social chat, but resisted the idea, and finally went out to the garage, turned on all the lights, climbed in his boat and began detailing the interior.

Virgil was a modestly tidy person, as much as most bachelors are, anyway, but he was serious about his boat. The last time he'd been musky fishing on Eagle Lake, up in Northwest Ontario, he'd hooked into a fish in the fifty-inch range. But the guide, who was not reasonably tidy, had left a net sitting on the front casting deck, and Virgil had stepped in it while fighting the fish. The guide, excited at seeing the fish, had pulled at the net handle and said, "Move your feet," and Virgil, feeling that he was losing his balance, looked down at the net and then tried to pick up both feet at once, doing a little dance, lost his focus on the fish, felt the line go slack, and then watched the fish dive away.

Both Virgil and the guide could see Virgil's bucktail hanging loose in the water, and the guide, standing there slack-jawed with the net in his hand, asked, "Why'd you do that? That was a nice fish."

Wouldn't have happened in Virgil's boat.

TAG BAUER opened the motel room door and found himself looking at a slender dark woman who he suspected was not a fan. "Can I help you?"

Tal Zahavi put her index finger against his chest and pushed him back into the room, looked around, then kicked the door closed with her foot. "I'm from Israel," she said. "I am looking for the Solomon stone."

Tag shook a finger at her: "Ah. Yes. The Mossad agent. I've heard about you."

"I would like to make you an offer."

Bauer interrupted: "How'd you find me?"

"I called a source . . . and got the make and license number of your car. There are not many hotels here—I drove around until I found it."

"How'd you find my room?"

"I paid a cleaning lady for the number," she said.

"Okay. So what's the offer?"

"I watched you on television and then I watched some of your TV shows on YouTube," Zahavi said. "From some of the shows it seems that you shoot your own video at times. You have your own camera?"

"Of a sort," Bauer said. "It's a small Panasonic, but it takes excellent video. Of course, the results are not as good as real movies, it's all handheld and so on."

"This Flowers will not help you obtain the stone," Zahavi said. "He is a liar and a sneak, and if he gets the stone, it will disappear into a police station and never come back out."

"He says all he wants to do is send it back to Israel."

"Yes, yes, with this Yael Aronov." Zahavi nodded. "She is a pest. I can tell you, hers are the wrong hands. This stone is a very powerful propaganda weapon, and it cannot fall into the wrong hands, even if they are Israeli."

"This is all very interesting, but I don't see how it impacts me, or my camera," Bauer said. He backed up and sat on the bed. "I'm actually thinking it might be time for me to get out of town . . . unless you can tell me why I shouldn't."

"I make you an offer. If you help me get the stone—if you provide information that will help me—I will help you make a movie about it. Here, in the U.S. And I will be able to provide further benefits, at a later date, in Israel. There are many things in Israel that would shine on your show. The copper scroll—"

"The treasure of the copper scroll . . ." Bauer said, his eyes narrowing at the thought.

"May be a myth," Zahavi said. "But, we could provide you many sources knowledgeable about the copper scroll—the greatest experts in the field—and access to the scroll itself."

"The scroll's in Jordan."

"We have resources in Amman," Zahavi said.

Bauer pushed himself back on the bed until his head was on a pillow, and thought about it. Zahavi leaned her butt against a bureau, crossed her arms, and let him think. Eventually she added, "Of course, you are free to decline, and we Israelis are free to decline access to our valuable archaeological country."

Bauer said, "First the carrot, then the stick." More thought, then, "I do have some information that could prove useful."

Zahavi smiled: "That makes me very happy."

"I'm not sure that I would want to be involved in the actual acquisition of the stone."

"You wouldn't have to be, if there's a way I could get it on my own."

"On the other hand," Bauer said, "I'm not sure I'd trust you to help me make the movie, once you got your hands on the stone, if I wasn't there to insist."

"When I make a deal, I honor it," Zahavi said.

"What else could you say?" Bauer asked.

"My organization has a reputation to uphold," she said. "When we promise to pay, we pay—otherwise, people would stop talking to us."

He mulled it over for a while, and eventually said, "Jones has had help in concealing both himself and the stone. A woman.

Flowers is working with this woman. Tonight, she agreed to help him recover it. I don't think she was telling the complete truth, but in any case, at some point tomorrow night, she will be alone with the stone. She doesn't have it yet, she'll have to pick it up somewhere. I wouldn't be surprised if Flowers has her under surveillance—or will have her under surveillance tomorrow."

"Why would this woman have the stone?"

"As I understand it, and I don't have the final details, the bidders will bring their money to the auction, which will be held in a public place. When Jones has seen the money and has accepted the bid, the woman will appear with the stone, and display it. Then Jones will be given the money, and Ma . . . and the woman will deliver the stone. Everybody will probably have guns."

"Do you have the money to win the bid?"

Bauer hesitated, but then thought, *Flowers knows anyway, and if Flowers knows, then the Mossad could know.* "No. I don't. I planned to show up in my truck, and put the headlights on Jones and the bidders. My camera will be mounted in the truck window, and I'll make movies of the exchange—I'll plead with Jones to give me the stone, so it can be saved for posterity. He won't, of course, but that's about all I got. I'd rather have the stone. Even temporarily."

"If you tell me about this woman, you could have the stone long enough to make a video."

Bauer chewed his lower lip, then said, "The exchange is tomorrow at nine o'clock at night. The woman will have to get the stone before then, maybe several hours before. I guess it's possible that she already has it. She has—"

He stopped suddenly, and Zahavi cocked her head: "What? Tell me."

"I've already made arrangements with her to see the stone, and maybe take a few pictures. Not film, just a quick photo."

"And who knows this?"

"Just me . . . and the woman, of course."

Zahavi smiled: "So we have it . . . unless Flowers is with her."

"No. She won't let him ride with her—because if she did, he'd just take the stone and the auction would be finished."

"But he could have her under surveillance."

"He could. But I can tell you something else that would be valuable to you. I found all of this out at the woman's house. I was talking to her when Flowers showed up, and he forced us to take a deal on giving up the stone. She was going to refuse, unless she got her way. And her way is, let the exchange take place, and then take the stone away from the high bidders. Flowers wasn't happy about it, but he agreed."

"Yes, yes, yes, but what is this valuable other thing?"

"He wants to make sure that when it all takes place, that he gets the right stone, and nobody tries to give him a fake. So he will have Yael Aronov with him tomorrow evening, to verify the stone. And since Aronov is Israeli, you may have some influence over her. If she could tell us where Flowers is, and whether he's directing a surveillance of this woman . . ."

"You'll have to give me the other woman's name eventually," Zahavi said.

"Sure, but not yet," Bauer said, crossing his arms over his chest. A signal that he'd taken a position, and wouldn't give it up.

"So," Zahavi said. "Do you know where Yael Aronov stays?"

"As a matter of fact, I do," Bauer said.

VIRGIL WAS still working on the boat, checking screws on the oarlocks, when Awad called, shouting over the sounds of a cowboy band. "I have an emergency. Al-Lubnani is at my apartment. He wishes to speak to me, but I do not wish to speak to him because I am very very very busy. I tell him to speak to you and he says he will."

"All right. I'll go there now," Virgil said.

"Thank you. Thank you, my friend. I go now."

"Good luck," Virgil said.

Al-Lubnani let Virgil into Awad's apartment and asked, "Do you wish a screwdriver?"

"Got a beer?"

"Alas, I do not," al-Lubnani said.

Virgil looked in the refrigerator, found a Pepsi, and he and al-Lubnani, carrying a screwdriver, moved to the couch and easy chair. Virgil put his feet on the coffee table and asked, "What happened?"

"I meet this Hatchet," al-Lubnani said, sipping at his drink. "He shows me the money. He has a pack for your back, and he opens it, and inside, it is filled with packets of dollars. One-hundred-dollar bills. Three hundred packets with one hundred bills in each packet. This is a very interesting sight."

"I bet it was," Virgil said. "Do you have it?"

"I do not. This is what he told me: when we have a rendezvous tomorrow, he will be my backup. He will go with me, but will not come exactly to the meeting. He will wait nearby. I am wondering, does he have a gun? Does he rob the meeting, to keep both the money and the stone? Will he shoot everybody, including me?"

"Good questions," Virgil said. "I will take these under advisement. Do you know where you are meeting?"

"Not yet. Jones will call me at nine o'clock tomorrow and tell me where to meet. I said, 'It is dark at nine o'clock,' and he said, 'That is why we wait until nine o'clock.'"

"Hmm."

"You say you take this under advisement. I ask you, are your arrangements . . . Is everything under control?"

"Yes. I believe we are watched even now."

Al-Lubnani looked at the ceiling. "CIA?"

"They won't tell me," Virgil said. "As far as I know, it could be Snow White and the Seven Dwarves."

"I wish I was in Paris," al-Lubnani said. "Instead, I am in a ridiculous Hollywood movie."

"Know how you feel, pal."

WHEN VIRGIL LEFT, he heard the door close behind him, but when he was thirty feet down the hall, heard it open again and turned and saw al-Lubnani coming after him.

"I forget to tell you," he said. "When I go to meet the Hatchet, I find him in a limo. You know these black limos, like they have in New York City? Towns, I think?"

"Town cars," Virgil said. "I know them."

"This town car has a driver and the Hatchet sits in the rear seat. But, as we are looking at the money, I see that the driver is listening to us. A window is between us, but I can see him listening. So I think the driver is not entirely a driver. I think he is with the Hatchet. Or, excuse me if this sounds crazy, it is possible that the Hatchet is very, very careful, and the man in the backseat is an actor, yes? He is an actor, and the driver is the Hatchet."

"Why do you think that?"

Al-Lubnani scratched his beard, thoroughly, then said, "I can't tell you this, except to say, I have lived in Beirut a long time, and there, you learn to know when something is wrong. There is a . . . wrongness. Is this a word?"

"I don't know, but I know what you mean," Virgil said. He scratched his own chin, thinking about it, then said, "I will also take this under advisement."

OUT IN THE TRUCK, he got the double-secret phone from under the seat and pushed "1."

Again, Lincoln answered in two seconds: "Yes?"

"Did you hear me talking to al-Lubnani?"

"No. We have his phones, but we don't yet have his apartment. We will remedy that as soon as we have the warrant, which should be at any minute."

"All right. Well, al-Lubnani didn't get the money, though he saw it. He says three hundred packets of ten thousand dollars each. The Hatchet kept it, and will turn it over to al-Lubnani tomorrow night, just before the exchange, which is set for nine o'clock."

"Yes." Lincoln's voice was neutral: Virgil couldn't tell whether that was new information or not.

"So, have you got the Hatchet covered?"

"We have the man who met al-Lubnani covered. We hope to confirm his identity tonight."

"Have you run a check on the limo driver?"

"Yes."

"Could you give me like five words on him? Local? Islamic or not? Where did they get the limo?"

"Local, Islamic. Name—you won't believe it, but I'll tell you anyway—is Max Kaar. Eleven years with the company."

"Anything else?"

"Yes. Keep your pretty little head out of this, Flowers. We've got it. Just get the stone, without interfering with the target, and everybody will be happy."

Pretty little head? It pissed him off.

WHILE VIRGIL was talking to al-Lubnani, Yael Aronov was sitting on her motel bed, pondering the possibilities. She had one moderately large suitcase that she'd bought herself, plus the two enormous suitcases she'd gotten from Tal Zahavi's room.

When she first saw them, she'd considered them an opportunity. Now, she wasn't so sure. Though she'd towed some pretty large suitcases through the green "nothing to declare" zone at Ben Gurion, these seemed excessive: maybe Zahavi, if she were truly with the Mossad, could have gotten away with it—perhaps she could have avoided customs altogether.

Yael might not be able to do that, with the elephant-sized bag.

Yael had just bought twenty iPad Minis at Sam's Club, and if she could get them back in Israel, she could make a hundred dollars each on them—and two thousand was a lot to risk, simply to pile more stuff in an enormous suitcase.

But the temptation was strong. She'd never been stopped at customs. . . .

Her contemplation of the bags was interrupted by a sharp rap on the door, a quick chink-chink-chink of a maid using a key. She was not a cop or a spy, so she didn't even think about her response: she went to the door and opened it.

A thin, dark-haired woman said in Hebrew, "I am Mossad," and pushed Yael back into her room.

Yael said, "Tal Zahavi—I have seen you on TV."

"Yes. That putz Flowers, I can't believe this," Zahavi said.

"But you kidnapped—"

"Borrowed her, for a few hours," Zahavi said. She saw the suitcases on the bed and said, "Those are my suitcases."

"Virgil said I should keep them, since . . . well, we're both Israelis," Yael said. "But I don't want them. What would I do with them?"

"I was planning to buy Fruit of the Loom underwear, which my uncle can sell in his store," Zahavi said.

Yael made a moue. "Not a bad idea," she conceded. "My brother kills for Fruit of the Loom. If your uncle runs a clothing store—"

Zahavi poked a finger at Yael: "So now, I require your aid. This is official business. Tomorrow night, the Hezbollah will purchase this stele, for as much as three million dollars in cash. We will stop this—but we can't outbid them, because we have no money. So, we will intercept the stone."

"You maybe, but not me," Yael said. "I do not work for the Mossad, and I will not. I am surprised that you still work for the Mossad, after this . . . borrowing of Ellen Case."

"You are not required to work with me, you are only required to tell me where this Flowers is. I have information that you will be with him tomorrow night as he attempts, also, to intercept the stone. I need to know where he is."

"And how do I do that?" Yael asked, her fists on her hips. "He will be there. I say, 'Excuse me, I have to make a telephone call to betray you?'"

"You say nothing. When he begins to chase the stone, when he knows where it is and who has it, you press my phone number on your telephone. You do not have to say anything: just call, and I will know he is chasing the stone."

"This is crazy," Yael said. Then, "Are you still on assignment? I would think that your superiors would have put you on a plane back to Tel Aviv when they saw the TV reports."

"This is not your business," Zahavi snapped. "The operation continues."

Yael said nothing, but the skeptical look on her face suggested that she didn't believe what Zahavi said.

Zahavi: "I was given unreliable support, who abandoned me the minute the trouble started. But I can still do this—"

"I don't *want* you to do it," Yael said. "I want to take the stele back to the IAA myself, so it can be properly examined."

"And so you can publish it and so the Arabs can make propaganda from it forever."

"I think you have been in the sun too long," Yael said. She added, "But, I am a good Israeli, and I will call you tomorrow night, if Virgil leaves me. But I will file a big complaint, a big stink, if you lose or destroy the stone, and I will not stop just because you are the Mossad and you say so. I will go to the newspapers, and we will have it out in public."

"I will not lose or destroy it—when the stone is back in Israel, this will all be arranged by our bosses. You will have to be content with that."

They talked for another couple of minutes, about the auction for the stone, and then exchanged phone numbers. As Zahavi was preparing to leave, checking the parking lot from the room's only window, Yael asked, "Are you going to take the suitcases?"

"No. I will not be leaving here in an airliner, and I will have no time to pull two big bags. My uncle will have to make his own profits."

A moment later, she was gone. Yael watched from the window as she hurriedly climbed into the passenger side of a large white SUV, and was gone.

VIRGIL RARELY TOOK A BATH, preferring the speed and overall cleanliness of a shower, but this night he'd submerged in his oversized bathtub, a relic left behind by the previous renter, a dis-

abled man who'd had it installed to help with muscle cramp-
ing. He died, but Virgil didn't think it had to do with the tub. The
man had also left behind an oversized hot-water heater, which
meant that Virgil could submerge to his ears, and cook out his
frustrations.

The water had just begun to cool, and his toes were showing
wrinkles, when his cell phone rang. Because of the ongoing clusterfuck, he'd left it on a windowsill above the tub, where he could
pick it up. He did, and saw that Yael was calling.

"Did you buy a membership at Sam's Club?" he asked.

"Yes, I did, and this membership, which I use only one time,
cuts directly into my profit," she said. "But, I don't call to talk
about Sam. I just had a visitor. She swore me to secrecy as one
good Israeli to another."

Virgil said, "You gotta be kidding me. I thought she'd be on the
other side of the ocean by now."

"I think she is in very large trouble, and she tries to save herself. But, that is her problem. My problem, my only problem, is to
get this stele. I think tomorrow night that she will try to take it, by
force if necessary. I am supposed to alert her, when you leave me
to attack the stone carrier."

"Hmmm," Virgil said. "All right. She had a male assistant when
she kidnapped Ellen Case. Is he still with her?"

"Somebody is with her. When she left, she got in the passenger
side of a very large white car. But, she said to me that her assistant had abandoned her. I believe that, because . . . she seemed to
tell the truth. She was very angry about it. Now, her new assistant
will tell her where the exchange takes place, this auction. She

says it will be at nine o'clock, but that the minister will not have the stele."

"This car . . . was it like a safari vehicle?"

"Exactly. You know it?"

"I do. Okay, I will work through this. I will call you tomorrow and tell you what we're going to do."

He punched off, put the phone back on the windowsill, said, aloud, "That fuckin' Bauer," and resubmerged to think about it some more.

21

Virgil got up the next morning with quite a few thoughts. The first was, if Tal Zahavi was with Bauer, he could bust her and take her up to the Ramsey County Jail in St. Paul and let Davenport worry about it.

After a fast cleanup, he was out in his truck, where he dug out the tracker, found the signal from Bauer's Range Rover, which was parked in a residential neighborhood on the west side of town. Virgil drove over . . . and couldn't find the Range Rover.

Eventually, with a little fast triangulation, he determined that the Range Rover was parked in exactly the same residential driveway occupied by an orange Mini Cooper convertible. He stared at it for a moment, wishing it away, then parked, walked up to the house where the Mini was parked, and rang the doorbell. A moment later, a tall bony fortyish woman wearing a pince-nez on her tall bony nose came to the door, carrying an open *New York Times* and a coffee cup, peered at him and asked, "What?" as though he were peddling cable-TV connections.

"I'm an agent with the Bureau of Criminal Apprehension." He

held up his ID so she could inspect it through the screen door. "Is this your Mini?"

"Yes, is there a problem?"

"I was tracking a man using an electronic tracker, and this morning it led me to your car . . . I think. I need to look at your car to see if he found the tracker on his, and moved it to yours."

"When would he have done that?" she asked, interested now.

"I don't know. Sometime last night, probably."

"Around nine o'clock at the Apache Mall?"

"Did you notice something there?" Virgil asked.

"When I came out from shopping, there was a big white SUV of some sort parked next to me," she said. "The man said he was looking at his tire, he said it felt soft, but I had the impression he'd done something to my car. But he didn't try to stop me from driving away, or anything. There didn't seem to be anything wrong with it."

"Driver's side, or passenger side?"

"Passenger side—right by the door."

Virgil went out to the Mini and found the tracker in ten seconds, taped to the Mini's frame.

"That goddamned Zahavi," he said. He was lying on his back in the driveway, looking at the tracking unit, and thinking that a spy would check.

"Fooled you, huh?" the woman said. She seemed amused.

"Fooled me, fooled himself," Virgil said. "It's a regular fools' paradise around here."

The woman said, "If ye should lead her into a fool's paradise, as they say, it were a very gross kind of behavior."

Virgil got to his feet and said, "Really? Shakespeare?"

"*Romeo and Juliet*," the woman said. "I'm surprised you recognized it at all."

"Not that many people say, 'it were,'" Virgil said. He dusted off the seat of his pants and added, "And I can tell you, just between us, there's about to be some seriously gross behavior."

WHEN HE went back to his truck, he called Davenport, who said, "You got lucky: I've been up for ten minutes."

"You know, Lucas, I don't really give a shit about that. I got all kinds of trouble, here. I need to borrow Jenkins and Shrake. I'm on my way up to the Twin Cities, and somebody needs to look up a limo driver named Max Car."

"Max Car, the limo driver?"

"That's what I said. Call me when Jenkins and Shrake are awake, and find Max Car."

"I'm far too important to do that, but I'll have it done," Davenport said. "You okay?"

"No. I'll be up there in an hour and a half."

AN HOUR LATER, Virgil was coming up to I-494, the interstate loop highway around the Twin Cities, when he got a call from Davenport's researcher, Sandy.

"Max Car, C-a-r, is actually Maxamed Ali Kaar, K-a-a-r, and it would have been a lot easier to find him if we'd known that."

"If I'd known that, I would have told you," Virgil snapped.

"Don't get shirty with me, Flowers," she said. They'd once had an extremely brief fling—four hours and nine minutes, by Virgil's cell phone clock—and she was less patient with him than other people might have been.

Virgil backed away: "He's a limo driver, right?"

"With Polaris Service, out of south Minneapolis."

"Text me a screen shot of his driver's license," Virgil said. "Have you heard from Jenkins and Shrake?"

"Yes. They're up and complaining."

"Good. Tell them to meet me at Kaar's address."

HE RANG OFF, and a minute later the phone vibrated, with a message: Kaar's address and cell phone number, and a note from Sandy: she'd taken a quick look at Google Maps, which showed his address as a small detached house not far from the car service, and adjacent to an industrial area in south Minneapolis.

"Careful going in," she'd texted. "Looks like a bear trap."

Five minutes after that, a screen shot of his driver's license came in. Kaar was a thin, dark-haired, dark-eyed, bewildered-looking man who wore a gray work shirt for his photo.

VIRGIL WAS at the address forty minutes later. Kaar's house was an old shaky white clapboard place with a tiny porch and a surprisingly green lawn, which, at the moment, was being mowed by a heavy white man in red tank top and cargo shorts. The mower was a manual reel-type.

Neither Shrake nor Jenkins was around, so Virgil called Shrake, who said they were in separate cars, maybe five minutes away. Five minutes later, they pulled in beside Virgil's truck, a half-block and around the corner from Kaar's house. They all got out to talk.

"I need to talk to a guy name Maxamed Ali Kaar, who's a driver here. He's supposedly in Mankato, but I was thinking about it last night, and I somewhat doubt it."

"But not entirely doubt it?" Jenkins asked.

"Not entirely. Anyway, his house is right down the street, and the lawn is being mowed by a fat guy in an undershirt, who doesn't look like the lawn service, but who also doesn't look like a Maxamed Ali anything. So, there's a question. Maybe Kaar doesn't live there at all. But if he does, and if he's here, we can't let him see us—but if he does see us, we need to grab him before he can make a phone call. That's critical."

"So let's one of us brace the fat guy, while the other two wait," Shrake said. "Find out what's up, and if he's there, we rush him."

Virgil nodded. "Can't let him make a phone call."

"So who talks to the fat guy?" Shrake asked.

VIRGIL AMBLED around the corner to Kaar's house. Jenkins and Shrake, now in Jenkins's personal Crown Vic, hovered at the corner where they could both see Virgil, but nobody in the house could see them. They could be at the house, Jenkins swore, in four seconds.

The fat guy was sweating heavily, and as Virgil came up, took off his Twins hat and wiped his face with a hairy forearm. Virgil could smell him from ten feet away: not dirt, just hot sweat. As Virgil came up, the man asked, "How you doin'?"

"Okay," Virgil said. He stopped, and pivoted, which put his back to the house. "I'm a cop. Does Max Kaar live here?"

"Thought you might be a cop," the man said. "What'd Max do?"

"Is he here?" Virgil repeated.

"He was fifteen minutes ago, and still is, unless he went out through the back fence. He lives in the casita out back."

"Casita?"

"The guesthouse."

Virgil stepped back and looked down the narrow driveway. "You mean the garage?"

"I converted it," the man said. "It's really pretty . . . okay . . . inside."

"What's your name?" Virgil asked.

"Larry Swanson."

Virgil waved at Jenkins and Shrake, and gestured past himself, so they'd roll on by the driveway where they couldn't be seen from the garage. They did, and got out, and Virgil explained the situation, and introduced Swanson.

"You're sure the man you saw fifteen minutes ago was Max Kaar?"

"Well, yeah. I've been renting to him for two years."

"Was he here yesterday?"

"Yeah, he said he had a couple of days off. I mean really, is this some kind of terrorist thing? 'Cause he seems like a nice enough guy."

Virgil said, "Listen, you guys hang here for a minute, I need to make a phone call."

He went back to his car to make it, wound up on hold for a moment, then was put through to an assistant attorney general named Pat Golden, who said, "They tell me it's that fuckin' Flowers, lookin' to get me in trouble."

"Pat, I'm really pushed, and I don't have time to explain it all to you, but I will later, or someday, if I'm allowed to. . . ."

VIRGIL WAS back out of the car a couple of minutes later and Jenkins said, "There's no window on the front of the garage, but there's one down the right side where the main entry door is."

Virgil waved him off and asked, "Mr. Swanson, are you married? Is there anyone else in your house?"

"No, I'm divorced, there's nobody else here."

"Good. I'd like you to put away your lawn mower, get a shirt, and lock your door, right now. Quickly as possible. You're not being arrested at the moment, but I will arrest you if I need to. Either way, you're coming with us."

"What'd I do? What'd I do?"

"I'll explain on the way. Now hurry. Hurry!"

Jenkins and Shrake were as confused as Swanson, but they asked no questions, just hurried the fat man through a quick armpit-wash and clean shirt, and out the door and into the back of Jenkins's car. Virgil said, "I'll see you guys at the BCA. Fifteen minutes."

"What'd I do?"

Virgil and Shrake walked all the way around the block to get back to their cars, taking no chance of being seen should Kaar step out in the yard.

When Virgil was back in the truck, he did a U-turn and drove north toward I-94, then took the double-secret phone out from under his seat and poked "1."

Lincoln answered. "What?"

"I think we need to confer," Virgil said. "As you undoubtedly know by now, the stele exchange takes place sometime around nine o'clock tonight."

"We're all over it."

"Are you watching the Hatchet and the driver, both?"

"Why do you ask?"

"Because I had a very bad night, and spent a lot of time thinking it all over, and so this morning I came up to the Cities and talked to Max Kaar's landlord, who said he saw Max about fifteen minutes ago. Here, at his house. He said Kaar was here all day yesterday. What I'm saying is, after due consideration, I suspect that the driver is the Hatchet, and the man in the backseat is a decoy."

After a long silence, Lincoln said, "I will call you back in two minutes."

FIVE MINUTES LATER, she called back and said, "You're on a speaker here, so speak clearly. Please, please tell me that you didn't arrest Kaar."

"Of course not," Virgil said. "I was afraid he'd tip off the Hatchet, one way or another."

"Thank God. Now, we need to make sure that the landlord is okay, that he doesn't somehow tip off Kaar that people were looking at him."

"I put the landlord in a cop's car and he's being transported back to the BCA right now. I've been told by an assistant attorney general that I can bust him on suspicion of sheltering a foreign terrorist and hold him incommunicado for a few days under the Patriot Act, but then he'd sue us, and every taxpayer in the State of Minnesota would have to send him money. What I'm hoping to do is to send him back home, with some coaching about how to handle Max the next time he sees him."

There was a rustle of voices in the background, and a name popped out: Morganthaler. Then there was more rustling, and finally Lincoln said, "A man named Joe Morganthaler will be at the BCA this afternoon. He will coach the landlord. All you need do is hold him until then."

"Good," Virgil said.

"I asked you to stay out of this, and now I'm ordering you: stay out of it. Stay out of it!"

"You didn't know that the Hatchet was the driver, did you? You would have trailed some chump to North Dakota or something while the real Hatchet was on his way back."

She clicked off. Virgil smiled at the phone, and put it back under the seat.

AT THE BCA, Virgil walked Swanson up the stairs and half-explained the situation to him. "We don't want to arrest you, because you haven't done anything wrong. On the other hand, we *can* arrest you, if we needed to, though you'd probably beat the charges. What we really want to do is put you back in your house, after you get some coaching on behavior."

"That's good, I'll do whatever you want," Swanson said. "But my behavior—"

"It's not bad or good behavior, it's how you react to Kaar the next time you see him, knowing that he might be cooperating with some really bad people. A guy is flying in just to talk to you, to give you a few moves."

"So what do I do now?"

"Well, you just kind of sit around, I'll get somebody to take you out to lunch, get you a tour of the crime lab upstairs . . ." Virgil outlined a few other entertainment possibilities as he walked Swanson to Davenport's office. Davenport was banging on a computer when Virgil arrived and knocked on his office doorjamb.

"Lucas, I'd like you to meet Larry Swanson."

AFTER SWANSON was settled under the watchful eye of Davenport's secretary, Virgil, Jenkins, Shrake, and Davenport gathered in Davenport's office to decide what to do about the evening's festivities.

"Sure would be a lot easier if we could just pick up Jones before he got to the delivery site," Davenport said.

"It would be, but we don't know what he's driving, or where he's hiding out, or how he plans to do this. I can guarantee it'll be something tricky. I don't think we have the time to figure all that out—but we will have the inside information on where it's going to happen," Virgil said.

"How much notice will you get?"

"As much as the people delivering the money, so we'll all probably get there at once, wherever it is."

"But if they want to do it on a country road somewhere, in the dark, and they see six cars coming instead of two—"

"Jones is a smart guy," Virgil said. "He won't want to be alone in the dark with Hezbollah."

"Take lots of guns," Davenport said.

"Gives me little goose bumps when you say things like that," Jenkins said.

VIRGIL, JENKINS, AND SHRAKE went back to Mankato in a caravan of three cars. At Mankato, Jenkins and Shrake dumped their cars in the parking lot of a Happy Chef Restaurant, consolidated in Virgil's car, and they all drove out in the countryside to visit Ma Nobles.

Virgil had explained how Bauer and Ma had pledged to help him, and how Bauer had apparently already sold him out. "All we want to do with Ma is make sure that Jones isn't at her place. And he might be. I don't know what's going on with those two, but something is."

"Does she go to church?" Jenkins asked.

"Not so you'd notice. Besides, Jones doesn't have a church. I don't know if he ever did. He's been a professor forever."

"I bet I know where he is," Jenkins said.

"Yeah?"

"Yeah. College professors always go somewhere in the summer. You know, they've got to do research in Paris, London, and Rome, and they write it off their taxes. So, he did just what he did with this woman in Israel. He knows *another* guy who's out of town right now, and he's broken in there, and he's driving that guy's car."

Virgil thought about it for two seconds, then said, "Probably. Unless he's at Ma's. If we had just a little more time, we could go jack up the people at Gustavus, find out who's out of town, start going door-to-door."

"You say we might not do much this afternoon. . . . Shrake and I could run up there, see what we can see," Jenkins said.

"It's a plan," Virgil said. "Let's see what Ma has to say."

THEY FOUND ROLF, Ma's oldest boy, unloading salvage lumber from a Ford flatbed truck—dry salvage, that he said came from Elijah Jones's old farmhouse—into the barn. Ma, he said, had gone out to the creek, but she had her cell phone with her. Another of Ma's kids came out, a big kid, said his name was Tall Bear, and when Shrake asked him if he had a minister hiding under his bed, Tall Bear said, "No, but Mom said Virgil is busting her balls about him."

Virgil got Ma on the phone and told her that he was at her house, and if she didn't mind, he and a couple of other cops were going to look under the beds, in the closets, and out in the barn.

"Pisses me off, but go ahead," Ma said. "I'll be there in ten minutes."

Virgil clicked off and said, "She says go ahead, which means we don't have to."

"Maybe we ought to, just for form's sake," Jenkins said, looking up at the house.

"Go ahead if you want," Virgil said. "I'll be out here."

Jenkins got Tall Bear to show him around, and Shrake and Virgil stood around watching Rolf unload lumber, and then Shrake took off his tie and said, "Well, shit, let's give him a hand," and so they did.

When Ma got back, she looked at them unloading lumber, shook her wet head, and said, "Sometimes you people . . . Virgil . . ."

JENKINS HADN'T FOUND anything at all in the house, and on the way back to town, said, "Nice boy, that Tall Bear. He said Ma was out swimming in the creek."

"Boy, I'd bet that'd be a sight," Shrake said. He looked casually over at Virgil and said, "Wouldn't that be a sight, Virgie? Those nice little pink tits, she's floating around on her back . . . Wait, what am I saying, 'little'? Anyway, the sight—"

"Yeah, that'd be a sight," Virgil said.

Shrake said to Jenkins, "Virgil agrees that would be a sight."

After a minute, Virgil said, "Fuck you," but he didn't laugh, though Jenkins and Shrake did. A lot.

22

Jenkins and Shrake spent the afternoon checking the homes of college professors who were believed to be traveling. They got the list after consulting with administrators at Gustavus Adolphus, and twice thought they might be on to something—the houses were occupied, one by the owners, who'd come back before they were expected, and one by the owners' adult children, who'd stayed behind while their parents visited Budapest.

At six o'clock, they gathered out back of Virgil's house for brats and beer and tried to figure out what they'd be doing that evening. Virgil changed into cargo shorts, a Hawaiian shirt, and sandals for the occasion.

"I'm mostly worried about Ma," he said. "I don't know exactly why she's involved with Jones, but there's something going on. Anyway, we'll track her. She told me herself that Jones had something tricky planned for the exchange. I think I've got it all covered, but we'll see."

"So we just sit on our asses until she starts moving?"

"That's about it," Virgil said. "I gotta tell you—I'm a little suspicious about this whole auction thing. Why would he even bother to have it? But I have two different bidders telling me that's what's going to happen, so we're going with it."

Shrake said, "I don't worry so much about Ma. I worry more about this Mossad chick. From what you say, she wants to try out a little combat."

"I don't want anybody to get shot, and I don't doubt that she can shoot," Virgil said. "If she pulls a gun, and if it's safe to do, we might want to give her a little firepower demonstration."

Shrake brightened. "We talking tracers?"

"You got some of those fast-ignition rounds?" Virgil asked.

"Does a bear excrete in the woods?"

"Have another brat," said Virgil.

Sitting around the grill, waiting for the trouble, reminded Virgil of his childhood, sitting around in lawn chairs on a hot summer Fourth of July, waiting for the light to die so the fireworks could start. He called Awad three times and Bauer another three, asking, "Anything yet?" and being told, "No," just like when he was a kid asking, "Don't you think it's dark enough?"

Just as when he was a kid, the light finally died. There was a storm front off to the west, and while they couldn't yet hear the thunder, they could see the far-distant flashes of lightning; just like when he was a kid, waiting with suppressed excitement for the big winds and the storm. Virgil changed into combat gear— jeans and a T-shirt—and with the three of them feeling restless, they all got together and cleaned up Virgil's kitchen, keeping an eye on Ma's truck. At eight-fifteen, the truck started to move.

"Let's go," said Shrake, and he and Jenkins jogged out to their vehicles and took off. Virgil watched them go, and then called Awad a fourth time: "Anything yet?"

"Nothing yet. We are ready here."

"Raj, if you guys fuck with me . . ."

"Virgil, my friend, we are in your hands, you are not in ours," Awad said.

"Keep that in mind," Virgil said, feeling a little mean.

MA TURNED onto the road outside her house, and thought, *What a great country night*. She could hear frogs in the roadside ditches, smell the humidity mixed with the gravel dust. The western sky had gone black, with flicks of lightning moving closer, but to the east, the stars were bright as headlights.

A gorgeous night, but pregnant with the feeling that something was about to happen. She'd had the feeling before—waiting out a tornado watch, or heading out to a roadhouse late at night, wondering what would happen in the next few hours. What?

She also had the feeling of being watched, and instead of creeping her out, it made her feel secure. Virgil was out there somewhere, she thought.

JENKINS AND SHRAKE headed out into the countryside in their separate cars. Jenkins had the tablet tracker, kept one eye on that and one on the road. He had a radio plugged into his cigarette lighter, as did Shrake and Virgil, and they could use them like intercoms, with the press of the button.

Ma started out going north from her house. Jenkins watched the illuminated dot crawl along a country road, then pause at a T intersection. He pushed the button on the radio and said, "She's stopped."

Virgil: "Where?"

Jenkins told him, and Virgil followed it on a Google map. "Unless she comes straight back, she'll have to go east or west from there. If she goes east, she'll be up against the river, and you guys will be right on top of her, and pretty quick," he said.

Jenkins said, "She's moving again, she's headed east. We're taking 169."

They watched her for twenty minutes, zigzagging around the countryside, making stops, taking small roads apparently to check her back trail; eventually, apparently satisfied that she was alone, she ventured out on Highway 169 and turned south toward Jenkins and Shrake, who were less than a mile away when she made the turn.

"We gotta get off," Jenkins called to Shrake. "Right up ahead, whatever that is, right next to those cars."

They never found out what the business was, some kind of manufacturing plant, Jenkins thought. The parking lot was mostly empty, but a half-dozen cars sat facing what might have been the office area. He and Shrake pulled into the line of cars and killed their lights. Ma went by a half-minute later, and they gave her a half-mile, and then pulled out behind her.

They all went south on the highway, until Ma slowed, then pulled into the parking lot at the same Perkins restaurant where Virgil and Ma had met the week before, to discuss lumber.

Shrake, who was driving a pickup, pulled into the parking lot, rolled past Ma, and parked. Jenkins, in his Crown Vic, pulled off the highway, two hundred yards away, and killed his lights.

MA SAT in the parking lot for just over a minute, and Shrake called and told Virgil, "It's another fake pickup. . . . She probably . . . Wait a minute."

As he was talking, a white Range Rover pulled in next to Ma's red truck.

"We've got that white Range Rover."

"Ah, jeez, I'm coming, I'm coming," Virgil said. "That could be the Israeli Mossad with a gun."

Virgil was in his truck, waiting downtown for the nine o'clock phone call from Awad, and maybe Bauer, probably two miles and probably three or four minutes from the Perkins, if he put his foot on the floor, which he did.

He had flashers, and he turned them on as he bolted away from the curb, onto Mulberry, across the bridge, onto the 169 ramp, and up the highway.

As he rolled, Virgil shouted, "Keep talking to me . . . keep talking."

Shrake called to Jenkins, "You better get down here, something's happening."

MA PULLED into the Perkins parking lot, again with the feeling that something was about to happen. She didn't trust Bauer, but

then, she didn't have to trust him. Just getting him here was part
of her function. She pulled in, waited; another minute, and another pickup pulled in, went past her, parked, and a large man
got out and walked into the restaurant. Through the lighted windows, she saw him talking to the cashier, and then follow her
back to a booth, and take a menu.

Fat raindrops began splattering off the tarmac, and off the
windshield, drops the size of marbles, bringing with it the fresh-
air smell of an incoming storm. She'd seen it on the television
radar, earlier, and it wasn't much, but it would rain hard for a
while.

Another minute, and Bauer pulled in, and up next to her driver's side.

Bauer got out of the far side of the Range Rover, holding a
folded newspaper over his head to fend off the rain, and walked
around, and she dropped her window and he asked, "You got it?"

"I do," she said. "Come on around to the other side."

"Let's get it out where I can see it."

"It'll be pouring in a minute—why don't you get your camera,
and we'll just get in, and we'll—" She saw movement in the Range
Rover, through the glass on the passenger-side window. "Who's
that with you?"

Bauer said, "Nobody."

Ma noticed that the window was down an inch or so, so that a
person inside the Range Rover could hear their conversation.

She said, "What's this?" and reached for the keys, but as she
started the engine, the passenger door on the Range Rover
popped open and a woman jumped out and she had a gun in her

hand and she pointed it at Ma's face and the woman screamed, "The stone! Give us the stone!"

Ma, suddenly over her head, shifted into reverse, but that wouldn't work, and Bauer said, "The stone, the stone," and to the woman, "Don't point the gun! Don't point the gun—"

The woman screamed again and Ma shouted back, "Okay, okay, okay . . ."

She reached into the foot well on the passenger seat and came up with the bowling bag. As she passed it out the window to the woman, the woman screamed at Bauer, "Drive! Drive!" Bauer hurried around the back of the Range Rover and climbed inside, and the woman got in, taking the gun with her.

Ma said, "Bullshit," and hit the gas, backing the truck around in a circle until it was directly behind the Range Rover. Out her driver's-side window, she saw the big man who'd arrived in the pickup burst out of the restaurant, and at the same moment, a cop-looking car, like an old-model highway patrol car, bumped one wheel over a curb and banged into the parking lot, coming fast.

Virgil, she thought.

BAUER SAW THE CAR COMING, and Ma's truck now parked behind him, Zahavi shouting, "Go! Go!" and Bauer said, "That fuckin' Flowers."

His Range Rover was facing a highway ditch just past a flag-pole, and with Ma where she was, he couldn't go anywhere but forward. He did that, flooring it, and the truck lurched forward, plowed across the ditch, and swerved onto the highway. Six seconds later he was accelerating through sixty miles an hour. In his rearview mirror, he saw Ma buck onto the highway—she'd taken the same shortcut as he had—and then a car swerve out after them. They were a quarter mile behind, though, and he was still gaining.

"Get out in the country and I'll find a road that'll trash them," he said to Zahavi. "Look for a turnoff."

She said, "Police."

The rain was coming hard now, in sheets, the lightning almost constant, thunder banging on the roof of the car like a bass drum. Bauer saw emergency flashers, closing fast. Much closer, a road cut off to the right. "Hang on," he said. They took the turn, accelerated again, down a street with houses on one side, commercial buildings on the other. Bauer checked the nav system and could see that he was coming to a T intersection.

"Gotta make a decision here," he said, and at the T, he turned right, toward what the navigation map showed as a dead end. He saw headlights behind him, one set, then another set with flashers, then a third set, and then he was at the end of the street. He continued straight ahead, through some small trees and brush, over a few bumps, through a barbwire fence, which was flicked aside by the bull bars, and then they were on a highway exit ramp, or maybe a frontage road, and he accelerated again and said, "Let them suck on that."

A minute later, one set of headlights burst onto the frontage road, then the flashers. "Well, goddamnit," he said. A bigger highway was coming up, and he recognized it as the one he'd just left, 169. They'd come in a circle.

Zahavi said, "Left—right is toward the town."

There was some traffic, but he timed it right and sailed through the intersection, and turned north, heading out of town, throwing up a rooster tail of water from the wide tires. "Watch the nav system, watch the nav."

WHEN BAUER TOOK OFF, Ma was right behind him. She tracked him around the first curve, saw the flashers coming up from the south, got her cell phone out, and called Virgil. "That you with the flashers?"

"Pull off, Ma, pull off."

"Screw that," she said. "They pointed a gun at me. I'm gonna put them in a ditch."

Virgil saw the T intersection coming up on his nav, and then Bauer turned right. "He's headed for a dead end. He's gotta have nav, I think he's going through."

Jenkins: "I can't take that."

"Turn around, go back. He's headed out to 169."

"I'm out there now," Shrake said.

"Wait until we call you."

VIRGIL SAW BAUER go right through the end of the street, followed by Ma in her pickup, and then he was there, banging through the ditch and onto the road.

Virgil shouted, "We're coming out," and Shrake called back,

"I'm coming up, I'm right there," and then, "He's out heading north, I'm right on his ass—he's pulled away, though."

ZAHAVI WAS turned on her seat, looking out the back, saw the flashers turn onto the highway, but well back, behind another truck; but the other truck was matching their speed. She said, "We have another follower."

Bauer let the Range Rover out, and the pursuing lights fell behind. Two minutes, three, four, and then Bauer said, ""Here's what we want. Hang on."

A minute later, he took a left turn, and they were on gravel.

SHRAKE SAID into his radio, "He's got a lot more speed than we have. I'm going with the light show."

"Be careful, for Christ's sakes," Virgil said. "There are houses out here."

IN HIS TRUCK, Shrake dropped the window, took a blast of rain, got the M16 off the floor, stuck it one-handed out the window, propped the forestock on the wing mirror support, aimed low, and pulled the trigger. A dozen rounds went out, the tracers streaking downrange like supersonic fireflies, into the roadside ditch ahead of the fleeing Range Rover.

———

BAUER SAW the tracers flash by and shouted, "Whoa, whoa, whoa," and yanked the truck to the side of the road.

"What are you doing? What are you doing?" Zahavi screamed.

"That was a machine gun," Bauer shouted back. "Fuck this," and he popped the door and was out with his hands over his head, the rain pounding down on his head.

Two seconds later, the pursuing truck stopped down the road, and a man jumped out and in the oncoming lights of the truck with the flashers, Bauer could see the man's silhouette with the long gun. He shouted, "We give up."

VIRGIL STOPPED beside Shrake's truck, and then Ma pulled up, and then Jenkins. Virgil and Jenkins pulled on rain jackets, and Ma pulled a plastic garbage bag over her head. Jenkins took the rifle from Shrake, and the three of them walked up to Bauer and Za-havi, who both had their hands over their heads. Shrake was a few steps behind, pulling on a jacket. Bauer and Zahavi looked like drowned rats.

"Crazy motherfuckers," Virgil said. "You're both under arrest for everything. Shrake, read them their rights."

"I am a diplomat and I invoke immunity," Zahavi said.

"Immune this," Ma, said, and she hit Zahavi in the eye with a balled fist, and the Israeli went down. One second later she was back up, ready to go, but Jenkins got her around the waist and said, "Let's not."

Virgil had hold of Ma, who twisted around and said, "She put a gun in my face."

Bauer said, "Yeah, she had a gun. She made me do it."

"I am a diplomat—"

Virgil: "Fuck a bunch of immunity." To Jenkins and Shrake: "Cuff them and transport them up to Ramsey. Aggravated assault, et cetera. I'll talk to you later."

"Where are you going?"

Virgil looked at his watch. Five minutes to nine. "I oughta know in the next couple of minutes." Then he remembered, looked at Bauer, and asked, "Where's the stone?"

"Floor of the truck."

Virgil and Ma walked up to the truck, and Virgil saw the bowling bag. He picked it up, and turned to Ma.

"So there's no auction?"

She took the bag from him, unzipped it, walked to the front of Bauer's truck, and smashed the stone against the bull bars on the front. The stone cracked in half, showing a white interior.

"It's an imitation, made out of plaster of paris," she said. "I told you Reverend Jones would do something tricky. The auction is over. The money and the stone are gone."

They all looked at the shattered fake, and then Bauer said, "Aw, shit."

Virgil asked Ma, "Where's Jones?"

"He's turning himself in—to you. He should be down at the Perkins at any minute. He'll need to go to a hospital, not to a jail. He's in terrible shape. I don't know how he holds together. Only willpower now, the medicine doesn't work anymore."

"Okay," Virgil said. To Jenkins and Shrake: "Change in plan. Jenkins takes these two up to Ramsey. Shrake comes with me and we'll bust Jones, and Shrake will transport him to Regions. He walked out of Mankato once, I'm not going to give him another chance."

Ma asked, "What about me?"

Virgil shrugged: "The way I see it, you just carried out the plan we talked about last night. As long as we get lots and lots of cooperation."

"Sure," she said.

"Let's do this," Virgil said. "We'll lock the Range Rover and leave it. I'll get it towed tonight. Ma, you can follow us down to the Perkins. Let's get out of the rain."

So Bauer and Zahavi were cuffed, Zahavi silent for once, and they all walked to whatever vehicles they were going to, and Ma said to Virgil, "You are strangely cheerful, and that worries me."

"Yeah, well, you know," Virgil said, but he couldn't help grinning at her. "You win some, and you lose some." He looked up at the dark sky, the leading edge of the storm now well to the east, took a deep breath, enjoying the smell of the rain on the gravel and the corn, and said, "What a great night, huh?"

On the way back to town, Virgil got on the secret phone. When Lincoln answered, he said, "I've busted Bauer and Zahavi, the Israeli Mossad agent. She's claiming diplomatic immunity, but you might be able to trade something for her . . . reasonable treatment."

"Somebody will think about that."

"You got your guy?"

"That's classified," she said, and hung up.

In other words, Virgil thought, *Yes*.

VIRGIL AND SHRAKE pulled into the Perkins, but Ma did not. Virgil saw her taillights disappearing down the highway and called to Shrake, "Where the hell is she going?"

"Probably gonna pull some more bullshit," Shrake said.

"Jones better be here, or I'll bust her ass, too," Virgil said.

There was a lot of water in the restaurant parking lot, but the rain had slowed. They went inside. No Jones. "Sonofabitch," Virgil said.

Then a moonfaced man with a buzz cut waved a hand at them and called, "Virgil?"

Virgil recognized the voice, walked over and said, "You've changed."

Jones was sitting in front of a half-full cup of coffee and an empty pie plate, looking up at Virgil. He said, "I wanted to say good-bye to my wife. I couldn't go as usual—this is my disguise."

Virgil said, "Well, sir, you're under arrest. We're going to take you up to Regions Hospital in St. Paul. You'll be held in a security ward."

"I think you're too late," Jones said.

"Never too late to go to jail," said Shrake.

"Well, big man, I have to tell you. I think you're wrong about that." Jones sighed, his eyes turned up, and he slipped out of the booth. Shrake tried to catch him, but he landed squarely on his moon face.

Virgil tried to pick him up, but it was like trying to get hold of a two-hundred-pound lump of Jell-O. Virgil called 911, identified himself, and asked for an ambulance: "You better hurry."

WHEN JONES was on his way to the hospital, with Shrake following behind the ambulance, Virgil called Ma, but got no answer, so he headed over to Awad's apartment.

Awad came to the door, and was effusive: "This was wonderful. Wonderful." He embraced Virgil, who pulled his head back, afraid he was about to be kissed on both cheeks. "What can I tell you, as Americans say? I have already chosen the airplane. This is a 1999 Cessna 206H, slightly used, I am offered a deal of the lifetime."

"Better not tell me about it," Virgil said. "I'm a cop."

"Ah, of course," Awad said. "But . . ."

Al-Lubnani was packing clothes into a suitcase.

"You're out of here?" Virgil asked.

"Indeed. Tonight. I will drive the Kia to Chicago. I hope the Hatchet will not interfere?"

"I have good reason to believe that he will not," Virgil said.

"Good," al-Lubnani said. "I need two days of freedom in France. After that, they will not find me."

"I don't suppose you kept the money here," Virgil said.

"With the possibility that you would come? Of course not," al-Lubnani said. "I trust you like my brother . . . but I'm afraid my brother is a rascal."

"Well, like I said, I don't really care. Where's the stone?"

Al-Lubnani and Awad exchanged glances, and Virgil thought al-Lubnani might have gone a shade paler. "You don't have it? Your assistant was here—"

"I don't have an assistant," Virgil snapped. "What the hell is going on? We had a deal."

"But she said it was over—that you arrested the Mossad agent and this Bauer, that you were arresting Jones. That you sent her to get the stone."

"Aw, for Christ sakes," Virgil said. He cupped his hands. "Was she . . . ?"

They both nodded.

ONE LAST TRIP that night, out to Ma's place. The truck was parked in the yard, and there were lights on all over the house. It was still raining, but now, more of a drip than a drumbeat. Ma met him at the door: "My goodness, look what the cat dragged in. Come on inside, we just finished making caramel corn."

Inside, Virgil found her three youngest, eating caramel corn out of plastic bowls and watching *Iron Man 2*. Sam said, "We're coming to a good part. You wanna watch?"

Virgil said, "I've got to talk to your mom."

"We better go outside," Ma said.

Virgil followed her out. She was moving right along, out across the yard to the barn. Virgil trotted to catch up, and inside the barn, she flicked on a light, a single bulb that showed up a tractor, a Bobcat, and a bunch of related machinery. She said, "Back here," and threaded past the machinery to a ladder that went up into the loft.

Virgil said, "Ma, we gotta—"

"Up here," she said. Virgil climbed up into the loft, into the slightly acid smell of the hay that was stored there. There was no light in the loft, except what came through the loft door from a pole light out by the driveway; the rain made a pleasant tickling sound on the roof.

Ma was sitting on what appeared to be a mattress. She said, "Rolf and Tall Bear sometimes bring their girlfriends up here."

Virgil said, "Ma . . ."

Ma patted the mattress and said, "Virgie, there's only one way you're gonna get that stone."

23

Sometimes, a man's gotta do what a man's gotta do.

24

Virgil had found a pair of water wings in the barn, the cheap plastic kind that you blow up and roll up your arms, and he lay back in the creek water. With the barest flutter of his feet, and the support of the water wings, he could keep himself moving. The air temperature had to be in the high nineties, he thought, and when the sun beat down, his body had to be near the boiling point. And when he kicked through the shade of an overhanging burr oak, he felt as though he'd been doused with cool water. At this point in time, there couldn't be a better place to be, not in the whole universe.

"We better stay in the shade as much as we can, or we'll burn into a couple of cinders," Ma said. "That sun is scorching hot."

She had no trouble floating, Virgil thought, probably because she had built-in water wings. In any case, she was an attractive sight, as they flutter-kicked around the swimming hole. The whole environment was reminiscent of a moment from a Disney movie, Virgil thought, with the lush dark green woods all around, the gurgling of the stream over the broken-down dam, the occasional tiger swallowtail fluttering by; like when Bambi was meeting his first butterfly.

"So what'd that bitch do when you got her to St. Paul?" Ma asked, un-Bambi-like. She was referring to Tal Zahavi.

"Threatened everybody in sight," Virgil said. "Diplomatic immunity, and all that. They're gonna lay down for it. Or maybe they don't have a choice. Whatever happens, it won't do her spy career a lot of good. They took her to court for an appearance, and there are now twelve thousand news photos of her."

"Good. She pointed a gun right at my nose. That really . . . I mean, I thought I might die right there."

"You could of."

"Have you ever thought you might die?" she asked. "When you were in a shoot-out?"

He had to think about it. "I'm not sure. I never *really* thought I was about to die, but I might have thought, *Holy shit, you're about to die*, but not believed it, if you know what I mean. You've got this voice telling you that, but the voice sounds sarcastic."

"Mmm."

"Zahavi would have scared me, too," Virgil said. "She was a little nuts. Maybe out in the cold too long. She *wanted* to shoot somebody—wanted to try it out, see how it felt."

"You're not gonna put Tag in prison, are you?" Ma asked.

"I don't know what'll happen to him," Virgil said.

"He's too cute to put in prison," Ma said. "A double-crossing piece of scum, but I can excuse that, if a man is cute enough."

"Glad to hear it," Virgil said. "Davenport says Tag'll make bail this afternoon, and he's already scheduled a press conference. He claims he didn't have any idea that Zahavi had a gun. He was just along for the ride, so that he could be shown handing the stone over to the Israelis. I don't believe him, but a jury might. If you say you won't testify against him . . ."

"Virgil, I just want it to be over," Ma said. "I've got my life to live. I'd just send him home."

"I kinda think that's what will happen. Movie stars . . . prosecutors like movie stars," Virgil said. "They think if they're nice to them, maybe they'll get to be in a movie."

"Good luck to them," Ma said. "Whatever happens, Tag brought it on himself. It's not like you didn't warn him."

THEY PADDLED around a bit more, and then Virgil said, "Not like I didn't warn *you*."

"Aw, let's not go there, Virgie," Ma said. "Not after last night. I never was going to keep the stone. But you surely scratched my itch, and I can't tell you how nice that was."

"Not to brag, but I have to say, I think I probably took care of your itch for several months, possibly even a couple of years," Virgil said.

"Mmm. No. In fact, I feel it coming back on."

"We'll think of something," Virgil said. "Say, you want another beer?"

"You're not peeing in the water, are you?"

"Ma . . ."

THE NIGHT BEFORE, after Virgil recovered the stone, he'd spent a half hour talking to everyone involved, making sure that

those who needed to be in jail were in jail, and that those who
didn't, weren't. When all that was done, he told the kids that
he was going to take Ma out to get a hot fudge sundae, took
her to his house, as he told her, "to get you even further in my
debt."

The next morning, early, he drove up to the Cities without the
stone, to work through the paper. The feds were asking about
what happened to al-Lubnani, who might be considered an
enemy alien, and Virgil explained that he'd disappeared. When
they asked about Awad, Virgil said that Awad had worked as his
informant during the whole episode—but if word of that got out,
he might be murdered. They went away to think about it, and
Virgil was confident that Awad was safe.

Awad himself was being hustled on the purchase of a
fourteen-year-old utility plane, which Virgil thought he'd probably buy—with hundred-dollar bills, of course.

MA FLOATED UP and put her feet on the stony creek bottom. She
was short enough that the water would have come up over her
nose, so she had to bounce as she pushed up between Virgil's ankles. "I do feel bad about Reverend Jones."

"Nothing anybody can do about that," Virgil said. Jones was in
the security ward at Regions Hospital in St. Paul, after being
transferred up from Mankato. He never recovered full conscious-
ness. The docs at Regions had his Mayo medical file electronically
transferred, looked at it, looked at Jones, and suggested that the
old man be sent home.

"He's right there at the end," an oncologist told Virgil. "He'll never be back, now. His coma is getting deeper. He'll be dead in a week. He'll need a lot of morphine, and it'll save everybody a lot of money if he got it through a hospice service, instead of here."

Virgil related that to Ma, who teared up for a moment, then splashed some creek water in her eyes and washed the tears away. "That man saved my life," she said. She'd told Virgil all about it during their extended slumber party. "He hadn't come along, I had the potential to turn into a real piece of trailer trash."

"I doubt it—you're a survivor." Virgil looked at his watch and said, "Your kids still gone?"

"Another hour or two. Why?"

"We could get back to the house . . . and then I've got to head back to the Cities, now that I've recovered the stone."

"Are you going to tell them the truth about the stone? Your cop buddies?"

"I have to, Ma. You called me this morning and said you'd found it at Jones's old family place, while you were tearing it down. He must've ditched it there. Rolf was a witness—not that anyone will care, since they'll have the stone."

"I was amazed when that thing popped out of the wall," she said. She got in the shallow water, stood up, arched her back, and stretched and yawned. "If we're gonna do it, we better get 'er done, before the boys get back."

"Yes, ma'am," Virgil said.

She was a sight.

———

ON THE WAY back to the house, Virgil said, "I got a question for you, Ma. I know you're smart, because somebody told me. I don't mean a little smart, or somewhat smart, but really, really smart. When we're talking, sometimes you use perfect grammar and syntax, and sometime it's this rednecky 'slicker'n snot on a door-knob,' 'dumber'n a bag a hammers,' and all that. Why do you do that? Switch back and forth?"

She glanced at him and said, "You're not totally unperceptive. I'd noticed that."

"So why?"

"I don't know. Because people expect it, I guess," she said. "I drive around in a pickup truck and tear down buildings and I got five boys without daddies . . . so that's what they expect. 'Dumber'n a bag of hammers, dumber'n a barrel of hair, slicker'n owl shit . . .' If I act that way . . . well, they won't see me coming, if I'm ever in a spot where I don't want them to see me coming."

Virgil cupped a hand over his ear and pumped a drop of water out, and said, "Okay. I can buy that."

"I'm sure you can, since you do the same thing—laid-back surfer-boy bullshit, those band T-shirts and that long blond hair, until you have to be mean. Then you can be meaner than the average rattlesnake."

"I resemble that remark," Virgil said.

"Yes, you do," she said. "So, let's walk faster. I've got a couple new things I want to try. As it turns out, lucky for me, you're not the bashful sort."

_____

AN HOUR LATER, Virgil called Yael and asked, "You packed?"

"I am ready. Do you still have the stone?"

Virgil had called to tell her that he'd recovered the Solomon stone. "Of course. You thought I'd lost it again?"

"Not exactly, but I thought I should inquire, in case I shouldn't check out."

"I'll be there in twenty minutes," Virgil said.

He kissed Ma good-bye on the front porch, and as he was walking out to his truck, saw Sam coming down the driveway on his bike, in his Cub Scout uniform. Virgil turned the truck around, stopped next to the kid, and asked, "You fish?"

"When I can."

"I got a boat. If your mom says okay, we'll go up to the St. Croix and knock down some muskys," Virgil said.

"Can you eat muskys?" Sam asked.

Virgil crossed himself. "Never, never ask anything like that. No, you can't eat muskys. Maybe we should go for walleyes."

"Either one is good with me," Sam said. He looked down at the house, then back at Virgil. "You didn't knock her up, did you?"

"Jesus, I hope not," Virgil said. "You don't need another redneck in this family."

"That's the goddamned truth," Sam said, and pedaled on.

ON THE WAY to pick up Yael, Virgil called Davenport, who came on and said, "Now if we just had that stone, everything would be somewhat perfect."

"I've got it. Jones apparently ditched it at his old farmstead, and a woman I know is tearing the place down," Virgil said. "It popped right out of the wall."

"An amazing coincidence," Davenport said. "Astonishing, really."

"Oh, I don't know," Virgil said. "I suspect Jones wanted it found. The money's probably where he wanted it to go, so . . . he doesn't care about the stone anymore. Or maybe he does care, maybe he never wanted to betray his old friends in archaeology. So he left it where we'd find it."

"Okay," Davenport said. "Although, I've got a feeling that you haven't looked under all the available rocks."

"I'll tell you, Lucas, we really don't want to do that. At least, not until we hear what's finally happened with the Hatchet."

"Got it," Davenport said. "Speaking of Jones, his daughter's asking for you. She's over at the hospital."

"I'll stop this afternoon," Virgil said. "But first, I'm gonna bring the stone up and stick it in the evidence locker, and let you geniuses figure out what to do with it. I'm done with it."

"See you when you get here."

AND HE MADE a call to Lincoln, the intelligence agent, or whatever she was. He pressed "1" on the double-secret telephone, and she answered two seconds later. "What?"

"I thought I'd give you a chance to say, 'Thank you,'" Virgil said.

"Thank you."

"You've still got him?"

"Got who?"

"All right. I hope it works out for you," Virgil said. "Is there any possibility that I'll ever know how it turns out?"

He could hear her thinking, and then she said, "I'll tell you what, Virgil. There are some possibilities out there, where we just couldn't talk to you. I'm not talking about us doing anything illegal, I'm just saying, there are some possibilities."

"Give me a hypothetical."

"Hypothetically, if you were in this sort of situation, say, and the target was picked up and eventually agreed to turn—"

"Okay. I got that," Virgil said. "But listen: if it's just a straight bust, or you take down a group, but it doesn't make the papers . . . give me a ring. I don't need details, I'd just like to know what happened. How the story came out."

"I'll do what I can," she said. "I have to say, Virgil, you are a journey all of your own, and I hope you enjoy yourself in the rest of it."

"What do you want me to do with the secret phone?"

"Nothing. In a day or two, it'll turn itself off, and it'll never come back. If you open it up, you'll find that the electronics have been reduced to a brownish goop. I wouldn't taste it. If, for some reason, we need to talk to you again, we'll know where to find you."

"But I won't know where to find you."

"That's correct."

And she was gone.

WHEN HE GOT to Mankato, he found Sewickey sitting in the parking lot, in his Caddy, with the engine running. Sewickey got out and said, "Thank God. I've been here for four hours. I saw all that about the Mossad woman and Bauer on TV, and I figured you'd show up to talk with the Israeli."

"You're looking for the photographs?" Virgil asked, remembering that he'd promised them to Sewickey, if Sewickey stayed out of Virgil's hair.

Sewickey said, "Exactly. I need to get back to Austin. There're rumors that a piece of parchment has come up on Santorini that mentions a town called 'Atalant,' obviously a reference to Atlantis. I'm going, and right quick, but I need to get to Austin first."

"If you had a camera . . ."

"I do. A brand-new one. In the Caddy," he said.

"I've got the stone, right here in the truck," Virgil said. "Get your camera, you can take some shots, and I'll take a couple of you examining the stone, and we'll be all square."

"Virgil, you are a prince among men," Sewickey said.

"Not so much," Virgil said. "I figure if you get these photographs, you'll stick them straight up Bauer's ass."

Sewickey laughed. "I will indeed. And make the oil and gas guys happy, at the same time. Who knows, maybe I'll get my own TV show."

They went up to Yael's room with the stone and made three dozen photographs, using a bedsheet as a seamless backdrop, and then a dozen more of Sewickey examining the stone with a magnifying glass, while wearing an Aussie outback hat. Yael did not approve, but conceded that Virgil may have owed something to Sewickey.

Sewickey followed Virgil back to his truck, Virgil carrying the stone, Sewickey towing Yael's suitcase, while she checked out. As they waited for her, Virgil asked, "Where was this Atlantis parchment found?"

"Santorini. Also known as Thera. It's in the Cyclades, off Greece. The island is the remains of a volcanic caldera. The volcano blew about three thousand six hundred years ago, and is possibly the origin of the Atlantis myth. If this parchment can be nailed down, that'd certainly support the theory that Santorini was Atlantis."

Virgil nodded and said, "Pretty nice time of year in the Greek Islands. I took a leave there, when I was in the army."

"Pleasant," Sewickey said. "Very pleasant, in fact."

"Lots of northern Europeans on vacation. Swedes, Norwegians, Finns, Germans, Danes . . ."

"All blond, all the time," Sewickey said, rubbing his hands together. "Of course, I'll be there for scholarly reasons and would have no reason to visit the beaches."

ON THE WAY north to the Cities, Virgil filled Yael in on the aftermath of the confrontation the night before, and told her that he'd be leaving the stone with the BCA. The negotiations for its return would be carried out between her, his bosses, the Israeli embassy, and somebody from the State Department. "You'll probably have to stay here for few more days, but it's a done deal. You can spend a little more time shopping. Go out to the Mall of America."

"What about Tal Zahavi?"

"Diplomatic immunity," Virgil said.

Yael shook her head: "This is one person I do not need to meet when I get back home."

"I doubt she'll want to have anything to do with the stone," Virgil said.

"I was thinking more along the lines of revenge," Yael said. "I'll be the only one she can reach."

VIRGIL DROPPED HER at the St. Paul Hotel, and continued on to the BCA, where he placed the stele on Davenport's desk. Davenport peered at it for a moment and said, "That'd look good on my mantel."

Tal Zahavi, he said, was still in the Ramsey County lockup, and would be for a few more days. According to reports from the jailers, she was in an around-the-clock rage, not that they gave a rat's ass.

The FBI had called. They'd send somebody down to consult with Raj Awad, Davenport said, but Awad was in the clear.

"I think Awad might be suddenly affluent," Virgil said.

"Who cares?" Davenport said. "None of this shit has anything to do with us. I just wish they'd keep it over there, wherever that is."

"I wash my hands of it," Virgil said. "I'll go talk to Ellen, see what she has to say, and then I'm gone."

"Got a date?"

"Hope so," Virgil said.

VIRGIL WENT over to Regions Hospital, a sprawling brick medical palace down the hill from the state capitol. The hospital had a locked ward for the criminal kind, and after going through some rigmarole, Virgil was taken in by a guard. Jones was flat on his back, more tubes going in and out, just as they had been in Mankato. His eyes were closed, and he looked shrunken, as though he'd lost five pounds since the night before.

Ellen was sitting next to him, reading a book. She saw Virgil and he raised his eyebrows, and she looked at her father and shook her head. "We're arranging for a hospice."

"I heard from the docs, this morning," Virgil said.

"I just . . . I just . . ."

"I'm sorry."

She said, "When he was waiting for you at that restaurant, he called me—he called Danny, too, he's on his way—and told me that he really didn't want anyone hurt, but he had obligations that he couldn't escape."

"I appreciate that, Ellen. I can't lie to you—he's still pretty much of an asshole in my book. Ma could have been killed last night, trying to help him out. Part of it was her own fault, but part of it was your father's, too. Ma felt an obligation to him, and he exploited that."

"He wasn't a bad man," she insisted.

"That's what Ma says, too."

———

"I NEED A FAVOR FROM YOU," Ellen said. "A big one."

Virgil shrugged: "I'll listen. I'll do what I can."

"When I was talking to Dad last night, he said he'd made a will, specifying that his body be cremated, and the ashes taken to a grave he's already arranged, in Israel. It'll be the grave for Mom, too, when she dies."

"Yeah?"

"He wants you to take his ashes there," Ellen said.

"Aw, Ellen . . ."

"I'd go, but he said I couldn't—that the Israelis would wind up arresting me and investigating me for this stone business. Same thing for Dan." She reached out and took Virgil's wrist. "He said to tell you that you have to do it. That's the word he used. He said you *have* to. He said to tell you that you haven't reached the end of the story yet, and you'll never know the end until you put his ashes in that grave."

"Ellen—"

"He said to ask you as the son of an old friend and colleague."

"Ah, jeez." Virgil looked down at the dying man and shook his head.

"YOU HAVEN'T reached the end of the story. . . ."

That gave Virgil something to think about on the way back to Mankato, and it stayed with him, especially at night, before he went to sleep. He hadn't reached the end of the story?

The story itself went national—not the hassle in Mankato, but the stele itself, and the implications of the inscription.

The *Wall Street Journal* did the first story, which was amplified by the *New York Times*, and then it was off to the races. The end of Judaism? They were all Egyptians together? A few of the saner voices suggested that the story, along with the implications, would be gone in a month, and Virgil suspected they were correct; but then, whoever listened to saner voices?

THE DALLIANCE with Ma continued, although he stopped calling her Ma. He didn't tell her, but "Florence" never seemed right to him—she didn't look like a Florence or a Flo, he thought, probably because he had an aunt named Florence and Ma didn't look like her; if anything, Ma was an anti-Florence. Then he found out her middle name was Frances, and he started calling her Frankie, which amused her, but seemed okay with everybody.

He even got along with her kids.

Ma and Rolf cleaned up the equipment at the river site, and Virgil tipped off the Blue Earth County deputy who'd been looking for it. The deputy went out, found the lumber, and had it pulled from the river. The wood was stacked out behind the office at the Ponderosa landfill, where, Rolf said, it'd probably rot.

TAL ZAHAVI was kicked out of the country, Tag Bauer bailed out, and Virgil suspected he'd never come to trial; what Virgil said he'd done just wasn't important enough to waste money on, especially since the case would be difficult, with the witnesses scattered all over the world.

A week after the auction night, Ellen called to tell him that Jones had died. "He went peacefully," Ellen said.

"I'm glad he died peacefully," Virgil said. He didn't want to say anything more, because he really hadn't liked Jones.

"You promised to take his ashes to Israel."

"Well, I didn't, Ellen. You tried to get me to, but I didn't."

"He said you have to go. He said the case wasn't over yet, and you are the only one who could solve it."

"Ellen . . ."

VIRGIL'S FATHER was at an interfaith conference in the Twin Cities that week, and Davenport brought Virgil up to talk to an auctioneer named Burton Familie, with whom Virgil had had a previous relationship involving the dispersal of stolen machine-shop equipment through farm estate sales.

Familie had some information on a boxcar burglary ring, and Davenport wanted it. Familie, on the other hand, wanted an understanding, as he called it, with the BCA. Other people might have called that a criminal conspiracy; it all depended on your point of view. Virgil mediated.

When that was done, he called his old man, who said that he was at the Parrot Cafe and that he hadn't ordered yet. The Parrot was ten minutes from the BCA offices and Virgil drove over. He found his old man in a booth in the back, talking with a Catholic priest over cheeseburgers and fries.

Virgil squeezed in next to his old man, who introduced James McConville, who worked at St. Agnes Church in St. Paul, and was an old friend of his father's.

"I had a girlfriend, sort of a musical hippie, back a while ago, she'd take me over there for those orchestral masses," Virgil told McConville. "I gotta say, that whole Roman Catholic High Mass thing can get a grip on you, with the incense and the Bach and the vestments and the big gold crucifix. . . ."

"Easy there, Virgil," his old man said.

McConville chuckled and said, "We're still doing the music. Drop by anytime. So, what about this stele from Israel?"

They chatted for a few minutes about the stone, and Virgil's father shook his head and said, "Ultimately, it won't matter much, except to archaeologists and those sorts, and it'll be another bone picked over by the crazies. Judaism doesn't depend on the veracity of the Solomon stone any more than Christianity depends on the veracity of the Shroud of Turin. They are artifacts from a past we can't see."

"Jones would disagree," Virgil said.

"Because he spent his life digging up artifacts from the past we can't see," McConville said.

"He wasn't a bad man," Virgil's old man said. "I liked him right from the start. He was a tough guy, played rugby back when rugby players ate their dead. Had an intellect on him."

"Sort of went down in flames, though. He had a pretty good reputation over there, until he did this," Virgil said. "He wanted me to take his ashes to Israel for burial. . . . He said the case wouldn't be over until I did it." He told them about Ellen's plea involving her father's ashes.

"Are you going?" McConville asked.

"Nah."

"Why not?" Virgil's father asked.

"I don't know. It'd cost too much, for one thing. It's a long trip. I didn't really owe him anything."

McConville shrugged. "In my opinion, you've got to go. I mean, look at everything that happened. If he's as smart as Lew says he was, and if he says the case isn't over and only you can settle it . . . how can you *not* go? I'm not saying you've got an ethical obligation, you've just got an obligation to your own curiosity. Don't you?"

Virgil looked at his father and asked, "Why'd you have to be sitting with this guy? If I go, it'll cost me ten grand."

"The money's not a problem," his father said.

"It's not? I'm paying fourteen percent on my boat and I've got two years to go."

"The boat's your problem," his father said. "As for taking his ashes to Israel, I'll write you a check."

Virgil thought about that for a minute, then said, "I knew you had money, but I didn't know you had *money*."

"We're quite comfortable," his father said. "So you'll go?"

"I can't handle long flights in tourist class."

25

There were arrangements to be made, but Ellen handled them. She suggested that when he got to Jerusalem, he contact Yuli Gefen, Moshe Gefen's daughter, to take him out to the cemetery. That was the same Gefen that Yael had seen in Sam's Club: the bagwoman for Jones's scam.

So Virgil went to Israel with a jar full of ashes, business class.

He carried a letter from the Israeli embassy, about the ashes, to show at customs, if customs wondered what was in the jar. The flight took twelve hours or so from Newark, and landed in Israel in the morning. Virgil walked the ashes through customs, no questions asked, and caught a taxi to the American Colony Hotel in Jerusalem.

The hotel reminded him of a couple in Phoenix, with its thick walls and tiles. He got a few hours of sleep, since his body insisted that it was four o'clock in the morning, and then, after consulting with the front desk about the telephone, he called Yuli Gefen. She lived in Tel Aviv, she said, and had to take care of the kids that afternoon and evening, but was anxious to see him. Could she drive up in the morning?

Virgil said that would be good. Still jet-lagged and out of sorts, he got directions from the desk man again, and walked up a long hill, and eventually found himself in the Old City. In the Old City, he bought a map and went to look at the Western Wall, and did the Stations of the Cross, checked out the Church of the Holy Sepulchre, where he saw a pilgrim crawling on her knees across the square outside.

Then he walked through a maze of narrow passages, past merchants selling mostly junk, but also meat and spices and rugs and jewelry and T-shirts and ball caps and almost everything he could think of, but no fishing or boating equipment that he could find, and finally came out at the Dome of the Rock.

He couldn't go inside, because it was too late in the day; but from the outside, he thought it one of the most magnificent buildings he'd ever seen.

AFTER most of a bad night, dreams jumbled with waking moments, he finally got to sleep, and two minutes later, it seemed, was awakened by the call to prayer from a nearby minaret. As he lay there listening to it, he realized that he was no longer in Kansas. Or Minnesota.

YULI GEFEN was a cheerful, slightly heavy woman who drove a battered Volvo station wagon. "I missed you at Sam's Club," Virgil said, and she laughed and said, "Sam's Club. This is what Israel needs. Pure genius."

She denied nothing, but then again, she admitted nothing.

"I'm past accusing anyone of anything having to do with the stone," Virgil said. "I'm just curious. Why would you take this risk, even if Magda Jones was a friend of your parents? You could have been arrested and put in jail."

She was silent for a while, then asked, "Did Ellen tell you about my son?"

"Your son? No."

"He's autistic," she said. "Severely so. He's smart, you can tell that, but . . . he needs help. He needs a special school where they can help him. My husband is a wonderful man, a scholar, but he doesn't make anything like the money we would need to send Moshe to the school."

"Ah," Virgil said. "Your son, and Magda . . ."

"You're beginning to see the dimensions of this," she said. "When Elijah called me, what could I say? This is my son, this is his chance."

THE CEMETERY was set into a rocky hillside, and a caretaker met them at the gate and said that the grave was ready. There was already a stone on top of the empty grave, and it would be lifted by a couple of laborers, and Virgil would stick the jar inside a niche.

"My mother and father lie in the next grave," Yuli said. "So these friends travel together to . . . wherever they go."

"They all must have been really close," Virgil said, as they walked down a narrow path on the hillside.

"Friends as good as you can have in this world," Yuli said. "You know how, sometimes you meet people, even just one time, and then see them years later, and you are still friends? They were like that: instant friends, but then, they saw each other two or three times a year. It was so sad when Magda began to decline with the Alzheimer's. It stole her personality away. She was so . . . ebullient."

"I understand she will be cared for," Virgil ventured.

"Yes. She will."

When they got to the grave, Virgil saw that it consisted of two parts: a longer horizontal slab, and a shorter vertical stone. The vertical stone had a simple "Jones" cut into the face. The two laborers lifted the horizontal stone, using pry-bars and blocks, exposing a small square-cut niche below it. Virgil gently fit the copper jar into the space; there was just enough extra room for another jar. The laborers dropped the stone back in place, and the caretaker said, "May God bless all of us."

"Amen," Virgil said.

Yuli had stepped over to her parents' gravesite, which, like the Joneses' plot, had both vertical and horizontal stones, and brushed some leaves away from the inscription. Virgil looked at the vertical stone and said, "Ah, man."

"What?" Yuli picked up the tone.

"Can I use your cell phone?"

VIRGIL HAD BEEN scheduled to meet Yael that evening for dinner, and now he called her cell. She picked up and said, "Ken?"

"No, this is Virgil. Listen, do you have the stone?"

"Well, I don't have the stone, but yes, it is here."

"You've got to get the stone and come over," Virgil said.

"I can't take the stone anywhere," she said. "It is in the vault."

"Who can get it out?"

"Well, the director."

"Tell the director to get the stone and get his ass over here," Virgil said. "Tell him that it will be the most important thing he does this year. Make it fast. It's really hot here."

VIRGIL AND YULI left the cemetery and walked down the street to a little Arab restaurant, sat in the garden and drank apricot juice, and then Diet Coke, and Yuli told Virgil about her father's life and work, and more about Jones than Virgil had ever wanted to know. They were there for an hour when Yael showed up with a tall bulky man in an olive drab short-sleeved shirt and khaki pants, looking like he'd once operated a tank, and enjoyed it, and a thin bearded man wearing round glasses and carrying a bag that looked heavy.

"The stone," he said to Virgil.

The bulky man, who Yael introduced as the director, said, "I hope I don't waste my time. I had appointments."

Yuli said, "This way."

They walked back to the cemetery and down the hill to the gravesite. Yael said, "Ahhh," and the bulky man brightened and said, "I see."

"Let's make sure," Virgil said.

The thin man put the bag on the ground, unzipped it, took the stone out, and handed it to Virgil. Virgil stepped over to the black vertical stone over Moshe Gefen's grave. The rough-cut gravestone had a distinctive protrusion at one end. Virgil took a minute to get it done, but in the end fit the cavity in the bottom of the Solomon stone over the protrusion in the gravestone. The fit was so tight that an ant couldn't have gotten through on its hands and knees.

Virgil stepped back and they all looked at it, and then the bulky man laughed. "The grave of the greatest paleographer in Israel, yes? The one man who could make the Solomon stone in his workroom." He clapped Virgil on the back. "We make a medal for this fuckin' Flowers, hey?"

Virgil looked at Yael and said, "You had to tell him, huh?"

VIRGIL SPENT three more days in Israel, touring. He went down to the Dead Sea, rode a camel, visited Masada, drove up the Jordan Valley past Jericho and all the way to the Sea of Galilee, then toward the Mediterranean through the Jezreel Valley and passed by, but didn't notice, a hillside that once supported a royal city, where Jezebel the queen had been thrown out a window to be eaten by dogs; now nothing but a rocky hillside. Back in Jerusalem, he found an Arab guide to take him into the Dome of the Rock and saw the stone where Abraham had prepared to sacrifice Isaac; or Ishmael, take your pick.

But three days was all the time he had on his ticket, so he went home, tired, and the day after he got back, slipped back into the swimming hole.

————

Ma had gotten a set of swim fins from one of her kids, and while that was the only thing she was wearing, it gave her a decided advantage over Virgil and she was swimming circles around him.

"So that finally proved it was a fake, huh?"

"Hezbollah is saying that they faked the headstone. So, in Israel and in the West, it's a fake. North, south, and east of Israel, the headstone's a fake. The question now is, who's got better propaganda?"

"That's the question, huh?"

"And you want to know the answer?"

"Sure."

"I don't care. Don't care who wins. It's just a lot of people throwing bullshit at each other. Even if the stone had been real, it would have been some pharaoh throwing bullshit at the locals. The BC version of Fox News."

Virgil paddled out from under the shade tree and put up a hand to block out the sun. Ma said, "Tag called me."

"Yeah? What'd he want?"

"Wants me to appear on his television show," she said. "They want to reenact his car getting shot at. They want me to come on with my shotgun."

"What'd you tell him?"

"To go fuck himself."

"Good for you. You have the Flowers seal of approval."

"What more could a girl hope for?" she said, and then: "Oh, wait—I just thought of something. . . ."

About the Author

Pulitzer prize-winning journalist John Sandford is the author of the Prey series, four Kidd novels and the Virgil Flowers series. He lives in Minnesota. Visit www.johnsandford.org

This book and other novels by **John Sandford** are available
from your local bookshop or can be ordered direct
from the publisher.

978 0 85720 912 2	Shock Wave	£7.99
978 0 85720 399 1	Bad Blood	£7.99
978 1 84739 768 3	Rough Country	£6.99
978 1 84739 469 9	Heat Lightning	£6.99
978 1 84739 185 8	Dark of the Moon	£6.99
978 1 47112 964 3	Silken Prey	£7.99
978 1 84983 939 6	Stolen Prey	£7.99
978 1 84983 900 6	Buried Prey	£7.99
978 1 84739 769 0	Storm Prey	£6.99
978 1 84983 479 7	Winter Prey	£7.99
978 1 84983 477 3	Broken Prey	£7.99
978 1 84983 481 0	Mortal Prey	£7.99
978 1 84739 471 2	Wicked Prey	£6.99

IF YOU ENJOY GOOD BOOKS,
YOU'LL LOVE OUR GREAT OFFER
25% OFF THE RRP ON ALL
SIMON & SCHUSTER UK TITLES
WITH FREE POSTAGE AND PACKING (UK ONLY)

How to buy your books

Credit and debit cards
Telephone Simon & Schuster Cash Sales at Sparkle Direct on 01326
569444

Cheque
Send a cheque payable to Simon & Schuster Bookshop to:
Simon & Schuster Bookshop, PO Box 60, Helston, TR13 0TP
Email: sales@sparkledirect.co.uk
Website: www.sparkledirect.com

Prices and availability are subject to change without notice.